Praise for Marie Kiraly
and her masterpiece of dark sensuality
and forbidden passion . . .

MINA
THE DRACULA STORY CONTINUES

"Chilling, fast-paced, a real page-turner."
—P.N. Elrod, author of
The Vampire Files

"A stunning reading experience . . . This is a most excitingly written adventure story, filled with sensuality, a raw intensity of emotion and a suspense that will match and surpass Bram Stoker's original story."
—*Affaire de Coeur*

"Strong . . . sensual . . . surprisingly tender . . . *Mina* displays a resonance unlike its source material, humanizing people Stoker merely used as pawns."
—*BookLovers*

"Kiraly takes the Dracula legend beyond its original ending . . . a nicely twisting sequel."
—*Milwaukee Journal*

"Throbbing with the rich sexuality which marked Bram Stoker's *Dracula*, *Mina* is an erotic ride through the life of a liberated Victorian woman who no longer desires to repress her dark passions."
—*Shadowdance*

"*Mina* is a tremendous novel that Stoker would have been very proud to have authored. Marie Kiraly successfully incorporates the events of the original novel [and] splendidly goes beyond . . ."
—*The Talisman*

"Destined to be considered a literary classic . . . a wonderful read."
—*Eclipse*

Berkley Books by Marie Kiraly

MINA: THE DRACULA STORY CONTINUES
MADELINE: AFTER THE FALL OF USHER

MADELINE

After the Fall of Usher

Marie Kiraly

BERKLEY BOOKS, NEW YORK

MADELINE: AFTER THE FALL OF USHER

A Berkley Book/published by arrangement with
the author

PRINTING HISTORY
Berkley edition/December 1996

The Putnam Berkley World Wide Web site address is
http://www.berkley.com/berkley

ISBN: 0-425-15573-0

BERKLEY®
Berkley Books are published by The Berkley Publishing Group,
200 Madison Avenue, New York, New York 10016.
BERKLEY and the "B" design
are trademarks belonging to Berkley Publishing Corporation.

PRINTED IN THE UNITED STATES OF AMERICA

10 9 8 7 6 5 4 3 2 1

Dedicated with love to my parents,
Howard and Eleanor Schmieler,
who on this day this novel was finished
celebrated fifty years together

prologue

"*I cannot explain* precisely why I came to you except that my situation seems so desperate," my late-night visitor began. She was a tiny woman in her early twenties, with plain brown hair pulled back in a tight bun, sharp though attractive features and nervously fluttering hands. Obviously aware of the last, she kept them tightly folded in her lap when she spoke, looking down at them as if they would somehow fly away from her if she did not give them some constant bit of attention. Because her head was lowered and she had a tendency to speak softly, I had to strain to listen to her words.

"And even though it is only a feeling," she went on, "I believe it with all my heart, and all my instincts. Mr. Poe, you are my one real hope."

I was her one real hope? If so, her situation must be terrible indeed, for hadn't I said those same words so many times to so many different people? On the other hand, I had never looked so prosperous when I uttered them, or inexplicably, so needy. Her dress was deep blue, fashionably cut and well made with a high neckline trimmed in Irish lace. The brooch at her neck was mounted in gold, and the black shawl she wore was soft and dense, as functional on this cool summer night as it was beautiful. She hardly looked like a woman without means, yet there was a controlled hysteria in her stiffly held body. And she had come here for the express purpose of meeting me, something that I still could not comprehend. "How did you find me?" I asked.

"I was on a train heading for the port at Wilmington when I read that you were staying here in Richmond. I decided to spend the day in town and try to find you. They told me at the American Hotel that you had moved here to the Swan."

"I think I'll be returning to New York soon," I said. My money was already running out, and the prospects for earning more were rapidly dwindling along with my health in this cursed southern heat. Cholera was claiming its usual victims in the poorer sections of town, and the area in which I was staying was hardly better. Even before I left Philadelphia for the journey south, I'd had a vivid premonition that I would never see my aunt Muddy again. Muddy is getting old, and I thought that it was she who would die. Yet now I am ill, and she writes me letters to cheer me. But the premonition remains, as strong as ever, though I try to ignore it.

"Then I'm so thankful I found you!" The woman's hands, unclasped, reached out toward me. Her eyes met mine for the first time. They were a curious color, like cream and strong coffee, arresting in a strange sort of way, perhaps because she seemed on the edge of tears.

"I have few financial means, and certainly no great connections. What problem made you seek me out?" I asked.

She hesitated before replying, and took a deep breath. I thought she was calming herself, but instead she seemed to be collecting air for another outburst. "My child is missing, Mr. Poe. You may know something about where he's gone, you must help me. You are . . ."

I began to realize, with falling spirits, that if my visitor went on like this, I would be up most of the night. I was hardly well enough to survive without rest, and if the woman I intended to marry heard rumor of this late-night visit, I would be hard-pressed to explain it. I gripped the woman's hands, and held them firmly. They were icy, and I wondered if it was fear that made them so or if she was also ill. "Your one hope," I said. "Yes, you have told me that already. Now

all problems have roots somewhere. Since the recent past un-
settles you, perhaps you should start your story at the beginning and we'll look for the solution to your situation
together."

"Like your Monsieur Dupin?" she asked, seeming to relax
for the first time.

I hadn't thought of my suggestion in that light, but it made
perfect sense. Pleased that she was familiar with one of my
lesser-known works, I smiled. "Just so," I replied in a tone I
hoped would put her at ease.

This time her hesitation did signal a search for calm.
When she finally continued, it was in that same small voice
she'd used when she first arrived.

"I never knew my mother," she began. "She had, I was
told, breezed into my father's life like some tremendous
storm. I never had a picture of her, but my father told me
more than once that Mother was not a beautiful woman.
They met . . ."

"Is this truly the beginning or can you perhaps . . ." I
coughed, tried to suppress it, and found I could not stop. My
hands shook as I reached into my pocket for a kerchief.

"You're ill!" she said, rushing to my side.

I smelled lavender cologne. Sissy used to wear that scent.
Even after nearly three years something as simple as this
brings my wife's face so clearly to my mind, along with the
too-vivid memory of my despair when she died.

"I saw a doctor just before the lecture. He tells me it's
nothing more than catarrh brought on by the dampness of the
weather." I lied to put her at ease. In truth, I'd been ill for
days and had no money to see anyone. If I did, I suspect the
diagnosis would be far worse.

She took off her own cloak and draped it over my shoulders. I was touched by her kindness, and far more willing to
be patient and let the story unfold. But it seemed that instead,
I had brought out the maternal instincts of my visitor. She
glanced around the room, her attention finally settling on a
bottle just visible in the top of my valise. "Would you like
some of the port to sip for the cough?"

Knowing where one sip would lead when I was already so

ill, I shook my head. "Pour yourself some, though. Your hands are so cold," I replied, more than a little shocked when she actually did so. Once she'd settled into a chair across the table from me, I made a simple request: "You could begin your story by telling me your name."

"I didn't?" Her eyes widened. "I'm so sorry, Mr. Poe. I'm Pamela Donaldson, Mrs. Donaldson. The name is hardly familiar to you, but another certainly will be. You see, I believe my child has been taken on the wishes of someone you know all too well. Madeline Usher."

As the woman intended, the revelation astonished me. I sat back in my chair, now ready to spend a fortnight if necessary listening to her tale.

And what a story it turned out to be! I used the better part of the week after she left scouring my memory for every detail of her account, organizing the facts that she conveyed to me into a jumble of quotes and hastily written description. There is no poetry in the narration, though I confess to embellishing the tale with occasional flights of my own fancy. But the core of it is the truth, and for good or ill, the end has yet to be written.

I am certain that I shall be drawn into this adventure and pray that when it is done, I will be alive to finish this tale.

part one

❧

THE VISITOR

(taken from the notes of Edgar Poe)

chapter 1

"*My maiden name* was Montgomery," she began. "My father, William, owns a plantation in Buckingham County, Virginia, and because of his wealth, I wanted for nothing. I had servants to care for me from the time I was born, and later in life I attended one of the finest girls' schools in the country.

"My father's family had not always been so rich, however. The original brick house had been built three generations before my birth, but the family had never been able to expand their holdings beyond a few hundred acres.

"All that changed soon after my father was born. In 1803 my grandfather acquired a sizable sum of money that enabled my family to double the size of their farm and to purchase the slaves necessary to work it. I never knew who left him the legacy. Perhaps Grandfather borrowed the money, but if so he was too proud to admit it to anyone and apparently paid the debt back quickly.

"When I was very young, one of the house slaves who had been born on our plantation took me on a walk around the house and described how the family fortunes seemed to have changed in only a few days. I can still recall everything Emmie said as she pointed out the old sections of our house and told how the new had been built around it.

"'There used to be rosebushes here . . .' Emmie had told me and pointed to the place where my father's bedroom was. 'And lilacs there . . . and the kitchen garden there. I was only six or so when a pair of wagons came down the road bringing workmen who pulled everything up. Your father lay upstairs in his cradle screaming at the noise. He didn't stop until the work was done. He was excitable even when young, that one.'

"'And Mother?' I asked hopefully, but Emmie only looked away. In the years after Mother disappeared, no one was allowed to discuss her—not in Father's presence, and especially not in mine. I turned to face the road and saw him walking toward us, looking old and stooped, though he was scarcely thirty.

"I suppose that Mother broke his heart, but I was never sure. She may just as easily have wounded his pride, which always seemed present in him in too great an abundance. I only remember hearing from more than one person, and always when my father was out of the room, that Anna, my mother, was not a beautiful woman, nor even a charming one. Yet from those scraps of information it certainly seems that Mother had all the effect of a whirlpool on him."

Franklin Montgomery, William's father, lived well into his seventies, so Pamela got a chance to know him well. He was a strict and somewhat ill-tempered man who had raised William on his own since his wife had died when William was ten. He was probably too busy to control his son's behavior, and was more than generous with pocket money. His only non-negotiable demand was that his son receive the best education available, though he'd gotten none himself and did not seem to value it in others.

Young William, in the enviable position of being wealthy, educated, and unencumbered by any constraints on his behavior, grew into something of a wastrel, fond of gambling and drink, trying his father's patience with endless demands for funds.

William was scarcely twenty when he met his future bride, Anna Broussard, at a theater in Appomattox. He encountered her again when he and a friend went out for a late-night supper after the performance. Both times she made a point of initiating a conversation. William admired her boldness and took her up on the invitation that he stop by the boarding-house where she and her mother were living anytime he was nearby. He apparently did so once or twice, and was so cordially received by them that he became suspicious of their intent and stopped the calls.

Apparently the Broussards had been keeping track of him, because as soon as he returned home, he received an affectionate letter from Anna, so affectionate that he made a point of reading it to his parents and commenting on the girl's forwardness. "You always told me to be wary of fortune hunters," he said. "I suspect I've finally met one."

"That's hardly clear at this point," his father replied. "Be polite and write her back."

This was said in the tone of an order. William, accustomed to obeying his father's infrequent orders, did as he was told. His letter was written to discourage Anna but had exactly the opposite effect. Anna, and her mother, arrived a week later. The older woman met privately with Franklin Montgomery, while Anna asked William to take her on a tour of the estate.

By then William was convinced that the woman was indeed a fortune hunter, and certain his father would recognize this soon enough. With that thought in his mind he decided to humor her and ordered two horses saddled. At some point in their ride they stopped to rest.

It is not difficult to picture her clearly, so tiny next to him, her hand on his sleeve, her face upturned. He kissed her, expecting to get his face slapped for his insolence. Instead, she responded, surprising him with a frank passion that would be out of place in a woman even today. When they returned to the house, his head was spinning with confusion and unexpected lust. He was convinced that his father would forbid him ever to see her again, and not at all certain that was what he wanted any longer. Instead, he discovered his father and Anna's mother sitting in the parlor sipping sherry. They looked, William commented years later in one of his rare moments of candor to his second wife, as if they'd known each other for a long time. If so the earlier relationship had not been a pleasant one. Franklin sat with a strange, strained smile, as if he had not liked the woman in the past and only suffered her presence now.

The Broussards stayed for three days. After they left, Franklin suggested that William see more of Anna. When William appeared cool to the idea, his father insisted.

Anna Broussard and William Montgomery were married four months later in a celebration that brought landowners from six counties to Montgomery House. The couple then traveled abroad for half a year before returning there.

For the next two years they were a devoted couple. William began taking an interest in the management of the estate he would one day own, and gave strong indication of wanting to settle into the quiet, simple life of a country gentleman. With his father's permission, he redecorated the large front bedroom in the east wing according to his wife's taste. Then he had her portrait painted to hang above the sideboard in the dining room.

She was wearing a dress that was pale peach, and her auburn hair fell in bright ringlets over her bare shoulders. Her pose, it was said, was almost scandalous.

Scandalous? Possibly. But certainly in keeping with the whims of a proud man passionately in love with his wife. He would have stared at that portrait when she was away and thought how fate—so often perverse—had been so kind to him.

Then what he had hoped for happened. Anna became pregnant.

As the child grew within her, her disposition changed. She would write a dozen letters home to her mother, then not correspond with the woman for weeks at a time. She became moody—given to bouts of laughter alternating with desperate tears. She would cling to her husband, refusing to let him leave her side for hours at a time, then, in a fit of what seemed like courage, would request that he go.

More than one physician was sent for, but none could determine the source of Anna's strange mania, if only because the woman refused to admit that anything was wrong. Her doctors prescribed elixirs to calm her nerves and help her sleep and told William that she would undoubtedly be quite all right after the child was born.

Franklin Montgomery fell ill about that time, and William had to take over many of his duties. The work gave him a means to ignore his wife's mania, and she kept to her rooms for the last two months of her pregnancy. As her delivery date grew closer, Emmie would often look up from her work in the kitchen and see Anna standing on her balcony with tears running down her face, though there was no reason at all why she should be crying.

Pamela Montgomery was born in late May. Anna paid little attention to her daughter, refusing even to nurse her. Emmie, who had been a scullery maid, had recently given birth to a stillborn infant. Her breasts nursed Pamela, her arms held the infant and rocked her to sleep. Because of the bond that formed between them, Emmie's status in the hierarchy of slaves rose. She moved from the kitchen to the nursery and became Pamela's one true friend, shielding the child as best she could while the drama between husband and wife played on.

For some weeks after the birth Anna remained in bed, refusing to eat more than enough to sustain her, refusing to see any of her friends in the area, refusing even to spend time with her husband. The only interest she took was in reading the letters her mother wrote her from Charlottesville and in responding to them, giving detailed accounts of her daughter's health, while saying little about her own. The physicians William consulted about his wife's condition said her depression was not uncommon and to give her time.

So he did. Months passed, and as the doctors had predicted, Anna began to rouse herself from her lethargy. A year after Pamela was born, she asked if she could visit her mother in Charlottesville. Her husband apparently saw her desire to travel as a good sign and agreed.

Anna and her mother both vanished soon after. When he got news of her disappearance, William Montgomery went through his wife's room and discovered that everything of value was missing. She hadn't met with any foul play; her leaving had been planned.

"You look at me so oddly when I speak of my mother's disappearance. What is it that troubles you so?" Pamela asked me.

"That you could never recall her sweet face save through a portrait," I replied.

"Sweet face? I hardly think so, not when she cared so little for me that she never even held me," Pamela replied bitterly. "As for her portrait, I only heard of it, Mr. Poe." Pamela abandoned her place by the grate and began pacing my little room. Even moving her tale forward to the time after she was born had begun to agitate her. I started to wonder if her hold on sanity was tenuous. She might have never been married or had a child to lose. She might have become obsessed with one of my poems and made up the story as a means to see me. Or she might have been delusional, believing in a past that was no more than a fabrication of her overwrought imagination.

"You see, after my mother disappeared, my father began a thorough search for her, just the sort of thing your Monsieur Dupin might do. Though it was unlikely that she had wandered off, he began on the estate, riding over every acre personally. When he found no trace of her there, he sent letters to acquaintances in every major city within two hundred miles. You can undoubtedly imagine how publicizing such a scandal made him feel, but he kept up the search for nearly three years. Emmie said that by the time he finally gave up, all traces of his love for her vanished. I've always suspected that he did find her and that she refused to return to the estate with him. I suppose I'll never know, but his attitude toward her changed so swiftly that I'm sure I'm right.

"After one long, final journey he returned home and ordered her portrait to be taken down and destroyed, her rooms to be closed and locked. For the next few years any house slave who mentioned her name was whipped. Because of this, I gave little thought to my mother when I was young, and when I asked questions about her, I quickly learned to ask them of Emmie rather than my father."

"He would grow angry?" I asked.

"He would beat me as he did the others he owned, Mr. Poe. I still have proof of this part of my story."

She pulled up the sleeve of her dress and showed me her forearm, covered with three deep, jagged scars.

"What did this?" I asked.

"I was with my father when he was inspecting the tobacco fields. One of the fieldhands commented that I'd grow up to be as pretty as my mama. Father turned the dogs on him. One of the hounds misunderstood and attacked me. The mistake saved the slave's life, so I don't regret the pain. My father refused to have the wound treated until it infected."

"A monster!" I whispered.

"So he became," she replied. "And the real tragedy was that I could just barely remember what he'd been like before. It seemed that all the love he had felt for my mother had twisted into terrible bitterness. It filled his soul and left no room for anything else. Perhaps if there had been some relations nearby, or a grandmother or maiden aunt staying at the house, my life might have been easier. But there was no one save the house slaves. They were kind but distant—always aware of the differences in our positions and how harsh a master my father could be."

The confession had been a painful one. I could see it in her eyes and in the quaver in her voice as she went on. "My childhood, then, had a hidden side that was far from idyllic. For the first few years after he gave up his search, I rarely even saw my father except at gatherings where it was impossible to keep me locked away.

"Then, as abruptly as he had given up the search for my mother, father remarried. I had no indication of his plans; he simply went away for a fortnight and returned with a new wife."

"How could he marry again?" I asked.

"He bribed a judge and had my mother declared dead. A less wealthy man might have had to wait another few years, but Father paid the official well. It's amazing to me even now how much justice two hundred dollars can buy."

Judges were expensive. Poets could be had for far less. I could recall a few times when I'd sold my overused soul for as little as five dollars.

"Mother had auburn hair like mine," Pamela continued. "Caitlin was blond and very fair and so incredibly happy. I would hear her singing as she bathed in the morning, and at night after supper she would sit at the piano and play for us.

"Yes, us. Father loved her, enough that when she declared that we three must dine together as civilized families do, he capitulated. Even so, he never looked at me directly save when it was absolutely necessary, and never complimented me on my achievements. I sensed that he was both angry and disappointed in me. I could not imagine what I had done wrong save that I existed.

"Later, when Emmie thought me old enough to understand discretion, she told me that I resembled my mother too much and that was why Father detested my presence. I made her detail all the similarities.

"I couldn't change the color of my eyes or the shape of my lips, but as soon as I was alone, I took a scissors and cut off my long hair, arranging what was left in a way my mother never would have done. Caitlin discovered me and helped me finish. Though I told her why I'd done it, she never said a word to Father about my reasons. I decided then that I loved her more than any other person I had ever known. In time she became my confidante as well. Most of what I know about Mother I learned from her, and Emmie.

"Father and I settled into an unspoken truce, one I was certain would be broken when I least expected it. The constant waiting made me anxious. I had nightmares, terrible ones, and when I would wake there was no one I could call to come and sit with me."

She seemed to be shaking from just the memory when she spoke those last words. I wanted to ask what sort of nightmares she had but did not want to make her anxiousness worse by having her recall them. Instead, I did what so many have done to me—I ignored her trembling and her tears until she composed herself and went on.

"And so my childhood was divided between servants and tutors, pleasant afternoons with Caitlin, and meals with Father. When the sudden opportunity came for me to go away to school, I agreed immediately. Even today, after all that has happened, I don't regret it.

"The Hudson School for Young Ladies is located in the hilly country just west of Albany, New York. The frigid winds of the north, the distance from my home, and the spartan atmosphere of the place made me wonder if Father had found a more subtle means of punishing me. However, in time I grew to love the place and the girls. And the happiest years of my life began there."

chapter 2

"*The Hudson School* had been founded by Dutch settlers nearly seventy years ago. Since then it has evolved from the cloistered atmosphere preferred by its founders to one gayer, more in keeping with social and political norms of the present. As a result the number of students has grown. The school's annual social has been held the third weekend in May every year since the school was founded. The rose hedges are in bloom then, and if nature is kind, the cherry trees and lilacs are as well, making the grounds particularly beautiful. Appearances are important because the social is held as much to publicize the school to the wealthier families in the state as it is for the girls' benefit. Many of my friends were at Hudson because a brother, a younger uncle, or even a widowed father had attended this event. And of course, many a suitable beaux met his future bride beneath those fragrant branches.

"My years under father's withering scrutiny had made me shy, and nearly two years at school had done little to dispel it. I kept to the edge of the crowd, speaking only when spoken to and then as little as possible. As a result, I was sitting alone when Elliot Donaldson arrived.

"Everyone who saw him there agreed that he seemed awkward and out of place in so civilized a gathering. Though his dark hair, bronzed skin, and intense brown eyes made a handsome enough combination to attract the attention of many of the girls, his black suit was out of fashion and dusty and his tie slightly askew as if he had knotted it quickly just before joining the group. He paused to speak to the owners of the school. They pointed me out to him, and he walked directly to me and took my hand.

"'I understand that we are cousins, though I hardly know how, but Mother did ask that I come and meet you since I was going to be in the area anyway.'

"I sensed something strained and awkward in the way he spoke and could not help but smile. That rough-edged young man still did his mother's bidding. I thought it charming and took his arm gladly when he offered to walk with me awhile.

"His relationship to me was distant and on my mother's side. Since I never knew the woman, let alone her kin, I had a thousand questions to ask but no idea where to begin. We finally dropped the matter. Conversation became awkward until he began speaking of the vineyards he'd planted on his lands around the frontier town of Watkin's Glen and the wines his grapes were just beginning to produce. He'd brought a few bottles to the social, and though drinking by the girls was usually prohibited, he persuaded the headmistress, Mrs. Lowell, to open one so the group could sample it.

"I'd often had French sauternes with meals at home. This was different, dryer with a musky undertone he said was a feature of the fox grapes. Nonetheless, I could well believe that the wine would in time become popular, and somewhat giddy from the small amount I'd been allowed, I told him so.

"The compliment made him smile, and he began describing his home with such enthusiasm and earnestness that I started to feel some attraction to this distant relation.

"He had been raised in Louisiana. His mother was of French background, his father English, and he spoke both languages fluently. When he was only seventeen, he'd traveled north to claim the inheritance from his maternal grandfather. A trapper had been renting the house—which Elliot described as little more than a shack when he arrived. Elliot arranged to have the house cleaned and repaired, then began hiring hands to clear the land and start the planting. When he met me, he'd been there three years."

"All that work for such a young man," I commented.

"Young! Mr. Poe, I discovered that he'd taken possession of the land when he was the same age as I was when we met! I could hardly believe what he could accomplish, but then neither had his neighbors. Coarse men, most of them, and most would have been more than willing to take advantage of Elliot, but he was far too astute for them. He'd arrived in New York in early June of 1839. By October of that year, when the first snows fell, he had everything snug and secure, ten acres cleared, a good supply of wood ready for the hearths, and food and sustenance laid in for the winter. Within two years the land being farmed was paying for itself. That was when he'd planted the vineyard with Concord and Clinton grapes. When we met, he was only twenty-three, and already planning the next changes for his property.

"He stayed in a hotel near the school for two weeks. We saw each other almost every day and began corresponding after he left. He wrote weekly, long and loving letters that because of the isolation of his farm would be posted every few weeks. He took to numbering his envelopes, and I would write back in a similar fashion. We became informally engaged that fall. He wanted to write my father and ask for my hand. I finally confessed what my childhood had been like and made him swear that he would marry me no matter what my father's response. Perhaps Father's bitterness had shrunk with age, or perhaps he simply wanted to be rid of me. In any case, for the first time I could remember, he agreed to something I wanted and gave his blessing to the match.

"When I realized that I would never have to go back to the harsh house in which I had been raised, I felt a freedom I had never imagined, and longed to share it. I wrote Father and told him that I asked for nothing for my wedding save one gift. I wanted him to free Emmie and give her money to travel north to come and live with me.

"He denied the request as he had denied me almost everything else. Even Caitlin's entreaties on my behalf did nothing. At least he didn't make Emmie suffer for my affection for her. Later, after Caitlin died giving birth to his son, I learned that Father let Emmie remain in the house. She tended the infant for a year until the child followed his mother to her grave. She then stayed on as a house servant.

"I didn't hear of Caitlin's death from my father. A neighbor, a friend of Caitlin's who wrote me from time to time to give me news of the family, informed me of it. She hasn't written since and I know nothing of my father. That was four years ago. For all I know he could be dead."

"But you will hear news of that, won't you? You said he has no other heirs," I reminded her.

"Perhaps he'll adopt someone and bypass me altogether," she replied bitterly.

I winced. Had I been John Allan's true son, that's probably what he would have done.

Pamela Montgomery and Elliot Donaldson were married in the chapel of the Lowell School in the spring of 1845. The details of the wedding were hardly important, save that a teacher from the school acted as the groom's witness because Elliot had brought no friends to stand up for him. The couple left by train for Batavia the following morning.

The first part of the journey was pleasant, but in Batavia they transferred to a coach to take them south, then east to Elmira. "It was an uncomfortable, crowded ride," Pamela said. "One made all the more unpleasant by the incessant rain, the cold, and the constant stops for mailbags which were tossed in with us. We used them as pillows and footrests and later made room for them on the seats as if they were extra passengers crowding in. I thought of all the letters I had exchanged with my husband, and that they had probably traveled in these same mailbags. I tried to keep my spirits up as I grew more and more uncomfortable.

"In Elmira we found an unexpected wedding present waiting for us, a small wagon and pair of horses sent as a gift by Elliot's mother. The wagon, more a coach really, since it had a top and roll-down sides to protect us from the rain and snow, was marvelously designed with wide axles and leather straps to absorb the shocks.

"As I took my place beside my husband, I thought of the expense my mother-in-law had gone to just to have the wagon shipped here, and began to realize that I had married into a wealthy family. Elliot, on the other hand, did not seem to think much of his mother's lavish gift, complaining that the horses would have to be fed, that he had no room in the barn for them, and that the wagon would be too wide for the road. Since the wagon was scarcely wide enough for us to sit side by side I wondered how dangerous the last part of our route would be.

"It was even worse than I expected. The road was narrow and curved along the west bank of Lake Seneca, often winding across the high bluff above the lake. A storm the night before had brought down some saplings that had to be cleared from the road. However, the team was placid and strong, well up to the task.

"The journey took most of the day. The few houses near the town grew thinner, then vanished altogether, and we traveled on through woods that seemed to grow thicker with every mile. Our neighbors' farm was the last settled place on the lake, then the road narrowed even more as it cut inward through the trees for the last two miles."

I asked if Pamela had been terrified by the wilderness, and she actually managed to smile.

"The isolation of my new home meant little to me, Mr. Poe," she explained. "I was used to being alone. When we reached the house I found that my husband had much exaggerated its grandeur—no small feat since he had described it merely as snug and livable. He apologized and said he wanted me to make the final decisions as to paint and trim, the placement of the gardens, and the other final touches.

"Throughout that summer I planted snapdragons and balm in the sunny places and transplanted violets and ferns from the woods into the shadier spots. While I gardened, Elliot expanded the porch from the narrow stoop to one that ran the length of the house. I put pots of angelica at the porch corners for luck and started an herb garden behind the kitchen.

"The work kept us occupied through the long summer months while the grapes ripened. By late summer the farm gave hints of one day being beautiful, though never in the elegant way my father's estate had been.

"As the harvest neared, I went to the vineyard with Elliot each day, watching for the birds to begin their feast, a sign that the grapes had reached their peak of sweetness. Together, we harvested and crushed the grapes. Later, after the wine had fermented and the vines had frozen, we pruned the stock.

"Such isolation might have been impossible had we not been so well suited for each other. Our only frequent companions were Morgan and Mary Quinn, neighbors who lived two miles down the road. Morgan had agreed to help Elliot with the carpentry work on the house, and when he came, he would bring his wife to visit me. Later, we would take turns visiting each other's houses for dinner and stay the night since the trip home in the dark was so hazardous. I could say that Mary became my best friend, if it weren't for the fact that she was my only friend.

"Had it not been for our proximity, I might never have socialized with Mary at all, for our backgrounds were markedly different. I had been raised a freethinker while she was best described as Mennonite, and to my logical way of thinking backward and superstitious. She planted vegetable seeds for her kitchen garden by the phases of the moon, and waited for a sign before making any major decision. There were hex symbols painted on the Quinn barn and front door. She had teas for every illness, and poultices for injuries. Morgan Quinn, a staunch member of the Church of England, used to laugh at her customs, but gently for he admitted that her arts gave them the healthiest livestock in the area, and that more than once she had successfully used her potions to treat him for illnesses that would have killed a man far stronger than he.

"She had also been responsible for the placement of their well, and had helped Elliot locate his. Her talents were, Elliot admitted, uncanny."

"She was a witch, you mean?" I commented.

"I asked her that once, and she said she only remembered what others had forgotten and that her knowledge had been passed down from her mother, who had learned it from her mother, and so on. She said there was no witchcraft in healing people and in helping the land prosper."

"Some believe that there is white as well as black magic," I said.

"I don't believe in magic at all, Mr. Poe. Where people see acts of God or fate, I see coincidence."

"So do I," I said. I saw her startled expression and added, "I suspect that if I truly believed in the supernatural, I would never be able to write another word about it for fear of retaliation."

She laughed. "Well, Mary Quinn believes. She would argue that there is only power, and the good or evil that comes from that power is a matter of intent. She told me that as she was drawing out patterns for hex signs to place on our barn and house."

"For what purpose?" I asked.

"For protection. You see, we were so isolated that an occasional Indian would wander onto our farm, and they respected Mary's painted signs as if they had been placed there by one of their own holy men. Those scattered remnants of the once-terrifying Algonquin nation visited us often. Though they seemed friendly enough, I had been raised hearing tales of scalpings and massacres, so Mary made the hex sign to remind them that Elliot and I were her friends. Elliot thought he could trade with them, as some of the other settlers in the area did, and he was soon exchanging furs for food staples, knives, and the other things that wilderness dwellers need. He would stockpile the furs until he had a good supply, then travel into Watkin's Glen to sell them and return with sugar for the wine, staples for our larder, and often a gift for me. While he was gone, I would stay with the Quinns because I did not want to be alone.

"Within eighteen months my husband had expanded the holdings enough that we were able to hire a couple, the man to help my husband, his wife to give me some assistance with household chores. The Bouttes were French, homeless descendants of Acadians who had fled their lands rather than be relocated by the British. They spoke little English. In truth, I think that even if we hadn't had that barrier between us, Colette Boutte and I would not have been friends. She knew her station too well, deferring to me in everything with a supercilious obedience I found infuriating. But she and her husband, Charles, did their work thoroughly, and I had no reason to complain. Then, one tragedy after another struck, altering my life again, and taking away whatever security I had hoped to find in marriage, and in a life far removed from my native Virginia."

chapter 3

The last part of her story had taken nearly an hour to relate, with much rambling about the Indians, the state of the house, and her growing love for her husband. She told it well, however, and I let her speak as she wished.

Pamela paused in her account, and I could see that she was close to tears again. I began to recognize the nature of them. She had held in her emotions for too long, then finally seeing me—who she perceived as her savior—she gave vent to them.

I refilled her glass with the last of my port. I had a loaf of bread and some cheese I'd bought that afternoon and made her sit and eat with me before going on, though it meant that I would have to spend the last of my money buying a replacement meal tomorrow evening. My kindness made her relax somewhat, and she went on in a stronger voice than I'd expected.

"The Bouttes had been in our employ through most of the winter when Elliot and I decided to journey together to Watkin's Glen in early March. A business acquaintance of my husband was being married some weeks later, and Elliot wanted me to order a new gown for the wedding. Though the weather had been unseasonably warm, enough that ferns were already poking through the thawing soil, there was still thick ice on the river, and of course the ever-present threat of snow or sleet until well into spring.

"Elliot hitched our team to the wagon he'd loaded with the latest batch of furs he'd collected. We started out just after breakfast, reached the Quinn farm by midmorning. As was our custom, we stopped to say hello and ask if they needed anything from town before continuing on.

"The next two hours brought a marked change in the weather. The sky that had previously been clear clouded over. The wind shifted out of the northeast and thick damp snow began to fall. I wanted to turn back, but Elliot argued that we were already more than halfway to town, and that in a few miles the road would merge with another, one wider and more level than the road we were on. I've never taken the cold well, so I took some of the furs Elliot had collected and used them as a blanket, covering even my face as we drove on down the narrow, twisting road.

"The wind increased. It gained speed as it blew across the lake, buffeting us in the occasional clearings. Its whistle in the trees grew as the storm strengthened. We heard two crashes in the forest and knew that some of the older, taller trees were meeting their end in the gale. I wanted to stop until it abated, but Elliot argued that we might as well travel as far as we could. 'You don't know how dangerous this weather can be,' he told me. 'If it continues like this, we could be fighting our way through waist-high drifts by tomorrow, and we're hardly dressed for bitter cold.'

"'Could we leave the wagon and travel on horseback?' I asked.

"'We will if we have to,' Elliot replied.

"I kept quiet after that and hoped that our well-trained horses would get us through."

Though Pamela seemed overwrought by what she was about to relate, she managed to continue in a soft but even voice. "To reach the main road, we had to travel through a final winding section of trail, made even narrower than the rest of our route by a steep drop-off to the lake. This exposed us to the full force of the wind, and Elliot had to struggle to keep the team moving slowly since all their instincts were to quicken their pace and find shelter in the trees just ahead. As we approached them, a sapling blew down in front of us. It would have done little danger, but the horses shied and tried to back up, throwing the cart over the side of the drop. The cart rolled, pitching the horses sideways. Before they could right themselves, they slid into the icy-covered waters some twenty feet below the road dragging the cart, and Elliot and me, with them.

"Everything that followed happened so quickly that I can recall only pieces of the next few minutes. The ice held for a moment in spite of our weight, then broke. The water flowed over me, colder even than the wind, so cold it knocked the breath from my body. I was close to losing consciousness when I felt Elliot push me onto the shore. I turned and saw him wade back into the center of the river to free the team. One of the horses was badly hurt in the fall. The other was floundering in the deeper water, struggling to right himself. Elliot managed to cut the luckier horse free, and as the animal began lumbering up the slope, Elliot ordered me to take hold of what remained of the harness. I knew that my life depended on my actions in the next few minutes, and I gripped the leather strap with all my remaining strength, holding on until the horse reached the trail. My strength failed me then, and I let him go as I fell onto the frigid ground. The wind beat against me, and I was certain my clothes were about to freeze on my body. I turned toward the river, fully expecting to see Elliot struggling up the bank behind me. I was alone.

"I called his name. I tried to see where he might have fallen, but I saw nothing and heard no reply. Knowing that we would both perish if I didn't get help, I crawled the few feet to where the horse was standing. By then my clothes were freezing to my back and my numb fingers could not get a grip on his reins.

"What happened next will probably sound impossible to you, Mr. Poe, but I swear it's the truth. Someone lifted me onto that horse's back. Someone wrapped my unfeeling hands around the reins, turned the horse in the direction of the Quinn farm, and started the half-frozen beast moving.

Later, I was certain it was my Elliot, come back from the dead to help me, but in truth I did not see his face. I must have lost consciousness sometime during the journey because when I woke I was wrapped in furs, close to the hearth in the Quinn house being tended by Mary."

Pamela stopped and looked at me, waiting no doubt for me to make some sort of comment about what I thought had happened to her. "Sometimes, when people are faced with deadly physical challenges, their bodies are capable of great, almost superhuman, bursts of strength. Later, when they look back on the moment, their minds have to invent reasons for their acts," I said.

"Is that what you really believe?" she asked.

"I write about ghosts, and worse, but in truth I always look for a rational explanation for supernatural events, and I always find one. No, I do not believe in them."

She shrugged. "I said I was certain. The reason will be clear enough later," she said. I knew that her mind was set, and she would not alter her own explanation for surviving.

"Mary said that as soon as he saw me, her husband guessed what had happened. He and one of his farm workers had gone to search for Elliot. They looked for hours, then gave up when the storm made the work too dangerous. Elliot's body was found two weeks later when the ice on the lake melted.

"The terrible cold I'd experienced had made me ill. Mary tended me with great care, but even when I had my strength back, I still did not feel completely well. Even so, I would not impose on my neighbors for too long. Instead I went home to try to deal with my situation.

"I was a widow at twenty-three, with lands so remote that I could not work them alone and no means to hire the men necessary to help me. Hardly an auspicious situation for one who had placed so much hope on marriage. But I still had what my husband had left me. I decided to continue maintaining both the vineyard and the trading company as long as I could. I knew some of the Indians who traded with us as well as my husband did. I hardly had his sense for barter, but I could probably get by. Maintaining the vineyard would not be difficult, and I could count on the Bouttes for some of the harder work. But even my hopes for that were ended when I realized that the weakness I had been experiencing had a far-too-common cause. One morning, when Colette Boutte came into the cabin to help with her usual duties, I was sitting at the table with my face white, my stomach on edge and my head spinning. 'You're going to have a child,' she said in her usual, expressionless tone, as if one more difficulty was not only to be endured but expected.

"Because I had loved my husband dearly, I was thankful. Nonetheless, I knew that soon I would not be able to do the work I usually did, let alone take on any of the labors of my lost husband. Certain that all my dreams of freedom were useless, I wrote a letter to the bank in Watkin's Glen, telling them that I was pregnant and that I would have to abandon the farm before winter. I asked their assistance in selling the land."

"You could have written your husband's family," I said.

"You don't understand, Mr. Poe. I wouldn't have had the slightest idea where to send the letter. In the nearly three years I had lived with Elliot, he had written his relations only once—to thank them for the wedding gift—and rarely spoke of them. I knew nothing about them but that they lived some-where in Louisiana. I could only assume that they had no idea that Elliot had died, let alone that I was expecting his child.

"Because of this, the gracious and sympathetic letter I received from his mother was a pleasant surprise. In it, she said that the bank had contacted her about the property, and had conveyed my news to her. She told me that she was elated that a part of her Elliot would live on. She said that she would ask me to come south to stay with her but did not want me to risk the journey so soon after the accident. She enclosed a draft for fifty dollars, which seemed like a fortune in that part of the country, and asked me to write her. Unfortunately, she had mailed the note in the envelope the bank had provided for the draft, and had not enclosed her own ad-dress.

"Morgan Quinn brought the letter to me. He later went to

town on my behalf, returning with supplies to make life easier for me. Ten dollars went to pay the Boutte's back wages. We got on better after that until two months later when my mother-in-law arrived.

"She came as unexpectedly as the letter had, just before dark. She was apparently more comfortable on water than land, for she'd traveled by steamer up the Ohio River and made the last part of her journey across Lake Seneca to the Quinn farm where she hired Morgan to ride her over in his cart. She stood in the center of my tidy, whitewashed cabin and stared at me so intently that a blush rose on my cheeks. 'What is it?' I finally asked.

"'You carry all that remains of my son,' she said and held out her arms. Though I am not a demonstrative person, I rushed into them. We embraced each other. I think she began to cry first, though I am not certain of that.

"Later, when we'd composed ourselves, I poured us each a glass of my husband's wine and we toasted his memory. From that night on, we called each other mother and daughter. I was pleased at first to finally be able to use that word, since in all my life I'd never had a mother to speak it to.

"Since Vivienne Donaldson spoke French, she began translating for me to the Bouttes. Eventually, they stopped asking questions of me, and she took over running the farm and vineyards.

"I suppose it was natural for them to look to an older woman for their orders, but I didn't like being ignored by my own hired help. I spoke to Vivienne about it, and things were better, though only for a little while. 'Why should I trouble you about every little detail,' Vivienne told me. 'You have more important things to consider.'

"Indeed I did, chief among them the fact that the only reason this woman was here was to make certain her grandson was born safely. I could not blame her for this except that I had the feeling, that for all her kindness, she had some hidden motive in her incessant fussing for me to eat regularly when I could scarcely swallow a slice of bread for breakfast, to rest when lying down brought horrifying dreams."

"What sort of dreams?" I asked her, knowing how much dreams could reveal.

She smiled, faintly.

"I am very small, still unsteady on my feet. I go down the hall to my mother's room and find instead my mother-in-law lying in the bed, brushing out her chestnut hair. She looks at me not with love, or care, but with incredible sorrow. I start to cry and wipe my eyes on the hem of my skirt. When I look up, she is gone."

"What do you think it means?"

She laughed without mirth. "I thought it wishful thinking, a reminder that once the child was born she would go home."

"I thought you indicated that you liked her company?" I reminded her. "You called her Mother, after all."

"I did, but as the weeks passed, there were things about her that made me feel uneasy. Perhaps it was her attitude. My house was never cleaner than after she cleaned it. My little flower beds were tended with such compulsive care that blooms just past their prime were snipped off immediately, lest their fading glory ruin the look of the plantings. Vivienne did not do this with any love or pride, but rather with an anxiousness that made it seem as if she were waiting for someone to come and find her remiss in her work. I knew her expression all too well; it brought back unpleasant thoughts of Father. I came to resent her presence, and the past it evoked. I wished she would leave. I would have been alone then except for the Bouttes, but it would have been a peaceful loneliness. She must have sensed my feelings, because she grew remote and secretive, saying little to me and often seeming to ignore me.

"In the autumn she took the same care in seeing to the harvest, sending Charles Boutte to town to hire extra hands. Even if Elliot had been there, we would have needed the help. The vines had never produced such bounty, but I grieved as I watched the men carry the grapes to the press. Elliot was not there to witness it."

"Death is harder on those left behind," I said.

She looked at me thoughtfully. "Immortal grief," she whispered.

I viewed her differently after that. We both knew that kind of loss, and it made us kin of the spirit.

"When the wine had been fermented and the barrels had been rolled into the cellar to age, the hired men went back to town for a few weeks, then returned after the first hard freeze to prune the vines. At Vivienne's request, they brought with them a young French-Canadian midwife, named Blanche, to stay with us until the baby was born. Colette Boutte had said that she knew something of deliveries, but Vivienne explained that she wanted someone with more experience to attend. 'Elliot was my firstborn,' she said. 'I want nothing but the best for you and his child.'

"Something about the way she spoke the words made me wonder if she was lying, though I could see no reason why she would. Actually, though I was still more than a little angry that she hadn't consulted me first, I also felt some relief. I hadn't wanted to face having the child with just Colette and Vivienne to help me, but had resigned myself to it because I couldn't afford a midwife. I took Vivienne's hand and kissed her cheek and thanked her sincerely.

"We four women would sit by the fire, Blanche, Colette, and I knitting booties and blankets for the baby while Vivienne read to us from the books she had brought from home. One was a collection of clippings of poems and tales she loved. I recall that one evening she recited 'The Raven' so dramatically that when a gust of wind beat a branch against the roof, I cried out in fear. But more often the volumes were in French. I understood one word out of ten, but Blanche and Colette were so pleased I did not protest and instead tried to pick up a new word or phrase as she read.

"My son was born on the winter solstice. It was an unseasonably warm day, and as the labor progressed, I stared out the little windows in my bedroom and watched the snow dripping from the porch eaves. When he had been washed and wrapped in blankets and laid beside me in the bed, I studied his face, trying to decide who he looked like. He gave little evidence of looking like either one of us, though what hair he had was nearly the same color as Elliot's, just slightly darker than mine."

Since Pamela had never described her husband, I asked her to do so now. Her eyes seemed to lose their focus, her expression to be lost in the past and I knew she was recalling his features in her mind before she replied.

"Sometimes it seemed that we were too much alike. No, not in looks, though there were similarities in our hair and complexion. I am speaking more of habits and temperament."

"That is usually what makes people wed," I replied.

"It was more than that. We both despised the ostentatiousness of our past. We preferred the intimate companionship of each other and a few close friends to that of crowds of near strangers, who always made us uneasy. I think we had been raised the same way, so much so that neither of us discussed our parents. Far better to speak of books we had read, people we had met, or even the weather. I could never shake the feeling that I had done something to wrong my father. There was always some sense of guilt. I think Elliot felt the same way about his own relations."

"And, of course, you had both been conveniently exiled, so it's little wonder you found each other," I commented.

"Found is hardly the word. Elliot was ordered by his mother to meet me, and he did so. I knew he loved me as much as I did him, but I think if his mother had ordered him to marry me, he would have obeyed even if there were no affection between us.

"In those months after Vivienne came to live with me, I watched for some sign of a strong will, but there was none. Actually, my mother-in-law was much like me, given to indecision and emotional tears. When she held her grandson for the first time, she gave way to them, and minutes later we were both crying. 'We'll name him after Elliot,' I said.

"She looked at me oddly and I wondered if she had a different name in mind. 'And may his middle name be Roderick, after my uncle?' she asked.

"It was hardly a name I would have chosen, but the request was a simple one, easily granted. Better than using my father's name, I thought. Later, she took to calling him

Roddy. Once I started to do the same, the middle name stuck to him as the first never had. So Roddy it was.

"With my child in my arms, I lay back and let the exhaustion of his birth claim me. Later, when I woke, there was moonlight leaking through the shutters on the windows. The fire on the hearth had died to only a few glowing coals, and in their light I saw Blanche sleeping on the floor. Vivienne was sitting in the rocking chair Elliot had bought for me, Roddy in her arms. I looked at her and thought of how tomorrow it would be me sitting there rocking my child and that all the fears for my future, the loneliness and the hardship of life there, had led to that one beautiful conclusion. I stood and, after a moment's dizziness, went and took my son from her. 'Get some rest yourself,' I whispered to her and carried Roddy to the warmth of my bed."

The clock in the downstairs hall—it and the lace curtains on all the windows being two of the only signs of civilization my current landlady allowed—struck one just as Pamela was finishing that last sentence. We had both managed to talk through the earlier chimes, but this single note droning in the silence of the night could not be ignored. "It's much later than I thought," she said. "If you wish, I could leave you to your sleep and return and finish the story in the morning."

She did not reach for her gloves or shawl. "Do you have a place nearby to stay?" I asked, knowing somehow that she didn't, and had come to me with no thought to her own comfort.

She shook her head.

"Are you tired?" I asked.

"No, but I don't want to keep you awake, or cause any damage to your reputation."

My reputation! If she had made inquiries about it with as much determination as she had in finding me, my visitor would have discovered that it was already somewhat spotted. But one thing I had never been accused of was any lack of manners or hospitality. I intended to remind my fiancé of this if she ever brought up rumors of Mrs. Donaldson's visit. "My sweet little Pilgrim!" I told her. "I could not send you out into the streets alone. If you have no place, you could sleep here and I could spend the night reading in the parlor. You see, I'm not tired either, especially now that you've said a name I recognize."

"Then I'd like to go on and tell the rest. I have some tea in my traveling bag if you'd like."

"I prefer coffee," I said, "but I can heat water for both of us."

I went downstairs and filled my pot from the kitchen pump, then opened the woodstove and placed it directly on the cinders of last night's fire. While I was waiting for the water to boil, I spied a half loaf of bread left over from the evening dinner. Knowing Mrs. Blakely would only throw it to the birds and bake more in the morning for the Swan Tavern guests, I ate a slice, wrapped the rest in a napkin and placed it in my pocket. At least I would not go hungry tomorrow evening, or have to beg some from her in the morning. Having done that, I carried the pot of hot water upstairs.

As I pushed open the door, I saw Pamela jump with alarm as if she had been expecting an intruder rather than her host. If she had vanished in my absence, I would hardly have been surprised, though certainly disappointed. She'd aroused my curiosity. If she didn't finish the tale, my imagination would have to do the work. I was beginning to suspect that reality would be the more fantastic.

chapter 4

"*Many things changed* in the months after Roddy was born. Blanche returned to Watkin's Glen as soon as the weather was warm enough for travel. Colette Boutte went with her to take a seamstress job in town. Her husband, who had always been a taciturn man, did his usual duties with invisible efficiency. There was always wood outside our door each evening for our fires, and the livestock seemed well tended. Vivienne fussed about me as much as ever, making certain I did not exert myself, or catch a chill.

"But for all her concern for my well-being, she also ignored me and doted on her grandchild. To her, everything I did was wrong. If I took the child out for air, she would tell me it was too cold, but later she would go and walk outside with him as well. I began to think she was deliberately trying to undermine my confidence in my mothering instincts, and I began to count the days until her departure.

"She probably sensed my resentment. We stopped playing cards or reading to each other. I think we both found it more pleasant not to speak at all.

"In milder weather Mary Quinn would sometimes ride over for a visit. Vivienne rarely spoke more than a few words to my friend, but when Mary left, she would make a point of stopping her and giving her a packet of letters and money for postage so Morgan could mail her correspondence the next time he went to town.

"I asked her about the letters and she told me she was writing to Elliot's grandmama and other friends in the South who would want to know about the family's new addition. I thought this strange only because she rarely mentioned her family. A birth announcement would be natural, but so many letters mailed so often seemed odd. She must have sensed my suspicion because she told me, 'If I did not write her and tell her of the boy's progress, she would come here herself to see him. In truth, the house is not large enough to contain the two of us. As for the other letters, I did come here quite suddenly. Friends do worry, you know.'

"I guessed what she meant and did not question her again. Instead, I mentally noted each sign of approaching spring. Though I would be alone again, I could easily learn to live without her.

"Roddy was a strong child. He made it through the winter without so much as the sniffles. As the weather warmed and the skies cleared, I was the one who began to feel unwell. At first, my stomach felt on edge; later my head pounded. I had a curious lethargy that kept me in bed, and my milk began to dry up. Since I could not nurse my child, I sent an urgent message to the Quinns'. Mary immediately came with a quart of goat's milk, along with the goat itself so that Roddy would have fresh milk to drink while we weaned him quickly on mashed potatoes and carrots thinned with gravy. Though by now we were well into summer, I could not suggest that Vivienne leave. In my illness I had come to rely on her too much.

"One morning I went to get my child from his crib and saw that his face was hot and flushed, his arms covered with a rash. Vivienne came as soon as I called. 'Perhaps it's the measles,' she said after she examined him. 'Or he may not be tolerating something he's been eating."

"He's hot," I said, certain that he must have the same illness that had weakened me so much.

"'There's a doctor in Watkin's Glen, isn't there?' Vivienne asked.

"'It's so far,' I protested. 'And it's so cold and damp this morning.'

"Vivienne looked outside and frowned. 'You're right,' she admitted. 'But if he isn't better by tomorrow . . .'

"'Then by all means, go with him,' I said, finishing her thought.

"The next day was clear and Roddy seemed hotter than the day before, and listless as well. When Vivienne tried to feed him, he refused to eat. Seeing no other choice, I bundled him up, kissed him goodbye, and watched Vivienne ride off with Charles Boutte. After saying a prayer for their safe journey, I went back to bed and slept through the day. That night I ate the stew that Vivienne had left for me, but soon after I finished it, I felt so ill that I was almost too weak to rise from the table. I started for my bed, but as I did I saw Elliot standing beside it.

"Now I may have loved my husband, Mr. Poe, but his ghost was frightening, and the angry expression on his face did not lessen my fear. I backed away from him. As I did, the dizziness I felt seemed to coalesce in my stomach. I rushed outside and threw up all that I had eaten. I fell to my knees, suddenly so weak that I doubted I could stand and walk to the house."

"Did Elliot come to you again to help?" I asked.

"No, though I admit I almost expected him to. Instead, I managed to crawl inside, then with difficulty, I shut and barred the door and went to bed. I was certain I was going to die and so very thankful that Elliot's spirit was near me and someone was watching over my Roddy.

"Have you ever been so ill, Mr. Poe, that time slips by without notice? It was that way for me. I would wake, drink a bit of water or eat some bread, then return to sleep. I was roused from my uneasy rest by a pounding at the door. I called out, and finally stumbled to the door and unbarred it.

"Mary Quinn stood outside with a basket of bread, meat, and cheese. 'Have you gotten any news about Roddy?' she asked.

"I shook my head. 'Vivienne hasn't been gone long,' I said.

"'Long!' Mary exclaimed. 'It's been five days.'

"'Five,' I whispered, then convinced that my child must be dead, and I on my way to join him, my legs gave way. Mary caught me as I fell and helped me inside. Soon she'd built a fire to drive out the dampness, and fixed me a pot of her tea and some bread and honey. I lay in my bed, sobbing, unable to stop or to say a word to my friend, such was the depth of my despair."

"Vivienne Donaldson poisoned you, didn't she?" I asked.

"Is it as obvious as all that?" she replied with a sad laugh. "It wasn't so to me. Not then, nor for the days that Mary stayed and nursed me back to health with her teas and tonics and the pleasant warmth of her presence. By the time I was able to get out of bed, more than a week had passed. Vivienne had sent no word, nor had Charles Boutte returned. As soon as I was able, accompanied by Morgan Quinn, I went into town to look for my child.

"Vivienne Donaldson had been there, but only for one day. After resting in town for the night, she and Roddy had taken the coach to Elmira. I caught the driver just as he was pulling out for another run and learned that she had been dropped at the train station. The coachman could recall nothing else.

"That was the moment when I realized exactly what Vivienne Donaldson had done to me, and why. She had wanted my child. Now she had him and there was nothing I could do about it."

"Were there no authorities to help you?" I asked, amazed that she should be without any assistance.

"Watkin's Glen has an army outpost. I went to their colonel, but outside of sending out inquiries on my behalf, he could do nothing. I stood in his office, bereft of funds, of strength, of family, and fought back my tears. Tears were a sign of weakness, Mr. Poe, and I would not be weak. I cried while I told you this story, but it is the first time I have cried since Mary Quinn pounded on my door.

"With no choice left me, I decided to go after my child myself. I went outside and conferred with Morgan Quinn. Then the two of us walked the quarter mile to the one-room building that served as our local bank. Quinn intended to pull out part of his savings and arrange a loan to buy my land and cabin. The price we agreed to was probably half what it was worth, but I had no time to hunt up a richer buyer and five hundred dollars was all Quinn thought the bank would let him borrow.

"I had intended to set up a line of credit so that I could begin the search for my son, and perhaps offer a small reward for his return. But even this modest idea was denied me. Though the banker was sympathetic when he heard my story, he informed me that as the surviving spouse, I was entitled to all of Elliot's bank account; however, I could not sell the land because Elliot had never owned it.

"'Are you sure?' I asked the banker.

"'It's what he told me when he opened an account here. Maybe he took title to it since then. Do you have a deed, or some paper to use as proof?'

"I shook my head. I had never seen any legal papers in the house at all. When Elliot told me he'd come north to claim an inheritance, he hadn't said he owned the place, at least not precisely. I had only assumed.

"But if it hadn't belonged to him, it had to belong to somebody. Perhaps the banker had a name, or an address. 'Who owns the deed?' I asked him.

"'I remember that your husband showed me a letter allowing him to take possession of the property. It was signed by a woman.'

"'Was the name Vivienne?'

"'I don't recall, except that I thought it odd that a woman would own a piece of frontier land. The records aren't here. You'll have to go to the courthouse in Albany for them.'

"'This is an emergency!' I wanted to scream. 'Don't you understand what's happened!' But of course he did, and he was doing all he could to be helpful. It just wasn't enough. In that moment I thought of my father and how he had searched for so long for my mother. I thought of his pride, and his sorrow. For the first time in my life I sympathized with him. 'I believe that the land is owned by my deceased husband's family,' I said. 'May I continue to consider what the land produces to be my own?'

"'Until the family complains, of course you may. Your son will probably inherit it someday. In the meantime, if you work it, I would think the courts would agree that the income from it is yours.'

"'If someone works the land for me, may I transfer the profits from it to that person?'

"'Is that what you want to do?'

"I nodded and drew Quinn aside. 'Last year, Elliot made over a hundred dollars from those vineyards,' I said. 'The harvest will be better this year. If you loan me fifty dollars, I will sign over this year's profits to you.'

"'It's too much,' he protested, but again I knew it was all he could afford. I reminded him that I already had the forty-two dollars from Elliot's account, and that he would have to pay laborers to help with the harvest and pressing if he wanted any profit from the land. He agreed and drew out the money.

"Just before we left, I asked the banker one final, important question. 'When she came here, my mother-in-law told me she'd been informed of Elliot's death by the bank. Did someone here know her?"

"The only information that came out of here was a notice of your husband's death sent to the Capitol in Albany. It would have been their responsibility to notify the owners of the land. That would be how the family learned of his death. And of course that means . . ."

"He paused, his expression brightened as he realized I had already deduced what he was going to say. They had an address in Albany, or they would not have been able to write.

"Quinn and I returned to my home so that I could pack. In the company of Mary Quinn, I spent the last night in the house I had thought was mine. Mary sat beside me in front of the fire, holding my hands and trying to offer me what advice she could. Finally she pulled a knit drawstring bag from her pocket, asked me to hold it a moment, then spill its contents on the carpet. It contained about a dozen square wood tiles, decorated with symbols on each side. With the golden rays from the tiny blaze flickering over her face, Mary studied the pattern they made for nearly half an hour before speaking.

"'Everything should be scattered now, but the reading is oddly unified,' she told me. 'Your plight grows out of a single person . . . a man, I think. His deeds affected you long before you came here. Pamela, you must seek your son in the past. You must.'"

"'How can you be so certain?' I asked.

"'It is a gift I have been blessed with. I can see, and I know I'm right.' She began collecting her tiles, wiping each of them on the hem of her dress before putting them in the bag. 'Years ago each village would have one family whose members would act as both seer and healer, and the power would pass from the old seer to the one he, or more likely she, chose to train in the arts. Those times are over, but some of the knowledge persists. My grandmother taught me. I will teach my daughter or son. So the legacy passes.'

"The next day, with the Quinns' money in my pocket, and my bags packed with my few decent dresses, I bought a coach ticket to Albany. As I rode away, I looked down at the tiny lark and tulip design Mary had drawn on my bag—symbols of luck, love, and fortitude—and thought of her advice. Though I did not believe in fortune-telling, I remembered everything she said so clearly because I was so desperate, and because her words seemed to touch the empty core of my soul. In truth, they sounded so right.

"But I took greater comfort in the other, more tangible help Mary had given me. Unlike me, she was an inquisitive woman. She'd opened the packets Vivienne had given Morgan and read the addresses on the letters. Though she couldn't recall the names, most of them were to different people in New Orleans and Natchez, but four were to the same place, the State Bank of Albany. The last letter sent had been to them.

"I had somewhere to begin, and two sources for the information I needed most. I thought that better than leaving home with no hope at all."

*   *   *

It seemed from Pamela's description that Albany had not changed overly much since my own brief visit there a decade ago. It was still a town of dour, industrious men and women in their brick houses with the uniform tile roofs that must have reminded the original settlers of their Dutch homeland. We sat drinking our tea and coffee as she composed herself to continue her story.

"I had arrived in the city far too late to find the courthouse or law firm open," she said, "so I got off the coach a stop early and walked the short distance to the Hudson School.

"Mrs. Lowell herself answered the door. For a moment I thought she did not recognize me. Then she drew me inside, offered me a seat in the parlor, and without asking why I had shown up at her door unannounced and at such a late hour, she rang for tea.

"I told her as much of the story as I knew and asked if I could stay the night. 'There is always room for one of our girls,' she replied.

"I'd expected a room, and some food, nothing more. But the next morning Mrs Lowell ordered her coach made ready and rode with me to town.

"I haven't described Mrs. Lowell to you yet, but I feel I must now. She was a widow, once married to one of the wealthiest settlers in that area. When he died, leaving her without children, she decided to devote her life to other children of every social class. She took the sizable funds left her by her husband and purchased the Hudson School. Until then, the school had been in a slow decline. She revitalized it, giving it an energy it hadn't previously had. She is a Quaker, and an abolitionist. More than once I saw her ride off in the middle of the night, and the next morning we would have a new Negro serving girl in the house who would disappear some days later as suddenly as she had arrived. Since many of the politicians and wealthier merchants were also Quakers who shared her views at least privately, she educated many of the young women of the area, including the daughters of William Dow, president of the State Bank of Albany. Though nearing sixty, Mrs. Lowell still had a way of getting what she wanted—be it perfect deportment from her girls during the spring social, donations for the new school wing, or an immediate appointment with Mr. Dow.

"The more things went my way, the more my hopes rose, and the more emotional I became. I wanted to fling my arms around Mr. Dow's pudgy neck and cry on his shoulder, but instead I sat with my hands politely folded in my lap, my back straight as Hudson girls' backs always are, and told him my story. My voice stayed even; my eyes remained dry. I felt as if I were reading a play rather than telling the story of my own tragedies.

"When I had finished, Mr. Dow stood up and, without saying a word, left the room. As I watched him go, I thought I saw him pull a kerchief from his pocket.

"Apparently Mrs. Lowell had noticed the gesture as well. 'Were you in school with his daughter, Miranda, my dear?' she asked me.

"'Just the first year I was there,' I replied.

"'She died last year of influenza. The loss still grieves him.' She reached out and covered my gloved hand with one of hers. 'Emotional ties between people can be so important,' she added.

"Dow returned some minutes later with a huge account book. After studying the recent entries, he looked up at me and shrugged. 'I don't know how much I can help you,' he said. 'Vivienne Donaldson and her son opened a joint account here seven years ago. At her order the account was closed after the death of her son and the balance transferred to the law firm of Grymes and Livingston in New Orleans. It's really all I know.'

"'You have no address for the woman?' Mrs. Lowell asked.

"He shook his head. 'Have you been to the courthouse?' he asked.

"'We're going there now,' I said. He wrote down the name of the law firm—as if I could forget it! I thanked him and we left."

"Please stop a moment," I said, covering my eyes with my fingertips, trying to weigh just how much to ask her, and de-

ciding that for just this once she must be warned. "How did
your mother-in-law know to come north to be with you?"

"She said the bank . . . No, Mr. Poe, you're right. The
bank didn't know her address, though the one in Albany apparently sent some official notification of Elliot's death to
the woman's legal representative."

"But they wouldn't have known of your pregnancy?"

She looked at me, a puzzled look growing on her face as
she searched for a solution. "Someone must have known the
family and written."

"You said Elliot kept to himself," I reminded her gently.

"Someone was spying on us? But who, Mr. Poe, and
why?"

"Perhaps someone was paid to spy on him, probably by an
overprotective mother who was worried about a son who left
her when he'd scarcely reached manhood, went into the
wilderness alone, and never wrote home," I said.

As I'd hoped, she laughed but only for a moment. "I see
your point, though I still find the idea of someone spying on
us to be troubling. It could have been anyone."

"The Bouttes?" I suggested.

"I don't think they knew how to read and write. Perhaps it
was one of the clerks at the bank. We and the Quinns both
knew the local bankers well. If one of them had been paid to
send occasional letters to the family, he'd hardly let on about
it if he wanted to keep his job."

"Perhaps." I nodded. "Please continue."

"On the walk to the courthouse, Mrs. Lowell gave me as
much encouragement as she could, but in truth I did not need
it. Actually, I was trying not to get my hopes up too high. I
had one new piece of information. Even if there was nothing
to be found at the courthouse, I hadn't reached a dead end
yet."

Pamela paused in her speaking and looked at me curi-
ously. "Do you think that those who are raised harshly are
better able to withstand adversity?" she asked.

In truth I had never considered the matter, though I must
admit that I am proof of her point. I had been raised in a

wealthy home, and it had taken years of adversity before I became accustomed to it. "I don't know. Perhaps it's a matter of temperament," I replied.

"If so, I never should have reached Albany, but there I was, my voice steady as I asked to speak to a courthouse clerk.

"This time the information was harder to come by because we did not know the exact year when the land transferred to my husband's family, nor what the name of the relation owning it had been. After two hours and a consultation with his superior the clerk did manage to find some records of our farm and vineyard by going back to the earliest mention of it in the records and working forward. The land had originally been part of a grant from Queen Anne to Johannis Hardenbergh in the early 1700s. It had changed hands four times since, eventually from an English owner to a French one, named Villers, and finally to that of one Madeline Usher of New Orleans. There was no address for her, but I thought of the letters Vivienne had mailed, and her dealings with the New Orleans law firm, and decided that her relations would not be difficult to find."

"So it would seem. But what then brought you here?" I asked, trying to sound more curious than concerned, to give her not the slightest cause to think I had anything but the utmost fascination with her story.

"Doubts, Mr. Poe. And caution. I do not want to have one slender thread to hold on to when two would be so much better."

"You were thinking of your mother, weren't you?"

Again, she looked at me with such surprise at my understanding that I wondered if in all her life anyone had ever paid this much attention to her fears or her desires. "Exactly," she said. "There may be no lawyer in New Orleans. Even if there is, Vivienne could leave my life as utterly as fog in the morning sun.

"But I did not think of you immediately. Instead, as Mrs. Lowell and I walked to her carriage, I told her that the name on the deed was familiar but I could not recall why.

"'Under better circumstances you'd certainly recall it,'

Mrs. Lowell replied. 'Think of a terrifying story you once read in your contemporary literature class.'

(I must make a personal comment here. In spite of the compelling story she had told me, I felt a sudden thrill in knowing that the Hudson School had considered my work literature—something the critics had never seemed to note.)

"Of course I remembered the story then," Pamela continued. "When we returned to the school, I asked Mrs. Lowell if she'd kept a copy of it.

"That night I turned up the lamp and read the tale again, paying particular attention to the descriptions of brother and sister. Physically, they resembled many people, but their temperament, their heightened senses, nervousness, and retreat from the world reminded me most of my Elliot and his mother. The brief author's note which accompanied the story described it as a work of fiction, yet I could not help but question its origin, and the odd fact that the names were apparently the same as those of my husband's grandmother and great uncle. Were you writing about real people, Mr. Poe? If so, did you know them? Where was the house that fell?"

Real. Yes, those people had lived and breathed and I had known them all too well. But they had not been called Usher, but Allan. It had been my stepmother who lay dying, the fever and pain making her delirious. It had been my stepfather who had watched helplessly as she faded, taking out his grief and rage on every living person around him. And, it occurred to me, that I, too, was an Usher, for when I wrote the story my beloved wife was already in that inevitable consumptive decline. Though I turned a blind eye to the truth for as long as I could, it colored my dreams and through them my work.

I thought a moment, then replied, "Actually there were two families named Usher. One of them, a husband and wife, were actors in the same company as my mother. I never really knew them, though my brother, Henry, spoke of seeing them perform from time to time. It was their family name that stuck with me. Later, when someone who knew my sense of the macabre gave me an old, badly written news account of the apparent death of a brother and sister when their house collapsed around them during a storm, I noted their names, thought they might be relations of my mother's friends and read it. Years later I wrote a story based on that yellowed scrap of paper. That's all. So I never knew them."

"You used their real names?"

"I did. Though the body of the woman was never found, it was believed that she and her brother were both dead. Since they hadn't left any heirs, I thought to give them just a bit of immortality."

"Where did the story originate?"

I tried to remember, but all I could see in my mind was Roderick Usher in his crumbling, isolated mansion and the oppressive swamps around it. My setting had been the Dismal Swamp of southern Virginia, but the original event could have happened anywhere. It had been over ten years since I'd written the story, longer since I'd read the report that inspired it, but I've always prided myself on my memory for facts as well as verse. Have I been so ill of late that these things slip through my mind so easily? "I recall only that the story did not happen in this country," I replied, trying to think of something more helpful to add.

"How old was the story?"

"I believe that the events took place before eighteen hundred."

"Louisiana was not part of this country then. That could be the right place?"

I could see that she was getting far too optimistic. Yet, perhaps she had a right to. Louisiana had been under control of the Spanish at that time, or perhaps the French since the area had changed hands so quickly and so often at the turn of the century. "I keep notes on all my stories," I said. "If you'll be staying in the area for any length of time, I can ask to have them sent to me here."

"No, I can't wait. I have to go on, but I could write you as soon as I am able and provide an address where you can reach me when you receive the information."

I took a piece of note paper, wrote down two addresses, and handed it to her. "If I move from here to somewhere else in Richmond, I'll be sure to leave a forwarding address. If I leave the city, you can reach me through my home in Ford-ham."

She was staring down at the paper as if it contained some terribly profound information. As the silence grew, so did her agitation. "What if I get there and the lawyer simply denies that the family knows anything about Vivienne's where-abouts or my child? Do you think it would be better if I went to the local authorities before I meet with him?"

I considered that course and shook my head. "You have to make it in the family's self-interest to tell you the truth," I replied. "Judging from your husband's reticence to speak of them, I suspect that the family has had scandals enough in the past and hardly needs you starting another one. Now I know this will be difficult, but can you find some reason to forgive your mother-in-law for what she did?"

Pamela had a quick mind for she understood what I suggested almost immediately. "She has a highstrung sort of disposition. The isolation wore on her. Her son's death, followed so quickly by her grandson's serious illness, must have thrown her into a state of nervous collapse. For the sake of my son's future reputation, I wouldn't want her condition made public."

I clapped, softly so as not to disturb the Swan's other guests. "Exactly!" I declared.

"There's more." She smiled, openly and confidently, and I could see that this final conversation was the one which would give some peace of mind on the rest of her journey. "Until my mother-in-law disappeared with my son, she was very kind to me. She spoke of other relations. Since I've always had a great deal of curiosity about my husband's family, I look forward to meeting them and only wish it could have been under better circumstances."

"Say the last with some reticence, as if you still aren't sure," I commented.

"That will hardly be difficult." As she replied, the clock downstairs struck two. We both paused to take note of it.

"The next train leaves at seven-thirty," she said. "I'll go to the station now and wait for it."

"You'll do nothing of the sort," I replied. "I'll sleep in a chair downstairs, wake you at six and walk with you to the station."

I slept as best I could in one of the easy chairs in the parlor reserved for the boarding guests. As I'd expected, I woke each time that infernal grandfather clock chimed the hour, with some scrap of "The Raven" rolling round in my brain, repeating itself over and over like the refrain of the poem itself. I never regretted writing it, for I'd written it to make myself immortal and it was well on the way to doing just that. But I did wish that I had not been asked to recite it so often that I'd committed its addicting verse to memory. Finally, just after dawn, I fell into a deep sleep.

And a dream came back to me, similar to another I'd had only weeks ago. In the first, a woman had comforted me in my most desperate hour of need, while I was imprisoned in Philadelphia. Surrounded by ruffians and worse, I'd escaped into sleep and found *her*, a woman of incredible beauty and angelic serenity. She'd stood at the top of a long flight of stairs, her thin bare arms extended, her expression one of melancholy comfort. Yet she had brought no comfort, only a vision of the trials to follow, then gave no advice on how to avoid them.

I'd seen myself, transformed into my own immortal raven, circling higher, ever higher until I was lost in the clouds. And while I soared, beyond caring about mortal matters, black robed figures came and dragged away my dear Aunt Muddy, tormenting her. Her screams brought me back to earth and I was forced to watch. . . .

No, I will not record the rest of it, for to set the vision down will only commit it more firmly to my memory! I only mention it because the setting of the second dream was the same, only now it was Pamela at the top of the stairs, her arms reaching toward me. I could not see myself, yet I knew that madness had gripped me, and that she was fighting for my soul, my life. . . .

I held fast to this uneasy vision, not waking as the clock chimed the next few hours until it reached seven. I woke with a start and rushed upstairs, intending to wake Pamela and tell her to hurry. When she did not answer, I went into my room and found the bed neatly made. I might have assumed that her entire story had been one long and particularly vivid dream had it not been for one of my envelopes propped up in my pillow. She'd enclosed twenty dollars along with a note thanking me for listening, and for the room, and entreating me to please do what I could to discover the source of my story. The final words read simply, *Before I left Albany, Mrs. Lowell added greatly to my traveling funds. I hope I have more than enough for my journey. I want to pay for the room, and for whatever expenses you will have in getting the information. I am forever in your debt. Pamela Donaldson.*

She'd given me ten times what she should have, yet I needed the funds so badly. I thought of her thin face and how it had looked with eyes full of tears, or her lips turned up in one of those fleeting, brave smiles. I could not help but compare her tragic life with the stoic propriety of Elmira Royster, that childhood sweetheart whom I'd recently met again and hoped to marry.

But I do not need someone who experiences the same elation and despair that I do. I must remind myself of this often. I need a safe harbor when my mental flights of fancy play themselves out and I crash exhausted on the all-too-real rocks.

Yet, even if I never see Pamela Donaldson again, her memory will always be with me as is the memory of so many women, living and dead, who have touched my life.

I sat at the table and wrote immediately to my aunt Muddy, the woman I call "Mother" with as much joy as Pamela must have felt when she first used the word to her mother-in-law. I sent Muddy half the money Pamela had left me and asked her to go through my notes and find any information she could on the original house of Usher. Then, as I lay down for a few more hours of slumber, I said a prayer to whatever fates might listen, that Pamela would have success in her quest.

part two

❧

THE
FAMILY USHER

chapter 5

There is a languid silken texture to the ripples of frigid
waters that is not present in warmer ones. Pamela had first
noted the difference as she sailed up the Hudson River to Albany so many years before. She had seen it in the creek that
flowed through her husband's vineyard, and in the slate-col-
ored waters of Lake Seneca. She had no desire ever to look
on it again.

So rather than heading for the coast, she took the railroad
south to catch a steamer bound for New Orleans from a
warm-water port and met the famous Edgar Poe. He had not
seemed a harsh or ill-tempered man, as some of the things
she had read about him in the past had led her to expect.

Nor had she found the lunatic Mrs. Lowell had thought he
might be. Yes, there had been an unsettling intensity in his
eyes, so strong that he seemed to be trying to read her
thoughts or see into her soul. Mrs. Lowell had mentioned rumors of laudanum use, but Poe had not seemed delusional.
Far from it! His thoughts had been perfectly rational, his sug-
gestions all logical, and his offer to help so completely sincere that she had no doubt that he would aid her. She found
herself thinking of him often on the long ride south, surprised to find that the vibration of the rails lulled her into a
kind of waking sleep in whose reverie she'd carry on a men-

tal conversation with Poe as if she were relating the details of her ongoing journey as she had her past life.

And in that conversation she also confessed all the little particulars her polite upbringing had prohibited her from speaking aloud. In truth, she had married a man very much like her father.

Oh, Elliot had courted her sweetly enough, and the letters he wrote during their long separation were loving, understanding and, she believed, sincere. They spent their wedding night in Albany's best hotel, his chaste kisses progressing slowly to more passionate ones. His caresses were light at first, and she was aware of how carefully he gauged her passion before demanding more. When finally he removed her embroidered nightdress, she scarcely blushed at all. Later, far later than she would have expected, she felt so much pleasure that she hardly noticed that brief moment of pain.

So of course he'd had experience with women, but it was not her place to ask. Besides, he had been southern raised, and wealthy. Southern men, she knew, had their pick of women—those they bought by the night as well as the dark-skinned ones whose lives they owned, often from birth.

No, it was not her place to ask any questions of him, only to be thankful that he had found her, claimed her, rescued her from an uncertain future. How foolish she'd been! How innocent.

Perhaps her status changed on her wedding night without her ever realizing it. Perhaps once Elliot possessed her, he'd thought of her as one more possession. She only knew that from the time their train pulled out of Albany, he became as distant from her as he was from the strangers in the seats around them. He was a quiet man, she'd told herself, shy rather than aloof, and when they were alone in their new home, things would be better.

In a way, they were. They worked together, slept together, shared thoughts of their future together. Yet, it always seemed to her that Elliot's mind was elsewhere, as if he were trying to solve a problem he could not share with her.

For a time she even thought that he was disappointed in her, but gradually, over the months they lived together, he became less remote, as if the passion he had confessed to in their courtship had finally grown into tenderness, into love.

They got on well so long as she didn't inquire about his family or his home; about any of the events in his life before he came to his small bit of land, his cottage and his vines. When she did, she was met with a silence, one that would often last for weeks at a time. In the beginning her prying was often deliberate. Later, it was usually an innocent slip of the tongue. Nonetheless, the result was the same. She never knew if he intended to punish her for bringing up the past or if its reminder simply brought on some deep melancholy that would grab hold of him until he rallied and fought it off. She only knew that as quickly as his silences came, they ended. Since he was all she had in that vast green wilderness, she soon learned to keep her questions to herself. Eventually her ignorance became natural, accepted.

Until Poe had asked her why she didn't write her in-laws directly, she hadn't even considered how strange this ignorance would seem to anyone. But she did understand why she hadn't found her husband's secrecy odd; she'd lived that way all her life.

Four days after her meeting with Edgar Poe, as she waited to board the steamer bound for New Orleans, she felt a sudden surge of fear. Clutching the wooden rail that provided some safety on the dock crowded with passengers and crates of goods waiting to be shipped, she forced herself to look down at the water, to think of her child and the quest she was on.

"A float, ma'am?" someone asked.

Pamela turned and saw a boy about thirteen holding an armful of canvas vests. "Filled with cork. Guaranteed to float. May you never need it." As she dubiously felt the thickness of it, he added, "And it's a good seat cushion for the hard wooden benches on board."

She glanced around and saw that the other vest sellers were doing a brisk business and decided that there was some use to them after all, if only to provide some extra measure of courage while she climbed the narrow, steeply pitched plank to the passenger deck.

Through the week that followed, she tried to keep to herself, but discovered that an unescorted young woman attracted the attention of everyone. Young single men paid her compliments and offered to share their food and drink with her. Older men wanted to protect her, one even going so far as to call her "daughter." She finally struck up an acquaintance with a woman in her sixties, also traveling alone. Isobelle Braud was a native of Louisiana, a descendent of the Acadians, returning to the city after a long absence to visit her daughter and son-in-law, and see the grandchildren she'd heard about only through letters. She did not pry into the reason for Pamela's journey but instead prattled on about her children, and their fates in the land to which their families had been exiled. One of them had married a distant cousin named Broussard, and Pamela could not help but ask, "Was he perhaps related to an Anna Broussard? She was my mother."

"Mother?" the woman frowned and touched her hair, a gesture she did so often that Pamela was certain that at one time she had worn it down and long and had developed the habit of running her fingers through it. "I don't know any Anna Broussard, though I am sure there are probably many with the name. You see, my husband's father was Acadian. Those people were from only a few large families, so there are many Broussards and Brasseauxs and Heberts and Brauds and Moutons, all intermarried into one huge family. I suppose you think them savages—"

"Not at all," Pamela quickly responded. "I think the Acadians are heroic for surviving all they've been through."

"Everyone has tragedies, my dear, and we all survive because we must. In that sense, my grandparents were no different from anyone else," Mrs. Braud replied, patting her hand with such sympathy that Pamela was certain the woman had seen right through her peaceful facade.

At night Pamela would sit with the other passengers in the dining hall, the oil lamps swaying above their heads as the guests pulled out fiddles, guitars and harmonicas and began to play well-known songs. Dancing was difficult on the swaying deck, so the passengers contented themselves with singing.

One evening, as Pamela sat alone on deck, someone too shy to perform for the crowd began to play a violin. As the full moon rose, drawing a line of silver across the placid gulf waters, she had a sudden vivid memory of an informal recital at home.

She could not have been more than two. She sat in one of the wooden parlor chairs with her feet straight out in front of her. She saw her father standing across the room, Emmie in the foyer just out of sight of the guests. Her mother sat beside her, her graceful hands nervously beating time to the music. It was the first time she had thought of Anna Broussard in any way at all pleasant in a long while.

As the boat moved south along the tip of Florida, the cool sea breezes gave way to a sultry heat. Men who had been formally dressed began appearing without coats and vests, while the women retired to the shady side of the boat to pull off their gloves and bonnets, roll up their sleeves, and do their best to keep cool.

Days passed, days in which the air only moved because the boat moved and the breeze reeked of coal tar from the smokestacks. Mrs. Braud had brought copies of *Jane Eyre* and *Wuthering Heights*, and Pamela soon found herself called upon to take her turn at reading from the sad novels of doomed love and revenge. So far her life had that same inevitable tragedy, but it would change, she vowed, it would change.

When the ship angled northward and into the Mississippi, the gnats and mosquitoes descended on the passengers like some biblical plague. Mrs. Braud invited Pamela to sit in her tiny private cabin, and they spent the last two hours of the journey in a space so sultry, Pamela found herself fighting to breathe.

They pulled into New Orleans late in the afternoon onto a wharf swarming with people and goods. Many of the passengers were going upriver to Natchez and beyond. They moved quickly from the steamer to the *Hecla*, a riverboat belching smoke and cinders from its stacks as it made ready to shove off. Fortunately, the wind was blowing from the north, sparing them the smoke, and bringing with it scents of baking bread, oranges, and jasmine.

Over a half dozen of Mrs. Braud's relatives were at the dock to meet her. In spite of the pressing heat, her daughter had even brought the children, including an infant that she laid in Mrs. Braud's arms before they started up the broad stairs leading to the top of the levee.

Pamela had wanted to say goodbye, but did not want to intrude on the reunion, nor to call out as they left for fear they would think she wanted an invitation to stay with them. However, her shyness made no difference. Mrs. Braud paused, searched for her in the crowd, and walked back to her. Looking down at the infant in her arms, she asked, "Isn't she a beautiful child?"

The child was sleeping peacefully in spite of the heat, and the rash the heat had caused on her neck. Nonetheless, she was beautiful. Pamela nodded.

"Do you have a place to stay?" Mrs. Braud asked.

"I was hoping to ask your advice on where to go. I'll be in town for some weeks."

"Well, tonight at least, you can stay with me." Mrs. Braud motioned at one of the younger men in her party, who took Pamela's bags from her. They all piled into a pair of coaches, with the children sitting on their elders' laps to make room for Pamela. "Go past the market so that Mrs. Donaldson can see it, Thomas," Mrs. Braud called to their driver.

He obliged, and they traveled past the source of all those marvelous scents—vendors at wooden stalls sold everything from food and clothing to apparently their children—or at least that was what Mrs. Braud made clear as she pointed out a pair of beautiful mulatto girls of about fifteen, who were being paraded by their grandmother past a group of creole dandies dressed in the height of fashion.

What astonished Pamela the most were the number of well-dressed Negroes and the way they walked with their heads high, rubbing elbows with equally well-dressed white men. "*Gens de colour*, free men," Mrs. Braud explained. "It seems as if half of New Orleans' Negroes are free; the others only act that way." She laughed, then added, "There's no avoiding them here. If you want musicians for a wedding, a daguerreotype of the happy couple, a specially made gift for them, or some personalized poetry to read at the ceremony, you go to them and are thankful that they exist. Free men are creative men. The rest of the South could learn from that, I think, though I rarely say it aloud outside of my family." She ended with a chuckle that softened the impact of her words.

Pamela stared into the crowd, noting the constant animation of it. This was a city of quick laughter, of open tears, of sudden rage. Was this really the place her Elliot had come from? If so, why had he been so stoic, so shy, so guarded? Why had he left at all?

They circled round the French Market, along the back of a charming white church and down a narrow road, remarkable only for its deep water-filled ruts, the thick frosting of mud on the door stoops, and the delicately curved iron railings of the balconies hanging so beautifully above them.

Pamela expected them to leave town and drive to the plantation Mrs. Braud had spoken of so often. Instead, the carriages pulled up in front of a two-story building with tall open windows facing the street. Everyone piled out and waited for Mrs. Braud to throw open the doors, then followed her into an airy house with wide archways between the foyer, parlor, dining room, and sunroom. A narrow hall to the right led straight back to the kitchen and an open staircase undoubtedly leading to the bedrooms above.

"Oh, my dears. I'd expected to have some work to do. You've done it all!" the woman exclaimed, looking at the polished floors and furniture, the magnificent oriental carpets, the silver coffee service on the table polished and ready for use, the plate of muffins beside it. A servant about Mrs. Braud's age came down the stairs, her status evident less in her clothing—which was more stylish than most of the dresses Pamela owned—than in the chocolate color of her skin and the apron she wore. She curtsied in front of Mrs. Braud, then stood at attention, waiting for an order.

"Sally! For pity's sake," Mrs. Braud said. "When have we

ever been so formal?" With that she hugged the woman and kissed her on the cheek.

Hardly the sort of greeting her father would give to a house slave, Pamela thought, rubbing the scar on her arm.

Mrs. Braud's two older grandchildren ran to the piano in the foyer and began arguing over who would play the first tune, then decided on a duet. They played it with deafening enthusiasm, but no one seemed to mind. While Sally went to fill the coffeepot, the adults settled into the parlor. The conversation—half French, half English—was lively and quick. Pamela, weary from the long journey, could not keep up with it. She spoke when spoken to and that was all. In truth, she couldn't remember their names, their relationship to Mrs. Braud, or even who the mother of that charming baby girl might be.

The snack and coffee gave way to a light dinner of seafood stew and cornbread and fresh peach pie. Then, as quickly as the house had filled, it emptied, leaving Pamela alone with her hostess. "I thought they'd spend the night," Pamela said.

"They'll have plenty of light to travel," Mrs. Braud replied. "The little ones can sleep in their own beds. They're less trouble that way." She picked up a decanter and two glasses and led Pamela through the sunroom and into the courtyard.

Sally had already lit the smudge pots that would keep away the bugs. They sat in a clear space scarcely larger than the parlor inside. Hibiscus and magnolia, honeysuckle and palmetto were planted in an artistic arrangement, as remarkable for their heavy sweet scents as the way they filled the little space so beautifully. They sipped their wine in silence until Mrs. Braud asked, "Forgive me for my curiosity, but you don't seem an adventurous sort. What brought you here from New York? If there's some problem, perhaps I can help."

Perhaps she could, but Pamela did not know the woman well enough to trust her discretion, and she hardly wanted the full measure of her tragedy starting rumors in the city. So she explained about her husband's death, how she had never met his relations and so had come to seek them out.

"And you have no address for them at all?" Mrs. Braud asked.

"They never wrote us," Pamela replied, thinking that was after all the truth.

"You say the family name was Donaldson?"

"Yes, and the grandmother was named Madeline Usher."

"Usher." Mrs. Braud smiled. "When I was very young, one of my uncles was involved in a duel with a man named Usher. He must have been a scoundrel because my family had never approved of such barbarism. I would not have remembered the event, except that someone in the family brought up the confrontation years later because of some lurid story he'd just read. He loaned it to me. When I saw that Edgar Poe had written it, I should have known better than to read it. I admit I had trouble sleeping for days after. Unfortunately, my uncle died years ago. Perhaps his wife may remember something of the Usher family. Do you have any other leads?"

"A law firm. Grymes and Livingston apparently handled the family's legal matters."

"Well, that is fortunate. John Grymes was retained by my family on many occasions. The man must be nearing seventy now, and I doubt he still practices, though he was a smart one for a Yankee. Every Creole family in these parts knew it and hired him whenever they were in some sort of legal fix, which was often enough when the country was changing hands every few months or so. He was our district attorney just before the war in 1812 but quit the job quite suddenly to represent Jean and Pierre Lafitte when they were brought up on piracy charges. It is said that Lafitte paid him in Spanish doubloons at Grande Terre and that on his journey back to the city he stopped at every plantation house on the river to show off his sudden wealth. The firm's business grew considerably after he won the case.

"His son, Randolph, is in charge of the firm now. He's a far less colorful person who once confessed to me that any one of his father's disreputable old clients gives him more trouble than a dozen of his own. I'm sure he can help you. Thomas can drive you to his office tomorrow. If you'd like some support, I'll be happy to come along."

Pamela would have preferred to walk there alone, and to present her demands without anyone knowing if she'd succeeded or failed. But she understood that this was a city where social ties mattered, and that Mrs. Braud's friendship might prove invaluable. Mrs. Braud saw her hesitation and took her hand. "I'm sorry, child. I'm so used to meddling in the affairs of my children that I sometimes forget the need for privacy."

"I'm glad you understand," Pamela replied.

Neither spoke for some time, then Mrs. Braud asked, "Do you suppose there's a connection between Poe's story and the family?"

Seeing a way to shift the subject to matters less personal, Pamela replied, "Mr. Poe said he based the tale on an old newspaper account."

The statement had the intended result. "You met Edgar Poe? How interesting! What was he like?"

"A southern gentleman—both by breeding and by his nature," Pamela replied, aware only after she'd said them that she'd chosen the exact words she'd often heard her father use to describe someone he was particularly fond of. "We spoke together for some time. Though I could see he was ill and needed to rest, he treated me with extraordinary kindness." She did not mention the aging boardinghouse, the threadbare appearance of Poe's clothing, the bottle of port, or anything else that might give a mixed impression of the man.

They sat together until quite late, Mrs. Braud telling Pamela stories of the British attack on New Orleans and valor of General Jackson and the pirate Lafitte. "Throughout that long night of the battle, I joined scores of women at a house not far from here. We sat together, praying as we waited for news. I had a pistol concealed in my skirts. I wasn't the only one. Thankfully, we never had to use them.

"In the morning we loaded bandages and bedding into our fine carriages and rode out to the battlefield to tend the wounded. I never had as much fortitude before or since as I did in those few days."

Later Mrs. Braud showed Pamela to an airy bedroom overlooking the courtyard and said good night. The torches were still burning outside, throwing leafy shadows through the open window. Pamela looked down and saw her hostess return to her seat, pour another glass of wine, and sit, appar-

ently deep in thought. Pamela felt as if she were spying on
the woman, so she turned up the light and began to undress.

A faint knock at the door came moments later. She opened
it and saw Sally standing there with towel and a washcloth in
her arms. "Madame sends her apologies for not asking
sooner, especially after such a long journey. Would you like
to bathe?" Sally didn't wait for an answer but went on. "You
have a choice of two tubs. The small one on this floor uses
unheated water from the cistern on the roof, but in the summer heat the temperature is quite pleasant. Downstairs, I can
provide hot water from the kitchen."

Though she'd washed earlier, Pamela's hair and clothing
still smelled like steamer smoke and her skin was sticky in
spite of the cool evening breeze. "Up here, please," she replied.

As Pamela slipped out of her clothes and stepped into tepid
water scented with lemon juice, Isobelle Braud sat in her
overgrown garden and considered what she'd learned. First
of all, Pamela had not told the entire truth about why she'd
come south. The falsehood had been evident in her voice and
in the way she'd held her hands folded in her lap as she told
her story. The girl was not a calm creature, but she'd forced
herself to appear that way, and had been almost calculating
in her choice of facts to reveal. This put Isobelle in a difficult
position. She could hardly accuse the girl of holding back
facts without seeming inhospitable and far too nosy. But at
the same time, a lack of knowledge made it impossible for
her to help Pamela.

And there was that name, Usher, still rolling around inside
her aged brain. Every time she tried to focus on where she'd
first heard it, all she could think of was the fictional Madeline, buried alive and obsessed with revenge.

Why had she ever read the tale? she wondered. Why
would anyone want to frighten herself that way?

chapter 6

The sun was fierce the following morning but in the humid tropical air could do little to dry the mud in the streets. The carriage seemed to move forward by inches, in a slow but constant motion that kept its wheels from becoming stuck completely. The journey took Pamela longer than if she had walked, but at least she got to her destination with her dress unsoiled. She asked Thomas to take the carriage home, took a deep breath to steady herself, and went inside.

There were no desks in Mr. Grymes's office, only a pair of divans, a long table and four chairs, and a bookcase filled not with legal volumes but with souvenirs from the 1812 war. A clerk came in and offered her coffee, and she sipped it while she waited, and waited.

The waiting was intended to put her off guard, she knew; and it was succeeding. She wished that she had been more open with Mrs. Braud and asked her to come. When over an hour had passed, Mr. Grymes joined her. He was nearly fifty—far older than Mrs. Braud had led her to expect—tall and somewhat fat. The heat seemed to trouble him, for he stopped often in their discussion to wipe his face and high bald forehead with a kerchief. She'd assumed she would be dealing with a younger man. Now she weighed her words even more carefully as she explained why she'd come.

"And you believe your mother-in-law took your child?" he asked when she'd finished.

Pamela tried to keep her voice even, to do her best not to sound angry or defensive at the man's evasive questions. "She was seen leaving Watkin's Glen. I can't think of where else she'd go but here to Louisiana. I want to make it clear that I will not press criminal charges. I only want my son back."

"Under the circumstances, I would be less forgiving," Grymes said gently.

"You might be of a different mind if you saw how Vivienne Donaldson behaved," Pamela replied. She was getting to the heart of her demand now, and she hoped her compromise would be accepted. "She cared a great deal for her grandson. When he became ill, I think she took on the role of Roddy's mother completely and became convinced that the warmth of the South would be better for Roddy than the chilly New York summers, a point I can scarcely comprehend now that I'm here. But whatever her reasons, I only want my son back, and once I have him, I am willing to forget everything that happened."

"And after you get him, where will you go?" Grymes asked, his voice still soothing.

Pamela was beginning to find the man's tone infuriating. She reminded herself of who Grymes represented as she replied, "I've been offered a teaching position. It's not the sort of life I am used to, but I will be able to provide for my child."

"I'm sure you can, but I think you might want to consider a second offer, particularly since you've seen to the heart of the problem." He handed her an envelope, saying as he did, "Inside is a copy of a letter mailed to you on July first."

Pamela opened it and read.

My dear child,

Vivienne has just brought my great-grandson home. Even after the long journey, she is quite distressed. She tells me that when she left you, you had a high fever and were delirious. She is certain that you died during her absence, but I believe that you are stronger than she thinks. Indeed I pray so, and that this letter reaches you and finds you well. I can imagine you, sitting alone in that little cabin, wondering what happened to your son, and I know that I must write you and put your mind at rest.

Your son is safe here in Louisiana and is almost completely recovered from his illness. Since you have also been in poor health, I would like you to stay where you are until you recover, then come south and stay with us. I am sending $50 for travel expenses. As soon as you are able to travel, please make your way to New Orleans. Go to the office of Grymes and Livingston. Mr. Grymes will direct you to our estate.

Madeline Usher

A fine letter, Pamela thought. It would have been a comfort had she been alive to receive it. But if it hadn't been for Mary Quinn, she would have been dead as Vivienne Donaldson believed her to be—a situation she was certain would be far more convenient for the Donaldson family .

"Since the mail upriver can often be unreliable, Madeline Usher came to New Orleans herself to post the letter by the quickest means possible and deliver this copy to me. I've known the woman for many years and can assure you that her feelings are genuine."

"May I ask what you think of her?"

"She is the third member of her family to be represented by this firm and the best of any of them. She has a good grasp of accounting and the law. She trusts me to handle her businesses, of which there are many, and listens to my advice."

There was a softness in the lawyer's expression, which made Pamela wonder if his relationship to Madeline Usher was entirely business. "I think she is too much the recluse," Grymes went on. "With her wealth and elegance and charm, she could be the toast of this city. Instead, she refuses to stay even one night in town, nor to allow me to mention her name to my other associates."

So her husband's guarded nature had been a family trait. Pamela was hardly surprised. "Mr. Grymes, may I make a request?" she asked.

"Of course, whatever you wish."

"I borrowed the money to come here. Since the postmaster in Watkins Glen is probably holding this letter for me, would you be so kind as to write him and ask that he give the money Mrs. Usher intended for me to Mary Quinn? She and her husband have a farm near Watkin's Glen. They loaned me the money to travel here."

"If you owe more, I'm sure that we can make arrangements," he replied.

"It won't be necessary. I gave them the rights to the profits on the vineyard in payment. This will help assure that they aren't caught short between now and harvest time."

For the first time she saw something akin to admiration in the lawyer's expression. "I'll do as you wish," he said. "Would you like to go upriver today? The *Doswell* will be pulling out at noon."

Mrs. Braud may have spoken highly of Grymes the father, but she had admitted to scarcely knowing Grymes the son. Pamela decided to be wary. "That's impossible," she said. "I am staying with Mrs. Isobelle Braud. I'll need to pack and say some proper goodbyes. Besides, now that I know my son is safe, there's less of a need to hurry. And I would not want my illness to return in this heat."

Grymes nodded. "That may actually be better. Now I can send word to the family so someone can meet you when your steamer docks. The next boat leaves at dusk, another at seven tomorrow morning. I suggest you take the morning steamer so that your traveling can be done through one day."

"Where exactly am I going?"

"Upriver to St. James and from there some twenty miles to the southwest beyond Bayou Lafourche, nearly to Lake Verret. Petite Terre is a newer house, and the plantation is one of the largest in an area of great wealth. I am told that it has a good deal of charm."

"You've never been there?"

"Madame Usher prefers to come to New Orleans whenever we discuss business matters face-to-face. Since I consider her far too much a recluse, while I am a reluctant traveler at best, I've never suggested that she do otherwise. Now, if you'll excuse me, I have a letter to write and deliver to the wharf in the next hour."

During the time Pamela had been meeting with Grymes, the heat had increased to scorching intensity. She walked back to Mrs. Braud's slowly, stopping to purchase paper, pen, and ink and a loosely woven broad-brimmed straw bonnet such as the local women wore to keep the sun off their faces and necks.

Mrs. Braud was sitting on her balcony when Pamela returned. She called down while Pamela was outside, requesting that she come upstairs. As Pamela expected, the woman wanted to know everything she'd discovered, and other than mentioning her child, Pamela did.

"You say they live west of St. James? That's so odd," the woman said when Pamela had finished.

"Mr. Grymes led me to believe it's some of the richest land in the state," Pamela replied.

"Exactly. If so, why don't I know the woman? I'm not being immodest, my dear. The planters in these parts are like one huge family. Anyone knows everyone."

"I assume that she must be nearly seventy. And Mr. Grymes told me that she prefers to keep to herself."

"Child, that makes her my age!" She frowned, then added, "I despise puzzles. Would you mind very much if I inquired about the family among some of the planters from that region? I'll be discreet, I promise."

"I wish you would. I want to know everything I can about my husband," Pamela replied. "Since I'm going to be away from town for a time, I'd like to write some letters before I go."

"Sit in the courtyard. The greenery is inspiring. I'll have Sally serve you lunch there."

Pamela wrote three letters—to Mary Quinn, Mrs. Lowell, and Edgar Poe. All of them began in a similar fashion, as she described the journey, meeting her hostess and discovering the whereabouts of her son, but she personalized each at the end. To Mary, she explained about the letter Madeline Usher had presumably sent, and asked that she watch for it. Since money was involved, she instructed Mary to write Mr. Grymes if she did not receive it. With Poe she was even more honest, adding detailed information about where she was going and some final concerns. *I had feared approaching Mr. Grymes. I thought the family would deny having seen Vivienne or my child, then make arrangements to hide him away before I sent the authorities to search. Instead, Madeline Usher has been so honest that I should be thankful. In truth, I am not. Everything is happening far too quickly, and far too easily. All the time I sat in that lawyer's office, I was thinking how much more convenient it would have been for Madeline Usher if I had died in that cabin. That may be what Vivienne had intended. If so, one of the people at Petite Terre is a potential murderer and the other may be an accomplice. Am I sounding too suspicious? As I read these words, it seems so, though I cannot help but feel this way after all that has happened.*

I would also like to ask a favor. I have written Mary Quinn to ask if she ever received the money Mrs. Usher said that she mailed me. However, I recalled your concern that someone in Watkin's Glen might have been spying on me. If someone was, he could easily intercept any note I send Mary. However, a note from you, postmarked from Virginia, will hardly arouse any suspicion. If you write her, I would be most thankful.

She hardly knew him, yet she felt compelled to add a few more requests. *I will write you again in one week's time. If you do not hear from me, assume that I am in trouble and contact the proper authorities. If you need to contact me and do not wish to send a letter to Petite Terre, write me through Mrs. Braud. I've been somewhat dishonest with the woman— first because I did not want to share my sorrow or bring scandal to my husband's relations, and now because I fear my suspicions will worry her. But if you believe there is a need to do so, you may write and tell her everything. I am certain she will assist me, for she is a very gracious woman. I hope that your health has improved since we met and that things are going well for you in Richmond.*

She left herself such thin lifelines, she thought as she addressed the envelopes; yet they were better than none. Though it hardly made any difference if she or Mrs. Braud posted the letters, Pamela did it herself while Mrs. Braud waited in the carriage. From there the woman took her on a longer tour of the city, then to an early dinner in a courtyard café shaded by the huge live oaks just outside its brick walls.

Before they went home, they stopped at St. Louis Cathedral, where Pamela knelt and lit two candles—one for success, the other for Elliot.

When they reached the house, Mrs. Braud remained in the carriage. "Go inside and get a good night's rest, child. You'll be thankful for it tomorrow. I have an appointment to keep, but I'll be up in the morning to see you off, I promise."

Pamela stood on the muddy stoop and watched her go, then cleaned her shoes off on the horsehair mat in front of the door and went inside.

chapter 7

The murky Mississippi waters grew clearer as the steamboat headed north. The heat did not subside, but the breeze gradually became dryer, so it was refreshing rather than oppressive. The river cut a wide slow channel between cleared fields of sugar cane and cotton tended by slaves in the worst human condition—many hatless and shirtless in the ferocious midday sun. Plantation homes, far grander than any Pamela had seen in her native Virginia, dotted both banks. For the most part, these were newly built, testimony to the recent rise of fortunes in the area. The piers sticking out into the river bore the homes' romantic names—Ormond, Trepagnier, Colomb, and more—each name blending with those preceding it into an exotic melange of sounds. Would that be the sort of house Elliot's family occupied? If so . . .

If so what? That their wealth would seduce her? That what they could offer her and her son would force her to forgive them for the terrible anguish they had inflicted on her?

And yet, as the boat moved on, a strange idea took hold of Pamela—one born no doubt in Mary Quinn's strange reading of her runes so many days before: She was coming home. Only for a visit, she quickly reminded herself, but home nonetheless.

In the interminably long and dismal days after Elliot had

died, she had actually considered writing her father, telling
him the sad news and asking to be allowed to live with him.
She was his only heir. He could hardly refuse her request,
though he undoubtedly would have made it clear enough that
she was not welcome. Given that certainty, this might turn
out to be a better homecoming than she would have received
in Virginia, at least on the surface. She would be wary, but
she would also hope for the best.

The boat reached the docks at St. James in late afternoon.
The sailors began unloading the cargo immediately, forcing
the few passengers leaving the ship to weave around them
and make their way to the shade of a pair of cypress on the
opposite side of the low levee. The ground was spongy beneath Pamela's feet, and the few houses built near the river
were set high on pilings. Pamela stood on the edge of the
weary crowd, looking up and down the road, hoping to spot
someone watching for her.

"We're at least a half hour early, ma'am," a young man
said, clicking his watch shut and returning it to a pocket of
his canary-yellow vest. "Don't be surprised that someone's
not waiting."

Did she look so anxious? She thanked him and took an
empty seat in the center of a wood bench. She was thankful
for the light chintz dress she wore, and for the bonnet, which
she took off and used as a fan while she waited.

The dandy had just checked his watch for the third time,
when Pamela saw a horse and buggy moving slowly down
the road. When no one waved to it, or walked toward the
road, Pamela stood and tentatively held up one hand.

The buggy that pulled up beside her seemed sound in spite
of its age. The straps were new, but the leather top was faded
and ripped at one corner. The driver was of some advanced
yet indeterminate age, his dark-skinned face as lined and
weathered by the sun as by his years. "Missus Donaldson?"
he asked.

"I am," she replied. Anxious to be on her way, she handed
up her traveling bags and got into the back. The driver stared
straight ahead, saying nothing. She had to ask twice before
he told her that his name was Bill, and that he had been born

on the Donaldson lands some sixty years before. "Course it wasn't the grand place it is now," he added.

"Petite Terre." She let the word play on her lips. "Is there a Grande Terre?"

"Course there is. But not here. Grande Terre's down in the Gulf."

"Does the Donaldson family own it?"

"Donaldsons!" He seemed to snort the word, then glanced back at her briefly. Though she tried to continue the conversation, he said nothing beyond a simple yes or no. She finally admitted defeat and sat silently watching the dreary landscape roll by. Often the swamps lay close to either side of the road. Even the grasses rising from the water seemed brown and dismal, the sky above them foggy gray, the line between them blurred in the damp evening air.

The road ended at a tiny cottage built well above ground on heavy oak footings. The cottage as well as the picket fence surrounding it had not been whitewashed in years. Clapboard covered the sides, but the front wall sheltered by the porch was made of some sort of fuzzy fiber held in place with narrow sticks. "Are we going farther today?" she asked, hoping by that indirect question to get some news of precisely where they were.

This time Bill didn't reply, though she could hear his muffled laughter as they rode through the gate and up to the house. He called out and a tall man came down the stairs to meet them. The sun had darkened his skin to a golden bronze, and the arms sticking out from the short sleeves of his brown homespun shirt were lean and muscular. He had curly black hair and a drooping mustache. "You made good time," he said to Bill in a soft patois so at odds with his huge appearance. He walked past them to open the rear gate. A path led down to a still body of water, wide enough to be a river but with no visible current. A raft large enough to accommodate the buggy and team was docked and ready at the tip of a broad, short pier, undoubtedly designed for just their sort of cargo. The ferryman took a pistol from his belt and fired a single shot in the air, then began laying down thick planks so that the team could roll the buggy aboard.

Pamela left the buggy while it was still on land and stood on one side of the pier looking out at the brackish water. It was so still that water lilies grew in the center and the shallows were choked with algae and moss. Dragonflies hovered nearly motionless just above the lily beds, darting quickly whenever a meal came within their range. Though the water seemed warm and calm, she could not dispel the memory that came uninvited to her mind as she watched the men guide the team onto the boat. The horses went aboard with no complaint. They'd undoubtedly made the crossing countless times before without a problem, she reminded herself, as she went down to join them.

"You can stay in the buggy and get some shade from the sun. Not that it's going to be sunny for long," the pilot suggested.

"I'd rather stand," she replied and followed his glance to the south where a line of dark clouds was growing on the horizon. She wondered if it would be silly to slip off her shoes and be ready for swimming should an accident occur or the storm hit before they crossed.

The man shrugged and untied a rope from the bow, then raised a pistol in the air and fired two shots. Minutes later the raft lurched away from the pier, then began moving slowly toward the center of the water while the pilot began letting out the rope behind them. There were lead weights every dozen feet or so, and the rope immediately disappeared below the surface where Pamela assumed it would be out of the way of any boats making a journey up or down river. Bill climbed back onto the buggy, lay sideways on the seat and closed his eyes.

Pamela joined the pilot. "What are we crossing?" she asked.

"The southern part of Lake Verret. This is the only crossing for miles in either direction."

"How will you get back?"

"I live on the west bank. If I end up on the other side at the end of the day, I can stay in the cabin or have the wife hitch up the mule and pull me over. With no load I can even pull myself easy enough on a calm day."

"Do you get many passengers?"

"Enough to make a living, not so many that I can't do an awful lot of something else."

"Have you ever been to Petite Terre?"

"Donaldson house? A few times when the old planter was alive, but that was years ago. Missus Donaldson, she don't like strangers." He noticed her expression, paused and asked, "You're Elliot's widow, ain't you? You going to stay there?"

"I'm not certain."

"Well, I can tell you this. No matter what anyone says, Elliot was the best of them. Damned fine, pardon the language."

Pamela understood what the man had implied. "No offense taken. You knew him well, Mister . . . ?"

"Blaine Stelley, and yeah, I knew him well enough." He glanced over to where Bill was snoring lightly with his mouth half open, then added softly, "You take care up there. They're odd people. In this country that's saying a lot."

"Odd in what way?"

She'd pried too hard. He looked down at the water as he replied, "Gossip's for the women. Ride over some time and sit down with my lady. Lacey's been known to gab." He pointed to the horizon and changed the subject. "Storm's coming. Best to sit it out with us than go on."

Beneath the placid bayou waters some animal swimming by set up a ripple on the surface. Pamela thought she glimpsed a shape long and fast and dark. She was about to ask what it was when the willows growing beside the landing brushed across her cheek. She choked back a scream.

"Shore sort of snuck up on us, it did. That's what talk leads to." He moved to the bow to open the gate, then began fastening the planks that would allow the team and buggy to leave. Though Bill woke as soon as they touched land, he merely sat up, grabbed the reins, and waited for the man to finish.

Pamela saw a thin woman with wispy blond hair standing at the land side of that pier, balancing a baby about nine months old on one hip. Her dress was made from the same cloth as Blaine Stelley's shirt, and she looked at him with equal parts of love and irritation. As soon as the boards were in place, Pamela went ashore and stood beside the young woman. "Stubborn fool should of stayed on t'other side with a storm comin' up," she mumbled, as much to herself as Pamela. She had a nasal voice that made her Louisiana accent all the more obvious.

"Are you Blaine Stelley's wife?" Pamela asked.

"I am. This is Jamie, our boy."

"I'm Mrs. Donaldson. I was married to Elliot."

Lacey looked toward her, but did not seem to be looking exactly at her, as if her eyes were focused on some point beyond Pamela's head. Pamela turned and saw that Bill had managed to move within listening distance of them. He glanced their way, then sat on one of the pilings supporting the dock and watched two men unload the team and buggy.

Once the buggy was on dry land, he took his place in the driver's seat and called to her, "Come on up, Missus Donaldson."

She started to do as he asked, but Stelley called out, "Storm's coming up fast. I'll help you put the team and buggy in the barn."

"Missus Madeline's expectin' us," Bill muttered.

"In one piece," Stelley replied. The wind increased. Bill glanced at the clouds and did as Stelley ordered, moving with a vague insolence, as if going to the barn was his own belated idea.

Lacey had already retreated to the porch of a house designed much like the cottage Pamela had seen on the opposite side of the lake, though this one was larger and in better condition. Besides the barn, there were also a pair of outbuildings, connected by a long covered breezeway. She saw traps hanging there, and a few empty drying racks. "Otter?" she asked.

"Muskrats mostly," Lacey replied. "It's a good living, but a hard one."

"My late husband traded furs," Pamela said. "You knew Elliot, didn't you?"

The rain was starting to fall. Lacey led her inside and handed Jamie to a stout old woman sitting in a rocker just inside the door. The old woman looked toward Pamela, though it was doubtful that she saw much through the milky haze of her cataracts. "Go and talk to her," she mumbled to Lacey.

The cabin was spacious, with tall windows to catch every breeze. The furniture, like that of Pamela's cottage at home, was functional and plain. A huge table flanked by two long benches dominated the center of the room. In the far corner, close to the light of a northern window, was a wide loom threaded with cream and brown yarn. Mounted on the wall beside it was a finished weaving, colorful and intricate. Pamela had little time to study any of it, for Lacey moved quickly through the room latching the shutters, which placed the interior in near darkness. "I'd leave 'em open to catch the wind but bousillage smells musty when it gets wet. Takes days for the smell to clear. These storms come and pass in an hour or so. Air'll cool down then; make for a nicer ride the rest of the way." She poured them both a mug of cider.

Pamela thought the woman was avoiding her earlier question, but once Lacey was seated, she answered it. "Blaine and Elliot and I grew up together. He wasn't supposed to spend time with us, but he'd sneak over to help Blaine tend his trap lines. Most of the time they'd both come back covered with mud and half freezin'. He must of been around fourteen when Bill found out what he was up to and told his mistress. We didn't see much of Elliot after that."

"What was he like, then?"

It was dark in the room, and the bit of light that leaked through the window was behind Lacey, making it even more difficult to see her expression. "Another scrawny kid, nothin' special," she said, but that guarded tone was clearer. Why shouldn't it be? Pamela decided that in similar circumstances she'd show the same caution.

The storm's strength increased. Rain beat against the roof and exposed side walls. The woman in the rocker lay with her head bowed while the baby slept in her arms. Lacey had fallen silent, though she seemed more lost in thought than concerned about the storm. Pamela tried to relax while gusts of wind shook the cabin until she feared that it would lift from its mountings. Then as quickly as it blew in, the gale subsided to a weak soft rain. Lacey moved through the room, throwing open the windows. The weather had cooled, and for the first time since she'd sat in Mrs. Braud's shady court-yard, Pamela felt comfortable.

The baby stirred. Lacey took it back. "Talk to her," the old woman repeated. She sounded as if they'd been sitting in si-lence. Perhaps, to her, they had.

Lacey returned to the chair beside Pamela's, undid the ties of her blouse, and began to nurse.

"I think your husband was lonely," Lacey said. "Petite Terre is no place for little ones; all those huge empty rooms with their old memories, like ghosts from another time."

"Have you been inside it?"

"My mother was. She told me all about it. Was that your son that came back with Vivienne Donaldson?"

Roddy! She'd seen Roddy. As casually as she was able, Pamela asked, "It's been some weeks since I've seen him. How was he?"

"A little hot. A little pale. Like you, I guess. It was Vivi-enne who worried me. She's a nervous one, but I never seen her as close to real prostration as then. I crossed the bayou with her, and all the way she held on to that child so tight I thought he'd smother. Sometimes she cried. Sometimes she talked to herself, but it was all foolishness to me."

"She was upset when Roddy and I became ill. What did she say?"

"Two words, over and over, 'She can't.' I asked what she meant and she said, 'I did what I had to do. She can't con-demn me.' I tried to find out what she meant, but she wouldn't say no more."

"Who do you think she meant?"

"With that woman, she could have been speaking of any-one about anything."

Pamela was about to ask another question when she heard Bill and Blaine Stelley leading the team to the house. She stood and smoothed down her skirts. "May I come and visit you again?" she asked Lacey. "I'd like to know everything you can remember about my Elliot. We were together such a short time."

"And that time is over. Best to look to the future, not the past, my father used to say. You got a fine boy; you just take good care of him."

Was that a warning or only a practical woman's advice? There was one question she might well ask at a later time.

"It's a long way to St. John's if you have to skirt the lake," Lacey added with barely concealed smugness, as if being the wife of the ferryman made her privy to all the gentry's secrets.

"You ready, Missus Pamela?" Bill called.

Pamela glanced at the mother and child and thought of her Roddy and how she would soon be holding him. Whatever came after would not mar the joy of that moment.

"Come back when you can," Lacey said. She didn't say goodbye. Perhaps that was a custom in this remote country, some sort of superstition.

The road Bill followed now was narrower than before, but perfectly flat and almost completely straight. As the darkness grew, Bill called back, "Don't mind the night, Missus Donaldson. The horses know their way in the dark." It occurred to her that this was the first kind thing he'd said to her, and she thanked him for putting her at ease.

What little Pamela could make out of the area they passed through before darkness fell completely was that most of the land had been cleared and planted. The few wild sections that seemed to have been overlooked by the plantations were water-filled indentations, surrounded by scrubby bushes, dying trees, and a few ancient cypress that somehow managed to cling tenaciously to life. As night descended, she heard the sounds of life coming from those dank oases—the croaks and pips of frogs and toads, cicadas, crickets, and a deep booming sound she could not place.

By the time they'd reached the house, a slivered moon had risen to throw a wan light on the landscape. Pamela saw an ornate iron fence, its gate covered with climbing vines. This was the last distinct feature she could make out because the lawn was dotted with huge live oaks through which only a few thin shafts of moonlight could leak. The house was long, a single story built high on pilings, with the ever-present covered porch running the length of it. A pair of lamps were lit on either side of the front door and light spilled from an open front window. Mosquito netting had been nailed to the inside of the window frame. Fat june bugs and moths beat against it, trying to get in.

Bill unloaded her bags and carried them up to the porch. Pamela took a deep breath to steel herself before knocking. Bill apparently misunderstood and knocked for her, then left her standing alone while he drove off with the team. She watched him leave, the noisy team and buggy masking the soft whisper of the opening door. Pamela turned when the light fell on her and saw a woman standing in the doorway, holding a lamp which she raised higher so she could get a better look at Pamela's face.

In form the woman looked much like Vivienne Donaldson—petite, and radiating that same nervous energy. Her hair was long and dark, streaked with gray at the temples. She wore it unbound, and it fell in a heavy mass over her shoulders. She had a broad, sensuous mouth, and high arched brows above prominent light brown eyes that gave her face a quizzical look. Once she must have been a beautiful woman, and much of that beauty remained. Pamela had assumed that Madeline Usher would be nearly seventy, but this woman appeared to be at least three decades younger, though the dim light might be hiding many of the signs of age.

Pamela discerned all this at first glance. Then the woman motioned her inside. "Come in quickly, child, or the bugs will follow," she said and closed and locked the door behind her.

Pamela stood with a valise in each hand. When the woman seemed to ignore them, she asked, "Are you Madeline Usher?"

"I am. Please call me by my first name and I'll use yours as well. Settling that now will save us a great deal of awkwardness later." The accent that Pamela had first detected seemed more pronounced now, yet impossible to place, as if the woman had lived in many countries, the language of each adding its own nuance to her voice.

"I've come a long way. I'd like to see my son." Pamela

did not ask, nor order, nor say please. She thought her words conveyed just the proper amount of polite determination. She was glad, because she had wanted to scream them.

"In a moment. Let me show you to your room first." As Pamela followed her down a long narrow hallway, Madeline went on, "I'm sorry you have to unpack yourself, but I allow no slaves in this house save for the girl who brings our meals from the kitchen and empties the chamber pots, and the housekeeping staff that cleans twice a week. One can never be too careful."

Pamela stored the comment for later, choosing instead to observe the decor. The portraits on the wall were of men universally stout and bald with affably bland expressions; all undoubtedly Donaldsons since they bore no resemblance to Madeline or her daughter. The ornamentation was more interesting—elegant dragon-shaped brass sconces with cut crystal globes, gilt mirrors, and delicately carved moldings above the wainscotting.

Pamela's room was at the end of the hall. Madeline carried the lamp inside and set it on the bureau. Its light was magnified in the mirror, showing a charming space with a red and yellow rug, and black enameled bed, armoire, and dressing table. There were two other entries to the room—a pair of French doors which led to the outside were closed and barred; the second, on an inside wall, was cracked open.

Madeline lit a second lamp. "Put down your bags and follow me," she whispered and stepped through it.

The adjoining room was smaller. Later, she'd notice that one wall was painted in a mural of bright purple bears beneath pink-leafed trees and brilliant azure sky, that the room held a buggy, a storage chest, and an assortment of stuffed animals and wooden pull toys. Now all she saw was the crib draped in white netting. Pamela rushed to it, pushed aside the netting, and looked down at her sleeping son. Though it had been less than a month since she'd seen him, Roddy seemed to have grown. His hair had thickened and was beginning to curl as his father's had.

Gently, so as not to wake him, Pamela picked him up and sat in a rocker close by the crib. Though nearly all her attention was centered on her son, she sensed that Madeline was watching her. She looked up at the woman. Were those tears in her eyes or merely some trick of the lamplight? Before she could decide, Madeline turned her face toward the door. "Vivienne had your room until this morning," Madeline said softly. "I made her move because I knew you would want to be close to your son. It is, after all, the mother's space."

Such persuasive sympathy in her voice, Pamela thought. So intense, and so real, though she could be mistaken about the last. Perhaps the hint of tears, the sudden shifting of the woman's eyes were meant to convince Pamela of her sincerity. If so, she would have to expend more effort than that.

"I'll leave you alone and see you in the morning. Breakfast is at nine. Before you go to bed, open the doors to let in the air," Madeline said and left her.

In the hour which followed, Roddy finally woke and yawned. He looked at Pamela with no surprise, as if being wrenched from her was the most natural thing in the world and their reunion equally expected. Eventually he gripped her finger and fell back asleep.

If the weather had been cool, she would have taken him to bed with her, but here in this sultry climate it was best that they sleep alone. Though reluctant to let go of him, she returned him to his crib, carefully arranging the netting as it had been.

She pulled her nightgown from her bags, then blew out the light and undressed in darkness. Just before she went to bed, she opened the windows and stood at them, looking out at the lawn. Fireflies winked in the dark shadows between the faded silver patches thrown by the dim moonlight. She saw a figure standing beside one of the huge oaks and took a step backward so she would not be seen. The man—or at least it appeared to be a man—began walking away from the house. As she watched, he gave a low whistle, and a huge hound came bounding across the grass, his light-colored coat glowing white in the moonlight. The pair headed down the path toward the barn and were soon lost in the shadows of the trees.

A cloud moved across the slivered moon bringing a sudden, profound darkness. Pamela shivered, turned from the window, and lit the candle on the table beside her bed. Then, taking great care not to wake Roddy, she maneuvered his crib into her own room, placing it close to the head of her bed in the corner farthest from the door.

Even with that precaution, she did not sleep well that night.

Sometime just after dawn Roddy woke and began to howl. She picked him up, took him to bed, and held him close. His hungry cries subsided for a while, then began anew. She had no idea what to feed him.

As she stood there, wondering if she should dress and take him to the kitchen, she heard a soft tapping at her outside door. Without waiting to be invited inside, a Negro woman walked silently in on bare feet and lifted Roddy from Pamela's arms. If she was surprised to see a strange woman in the bed, she gave no indication but instead sat in a rocking chair near the window and began to nurse him.

He was weaned weeks ago, Pamela thought. He shouldn't be feeding at some stranger's breast. I should be sitting there, nursing my son as I did at home.

Even as she thought the words, she knew how wrong they were. There was no midwife who would agree that solid food was any substitute for mother's milk in a child so young, and if there was milk to be had, so much the better. Hadn't she been raised in a similar way? Pamela lay on her side, watching the woman and her child. When the woman was done, she returned Roddy to Pamela and left as silently as she had come.

Alone once more with her child, Pamela tried to nurse if only to feel him nuzzling her breast as he had only months before. Roddy sucked weakly for a while, then, already sated, fell asleep in her arms.

chapter 8

Daylight showed Pamela more of the estate—a lush lawn shaded by immense live oaks, their branches seemingly weighted down by the strands of moss that covered them. Distant slave quarters; the two dozen or so little clapboard cottages giving signs of the wealth of the Donaldson family. Closer to the main house was a summer kitchen and well-tended herb garden. Smoke rose from the stovepipe, and the smell of baking herb bread was heavy in the air.

Last night's meeting with Madeline Usher had been brief. Today's was far more important. After washing and changing Roddy, she carried her son down the hall to the foyer, where she stood on the beautifully polished parquet floor and listened a moment. Hearing a murmur of voices, she walked through a doorway into a dining room. The red velvet curtains were tied back, the tall windows open to bring in light and air. A large thick rug in a strange pattern of leaves and branches covered most of the floor, and in its center was a long oak table, simply designed and beautifully polished. Sitting in the master's place, Madeline was reading a book while she ate.

She dined alone. Pamela had expected to confront her mother-in-law. Apparently, the meeting would be postponed for a time.

"Come in," Madeline said when she saw Pamela standing in the doorway, then called, "Justine." A mulatto woman with wide-spaced hazel eyes moved to the table. "This is Master Elliot's wife, Justine," Madeline said, then added something else in French.

The woman eyed Pamela with an emotion more intense than curiosity. Had this been one of Elliot's conquests? Pamela almost hoped her stare meant something as common as that. "What would Madame like?" Justine asked after a moment, her French accent so thick that Pamela had difficulty understanding her.

"Whatever your mistress had," she replied.

"Then you will eat lightly, Madame," Justine replied with just the hint of disapproval in her expression. "I will bring something more . . . *plus* . . ." She paused, apparently searching for a word and finding none.

"Whatever you wish to bring, Justine," Madeline said impatiently. Once the woman had gone, Madeline asked Pamela how she'd slept, then returned to her book. Pamela had so much she wanted to discuss but no idea how to begin. She picked aimlessly at the assortment of food Justine brought, and fed bits of cornbread to Roddy while she waited for a chance to reopen the conversation they'd barely begun the night before. Roddy showed little interest in the food; apparently all her frantic work to wean him had been undone in the last few weeks.

Justine had poured them each more coffee and was clearing the plates when Vivienne ran into the room. Her face was red as if she'd been running and her hands were clenched in tight fists. "Mother! I demand to know why I've been moved . . ." She noticed Pamela and paused in midsentence. "Praise God," she whispered and fainted into a heap of blue check chintz and white lace, so bright against the deep crimson and sienna tones of the carpet. Madeline stayed where she was and turned to Pamela. "No, I didn't tell her you were coming here. I wanted you to see exactly what her reaction would be."

Justine went to Vivienne's aid, wiping her forehead with a moist towel until the woman began to come around. "Help her to the table and seat her there," Madeline ordered, pointing to the chair directly across from Pamela. To Pamela there seemed to be something merciless in the order not only to remain but to sit in that place where she could not help but look at the woman she had wronged.

Vivienne sat, breathing heavily, and ever more quickly until a series of tiny strangled moans came from her throat, as if she weren't certain whether to laugh or cry. Madeline pulled a tiny crystal bottle from her pocket and passed it to her daughter. "Inhale it until you're calmer," she ordered.

Vivienne did as she was told. Her eyes, still fixed on Pamela, became relaxed, then almost dreamy. Ether, Pamela thought, only that would have so quick an effect on the nerves. She wondered if the woman had always been hysteric. If so, she'd managed to hide the fact well enough in the weeks they'd spent together.

"You read my letter, now you see that I told the truth," Madeline said. "I was astonished when Vivienne wanted to go to you, and outraged when she returned alone with the child."

"She left me to die and she very nearly succeeded," Pamela replied, astonished at Madeline's callousness.

"I didn't leave you. I just couldn't bear to return to that terrible place," Vivienne whispered, looking at her directly for the first time. "I wanted to take Roddy home, but I didn't leave you. I gave Charles Boutte money for you so you could come here when you were well."

"He never came back," Pamela responded, amazed that her voice could sound so calm when all she wanted to do was slap the woman for her lie. "Why should he have bothered, when you didn't care enough?"

Vivienne lowered her head to the white brocade tablecloth and began to cry.

"As soon as she arrived here in a state I can only call hysteria, I guessed what must have happened," Madeline said. "You should have sent a letter or a telegram. Since I heard nothing from you, I immediately wrote you, then set about restoring my grandson's health."

"I didn't know where you were," Pamela replied, realizing her ignorance had been Elliot's omission, not theirs.

Vivienne smiled and took a deep breath. "No matter. We're all where we belong now," she said, her voice dreamy from the ether. "We're all home just as Mama wants us to be."

It was not a time to discuss how short her stay would most likely be, Pamela decided. Perhaps there would never be a time, and she would simply pack her things, put her child in a basket, and walk the few miles down the road to the Stelley house. Let her leaving be as furtive as Vivienne's had been, and let them always wonder where she had gone.

She finished the meal, left the two of them sitting silently together, and took her son back to the rooms she shared with him. She'd stay here a day or two, just long enough to send word to Mrs. Braud. Once she and Roddy were safely in New Orleans, she would tell the woman everything and ask her aid in getting back to Albany.

When she tried to lay Roddy down, she realized how much he'd grown in the weeks they'd been separated. His howls were deliberate, angry, and he managed to stand on his pudgy legs and push so hard against the side of his prison she thought he would upset the crib. When she put him down, he immediately went to the bed, used the covers to pull himself up, then took an unsteady step toward her before falling forward. He hit his head on the wood floor and began to scream.

Pamela picked him up, hugged him, rocked him. He would not be comforted, at least not by her. Then the young mulatto woman who had nursed him earlier came through the door as silently as she had the night before and took him from Pamela's arms. "*Cheri, silence, si vous ples,*" she whispered. Roddy relaxed against her and pointed toward the door. "A wise child. He wants to be outside on such a beautiful day, and so should we," she said to Pamela.

She waited for Pamela to nod, then started toward the door, glancing back with obvious surprise when Pamela followed and sat beside her on the shady lawn. The woman pulled a rattle, a child-sized ball, and a little stuffed doll from her pocket. "Madame Usher thought you would want to rest," she said as she set the toys in front of Roddy.

"This is hardly work," Pamela replied, rolling the ball toward her son. "What's your name?"

"Abeille."

"That means 'bee,' doesn't it?"

"*Oui*. Even when I was tiny like your son, I was always—how do you say?—doing."

"Did you know my husband?"

"*Oui*. Everyone knew Monsieur Elliot. We were all sad to find him gone."

Sensing something important in that fact, Pamela pressed on. "I understand that he left here suddenly."

Abeille shrugged. "I don't know. I only know we weren't told he was leaving, not that we should have been."

Had Pamela been out of the South for so long that a slave had to remind her of their stations? Now that Abeille had, Pamela knew it was useless to question her further. She lay back on her elbows and stared up at the sky, the pale hazy blue of a southern summer. Roddy was crawling toward her when a large hound the size of the one she'd seen last night bounded across the grass. Pamela snatched up her child. "Abeille, is the dog safe?" she asked.

"Safe?" Abeille smiled. "Dirk is safer than most people."

Pamela tried not to cringe as the dog circled her. There was no reason to pass her fear onto her child, and she even managed to remain calm as the dog licked Roddy's hand. "Who owns him?"

"I do," a man said from behind her.

Pamela looked in his direction. For a moment she thought that reality and dreams had somehow switched places. She stared at a ghost!

The man whose hand was now buried in the hound's shaggy fur resembled her Elliot—not just his features, which were a nearly perfect match, but his stance, his expression as he stared back at her, hiding his confusion at her incredulity, her shock; the way he frowned before speaking. Only his eyes were different, a soft brown like her own rather than the deep rich shade of Elliot's. "What is it?" he asked.

Ah, yes! Elliot's voice!

"Are you all right?" he continued.

She managed to nod. Had she been standing, she was certain her legs would have given way as Vivienne's had when she found Pamela at her dining table. He moved toward her, arm outstretched. She motioned him to stay back, half convinced that if he touched her he would vanish or she would die.

"What is your name?" she asked when she could finally speak.

"Sean Donaldson. You're Elliot's wife?"

Though he seemed about her own age, the way he spoke the words made her feel so old, and so unattractive. "I am," she said.

"I'm his brother. People always told us we looked like twins, but I've never seen anyone so shocked by the resemblance."

"I'm sorry. I would have been less shocked if I'd known he had a brother."

"Half brother, actually. I use the Donaldson name because it's the only one I have." He sat beside her and waved an arm toward the distant fields. "Elliot was the Donaldson heir. Now your boy will inherit all of this someday."

He explained what that would mean while she sat, incredulously trying not to stare at him as she listened to Elliot's voice give an account of the vast Donaldson wealth. Two thousand acres. Ninety slaves. Three houses on the plantation, a third in Natchez. When she added to that her own future inheritance, she realized that her son's life, and through it her own, was far more complicated than the single room in Mrs. Lowell's school that she had planned for them.

Roddy was just a baby and would be as content in Albany as here. But later, when he was older, could she deny him all of this? Could she say so cavalierly that he must never know his father's kin, as she had never known her mother?

"Abeille, watch Roddy for us," Sean said. Without asking, he took Pamela's hand, pulled her to her feet and led her on a long walk down a winding path. His hand continued holding hers, and she did not pull away. There seemed to be some-

thing almost magically comforting in his touch, and after all
the lonely days in the last year, she would give in to this
small pleasure.

They passed the stables, where a half dozen horses were
being groomed by the hands, the slave quarters, the kitchen
and its spacious vegetable garden, the rose garden on the far
side of the house. He walked slowly, letting her take it all in,
then took her through another set of French doors. They were
in a gentleman's den. Books lined one wall. On the other
there were more pictures of the Donaldson family, all of
them showing the same pudgy features. None of the men
were over fifty.

"Did they all die young?" Pamela asked.

"There's some family illness. Elliot was apparently spared
it, though the fates decreed he was to die as young as the
other Donaldsons after all. Come."

He walked her down the long hall that ran the opposite
side of the house from her and Roddy's rooms, exiting finally close to the place where Roddy was playing with
Abeille looking on. They walked past the pair, down a gentle
slope to another quiet strip of water. A narrow footbridge
provided a crossing to a second grove of oaks. The trees
were thicker here, and so dense that no grass grew beneath
them. The ever-present Spanish moss had not been pulled
from the lower branches, and formed a barrier which had
been cut away only along the path which sloped suddenly
upward. At the crest of the hill was a stone wall about four
feet tall. Carved nude male and female figures, their legs
covered in dusky moss, stood with arms raised holding aloft
a string of carved snakes and vines which formed an arch
over the gate. Though the wall and carvings had been recently made, they seemed to have been drawn from some ancient, mystical source.

"What is this place?" Pamela asked.

"My grandmother's house," he replied and led her forward
through wooden gates decorated with the same vine and
snake design. Inside was a courtyard, though hardly the sort
of place that Mrs. Braud with her overdeveloped sense of
order would have liked.

Everything grew with wild abandon. Palmettos vied for light with overgrown hibiscus and mock orange. Ivy had abandoned its beds and thrown green tendrils along the flagstone path and patio. Near the courtyard's center were two lower walls. One contained a firepit, apparently often used. The second held a mound of stones. Water bubbled slowly from the top, trickled down the mound, and disappeared into it before it reached the ground.

"My grandmother's family is Welsh. There is a legend in Wales that a spring flowing to the surface is a hallowed place. When my grandmother discovered one on this hill, she claimed the spot for her own and had the house built." He took a cup from a hook in the wall, rinsed and filled it, and handed it to Pamela. The water was cooler and purer than that she'd had in the main house, and she shivered in spite of the midday heat. Sean watched her intently as she drank, as if his offer and her acceptance completed the first part of some complex, ancient ritual.

The place fascinated her, and the fascination made her uneasy, though she could think of no reason why it should. "Maybe we should go," she said.

"Grandmother asked that I show it to you. Do you want to go inside? She's probably there. If so she'll serve us tea."

The uneasiness increased to a strange unfocused fear. She felt it brushing against the nape of her neck, the fine hairs on her arms. "I would like to return to my son." She replied in the same tone as the night before when she'd demanded to see Roddy.

The effect was the same. "Of course. I forgot that you haven't seen him in weeks."

She brushed past him and through the gate, knowing that when she was alone, and certain that Madeline Usher was occupied elsewhere, she would return.

They returned the way they had come, moving from dense shade to dappled sun. He left her just after they'd crossed the footbridge, giving a low whistle. The dog appeared moments later, and they disappeared together into the woods.

Roddy and Abeille were not where she left them, nor anywhere in sight. She went back to the house and found them

inside, where Abeille was nursing Roddy. Pamela sat on the
edge of her bed and watched, thinking of the times she had
nursed her child until illness or deceit had ended that pleasure. She felt useless and angry at Vivienne, who, she was
certain, had ended her chance to be that close to her son.
"How old is your own child?" she asked.

"Three years old. I weaned her this spring," the woman
replied.

"This spring? But you're nursing."

"When she saw the poor little boy looking so thin and
sickly, Miss Madeline gave me something to drink. It
brought the milk up so I could feed him. I have to drink it
every day or the milk goes away."

"Could you bring me some?"

"It takes a few days for the drink to work. I don't have
enough for you."

Pamela was reluctant to ask the family for anything, but
that simple act had meant so much to her especially after the
separation. She waited until Roddy was sleeping, then went
in search of her hostess. She found Vivienne instead, sitting
close to a window in the library working on a piece of silk
embroidery. She glanced up as Pamela entered the room,
then returned to her work with polite indifference.

"I'm looking for your mother," Pamela said.

"She's napping. You should, too. In this heat it's for the
best."

"Then why aren't you?"

"I never sleep in the daytime; it's hard enough at night."
The words might have provided some opening for conversation if the woman had even glanced at her. Instead, Vivienne's
attention was on her work, the methodical in and out of the
needle, and the individual threads slowly coloring the fabric.
She and the woman seemed to be falling naturally into the
same pattern they'd had at the cabin, civil but distant, like
strangers waiting to be introduced. Pamela left without saying anything else. Vivienne gave no sign that she noticed or
cared.

On the wall outside the library was a finished silk picture
in an oval bentwood frame. It showed a pair of the oaks

flanking a tall Spanish style sepulcher on which was engraved the single name Roderick and beneath it the phrase *who waits for me to draw back the veil of death.*

A strange sentiment, Pamela thought; one fitting only for those morbid survivors who think to end their suffering by following their beloved to the grave. She had never felt that way, not even in those terrible hours after Elliot had disappeared beneath the ice-covered waters of the lake. She doubted that she ever would. With all the Donaldson ancestors looking contentedly at her from their places on the hallway wall, she returned to her room.

Roddy was sleeping in his crib, one finger in his mouth, his bare skin cool and dry. True to her name, Abeille had bathed him, then as Madeline Usher demanded had left the house.

Before she'd gone, she'd pulled back the coverlet on Pamela's bed, and refilled the washing pitcher.

It was hot, Pamela decided, and she was still tired from the journey. Though it was likewise against her nature to sleep in the afternoon, she bathed her face and arms in the cool water, stretched out on the bed, and shut her eyes.

chapter 9

The following morning she sought out Madeline Usher. She found the woman sitting in the shade of the little overgrown garden of her private house, a clear glass pitcher of tea on a table beside her chair, a book in her lap, which she'd nearly finished, another on the ground beside her. The books appeared old but well cared for and had no names on their binding. Just before Madeline closed the one she'd been reading, Pamela glimpsed a handwritten page. Symbols she did not recognize curled seductively over the yellowed parchment, reminding her of the carved snakes on the wall and gates. The symbols were interspersed with an occasional paragraph or two in English. Madeline smiled pleasantly, radiating as much warmth as she had when they first met. "Would you like to sit down and have some tea?" she asked.

Pamela nodded, expecting the woman to ring for it. Instead Madeline stood and went inside, the hem of her russet dress brushing the ground. Her mass of hair fell nearly to her waist. It seemed less gray in the sunlight, with a deep auburn glow. Her body was straight, her movements supple. Again, Pamela was struck by the discrepancy between the woman's appearance and her likely age. Perhaps the woman brewed her own special drinks, in which case, she should bottle and sell them and use herself as an example of their efficacy.

Pamela looked down at the books, curious about their contents. She was just reaching for one when her hostess returned. She'd brought out a second cup and poured from her pot. The water was tepid, tasting of mint and honey.

"I brew a pitcher in the sun every morning," Madeline explained. "In this heat the mint is refreshing, the cool water even more so. Now what brought you here so early in the day?"

"I've been speaking with Abeille. She said you gave her some drink so that she could nurse my son. You may have saved his life, and I'm thankful, but if it's possible, I'd like to take her place."

Madeline's mahogany-colored eyes, dark but warm like Elliot's, filled with understanding. "I fear that while it is possible, it may not be for the best," she said gently.

"What do you mean?"

"Put down your tea and come with me," Madeline said.

Pamela followed Madeline to the far corner of her garden, through a narrow door to a second, sunnier space on the south side of the house. The smells of mint and other herbs were thick in the sultry air. She saw clumps of unknown herbs interspersed with skirret and foxglove, and guessed that these were medicines that Madeline grew for her own treatments.

"The drink Abeille spoke of is a tea blended from herbs and seeds I grow myself in this garden," Madeline said, though she did not provide any details on the individual components. "I have only a bit of the tea left, and some of the plants necessary for the blend don't mature for a month or more. Still, there are ways I could grant your request, but it worries me."

"Worries you? Why?"

"From what my daughter tells me, you were ill in early spring, is that so?"

"Yes," Pamela said softly. She'd begun to understand what Madeline feared.

"And if you were not able to nurse afterward, there may have been good reason for it. Nature may be callous, but she protects her young. You are aware that some diseases can pass from a mother to a child that way?"

"I know that, but I feel quite normal."

"Perhaps. You look somewhat pale to me, but that could be due to those dark northern winters." She shrugged as if its unhealthiness was obvious, then went on. "And nursing wears down a woman. For your son's sake and for my own, I would not want to see you ill again."

"For yours?"

"For two reasons. First of all, I should never have let Vivienne go to you. It should have been me, or the two of us together. I have more skill for treating those who are ill, and a better temperament for isolation. I would have never left you alone and sick. Believe me, you would have recovered and come home with me to the place where Elliot and his wife belonged. And yes, I think you would be caring for your child."

"And the second reason?" Pamela asked.

"My daughter, as you undoubtedly have noticed, is high-strung and sometimes hysteric. When she insisted on going to be with you, I made her give me two solemn promises. The first was a natural enough one: that she would do her best to be as great a help to you as she could—no small feat for a woman raised all her life in the presence of servants."

"She simply took over my hired help as soon as she got there," Pamela commented.

"The second was that as soon as you and your child were able to travel, she was to bring you both south to stay with us.

"Apparently, you did not live harmoniously with her, and she doubted that you would ever come willingly with her. So when the opportunity presented itself, she took her grandson to force you to make the journey. Unfortunately, she didn't anticipate the Bouttes' dishonesty, and so you nearly died."

Madeline put her hand on Pamela's shoulder, staring at Pamela all the while as if fearful that Pamela might slap it away. "Before we talk of nursing your child, I want to see you completely well. In my grandfather's country they have a custom of blessing women just after marriage, not for the good of the union but to assure the health of the mother and for the children to come. If you and Elliot had been married here, I would have given that blessing. May I do so now for your sake, and your child's?" Madeline asked.

Pamela considered how the woman's daughter was unbalanced, and her grandson—probably wanting to get well away from his mother—had abandoned her. She could hardly refuse such a simple, and harmless, request coming so clearly from the woman's heart.

Madeline paused to pick sprigs of rosemary, thyme, and basil, then led Pamela through a second gate that returned them in a clockwise circle to the courtyard. She asked Pamela to stand upwind of the fire ring while she stirred the ashes in it, revealing a few glowing coals. To these she added a handful of kindling and two split logs. In a moment a small fire caught and grew.

"Stare into the flames," Madeline whispered. "Think of Elliot and your child."

As Pamela did, Madeline crushed the herbs in her hand and rolled them between her palms, releasing the oils, then throwing the herbs into the blaze. As the herbs dried and flamed, Madeline ran her scented fingers across Pamela's forehead, cheeks, and lips, down the side of her neck and the back of her hands.

The anointing finished, she put her hands on Pamela's shoulders, looked directly into her eyes, and began to speak. Her voice deepened half an octave into a soft, almost alluring whisper. Pamela had expected to hear English or French, but this language was utterly unfamiliar to her. She looked back at the woman, trying to be solemn and respectful of something she knew nothing about, when she felt a tightening in the center of her chest, a momentary shortness of breath. The sky seemed to cloud, or at least her perception of it did, and the steady breeze shifted sending a curl of scented smoke across her chest and face. Then the woman stopped speaking and the blazing sun came out once more. The shift in perception was so sudden and so strange that Pamela dismissed it as momentary dizziness or the hallucination of an overwrought imagination, hardly a surprise given the eccentric design of the house and the odd customs of its owner.

They returned to their seats in the overgrown garden and sipped their tea in silence. "What language were you speaking?" Pamela asked.

"I am Welsh," Madeline said.

"That wasn't English."

"It was Celtic, a language that was old before the Romans built Hadrian's Wall. My grandfather was born in the Berwyn Mountains of Wales, one of a long line of scholars and healers. He spent his life studying the old beliefs, and after so much study he adopted most of them. Many of the books in the library were culled from his collection, but I think that if I spend a lifetime in reading, I will never know half of what he did."

"May I borrow some of them?" Pamela asked.

"Pull whatever you like from the library shelves. All I ask is that you treat the books with care and return them to their place when you've finished with them. It's good to think of someone else reading them besides me."

"Doesn't Vivienne or your grandson?" It was the first time Pamela had said her mother-in-law's name since she'd come to this place. The word did not form easily on her lips. She doubted that it ever would.

"Vivienne reads the novels and stories, the more lurid the better. There aren't many books like that here, so she reads them more than once and has Sean buy her magazines whenever he goes to St. Joe's. She doesn't have an intellectual nature; there's nothing I can do to change that. As for Sean, he does not study as much as he used to. You might ask him to take you riding, though. Your Elliot, he was the scholar. I wish my grandfather had lived to know him."

Elliot had kept two books in their cabin—a Bible and an old French text on wine-making techniques. Pamela had never seen him read the first, though the second was consulted often. The thought of Elliot reading for pleasure or to acquire some arcane knowledge seemed ludicrous, though perhaps that was one of the many things he'd turned his back on when he'd moved north.

"I've never forgiven myself for his death," Madeline commented.

"You had no part in it," Pamela responded. "How can you blame yourself?"

"For one of those small coincidences that leads to something else without intention. I suggested that Vivienne buy you the coach and team for a wedding present. I knew something of hardship in my life, and I wanted you both to have some small luxury. When Elliot wrote to thank us, he mentioned that the carriage was too wide for the trails in that wilderness. After Vivienne learned how he'd died, she wrote me and I immediately thought of Elliot's concern. I want . . ." She paused and smiled, but sadly, and made a hopeless gesture with her hands as if she knew her guilt was foolish but could not dispel it. "Well, though an apology is hardly adequate, I want to extend one."

"No, there's no need," Pamela said. "We were caught in a sudden terrible storm. I don't think a regular wagon would have fared any better."

"If it would not distress you too much, tell me what happened," the older woman said.

Pamela did. Somewhere in the middle of her account, she noticed that Madeline was sitting stiffly in her chair, looking straight ahead as tears rolled down her cheeks. "When did you conceive your son?" she asked when Pamela had finished.

"I don't really know," Pamela replied, flustered by the question. No one in her family would have ever brought up such an intimate subject. It almost seemed perverted for the woman to ask such a thing.

But Pamela did know. She and Elliot had been discussing the plans for the following day. The discussion had naturally turned to the wedding they would attend, then to their own. "You were so lovely that night," he'd whispered, pulling back a stray lock of her hair so he could kiss the side of her neck in the spot that always made her nipples harden and her stomach flutter. It had seemed to her that it was unfair that a place on her body so exposed would be so sensitive. He'd kissed it again, and reached for the ribbon that fastened the collar of her dress.

His hands had been rough against her skin. Every time he'd made love to her, he'd apologized for his workman's hands.

As if she minded. As if the roughness itself didn't give its own pleasure. A blush spread across her face, growing more pronounced when she saw Madeline watching her intently, silently demanding an answer. "Roddy was conceived the night before Elliot died," she said. "I'm sure of it."

"There is a belief mentioned often in my father's books. It says that a child conceived so close to his father's death will surely possess the soul of an ancestor."

"How beautiful," Pamela said. "How comforting to think that the parent will live on that way. I had nearly the same thought the first time I held Roddy. He'd looked up at me the wise way that babies do, and I thought that the soul in that little body must have lived before."

Madeline gave a tiny laugh of delight. "You are so perceptive," she said. "I would have expected it of you, though. My Elliot would marry someone as intelligent as he was."

Perceptive seemed an odd word choice—unless Madeline believed as her grandfather had, Pamela reminded herself. She certainly seemed to. Because Pamela wanted to know everything she could about her husband and his family, she asked about the woman's religion.

For the next hour Madeline spoke not of legends or scripture but instead told of the world from the Celtic perspective—of the sky world, home of the gods and often more powerful goddesses of the sun and moon and stars, as well as magic and revelation; the earth world, home of the deities of nature, of man, and of the plants and animals that sustain him; of the underworld, where the deities of life and death and rebirth held sway. She finished with the story of one goddess and the terrible fate she meted to a warrior-king who did not recognize her.

"Rhiannon came alone to the field where King Liam had slain his enemies in a great battle. She came in disguise—her beautiful long hair thin and streaked with gray, her fine blue cloak tattered and dirty. The only thing she brought to give any clue to her identity was a herd of horses, the greatest she possessed, to test the king's honesty. He thought her an old hag and refused to discuss trade or payment. Instead, he called upon his men to go and steal the beasts.

"They did as their leader asked and ran into the field, but

the horses were all turned into huge, poisonous serpents who killed, then devoured the would-be thieves, leaving only the king alive. He recognized her then and bowed respectfully, apologizing for what he had done.

"She then went to his enemies, but they, too, saw her as merely a weak old woman and tried to steal the herd. Again, the horses were transformed and all the men were killed but the leader. But their leader was even more foolish than the first, for he still did not recognize Rhiannon and drew his sword to kill her. She pointed her hand toward him. A raven sprang forth from it and took out the man's eyes. King Liam came over the hill and saw the carnage but refused to kill his enemy, for the man had been cursed by the goddess and her punishment was grave enough."

"And then?" Pamela asked, hoping this was not the end.

"Then the goddess saw King Liam's wisdom and humility, and she went away with him and lay with him. From their coupling sprang a new clan to replenish those she had killed. This is said to be the origins of my family and our clan."

Pamela recalled the figures guarding the gate. "Are those the goddess and her consort?" she asked.

"Precisely."

"They're beautiful," Pamela said.

"I'm glad you like them. Sean did the carvings two years ago. He shows remarkable talent, I think. I placed them here because it seemed so fitting. They're a couple that belongs in a garden, aren't they?"

"Doesn't the moss hurt them?"

"They're cypress, like the pilings of many of the houses in this country. Even a flood couldn't hurt them, though a bad one might sweep them away. They are left to the earth's wishes, but the wood lets them keep their shape in spite of all the moss and the constant damp."

While they'd been talking, a soft northern breeze had blown away the hazy clouds and pulled the dampness from the air. Madeline glanced at a sundial buried at the edge of the flagstone terrace, half shaded by the overgrowth but still serviceable. "It's nearly one. Would you like to stay for lunch?" Madeline asked.

"Of course." Pamela had begun to enjoy the woman's presence, not in spite of the story Madeline Usher had told but because of it. It seemed as if the woman had nothing to hide, and that her affection for Pamela was genuine. If it weren't for the constant possibility of seeing her mother-in-law, she might even find the plantation a pleasant place.

They dined on fruit, fresh bread, and cheese, and a different tea pulled from a second pitcher, served with a spoonful of honey to mask its bitterness. "It has a tonic effect," Madeline explained when Pamela wrinkled her nose at the taste. "I use it to give me energy and keep me somewhat immune to the effects of this Louisiana sun. It might make you feel better. I'd like to see you drink a cup or two every day, and rest often."

"Actually, I think most of my weakness is from too little activity," Pamela replied. "I'm used to hard work, and I haven't done much since I became ill."

"Then you should take advantage of this beautiful weather and go walking or riding for a while."

"I love to ride. Will there be someone at the stable to help me saddle one of the horses?"

"I'm sure of it. Take my white mare. Cooley is very gentle and will go right back to the barn if you give her the lead. It's easy to get lost in this monotonous land. It's rather depressing, too, don't you think?"

"All the dead limbs sticking out of the water, reaching like black skeletal hands toward the sky," Pamela said, then laughed at the drama of her words. "It's as if the goddess you spoke of . . . Rhiannon? . . . had cursed it."

The warmth Pamela had sensed in Madeline Usher increased, and the look she gave Pamela was affectionate, almost loving in its focus. "You listened. I knew you would." After a pause she added, "My Elliot would have chosen someone like himself. Now go along and leave an old woman to her rest."

Old woman! Pamela thought. Would that she looked half so beautiful when she reached Madeline's age.

chapter 10

The stables were quiet and cool, and so well tended that the earthy scent of fresh manure was barely noticeable. Sean's hound lazed in the shade outside the barn door while inside a pair of children were standing on boxes currying one of the horses, a tall black mare with white markings on the neck. "Pardon me, but I need some help," she said.

One of the boys turned toward her, realized she was someone of importance, and pulled his oversize ragged shirt straighter on his thin body. "Ah can help," he said and ran to her.

"I'm going riding. Madame Usher said I can use Cooley."

"She said?" He looked doubtful. "No one but her ever rides Cooley."

"She said," Pamela replied. "Don't worry, it's all right."

"Who be you?" He had a soft blend of southern and island accent.

"That be Master Elliot's wife," the other boy said. "Best do as she says, Louis."

Louis's expression became one of respect. He worked quickly, checking the saddle straps carefully to make sure they were tight enough. "Go easy with her," he said as he helped her mount. "She be too old to run and the madame prizes that beast."

"I'll remember," Pamela said and led the horse outside.

Even the few extra feet of height the horse gave her was enough to expand her view of the flat country considerably. The fields were all around her. To the east, scrubby cotton plants stretched to a distant stand of cypress. To the south and west, tall stands of sugarcane, some of them twice Pamela's height, made seeing anything beyond them impossible. Two small fields were lush with hay, another with tobacco. Though the last seemed to thrive in the tropical air, she wondered where the fieldhands ever found a place dry enough to cure it.

She'd stopped in the nursery before coming to the barn. Having spent so much time with Madeline, she was hardly surprised to discover that Abeille had already fed Roddy. The boy was sitting with her on the shady lawn stacking blocks, each carved with a different figure. One showed a cow, another a horse, or cat, or dog, or chicken. She wasn't surprised by the barnyard menagerie but was astonished by the more fantastic figures of a snake, a dragon, and a griffin. Madeline had ordered them made, she decided, and wondered if it was right to feed the imagination of so small a child with such fantastic creatures and beliefs. As she lay him in his crib for an afternoon nap, she wondered if he dreamed about them.

Yet she had to admit that she was fascinated by the tales. As she rode down the long drive to the fence that seemed to surround the entire plantation, she found herself thinking of Rhiannon and her horses, and with satisfaction, as if she were the goddess, and this graceful but aged mount one of the magnificent horses that lured the men to their doom; and the besting of the men by the woman her personal triumph.

Staying just inside the fence, she began to circle the plantation. The route would give her some idea of how many acres the estate contained and how well it was managed, as well as the more practical information of where the nearest neighbors might be.

However, the fence that was so magnificent along the half mile or so of road ended a few dozen yards inland, turning into little more than a series of stakes in the ground, some connected by a thick rope, others by woven vines. Yet she had to admit that the plantation was magnificently managed and prosperous. This was shown in the healthy livestock grazing in the open range, and the efficient manner the slaves worked the well-tended fields, neither rushing as if fearful they would be punished if they fell behind nor slacking obstinately in their labors.

The land she rode through grew damper. The swamp often stretched to the edge of the embankment on which she rode and which seemed to mark the boundary of the estate. Dragonflies hovered, seemingly motionless above the silent water, darting only to feed or when some creature rose from its depths to take a quick breath of air. She saw snakes, turtles and, once, the long lethal snout of an alligator who eyed horse and rider speculatively then sank in the murky water, going off in search of easier prey.

This was not a place to linger. Sitting high in the saddle, she glimpsed the top of what seemed to be the barn and went off at an angle toward it riding slowly along the boundary between a cane and tobacco field.

During the hour she'd been riding, the breeze had died and the heat increased. She paused and dismounted in the shade of a trio of live oaks. In the center of the triangle they formed, a huge piece of granite seemed to rise from the earth forming a high natural table. Water bubbled from a crack along one side of it, pooled at the base, then slowly disappeared into earth that seemed far too sodden to hold it. Pamela started to tie the reins to a branch, then thought better of it and led the beast forward into the denser shade. Crouching, she cupped her hand under the spring's flow. The water was clear and tasted pure. She drank her fill, then unsnapped the bodice of her dress, dipped the hem of her skirt into the pool, and used it to wipe her chest, arms, and face. Refreshed, she sat beside the pool and let Cooley drink.

The air was much cooler in the shady stand of trees, almost cold, as if the huge rock had carried the chill of the deep earth to the surface. The rock was too high for her to see its top but there were indentations in it, sharply grooved as if recently cut. She climbed to the top and stood on the edge of a nearly smooth surface about a dozen feet square. In its center was a covered bronze urn. The curved sides were polished. The lid and decorative handles were formed of some other metal, probably pewter. The leaf and vine pattern of the handles was repeated along the edge of the lid. The escutcheons joining the handles to the bowl, and the circular handle of the lid were patterned with grapes. The urn had been recently placed here, or else had oiled to protect it against the dampness, for there was no rust pitting its surface and only a thick layer of dirt on the cover. Pamela pried it open and looked inside.

Two small snakes were entombed there, the bodies desiccated from age and decay so that only the skin and bones remained. She tipped the bowl slightly and saw two locks of hair beneath their skeletons. One was dark auburn, the other lighter red, and they had been tightly braided and tied with yellow ribbon.

A love charm, no doubt. She'd seen charms similar to this often enough on her father's plantation. Slaves brought their beliefs from Africa and the southern islands, but a slave would never own a container as beautiful and as expensive as this. Could someone have stolen it and brought it here? She might never know, but she had respect for the petitioner's belief. She replaced the lid and put the pot exactly where she'd found it and lay on her back and stared at the canopy the leaves and branches formed above her. She shut her eyes just for a moment and slipped easily into a deep sleep.

Pamela had no dreams, nor any concept of the passage of time until she heard someone calling her.

Even then, she woke with difficulty. For the first few moments she didn't recall where she was, then noticed the urn. The lid was slightly askew, and as she moved to place it tightly over the contents, it moved. She pulled back her hand as a pair of snakes wriggled free of their prison and slithered to the edge of the rock, disappearing into the crevasse above the spring.

She was too shocked even to cry out, but instead stared stupidly at the open pot and the pair of braids still intertwined inside it.

"Pamela!"

The voice came from behind her, drawing her out of what seemed to be a dream. She looked over her shoulder and saw Sean on a buff-colored horse, holding Cooley's reins. Dirk sat obediently nearby. Sean's shirt was dirty and stuck to his body as if he'd been working in the fields with the slaves.

"When Cooley showed up at home without you, I thought I'd better come looking for you. Fortunately Dirk has a bit of bloodhound in him." He dismounted and patted the hound, then moved to the base of the rock. "I'll help you down," he said.

"I think I can manage," Pamela replied.

As soon as she swung her body over the edge of the rock, she knew she was mistaken. Her legs felt weak and cramped, her arms shaky, unable to hold her. She missed the second foothold and would have fallen hard had Sean not caught her and held her a moment until she felt steady. As he did, she smelled his scent—the faint hint of spice to it. Even that reminded her of Elliot. She let him hold her a moment longer than was necessary before moving away.

"Can you ride?" he asked.

"Of course I can," she said. This was probably true, though she was thankful he helped her mount before turning his horse toward the barn and riding away without her.

Pamela followed as quickly as she was able. She let the animal lead, only holding Cooley back at times when she seemed ready to break into a gallop, an idea that, given the withering afternoon heat, hardly seemed healthful to an old horse. In spite of this, by the time they reached their destination Pamela's clothes were so wet that she eyed the watering trough outside the barn with desire. If the barn had been empty, she might have stretched out in it, clothes and all.

As soon as she dismounted, the stableboys came out to tend to Cooley. Pamela walked into the barn and saw Sean working in one of the stalls, tending to a mule that had cut its leg.

She walked into the adjoining stall, leaned over the dividing wall, and watched Sean work. He spoke gently to the mule as he washed its cut, then began wrapping it with a loose cotton bandage. "Elliot always left the wounds uncovered," she commented.

Some emotion crossed his face at the mention of his brother's name; not grief but pain as if he had always been held up to Elliot and found lacking. "Elliot didn't have bottle flies to contend with in New York State," he replied. "With the abscess the maggots would cause, she'd be lame for sure. Even with the bandage I'll have to keep her working away from the bayou for a few days. Gators are drawn to the smell of blood."

"They'd attack a mule?"

"Mules, horses, they'd even attack you if you gave them a chance. It isn't a good idea to ride alone here, and certainly not to fall asleep even in the shade."

"Your grandmother seemed to think it would be safe, even safe enough to offer me her horse."

"She's fearless, but then, she was raised in an area far wilder than this one. I saw you ride out. If I'd known you were heading inland, I would have accompanied you. I thought you'd stick to the road."

"To the road?"

"It's what I would do in your situation. I'd want to scout out the area and know where the nearest neighbors were, perhaps the nearest town. On the other hand, I wouldn't have been too surprised if you'd just gone."

Did he sound hopeful? Could he have good reason to be? "I wouldn't leave without Roddy," she said.

"You could have taken him. No one here would have stopped you."

He was tempting her, almost challenging her to leave. "Will all this be yours if we go?" she asked, letting her candor show the anger she felt.

"Never. As I told you when we met, I'm not a Donaldson. I hear there are some second cousins out East who would probably lay a claim, though they've never seen this place, let alone its owners," he said, his cold tone making it clear that she would learn nothing more from him. "It's getting late. You should probably go to your son.

"Thomas, take care of Cooley," he called to one of the stableboys who had been watching them from a polite distance. Though the boy could undoubtedly hear every word they'd said, he'd seemed to take little interest in them until he was called, then ran forward to lead the injured horse away.

Pamela could hear Roddy's angry howls when she was still some distance from the house. As she entered through the French doors, she saw Abeille sitting in the rocking chair, holding the child, trying to calm him.

"What's wrong? Is he hurt?" Pamela asked.

"He wants to play," Abeille responded. "You said you wanted to take him outside yourself when you returned, but he woke up early. He's used to getting his way." Her tone made it clear that she would not be criticized for doing what had been asked.

"I'm sorry. You're right, I should have returned earlier. Here, let me take him."

Roddy squirmed in her arms and pointed toward the door. "What else do you do to amuse him?" she asked.

"He likes to play in the water," Abeille responded.

"There's a place to swim? Is it safe?"

"Safe, *oui*, and private enough to bathe if you wanted to."

They loaded everything they needed in a wicker hamper. Abeille carried it while Pamela followed with Roddy. They walked past the kitchen and its little garden up a gently rising incline. In what seemed to be a custom in this country, the trees that grew on it had not been cut down. Instead they formed the usual thick canopy. In the center of the little glade was a high wooden fence, and inside it another spring. This time the earth around it had been bricked over and stone walls built to waist height so that the spring formed an oval man-made pool some twenty feet in length. Water bubbled slowly to the surface in the center of it and a small spout at one end allowed the top to drain at the same speed so the surface stayed clear of bugs and the water constantly replenished.

Pamela sat on the edge of it and dipped her hand into the water. It was warmer than the spring she'd found earlier today, but in the afternoon heat it seemed cool enough to be bracing.

"If you undress and get in, I can hand your son to you," Abeille suggested.

It had been years since Pamela had undressed in front of anyone besides Elliot, but she could hardly order a girl used to serving to allow her privacy. She pulled off her clothes, working quickly so that she would be in the water before Abeille finished undressing Roddy. Soon after, she forgot her modesty as Roddy kicked and splashed, squealing with happiness each time she bounced him in and out of the waist-deep water. "Are there springs all over this country?" she asked.

"Madame Usher says there are, but that people do not know how to find them as she does."

"I knew someone who could find water," Pamela responded, thinking of Mary Quinn. "She used a forked stick and told her husband where to dig their well."

"Ah! I have heard of that, but no, that is not how Madame Usher found the spring."

"Then how?"

"I do not know exactly. One day she came to the men and told them to dig here and they found it."

"The ground may have been damp."

"It is damp everywhere."

A true enough statement. "How do you think she found it?" she asked.

"She dreamed it," Abeille said.

"Dreamed it? What do you mean?"

"It is what she told me. She said she dreamed them all except for the first one."

"Where is that one?"

"I am sorry. I am not allowed to speak of this. I've said too much already."

Pamela had seen slaveowners in Virginia use the innocent superstitions of those they owned as a way to frighten them into submission. Slaves might be ignorant, but that did not make them less than human. Yet, from what she had seen of Madeline Usher, she was not the sort to do such a thing.

And there was the matter of the spring itself, Pamela had to admit. Whether Madeline had doused it or dreamed it, it was here. She grabbed a bar of soap from Abeille and washed her son, then passed him up to Abeille to be dressed. "Take him back to the room," she ordered. "I'll be along in a little while."

"As Madame wishes," Abeille said.

Once she was alone, Pamela lay back in the water and looked up at the patches of sky visible through the dense leafy boughs. Though the birds were singing and the air was still, the shivers she felt had nothing to do with the cool water. In spite of the high walls and the closed gate, she was convinced that she was being observed.

Perhaps Madeline is taking a nap and dreaming of me, she thought. She lay on her back with arms and legs stretched out and imagined the woman sleeping and dreaming this scene. Her imagination seemed so ridiculous that she laughed. It echoed off the water and fence; a hollow sound.

chapter 11

Vivienne came to the dinner table that evening. Pamela ate quickly, trying not to look at the woman. Even Madeline said little, only asking how Pamela liked her ride. As soon as Pamela finished, she left the table, giving a final glance at her mother-in-law. Were those tears in Vivienne's eyes? Did they show remorse or impotent fury? She'd never know and, she thought, she didn't care, though even as the words formed in her mind, she knew they were untrue. She wanted to learn what Vivienne thought, wanted to understand the reason for the great wrong the woman had done to her.

Someday, if her anger ever subsided enough so that she could speak a civil sentence to the woman, she just might shock Vivienne and ask.

"Before you go to bed tonight, I'd like you to have another glass of the tea I gave you this afternoon, but I have to warn you that you may have trouble sleeping or particularly vivid dreams," Madeline said.

"I hope they're not like the ones I had before Roddy was born," Pamela responded, "for all I dreamed of then was the accident, and Elliot slipping under the ice with his arm outstretched as if I would somehow be able to save him."

Vivienne made a tiny strangled sound deep in her throat.

The comment had all the effect Pamela had anticipated and one she had hardly expected. Madeline followed her to her room, stopping outside her door. "I'll leave you to your privacy, but I want you to know that if you do have nightmares, come to my room. I rarely sleep through the night anymore."

"Rarely?"

"My own dreams are often far from pleasant. At times such as those I relish the company of the living." She touched Pamela's cheek, looked at her affectionately, and said good night.

Dusk was quickly fading. Though the doors were open, Abeille had hung mosquito netting from hooks above it to keep out the bugs drawn to the lamplight. The glass of tea sat on the night table. Pamela picked it up and swirled the liquid around in it, watching the honey-sweetened liquid coat the sides. "Do you have any idea what's in it?" she asked.

Abeille shook her head. "I only know that Madame drinks it many times every day," she said.

Had Pamela fallen into some well-laid trap, some switch of the herbs designed to drug her into submission, or worse? She dipped her finger into the glass and tasted it. It had the same bitter undertone as the tea she'd had earlier, and Madeline had poured from the same jar to serve both of them. Pamela wondered about her sudden suspicion. If this family meant to poison her, they could do it with her drinking pitcher or through the meals they served her. There was no need for such an elaborate hoax.

No, she was being foolish. She picked up the glass and drank it, then sat on the side of her bed watching Abeille and her child, his pale face against her dark breast.

Later, after Abeille had gone and Roddy had fallen asleep in Pamela's arms, she looked down at the boy and thought of Elliot and the superstition Madeline had spoken of that morning. For the first time she faced the past squarely. "If you're here, my love, may you never feel the same sort of pain and loneliness I sensed in you before."

Though she whispered, Roddy reacted to her voice. He turned his face toward her. His eyelids fluttered, then he fell back asleep without waking completely.

She didn't feel tired, but it was late. Pamela put Roddy into his crib, blew out the light, and went to bed.

. . . She lays on the flat rock she'd discovered earlier in the day. Her eyes are closed and she is so motionless that only the slow rise and fall of her chest give evidence that she is alive. The covered bowl is beside her face. Its lid begins to move, then falls off altogether. From it the two live snakes emerge, their tongues darting in and out as they crawl to her, then over her.

She cannot wake from the dream she knows she is having. Though she is not constrained, she does not move as the serpents glide up her arms, to her chest, to her face, where they pull the breath from her mouth and nose. They steal life from her, growing larger, ever larger, while she slowly weakens, until with some strength born of fear she tries to push them away and finds she cannot do so.

Somewhere, miles away from the setting of her dream, someone is screaming. A shrill sound of terror . . .

With a sudden burst of will, she thrust herself into consciousness. Her heart pounded and her hands shook as she pushed back the netting and lit the lamp. Though she knew she'd been dreaming, every nuance of the dream remained in her mind, as real as any memory. The scream that had jarred her so mercifully awake continued onto the edge of consciousness, then died. Not certain of its origin, she held the lamp in front of her and checked every shadowed corner in her room and Roddy's, even feeling in his crib to make certain that nothing was there to harm him.

Still breathing fast, she sat on the edge of the bed. Even when she'd relaxed, Pamela guessed that sleep would be impossible for a while. She decided to accept one of Madeline's invitations, put on her robe, and went down the hall to the library.

A dim light fell through the open doorway. Pamela stopped in the shadows, prepared to leave if Vivienne was reading. Instead, she saw Sean sitting at a table, a notebook open in front of him. He appeared to be sketching rather than writing, his hand moving in short, delicate strokes over the page.

He sensed her staring at him, and looked up. "I thought you'd be Madeline," he said. "I heard her screaming from another of her nightmares. I guess she slept through this one." He smiled, clearly pleased to see her.

"I can't sleep. I've just come to borrow a book," she said as she entered the room.

"One of my grandmother's I suppose." He pointed to the shelf farthest from the window. "You might want to start with that thin book on the end. It's a Celtic history, good background for the rest."

"Your grandmother said you didn't read."

"Not as much as she would like me to, but enough." He held up the drawing he'd been working on. "Is it a good likeness?" he asked.

He'd drawn Elliot holding Roddy and it would have undoubtedly been a good likeness when Elliot was living here. "His face was a bit fuller, and his hair a little longer in the years I knew him," she replied. "You made him look younger, but I suppose that's how you remember him."

"I was only eleven when he left."

"Were you close?"

"I was hardly old enough for him to notice, much less care about. I wished we'd been close, though. After he left, I used to lay awake at night, waiting for him to show up at my window and ask me to come with him on some great adventure." He shrugged, as if saying that the past was immutable, and not worth grieving over.

"Elliot never spoke of his life here. Why did he leave?"

"I don't exactly know. All I can remember was that he was always being punished for taking off. Usually he went to visit friends in the area. He once told me that he'd stowed away on one of the riverboats and went down to New Orleans. Madeline sent word to Mr. Grymes, and he tracked Elliot down and sent him back. I guess you could say that he left home mentally long before his body made the journey."

"Then he went so far away."

"Madeline offered him the land." Again, the use of his

grandmother's Christian name. Was this a deliberate way for Sean to distance himself from the woman or was he acting at Madeline's request? Two plausible possibilities, and she felt uncomfortable asking about either. "I suppose she gave him enough money to work it, too. I guess she thought that preferable to having him just up and disappear someday with the family having no idea where he'd gone. As for Elliot, having a place to call his own until he came into sole possession of this one was better than drifting. Elliot wasn't the sort to take orders from anyone. You must have discovered that early on."

Pamela smiled. "I did." She took the book he'd suggested, and another on Celtic legends, and picked up her candle.

He put his sketch pad on one of the shelves and blew out the lamp. "My room is across from yours," he said. "I'll walk with you and share your light."

As they moved down the hall, she glanced sideways at him. The candlelight blurred his youthful features, making him seem even more like her Elliot. With a stab of anguish she realized that these were the halls they would have walked if Elliot had brought her here.

"Try to sleep," Sean whispered, hugged her, then kissed her on the forehead. It was a perfectly appropriate kiss, the sort a brother might give to his older sister, but his touch lingered. She closed the door behind her, ran her finger over the place he had kissed. There were tears in her eyes; coming suddenly like a surprise. Had she really been so lonely?

In bed, in the dark, she whispered her husband's name. It was no surprise then, when he entered her dreams, touching her as softly, as skillfully as he had in life.

. . . "Elliot!" she cries when she finds herself in his arms, for she knows the truth of her waking world. He is dead, unable to touch her, unable to feel.

Or to smile as he does, and look at her with such affection. They are in their house in the woods, lying on the rug in front of the fire as they often had before. Its light plays over his face, his bare body. He pulls off the lace nightshirt the girls at school had given her for a wedding gift and lets it fall gently over her face, blinding her to the sight of him.

She wants to brush it away, to look at him, to see him—perhaps for the last time even in memory. And if she did, would she see Elliot the man? Elliot the corpse? Elliot the ghost?

No, it is better to lie motionless, speechless, blind. There is no need to speak. His hands and his lips know her so well.

She cries out once, of that much she is certain, but what difference does it make? This is a dream. . . .

She woke to the familiar sound of Abeille entering her room through the open outer doors. The soft white net that surrounded her had been lifted on one side and the hem of it was tangled in her sheets. The inside of her thighs were wet and the bodice of her white cotton night shirt was open, one breast bare.

Of course she would have thrashed in her sleep. Why wouldn't she thrash when caught in a passion given all the perfection of her most cherished memories?

She straightened the netting, closed her shirt. If she slept in daylight, would she dream?

"Abeille," she called. "Take Roddy outside without me. I need a bit more rest."

"Did the boy keep you awake? Is he sick?"

"No, Abeille. Nothing like that. I just didn't sleep very well."

"Do you want breakfast here?"

"I'm not hungry."

The woman shrugged, as if to say that she disapproved but that it was not her place to contradict her mistress.

Pamela closed her eyes once more and thought of Elliot, but this time she slept without dreams, or at least any dreams she could remember, save one just before she woke.

. . . She sees Madeline in a forest-green gown. She is in the dining room placing plates of food on a tray. After adding a teapot at the end, she walks down the long hall toward Pamela's room. . . .

Someone knocked on her door. "Are you awake?" Madeline called.

Before Pamela could answer, Madeline entered the room, carrying a breakfast tray. She was wearing the same green dress as in the dream. The color and the simple design made her look less like a wealthy woman than some medieval renunciate or healer. If so, she should have been helping herself. Her eyes were red-rimmed and there were dark circles under them. Pamela recalled Sean's comment about the woman's nightmares and looked at her with sympathy.

Madeline set down the tray. "Abeille said you were staying in bed. Are you well?" she asked.

"Tired."

"Did you dream last night?" When Pamela nodded, Madeline pressed on, "About what?"

"Elliot."

Pamela's expression must have revealed some hint of the content. Madeline smiled. "To dream of your husband is natural enough," she said, then in reference to last night's comment, added, "Be thankful the dreams were pleasant for a change."

Pamela wanted to mention the coincidences between her last dream and Madeline's arrival, but decided to keep it to herself, at least for the moment. If she had tapped some latent power, it could be a possible defense or at least a means of gathering information about the family. In either case, she saw no reason to tell her quarry that she was armed.

Madeline buttered one of the rolls on the tray and held it out to Pamela. "The cook made spice rolls. They should be eaten while they're warm."

Pamela held it and watched while Madeline buttered a second roll for herself and poured them each a cup of tea. She kept on holding it until the woman began to eat and drink, then joined her.

"Abeille's taken Roddy out in his buggy so you can rest," Madeline said.

"Read, actually." Pamela pointed to the books on the bedside table. "When I'm finished, may I borrow Cooley again?"

"Of course. And come and see me. I'll be at the little house. Now, I'll leave you to your studies."

An odd choice of word, that last, Pamela thought, and she picked up the first book. The history didn't appeal to her, but the one Sean had recommended was a fascinating collection of folk tales. She read the first four, all about some demigod named Cuchulainn, who the notes preceding the stories explained had protected the fledgling race of Celts as they rose to power in Britain.

Finally, weary of so much inactivity, she dressed and went for a ride, taking a different route than the day before, staying well away from the swampy areas Sean had warned her of.

She stopped at only one familiar place—the spring flowing from the crack in the rock. After tying Cooley securely to a tree, she climbed to the top of it. She'd intended to look into the covered pot and see if the snakes were indeed gone, but as soon as she touched the flat top, the same terrible weariness she'd felt the day before returned. She felt dizzy, faint, and retreated. Once on the ground, she drank some of the water, then sat for a while in the shade until her strength returned, then grew. When she left the grove, she felt as if she had taken a long, satisfying nap.

After mounting once more, she took off in the opposite direction on a high bridal path between the cane and tobacco fields. She turned when she reached what seemed to be the eastern border of the plantation and headed toward the road, intending to make a circle back to the house and hopefully encounter Roddy and Abeille along the way.

Some time later she passed another wild section of land, but this one was higher and gave evidence of having once been tended. She skirted it just before she reached the road and started overland toward the main house. As she did, she spied a well-worn narrow path. The path, just wide enough for a person, made her curious, and she dismounted and led the horse down it. Though the mare was docile, the moss brushing against it made it shy more than once, then stubbornly refuse to go any farther. She tied the reins to a low-lying branch and went on without it.

A little house had been built on a rise, as houses in the area always seemed to be. It seemed older than the other houses on the plantation, with none of the grandeur of Petite Terre or the charms of Madeline Usher's private domain—no wall to separate it from the land around it, no garden, no fountain. Indeed, if it hadn't been for the obvious signs that the path to it was often used, she would have thought the place deserted. Convinced otherwise and far too curious to turn back, she went on.

Could the place shelter runaway slaves? That was doubtful, for its path was too obvious, and too well-worn, simply too well known, and no slave would long remain on the property of his master. Though she wished that she had taken Sean's advice and carried a pistol, she went up to the door and knocked.

chapter 12

An old woman, her natty hair white with age, a stark contrast against her dark skin, answered the door. Her expression changed quickly from irritation to curiosity when she saw Pamela, indicating that she belonged at the little house and rarely saw strangers.

Not at all surprising when the house was so remote.

"Who you be?" the woman asked rudely.

"Mrs. Donaldson. I was Elliot's wife."

The woman didn't seem to understand. "Is this still Donaldson land?" Pamela asked, wondering if she had somehow wandered onto neighboring property, but if so, astonished that someone would not recognize their wealthy neighbor's name. Perhaps the woman was senile, some old and well-loved mammy allowed to live out her last years in relative comfort and security.

"It is," the woman finally admitted, her hand still on the half-open door. She seemed unwilling to give Pamela any encouragement to enter, but was also reluctant to ask her to leave.

"Do you live here alone?"

Again, that pause. The woman was trying to weigh her answers, to decide how much to say. She nodded and started to close the door in Pamela's face when a quick rap made her turn and stare at the dark room behind her.

"Who's there, Selma?" someone called. The voice was nasal, shaky as if the speaker had been ill.

"Some stranger. I didn't want to bother you, ma'am."

"Stranger?" The voice sounded doubtful.

Pamela saw the confusion in the black woman's expression and took advantage of it. In a manner completely at odds with her usual shyness, she pushed the door open, sending a shaft of light into the room. "I'm Pamela Donaldson, Elliot's wife," she said loudly. "I've come to visit. May I come in?"

A tiny old woman stood in the light, her deep-set eyes tearing from its sudden brightness. The sound Pamela had heard had been her wooden cane beating on the tile floor. She hesitated, as the first woman had done, then began walking forward. Though her green dress was ordinary, there was a beautiful cameo pinned to its neck, and the ruby ring on the hand gripping the cane was large and brilliant.

"You should rest," Selma said.

"I'll rest when I damn well want to! Now you go and find some refreshments for my guest." She gripped Pamela's arm with a thin, surprisingly strong hand and led her deeper into the house, through a wide archway, and into a parlor. The windows were covered with heavy black velvet drapes, the walls painted a deep shade of green. Spiders had been at work in the ceiling's corners, their unfortunate prey dangling from the webs. The thick brocade carpet that covered the center of the room had a fine gray coating of dust. Both made it clear that while Selma looked after her mistress, she did not do the same to the house. A single lamp on a polished mahogany table provided the only illumination. Though the room was cooler than outside, its air was damp and stale, belonging more to a subterranean cave than someone's home.

"Sit down, child," the woman said, pointing to one of a pair of high-back leather wing chairs on either side of the table flanking the covered window. The woman took the other. Her legs were so short that they didn't touch the ground, and she swung them like an impatient little girl.

"Would you like a footstool?" Pamela asked after noticing one half-hidden under the table.

"That's Selma's job," the woman retorted, her voice loud enough to carry.

"I can only do one thing at once," Selma called from somewhere else in the house.

Pamela looked at the footstool but said nothing. Something about the old woman's attitude told her she might get kicked if she took on Selma's menial job. They sat in silence until Selma returned, carrying a pitcher of cider and two glasses. She set those on the table, moved the footstool in front of her mistress's chair, then moved to a place behind it, staying no doubt in case the old woman should need something more from her.

"I'm Judith Donaldson," the woman said. "I was married to Edward, who started this plantation some fifty years ago."

"Elliot's grandfather?" Pamela asked.

"He was nothing to Elliot, nor to Elliot's father."

Selma's eyes rolled upward. She slowly shook her head.

Something in Pamela's expression must have given the gesture away. "Go up to the kitchen and bring me and my guest back some supper," Judith ordered.

"I'm not supposed to leave you alone, Madame."

"Do I look like I'm alone, you damned idiot? Now go!"

The woman left, but not before another long glance at Pamela, another slight shake of her head. Was she trying to say that her mistress was senile? Judith Donaldson hardly seemed so, though her recollection of past events might be less than accurate.

"Now that we don't have that eavesdropping old imbecile around, we can talk in private. I was saying . . ."

"That Elliot was not your grandson?"

"Not by blood, but he's a good boy. I think my Edward would have loved him."

She spoke as if Elliot were still alive. Perhaps no one had told her of Elliot's death, or perhaps she had forgotten. Not knowing the state of the old woman's health, Pamela decided to leave her in ignorance.

"You see, Edward and I didn't have more than a few dollars between us when we moved here. This little cottage was our first house, and the first house in the area. Of course, it didn't have all the little luxuries then. The tables and chairs were rough-cut cypress, the draperies plain loomed cotton. I made them myself.

"We came here right after we married, hoping to start a family, but it never happened. Edward . . . Edward loved me, but he simply had no interest in physical love. I thought that he might have a mistress, but though I paid the slaves to spy on him, there was no one. But he was romantic, even passionate in an intellectual sort of way. We got along, though we were as poor as the Acadian exiles, and working just as hard for every meal.

"We'd been married for nearly twelve years when Edward received a letter from a cousin whom he'd mentioned to me solely because of the man's great wealth. The man had gotten one of his mistresses pregnant and the girl had died in childbirth, leaving him with a bastard son. Though his letter made it clear that he had some great attachment for the child because of his affection for the boy's mother, he would have found it difficult, if not impossible, to raise the child himself. He offered Edward a great deal of money if he would take the child and raise it as his ward."

"What was the man's name?" Pamela asked.

"Edward made me pledge never to speak it to a single soul, but after all that's happened, I see no reason not to show you." She turned sideways in her chair and held her cane over the dust-covered floor, then wrote a single name—Usher.

"Roderick Usher?" Pamela asked incredulously.

"How did you know?"

"I'd heard the name somewhere," Pamela replied.

"From where?" The woman was staring at her now, her expression demanding an answer.

"My son is named after him," Pamela replied.

"Elliot suggested that?"

Pamela shook her head. "His mother did," she said.

"Ah, her. She would want a thing like that." Her attention was still fixed on Pamela, her hand shaking as she reached for Pamela's wrist and squeezed hard. Her nails were thick and long, and curved downward over her fingertips, digging into Pamela's flesh as she said, "Call him anything but that. It's a bad name, a terrible name. I never knew such a horrible man."

"What made you think so?"

"The way he brought his son here. The year was 1798 and that summer was one of the worst on record for heat. Phillip was barely a week old and had been given nothing to eat on the long journey here but a bit of water he had sucked from a cotton cloth. His face was red from the sun, and he was running a fever. The man hadn't changed the child's linen, either, and the baby reeked of urine and shit. When I bathed him, I saw that his bottom was blistered from neglect. If we hadn't already made arrangements for a wet nurse to come and care for him, I think he would have died, and I doubt that Roderick Usher—for all his statements to the contrary—would have minded."

"Some men have no idea how to take care of an infant," Pamela replied carefully. She didn't want to sound as if she were defending the father, who'd obviously possessed no common sense, but wondered if there was something more to the old woman's dislike of him.

Judith chuckled. "He had no idea, I'll grant you that. Why should he?"

"How did he become so wealthy?"

"He aligned himself with criminals—smugglers and slave runners and pirates. He loaned money at usurious rates to those poor dispossessed wretches from the north. . . ."

"The Acadians?"

Judith nodded. "Then, when they couldn't pay him back, he'd take the land they'd struggled to clear and sell it to some already-wealthy planter. He'd received a small inheritance from his grandfather's estate. It was the same place my Edward had gotten the money to purchase our land, but while we labored to improve our situation, Usher took the quicker, less honest path."

"Roderick Usher and your husband were cousins?"

"Edward's mother was Roderick's great-aunt, which is

why, given the family tie, he came to us for help. In our care Phillip grew into a strong, beautiful boy. When Edward died, Phillip inherited the property. It was fitting, since we'd loved him as our own and since much of the property had been purchased and improved due to his real father's fortune and the money he gave us to take the child."

"Did Phillip know he was adopted?"

"No. At first I thought it was callous of Roderick not to allow his son to know the truth. Later, I was thankful for it. I would not have had Phillip learn that he was related to that man."

Pamela looked at the hand still gripping her wrist, at the small drops of blood from the wounds the woman had unintentionally inflicted. She looked at the woman's face, at the hatred so clearly visible in those hooded, ancient eyes. "How did he wrong you?" she asked softly as if they would conspire against him together.

"Roderick was only a small part of it," Judith replied. She let go of Pamela's arm and stared across the room, her expression vague.

Judith was deciding how much to tell her, as if the knowledge she might impart would still have the power to harm her family. Pamela could see only one way out of the dilemma. "Did you know that Elliot is dead?" she asked.

No, Judith hadn't. That much was clear in the sudden anguish in her expression, the tears that followed some moments later as if she had weighed Pamela's truthfulness before deciding to mourn. "How did they kill him?" she asked.

"It wasn't like that at all," Pamela said and told about the accident.

"Do you think they couldn't plan such a thing?" Judith said when she'd finished.

"It was the storm that killed him," Pamela responded. "Only God can plan the weather."

"And her. She's capable of that, believe me."

So the old woman was delusional. How much of her story was the truth, how much a fabrication? Who is capable? She wanted to ask, but before she could, the front door opened and shut.

"Missus Judith, I'm back," Selma called.

"Don't say a word about our conversation," Judith whispered. "She spies for them."

Pamela understood, then realized she wouldn't have to. The topic of their conversation was plain to anyone who could recognize the name. Thinking quickly, she reached toward her hostess, upsetting the pitcher of cider in the process. It fell sideways, the liquid obliterating the word written in dust—

Usher.

chapter 13

Though Pamela wanted to return and speak with Judith further, she was afraid to do so. If Selma had reported her visit to the Usher family, any undue interest Pamela might show in the woman would make them suspicious.

So for the next week, Pamela read in the library every morning, had lunch with Madeline Usher at noon, then went riding for an hour or two and spent the remainder of the day with her son. Her strength increased with every cup of tea she drank.

And her dreams became more vivid. At first the theme was always the same—her and Elliot, the scenes so intense and passionate that during the day she would sometimes think of them and blush. Later, they became less sexual but no less disturbing. She dreamed of winds howling through ancient groves of trees, of fires lit on hilltops, of warriors carried home from battle, their empty bodies coated with clay and wrapped in yards of white linen—the burial customs of a long-dead people. She would wake, trembling, certain she would never sleep again, only to lie back and close her eyes and dream again—perhaps of another scene, perhaps the same one continued.

It was the books she read, she was certain of this, but once the sun rose, the terror of the night was forgotten and she returned to take still another book down from the shelf and carry it to her room.

While her child played on the carpet, she would lay beside him, idly passing the ball back and forth to him with one hand while the other turned the pages.

Finally it seemed enough time had lapsed that she could pay a second social call on Judith Donaldson. When she arrived late in the afternoon, she found the household much changed. Rather than a pair of isolated elderly women, she saw a younger slave leaving the house with Madeline Usher.

There was no way to avoid meeting Madeline on such a narrow path, so Pamela walked boldly forward. "I thought I'd pay a visit to Mrs. Donaldson," she said to Madeline. "I'm sorry to see you leaving or we might have all sat together."

"You'll have to see her some other time, she's quite ill now. I'd ask you to sit with her, but I'm concerned that it might be something contagious. In this climate summer sickness often is."

"Could I go in for just a moment? I promise to keep my distance, but I'd like her to know that I came to visit again as I'd promised and to tell her that I'll come again when she's better."

"Better?" Madeline shook her head sadly. "Well, miracles have been known to happen, so go inside. Perhaps she will respond to a voice other than mine."

Pamela walked into the dark foyer and stood just inside the doorway to the room where she had sat with Judith. The old woman lay on her red brocade divan, her head propped on a pile of pillows, undoubtedly to help her breathe. Though her eyes were open, they did not seem focused on any of her possessions or on the slaves bathing her forehead and spooning cold tea into her mouth.

"Mrs. Donaldson, it's Pamela," she said. "I came to call and want you to know I'll come back when you're better."

Judith seemed to hear the words. Her lips trembled, her eyes tried to focus, but even that small effort was impossible and her expression relaxed once more.

Pamela went outside and found Madeline waiting to ride

back with her. "What are you giving her to drink?" she asked.

"Some of the tea I give you along with some additional infusions to bring down her fever," Madeline answered. "I know of no better tonic. I once suggested that she drink it every day, but Judith would have none of it, calling it a witch's brew. Now that she is too sick to refuse, I'm doing my best to save her life. I fear that it's too late."

They walked in silence for a time, their horses following behind. Finally Madeline answered the question Pamela longed to ask. "I think we did not get along at first because she did not approve of Vivienne. It's easy to understand when you know them both. Judith was a practical, hardworking woman. When possible, Vivienne is the opposite.

"Unfortunately, Phillip doted on my daughter's eccentricities. He did his best to keep peace between Vivienne and Judith while managing the estate with the legendary Donaldson efficiency. Unfortunately, that effort probably contributed to his death two years after his heir was born. The mortar sealing the family crypt was still fresh when the women began arguing again, ignoring the plantation completely. With everything falling to ruin, I stepped between them and tried to force peace. Vivienne was furious that I would not take her side and left the plantation, abandoning her home and her son. She lived in Natchez for a time, then traveled abroad. She might have never returned home, but her lover abandoned her when he learned that she was expecting his child and she had no where else to go. When Judith learned of the pregnancy and that Vivienne and I agreed that the most practical way of dealing with the scandal was to give the child the Donaldson name, she became furious and moved into her little house. I don't think I've spoken ten words to her since. Elliot used to visit her a few times every week. I suppose he reminded her of her son."

"Did she have any friends we should write to?"

"No one. I relish my solitude, but I can't imagine willingly living in such isolation."

They reached the end of the narrow path. Madeline swung herself smoothly into the saddle and waited for Pamela to do the same. They parted some distance down the road, Madeline heading for her retreat, Pamela for the main house and her son.

The following night Pamela dreamed of fire once again but in a far less romantic setting.

. . . It blazes above the tall oak trees, the sparks whirling stars in the blackness of the sky. Pamela runs outside in her nightdress, feels the dew so cool against her bare feet, the chilly night air so pleasant against her bare arms and legs. . . .

It seemed that she woke while she was running across the fields to the grove beyond which Judith Donaldson had lived the last years of her life.

Sean caught her as she tried to bolt down the path. "You can't go down there. The oaks look ready to flare," he said. For a moment she struggled to free herself, then realizing where she was, she slumped against him. Madeline came and laid a blanket over her shoulders.

"Why are you doing this?" Pamela asked, her voice dull with shock.

"She died so quickly and with such a high fever that Madeline thinks it may have been the plague," Sean responded. "We put her body in the crypt immediately, and burn the house as a precaution."

"Tell her all the truth, Sean. She'll understand." Madeline held Pamela tightly, comforting her as she said, "We also burn her home as a sign of respect," Madeline said.

"But all her possessions are in it, all the things she valued," Pamela protested.

"And now they go with her to the next life so that their existence does not tempt her back to this one before her rightful time."

"Isn't being reborn something to be wished for?" Pamela asked, for that is what the books she'd read had told her.

"The realm of just souls is a perfect one," Madeline replied. "Better to linger there and recover after a long, sad

life than to return too soon to our world with all its troubles."
Madeline stared at the flames. Even in the flickering, golden
light that could make the ugliest emotion seem soft and
beautiful, her expression remained hard and remorseless.
"Besides, she would not have wanted us to have them anyway," she added.

Pamela rested against Sean for some moments, taking as
much comfort in his presence as in the memory his presence
evoked. She stood until she realized that Madeline's attention was elsewhere, then turned and walked back to the plantation house.

Sean went with her, catching her once when she stumbled
in the dark, holding her just a moment too long. He paused
outside her bedroom door to pick a piece of ash from her
hair, then pulled back a lock of it that had fallen in her face.
"I always envied Elliot for leaving here," he said.

"You could go. No one's stopping you, either, are they?"

He shook his head. "I don't have his independence, or his
way of dealing with people. When someone tells me what to
do, I simply do it instead of questioning the act. Like tonight.
Madeline gave me the torch and ordered me to start the fire. I
didn't want to. I stood in Judith's hallway, looking at all her
treasures, thinking how much she had valued them and what
a waste it was to destroy them. Then I flamed the drapes and
went outside to watch the house burn.

"I didn't realize how ashamed I was of what I'd done until
you asked me why I did it and I lied."

"Did Judith die as Madeline told me?"

Sean nodded. "I discovered her retreat years ago and visited her occasionally. Sometimes she would call me by my
brother's name; at others she would use mine, so I guess her
mind's been muddled for years. She had the fever every
summer for the last few years. I think she knew that this time
she wouldn't recover, because when I was there two days
ago, she asked me to give some things to you. I have them in
my studio. Would you like to see where I work, or should I
go and get them for you?"

"I'll go with you," Pamela replied. She went into her room
and lit a lamp, then followed him across the hall.

His room was a mirror image of her own—the same small bureau and cupboard, the same spartan bed and tall doors leading outside. He took her hand as he had the first time she'd met him and led her through the room and into the one beyond it.

She'd expected it to be the same size as Roddy's, but the wall linking it with the next room had been removed, creating a space some twenty feet long. She saw an easel, canvasses, and paints near the window and carving tools on a narrow worktable. Beside them a lynx was beginning to emerge from a piece of golden maple, its face so perfectly carved that it seemed as if Sean had captured some part of the great cat's soul.

He held up the lamp so she could see the pieces arranged on shelves along one wall. There were trees and carved flowers so real that she could see the veins in their leaves. There were finely dressed women and sad old men, animals and dragons. "You made Roddy's blocks, didn't you?" she asked.

"I did." He seemed both astonished and pleased at her reaction to his work.

"But you do have a skill, a marvelous one." She turned her attention to the paintings. Landscapes, mostly, and from what she could see in the dim lamplight, as well done as the carvings. "People would pay so much for these things if they only knew about them," she said.

"I'd have no idea how much to ask, or where to go to sell them," he replied.

"There are shops in St. James. You could start by talking to the owners there."

"I tried once when I'd gone into town to get some magazines and books for Mother. But I'm no good at selling myself. Besides, it would take away from the time I spend carving, something I *enjoy* doing." He handed her one of the carvings, that of a young girl riding a horse.

As she looked down at it, he took her free hand and held it against his chest as he went on. "But I wish I had possessed the courage to leave, at least for a while. I could have gone north as Elliot did. I could have found you . . . or someone like you."

Their faces were close. For a moment she thought he might kiss her, and decided that she would like it if he did. Instead he flushed and looked away. "I told you that Judith gave me something for you," he said and pulled a cloth-wrapped package tied with string out of the cupboard.

She unfolded the cloth. Inside was a folded letter, a leather-bound Bible and a small carved wooden box that looked like it might have been made by Sean. She opened it and found a gold stickpin with Judith's initials carved in it. Turning her attention back to the Bible, she opened it and saw the beautifully illuminated pages outlining a family tree going back four generations. The last entry was her son's name; the space for the birthdate had not been filled in.

"The letter was dictated to me. I wrote the words exactly as they were spoken."

Pamela wanted to stay and talk to him longer, but it was late and she was anxious to read the letter. He followed her to the door. At the last minute she turned to him, stood on tiptoe, and kissed him on the lips. It was as close as she could come to admitting the truth to him: that she was as attracted to him as he was to her, not only because he looked so much like Elliot.

Elliot had been dead nearly two years. She was hardly an inconstant woman for considering someone to replace him. In truth, she found Sean's shyness exciting; it gave her a chance to take the initiative, to be bold.

As she walked across the hall, he stood in the doorway, and she could sense that his eyes were fixed on her back. He mumbled a good night and shut his door. She was certain that he had to be blushing.

The note was unsigned and written in a shaking hand. It said simply, *Madeline would undoubtedly say that one who has real power should let her dreams guide her course. On this, I agree, but I also know the importance of knowledge and faith. Read the journals bound in white leather. When you learn all that you must know, do not despair. There are more powers in heaven and earth.*

Pamela put down the paper and held the pin in her hand. If Judith Donaldson had known she was dying, and had much to discuss with Pamela, why such a cryptic message? Wouldn't a simple request that Pamela come and visit again have been far more informative?

Unless, of course, Judith had been unable to write—and that little house was as much a prison as a refuge. With that thought in mind, Pamela held the note to the top of the lamp's chimney until it flamed, then dropped it onto the hearth and watched it burn. Afterward, she fastened the pin to the neckline of her nightdress, blew out the lamp, and sat at the table by the window.

The moon was rising. Though the trees kept her from seeing it directly, she saw its silver rays slicing across the lawn and lighting the clear patches of sky.

The ever-present heat. The spreading trees. The silence. The incredibly long lazy days had given way to sultry nights. Her only duties were to care for her son, eat, and sleep. Once she had known this kind of life, but it had been long ago, and hardly a happy time for her. Now, in less than two weeks, she had fallen into that same deadening somnambulance again. It made her a prisoner in this place, as clearly as any chains or bars or guards would have done.

There was so much she didn't know about her husband and his family—things that she would never determine by talking to slaves or to Sean, all of whom might have reasons to lie. There were others she could talk to. She'd known of them but hadn't bothered to contact them. Even now, she felt like doing nothing so much as drinking Madeline's tea, going to bed, and letting her dreams take her where they would.

She fought the urge. Tomorrow she would not be led astray by a pleasant day of reading Madeline's delightful books or bathing or playing with her son. Tomorrow she would find the little journals and begin to learn what sort of family she'd married into.

No, she would begin now, she decided, then left the tea in the pitcher and went to bed.

The decision was not as easy as Pamela thought it would

be. There was undoubtedly some drug in the tea that helped her sleep, because without it she woke frequently, her heart pounding from dreams she could not recall, her body damp and itchy from the heat. She'd finally managed to settle into a light doze when she heard a soft tap on her door. Before she could respond, the door swung open and someone came inside.

"Pamela?" Sean whispered.

Pamela sat up. In spite of the darkness she clutched the blanket in front of her nightdress. "What is it?" she called.

"I thought I heard someone walking around outside my window. Are you all right?"

"I'm fine." She reached out and brushed against Roddy sprawled beneath the crib netting. "We're both fine."

He moved to the window and stared out at the lawn. "It's probably nothing but my imagination." He came to the bed, bent down, and kissed her on the forehead. "Could I ask you something personal? You don't have to answer, but please don't be offended."

"Of course," she replied.

"Did you love my brother?"

Hardly an easy question to answer, especially to Sean. "I respected him. I admired his passion for his work. In his own way he was an artist as much as you are. Though I wasn't smitten by him as other girls often are by their husbands to be, I came to love him. We complemented each other."

"Do you still mourn him?"

She knew why he asked this, and she did not want to discourage him until she'd sorted out her own feelings for him. "I'm sorry he never got a chance to see his son. I suppose I'll always miss him, but no, I'm not in mourning any longer."

A pause, then he kissed her, more passionately than Elliot ever had. Though he did not touch her, she knew how much he wanted to. "I want you to know how much I've come to care for you," he said and started to stand.

Of course he did. He had no one else. He'd admitted as much. Because of that more than anything, she grabbed his wrist, pulling him back beside her, kissing him again.

A breeze moved the netting on her bed and Roddy's. The

child stirred and rolled over. Without a word Sean picked up the crib, carried it into the nursery, and shut the door.

He returned to her, to where she lay waiting for him, and slowly began to unfasten the lacing of her gown, watching her face all the while as if expecting her to send him away.

In the darkness he looked so much like her Elliot that she forced herself to remain silent even in the height of passion, lest she forget that she was not in their bed in that little cabin and call out her husband's name.

part three

❧

EDGAR

(taken from the notes of Edgar Poe)

chapter 14

In the weeks since I met Pamela Donaldson, fortune has not smiled on me. As I had feared, Elmira managed to learn of Pamela's visit, though not until days after it. When Elmira brought the matter up, we were sitting in the little garden behind her house; a place where surrounded by roses and honeysuckle vines, we spent many hours recalling stories of the idyllic times when we were young and in love, and I free of the plague of poverty and bouts of feverish insanity that have descended on me with frightening regularity since Virginia died two years ago.

When Elmira asked me about Pamela's visit, she did so in a tone so cold and calm I knew my entire future with her depended on my reply.

I began by refusing to give Pamela's name, but explained in detail why she had come to see me. As I related her account in a general sort of way, Elmira's normally dour expression became angry. I hoped she was angry for Pamela, but instead she declared, "The young woman was all alone in the wilderness, burdened with a child she could scarcely care for, at the mercy of savage men and animals. I can see how the grandmother could become upset and want to take the child away."

"But when you consider the circumstances, you have to

admit that there was a terrible injustice done to the mother," I replied patiently, doing my best to conceal the anger I felt at her callousness.

"True," she replied. "But now the woman is on her way to the family. If the family is as well-to-do as the mother thinks . . . Well, God seems to be about to set things right, Eddy."

God, if he exists—a point I have never been completely certain about—has so far made a complete mess of the poor girl's life. It would hardly be the sort of thing to say to Elmira. Though the girl she had once been would have understood, the woman she had become would not. "I hope that you're right," I replied instead.

"If so, I don't see why you need to be involved any further in the matter, Eddy."

Because Pamela Donaldson has touched my heart. Of course I dared not say this, because Elmira would certainly misunderstand, as I suspect that she would misunderstand most of the beliefs that have sustained me through my volatile life. "I probably won't be," I replied. "But I will be anxious for her until she writes me to tell me everything is well."

"Of course you will, Eddy, for you have a generous nature. Actually, far too generous sometimes. I admire you for it, but I see how people make demands on you and how other people's small tragedies trouble you too deeply," she said and took my hand. I wanted to pull away from her grasp.

Later, as I walked the few blocks to my boardinghouse, I asked myself, and not for the first time, if I still loved Elmira. I did love her years ago when we were young, but so many of my feelings seem to stem from memories of happier pasts, of times that often seem more real to me than the present. When Elmira had been young, she'd been carefree, even daring. Now, like every woman I know, with the possible exception of Sarah Whitman, who seems to get more eccentric as she ages, Elmira has become conservative, prim, stodgy, cursed by the rigid demands of religion and society. I have to mind what I say in her presence and cannot imagine a future in which that uneasiness will ever change.

Nonetheless, she seems to care for me in her own way. We

corresponded for months before I came South, and her letters gave evidence of the youthful passion her presence does not reveal. She also understands my nature well enough to make no demands on me when a creative frenzy strikes. If I didn't write her for weeks, she didn't chastise me; but instead saved her displeasure for the long dry spells between those creative bursts, as if my worth like that of Dickens must be measured in the number of pages I manage to produce in a week, rather than in the exquisite purity of the finished product. Now I am forced to admit to myself, and to hide from her, the fact that those creative thrusts ended months ago. I feel worn out, used up, a corpse shamed by its lost life.

As always when the dry weeks strike, the dreams come, as if there are phantasms dwelling only in my mind which struggle to take on life through pen and ink. Last night I dreamed of my dearest Sissy—thin and pale in the final weeks of her agony; of my stepmother's funeral so many years ago; and of a tiny birdlike woman with large expressive eyes. I am certain that it was the mother I knew for all too short a time, her face recalled only in my dreams and in the tiny, overstylized miniature of her that my brother Henry left for me when he died.

Just before morning I dreamed of Pamela riding up to the house of Usher, her skin, like the narrow windows of the oppressive structure itself, colored bloodred by the setting sun. I saw her sitting in the upper chamber where Roderick Usher had slowly lost his mind. I watched the door to it open, saw Madeline standing in it with her tattered funeral dress. When she reached out her arms and came toward Pamela, I could not determine if she intended to embrace or kill the woman. For the most obvious reasons I woke in a cold sweat, not unlike that of a broken fever, convinced that I have failed Pamela, and my own better nature.

Though I could hardly have abandoned all my reasons for coming to Richmond to accompany Pamela on her journey, I feel that I should have done so. Elmira is right about that. I am too chivalrous, and too often acquire guilt when I have no reason to, but my conscience is still not satisfied.

Pamela Donaldson is in danger—I am certain of it—and I

should not have let her go South alone. Throughout the long day of paying calls on old friends and potential subscribers for the magazine I hope to begin publishing, the feeling stayed with me, as did the troubling dream, and I can only blame both for the events which followed.

I'd used less than three dollars of the money Pamela left for me, this to pay for another two weeks on my room and meals. Though at Elmira's insistence, I'd taken a vow of temperance only days before, I stopped outside the doors of a tavern near my boardinghouse to wave to a friend I saw dining inside. It seemed as if the smell of stale ale and spilled whiskey intoxicated me as much as the actual substances themselves, because the next thing I recall was sitting in one of the worn maple chairs, a mug of ale in front of me. Though it seems like the statement of a madman, in truth I had no idea how I came to walk the few steps from the door to the seat, and who had ordered the ale for me.

I looked around fearfully, convinced for a moment that some of the Usher family had been following Pamela, following her even to my door, and that they have since been dogging me. Anyone who knows who I am also knows my weakness, and so they had perversely sat me down in front of the one thing they knew could destroy me.

Had I already finished one mug or two? I felt in my pockets but the coins I had were still there. I had no taste of malt in my mouth, but that might mean nothing. I dared not ask the barkeep who had bought the drink for me, and I did not want to draw attention to myself by walking out without consuming what had been ordered.

Knowing full well the consequences, and damning myself for my weakness, I picked up my mug and drained it.

Someone standing at the bar was speaking some gibberish about going west to mine gold, and I found myself drawn into the conversation, long enough to discern that he at least knew who I was. Another round of drinks appeared, and another.

Then, while I was still sober enough to pass for an abstainer, I finished my journey to the Swan. Before I turned onto Broad Street, I glanced at my reflection in a window glass and adjusted my tie. As I approached the tavern, I saw a number of guests sitting on the deep porch that ran the length of the establishment. I tried to go past them without being observed, but the innkeeper, Mrs. Blakely, called to me. "You've not had your dinner, Mr. Poe."

"I've eaten elsewhere," I replied. I might have, but had no idea where or when, save that I was not hungry.

"Well, come back outside. I've some people who'd like to meet you."

"I'll buy you a drink, Edgar Poe," a man called, his voice slightly slurred. He was much further gone than I, which in a perverse sort of way made me feel virtuous, though I doubt that his hangover would be a third as bad as mine in the morning.

A woman shushed the man, then added, "Please, Mr. Poe. I've read all your poems. Come and sit with us awhile."

She had a beautiful voice, soft and feminine, with that Carolina accent I've always found so alluring. I joined her and took her hand. After I thanked her for her kind words, I did not let her hand go, but instead sat beside her. My mouth felt so dry that it seemed sealed shut, yet someone was asking if I would give them a poem. I stood up and recited the few lines on ale that I penned a year ago. As I closed with, "What care I how time advances, I am drinking ale today," someone ordered me a mug.

"Shall it be cider, Mr. Poe?" Mrs. Blakely asked. The dear woman was well aware of my too-feeble attempts at sobriety. I could hardly blame her for what she said, yet the words themselves, innocent enough, seemed to draw attention to a weakness—for that is what intemperance is—that I did not want to reveal.

"Not tonight," I replied, and managed to smile. "Certainly not after that poem."

Another mug followed. Someone asked me to recite "The Raven." I stood on the porch rail, gripping one of the supports to keep steady, and spoke in a tone deliberately flat and quick. I was not mocking my greatest work, but rather I was thinking of those who had recently paid for the privilege that I was now giving away for the price of a few drinks. I despised myself for my weakness, and as soon as I had finished the poem, I left the gathering.

I remember climbing the stairs, but not entering my room or lying fully dressed on the bed and falling asleep. I woke well after midnight, on top of my blanket, bathed in sweat.

Knowing my meticulous habits, the housemaid had filled the washbasin. I took off my rumpled clothing and hung them carefully in the cupboard. As I stood in front of the mirror toweling off Richmond's soot, I noted, not for the first time, the sad changes the years had brought me.

My skin has always been too fair, and I learned to avoid the sun at an early age. Once its pallor had looked striking against my dark curly hair. Now it has a chalky tone that frightens me, for it reminds me of the way Sissy looked in the months before she died. Arms that had once been muscular are thin. My chest is sunken. And my face, which has always seemed too delicately featured, has become puffy. Though the illness I had when Pamela Donaldson visited me has all but passed, the weakness has not. Once I swam six miles up the James River for no other reason than a dare. Now I would be hard-pressed to swim across it at its narrowest point to save my life.

Have I grown so old, so quickly?

I have to admit that my aunt Muddy has twice the stamina I do, but then she has always led a virtuous, temperate life. It occurred to me as I saw my sorry face looking back at me, that I will die before she does, and leave her nothing to live on but my reputation for erratic genius, forgotten when the next genius takes my place on the literary stage.

Have I been such a failure as that?

Tears welled in my eyes and I sat down on the edge of my bed, not surprised by the depth of my emotion, for when these dark thoughts come to me, they are always too intense, the distress they carry as painful as any physical illness.

Though my body felt leaden, I blew out the candle and groped my way to the window, pulling it open to let in the night air. A moth circled me in the near darkness, then drawn by a carriage lantern, left me alone to face the nightmares that drink always make more vivid.

I woke a second time to daylight and a pounding on my door. Before I could answer it, a pair of letters were slipped under it. The first was from my aunt. I did not recognize the writing on the second but saw that it had been posted from New Orleans. I tore open its envelope and sat at the window, squinting at the sun streaming through the faded curtains and falling onto the dim writing on the page.

I scanned it first, reading Pamela's account of the journey and subsequent invitation to Petite Terre with a mixture of relief and disappointment that my assistance was no longer needed. After, as I read it again, analyzing it as best I could, I became concerned. The quest had ended too easily, even Pamela admitted so in the final thoughts where she asked me to contact Mary Quinn, promised to be careful, and to write me again soon.

I opened my aunt's letter. Muddy had been successful in tracking down the boxes where I'd kept the notes to my stories but said that they were unreadable. *The pages had all been stored in the cellar of Christ Church in New York, where the damp and the vermin ruined them,* she wrote. *Reverend Booth was most apologetic and said that if he'd had any indication that what we'd left with him was so fragile, he would have stored the boxes elsewhere. I suggest you write him a few kind words, Eddy, as he is quite upset about the loss.*

How could I have left the boxes behind! I recalled scraps of information stored in them. The origins of the "Mask of the Red Death"—the brief newspaper account of a masked ball in Paris, where cholera had taken down the guests with savage speed. A London magazine account of a lurid murder that became the background for both stories about Auguste Dupin. The notes on science and philosophy that had been the foundation for so many of my scholarly articles. Gone. And Muddy wrote about how upset the reverend was about the loss, as if I was expected to take the matter stoically, without a hint of anger, just as she had taken all the losses of her life.

Pamela said that my stories had been analyzed in her literature courses. I recalled how I had once analyzed Shakespeare and Milton, Swift and Pope. The times when authors' notes accompanied the stories had been particularly interesting for me. This would not happen with my own work.

The irrationality of the thought struck me a moment later. I should be thankful that Muddy had discovered the ruined notes, for now I have a chance to reconstruct at least a part of them. In the next published collection of my work, I will be certain to include some comment on each story, and perhaps some additional thoughts on the other fiction as well. I can leave that legacy; all it will take is a bit of time, and luck.

Perhaps it was the ale I drank last night, not the thought of my impending marriage, but when I went downstairs a half hour later, I had little appetite for breakfast. Though Mrs. Blakely had cooked up her usual tremendous breakfast for her borders, I took only two cups of black coffee, these drunk alone at one of the tables well away from the glare of the windows. While I drank it, I wrote two letters—a brief one to my aunt, a second to Mary Quinn. I thought of my aunt's request, then decided to leave the poor reverend to his distress.

I pocketed one of Mrs. Blakely's fresh scones for later and went to post my letters. After, I wandered the streets of Richmond, my mind on the puzzle Pamela Donaldson's life presented, and on all the possible means at my disposal to solve at least part of it.

I concentrated on the details in her story that confused me most because she apparently had not thought of them.

First, there was the vague relationship between Pamela and her husband, a connection close enough that Elliot Donaldson would be asked to travel some distance to seek her out, yet not close enough for him to know precisely how they were related.

Second, there was the fact that Elliot Donaldson did not seem to have much affection for his family, yet he made the long journey from Watkin's Glen to Albany to meet Pamela because, as he told his wife, his mother had asked him to.

Third, and by far the most obvious—so obvious that I had to draw it to Pamela's attention lest she realize it herself later and think me a blockhead for not seeing it—Vivienne Donaldson's arrival at her son's farm had not been caused by any letter sent to her from the local bank. Even if the bankers in Watkin's Glen or Albany had known the woman's Louisiana address—a point each made clear he did not—they would have sent an official notice of death, nothing more.

I then considered how I could best help her and decided to take Mary Quinn's advice and investigate Pamela's past. This would be a relatively simple matter, one I could easily do during the many aimless days I was spending in Virginia.

From my own youthful experience in Richmond, I knew that merchants are all familiar with one another. Landowners are the same way. In the weeks since I'd arrived in the city, I'd been invited to the Norfolk area twice, both times by Harold Ingram, whose family had earned its wealth planting tobacco in the area north of Appomattox. Though Harold had been raised to be a southern gentleman and had even attended Jefferson University with me, where we'd both managed with deliberate wickedness to lose much of our gentility, all of our virginity, and huge sums of money, I'd matured in the years since school. Harold, on the other hand, has in the past written me letters giving evidence that his youthful escapades were only the beginning of a life of complete dissipation. His adventures in the years after he left school had seemed rather vulgar, and his wittiness was, in the absence of any noticeable spark of intellect, exceedingly drab. Yet his birthplace, the occupation he'd pursued for the first decade of his adult life until he sold the plantation to his brother, even his age—somewhere in his early forties—made me certain he'd known Pamela's father.

I wrote the man a hasty note accepting his invitation, and without waiting for a reply caught a boat heading downriver three days later. The weather was wretched, hot and rainy, which meant that my clothes were drenched for most of the journey. The wheezing cough that had so concerned Pamela Donaldson returned, each bout of it leaving me dizzy and weak. When I got off the steamer at Newport News, I'd expected to have to walk to the Ingram house some miles east of the landing, but saw Harold standing on the pier beneath an umbrella waiting for me.

chapter 15

Harold had not changed overly much in the twelve years since I had last seen him, nor even in the twenty odd years since I had first met him over a card game at school. His pudgy infantile face was still unlined, his thin hair still blond, his eyes—his best feature—still a brilliant innocent blue. Only his girth had changed. It seemed that it was now his belly which tried to break free of his trousers. "Eddy!" he exclaimed as he pumped my hand, then dropped the umbrella and threw his arms around my shoulders. "Eddy! Who would have thought that all the doggerel you wrote at school might turn out to be literature someday? I've read everything you've published, and it's all so marvelously frightening!"

I scanned the wharf, half expecting Harry to have hired a marching band to come with him. Instead, he'd brought his carriage and a bottle of amontillado which he immediately uncorked. Still shaking from that drunken bout some days before, I refused a glass, watching Harry drink as the coachman maneuvered the team through the narrow streets.

The Ingram house was some miles east of town, built on a high piece of land on Point Comfort near Fortress Monroe. That evening Harry and I dined on a veranda overlooking the water.

Across the bay I could see the massive battlements of the

fortress. Had twenty-three years really passed since Edgar Perry, the adolescent recruit with the assumed name, had landed there? I'd been so young, so intent on adventure. Instead I discovered such grueling and mindless routine that I quickly turned my back on that life. Even now, after years often spent on the edge of true poverty, I do not regret my choice. I've had adventures enough in my mind. Besides, my fortunes had recently taken a turn for the better if only because I'd just finished dining on the best supper I'd had in months—fresh bread and cheese, a thick chowder filled with seafood and chunks of salty ham, and chicken in a delicate wine sauce. Harry, who had always had the greatest interest in gustatory matters, found fault with every dish, but managed with effort to eat three servings in the time it took me to finish one.

"I never thought you'd take me up on my offer, Eddy," he said as he poured us each a glass of cordial to accompany the poached peaches that finished the meal.

"I would have come eventually," I replied. "I've been busy giving lectures to find subscribers for a new literary publication I'm starting."

"Well, if you'll be editing it, count me in. I can even invite some of my neighbors over on Sunday. You could do a reading and ask them to subscribe. Even those who don't read will sign up once they've heard you speak."

I made some polite, gracious reply and looked across the lawn, which sloped gently down to the water's edge. A pair of girls walked near the shore, their light-colored dresses seeming to glow in the evening light.

"Do you know I've actually had dreams about your tales, Eddy?" Harry went on.

"So have I," I replied dryly. I felt immensely pleased with Harry's idolization of my work, personally as well as because of the idea it had given me on how to get the information about Pamela.

"So as I said," I continued. "I would have come later, but something unusual happened. I met a woman who told me a remarkable story about her parents. I decided to use her information in a piece of fiction and was furiously working on it until I reached a sudden dead end. I came down now because I thought you might know her family and could tell me more."

As I expected, the notion that Harry would be helping me collect information for a story was the perfect half-truth. "Family? Why? Are they from Norfolk? I know almost everyone here, believe me, and the rest I'm acquainted with by rumor."

"They aren't from here, but from Buckingham County. Their name is Montgomery. The father was called William, the mother Anna."

"Anna and William Montgomery." Harold rolled the names around in his mouth as if they were another course of the meal, repeating them twice before recognition brightened his expression. "Of course! I wonder why I didn't recognize the names right away. The woman ran away from her husband. It was all the local planters could talk about, simply because nothing to equal it had happened there in years. So you met the daughter. Where?"

"She was part of a small group that dined with me after a lecture I gave in Richmond," I replied carefully. Pamela airing her family scandal in public was hardly polite, but visiting me at my boardinghouse in the middle of the night would be too choice a piece of gossip for someone like Harry to be trusted with.

"So she can talk about it. That's good, I suppose. I recall that she had a rough time of it after her mother left. Her father seemed to lose his mind for a time, or at least that's what we all thought. He treated her no better than I'd treat a slave; worse because I place value on those I own."

"Did he really lose his mind, or was he merely grief stricken at his wife's loss?" I asked.

"That's what it was in the beginning. Once, a friend of mine told me that he'd mentioned Anna's name to Will, and Will actually cried."

"Did he think she was dead?"

"Dead! No, by then he knew she'd abandoned him. He was crying because he missed her. 'Will the Wastrel' brought down to such a pitiful level by that bitch of a woman. Who'd have expected it? As you can imagine, everyone had his own opinion about the matter. Some of the planters' wives were convinced that Will had treated the woman badly, perhaps even beat her, but they couldn't comprehend why the wife hadn't taken her daughter with her when she ran. Most of the men thought him better off without her, though we rarely said so to his face. All I know is that he looked for his wife long after anyone with an ounce of self-respect would have thrown in the towel. What did he think he'd do when he found her—clap her in manacles and drag her back like some runaway slave?"

"His daughter thinks he did find her," I said.

"Of course he did. Everyone agrees on that. After a month-long journey to check still another sighting of that elusive creature, he returned and demanded that no one mention her name in his presence. That was when his darling snip of a daughter also lost her place in his heart. I think if he wouldn't have hung for it, he would have drowned the child like some unwanted puppy.

"I don't know what the girl told you, but the sentiment of the planters in the area was that he discovered the woman he'd married was probably a twopenny whore, which made the girl the daughter of a twopenny . . ." He saw the shocked expression on my face and stopped midsentence. "Well, you get my drift. But even that was strange because Will had bedded more than one of that sort of woman in his life and was never one to place a high value on his own reputation."

"Did you ever learn where he went on that last journey?"

"Now you're asking too much, Eddy. With stories like that you pass around the really titillating parts, not the petty details."

Like the Usher story, I thought. The place, the dates, even the person who had given me the clipping were lost to me, but the "really titillating parts" remained.

"If you like, I can drop a note to my sister-in-law. She'd be glad to put you up for a few days, maybe even take you over to the Montgomery place so you could meet Will and judge for yourself what happened."

I smiled. In a moment Harry would be ready to go with

me. I could picture us both, a pair of middle-aged snoops peeking into windows and tripping over our own feet in the dead of night. "People change after so many years," I commented.

"But the core remains. Yours. Mine . . ."

I couldn't help myself. I laughed.

Harry joined me. "Mine *is* much expanded. I did leave myself open for that, didn't I? But the point I'm making is valid."

"Of course it is, Harry. But it would hardly be polite for a stranger to go to a man's house, bring up unsettling matters from twenty years before, then demand that he explain his personal life all in the name of a work of fiction."

"You're right. Quite right, if politeness is what matters. But I'll tell you one thing and you can pass the advice on if you ever see Will's daughter again. She's lucky. Unlike mine and yours, her father is still alive. She should write him, and tell him how she feels about him. If she's up to it, she should go and face him."

I looked at my host in frank astonishment. "Harry, I feel as if I'm talking with a stranger. What brought on this sudden depth in you?" I asked.

"Age, I suppose, and a recent family reunion. When my father died, his wealth was equally divided between the land and his shipping business. I gave my brother Mark full title to the plantation because I couldn't tolerate living in a house where every room held some horror from my past. I didn't go back until four years ago after Mark died. He left a wife and three small sons, the oldest just six.

"You know those old southern houses. In a decade even the trees don't seem to grow. I stood on the porch where my father had caned me for every boyish prank as he tried to turn me into his idea of the perfect southern gentleman. I slept in my old room, where I'd been a prisoner for nearly all of one summer after he caught me in a compromising position with one of the colored girls and I had the cheek to tell him that even the mighty Jefferson had his mistress.

"My sisters came to the wake with their children. Since Mark's death had not been unexpected, our meeting was something of a reunion. After the children and spouses went to bed, we siblings sat at the oak dining table—itself a source of so much misery to us all—and talked about our past.

"After three nights of morbid conversation, I lay in my old bed and stared dry-eyed at the ceiling. An incredible weight that I had never known was a part of me pressed down my chest. I couldn't breathe. I couldn't even cry out for help. It was my father's ghost. I'm certain of this even today, but I felt no terror. Instead, in the longest night of my life, I fought with the bastard and banished him. That night changed me.

"Now, at forty-two, I feel as if I have finally grown up and the world is open to me at last. I may even marry someday, now that I'm a fit companion for a mature woman. I've begun courting my sister-in-law. Jane is a marvelous woman. I care for her a great deal and I love her sons as if they were my own. A man should know his heirs, however distant the relationship." He poured himself a second glass of cordial and passed the bottle to me. "Did you ever go home, Eddy?"

"Just once." I hesitated for a moment, weighing how much to reveal, deciding it was time to tell this story to another soul. Though I'd never expected that soul to be Harry Ingram, I began. "I'd heard that John Allan was dying and I wanted to see him before it was too late. I'd recently won first prize in a writing contest in the *Visitor*. I wanted to show him the story and the glowing praise written about it and to force him to realize that although I didn't choose the path he'd decided on for me, I'd chosen the right one."

"And what did he say?"

I hesitated. I remembered how much I'd had to drink that afternoon. I'd stopped at a tavern near my father's house. Too nervous to face him sober, I'd moved quickly from ale to whiskey. But I hadn't been drunk. If I had been, I would not be able to recall the incident so clearly, or with such a lack of remorse. "I handled it badly," I admitted. "My father's second wife answered the door. We'd never met, but she recognized me and tried to slam the door in my face. I pushed my way past her and ran up the stairs to his bedroom. I expected . . . well, I guess I'm a romantic because I expected to see him in bed, and to find him remorseful and ripe for some last-minute reconciliation. It didn't happen that way at all.

"I knew he had dropsy, so I should have been prepared for the sight, but I confess that I stood frozen in the doorway, with my hand on the knob not certain if I should stay or flee. He was sitting in a chair in the center of the room, his once lean hands and feet swollen from the disease. His face was puffy and red, and there was a large weeping sore on one cheek. I opened my mouth, but for the first time in all our years together, I was speechless. When he saw me, he reached for his cane and pushed himself to his feet. I fled not out of any fear of being beaten, or even arrested, but because I believed that the exertion would kill him, and no matter how badly he treated me, I would not have that on my conscience. For days after the incident I waited fearfully for some word that he had expired. When none came, I felt much relieved. He died two months later."

"But did the ill will remain?" Harry asked.

"For a time. I used to dream about that final visit, but gradually the memory faded. I hadn't thought about it until I returned to Richmond, and then not with any emotion until I heard the story of the Montgomery family and compared how the daughter had been treated to my own life.

"But I was not John Allan's real son, and I was totally unlike him in temperament and inclination. She was her father's daughter and, from what I could determine at our meeting, would have been an obedient one, so how could he treat her so harshly?" I paused, frowned. I hoped that my sudden conjecture was wrong, but I had to ask, "Harry, was there any rumor that Anna Montgomery was unfaithful to her husband?"

"Now, that would have made for truly interesting gossip. No, Eddy, there wasn't even a whisper of that sort of scandal. Everyone agreed that she loved him dearly right until she up and left him."

The two girls at the river's edge were joined by three more. The moon had risen, throwing specks of silver across on the placid bay water. The girls' pale arms and white dresses glowed, making them seem more spectral than real.

They strolled up to the house, sitting in a little gazebo some distance away. I watched their white hands move, listened to the distant indistinct sound of their voices. Beautiful youth. What injustices were committed on the innocent all in the name of parental expectation?

"How long was William Montgomery gone on his last journey?" I asked.

Harry's serious expression brightened. He grinned, then laughed. "That's twice you've asked about his last trip, Eddy! I believe you mean to solve this puzzle before you write about it. Well, I recall two small pieces of it. Will was gone just over two weeks. I know this because a cousin from Buckingham was getting married and Franklin Montgomery was a close friend of my uncle. He came to the wedding and said his son had just returned from the South but wasn't up to attending. Later, when we discovered how his attitude had changed, it was easy to understand why the last place he would have wanted to be was at a marriage."

"And he went South."

"So his father said. Since Anna was of French descent, could he have traveled to Santo Domingo? The island is always in some state of upheaval, which would explain why Anna left the child behind when she fled."

"Or she may have gone to New Orleans," I responded, thinking of the relationship between Pamela's mother and her husband's family. "What do you think?"

Harold shrugged. "If you think New Orleans is the place to find the woman, why don't you go there and look for her, Eddy? You can work anywhere. Nothing ties you to any one place."

Nothing but poverty, I thought, though it was hardly something I could admit, at least not directly. "I came South to raise money for the magazine," I replied. "I can't abandon that goal."

"You wouldn't be. I've been to New Orleans. It may have a hellish climate, but the wealthy are as civilized as any you'll find in Virginia, though they don't have the luxuries we do. Do a reading or two there, Eddy, and you'll pack the house. Sell them your subscriptions, and they'll buy because the editor cared enough to come and ask them in person."

"I'm tempted, but I haven't the money to undertake such a long journey," I confessed, hoping that I had downplayed my poverty to the correct degree.

"Well, dammit, I do. Write me into your story, Eddy, and I'll fund the whole thing. Go to France to find her, if you must. If it weren't for my business, I'd free up the months and go with you."

Fueled by my friend's enthusiasm, and my own growing restlessness with life in Richmond, I was almost ready to act. But then, as always, the thought of going so far away, so out of the reach of my aunt and others who care about me, made me pause. And there was my reputation to consider. If I abandoned the well-planned business trip I had lined up to pursue some wild story, I would likely lose the backing for the magazine. "I have a lecture to give in Richmond the beginning of next week," I said. "The advertisements are already in the local paper; I can't back out now to pursue some creative whim. And if you'd seen the state I was in just days ago, you'd know that the last thing I need is to travel to a place with a hellish climate."

"You're right, but the offer remains. In the meantime, think about going to Charlottesville. The food will be fresh instead of the half-stale swill we get in town, and the country air is fresher. If you don't want to meet Will Montgomery, Jane can introduce you to some of the older planters who may have information to help you. If I write Jane now, you can leave as soon as you've finished the lecture. I'll be going up myself in ten days' time. It's primarily a business trip, but while I'm there there's a little hobby of mine I'd like to share with you."

"Hobby?"

"No, no. I'm not saying a word. I want to surprise you."

"Pleasantly, I hope."

"Pleasantly enough. Actually, I got the idea from one of your essays."

"An essay?"

Harry smiled cryptically, his lips shut, his eyes sparkling

with anticipation. I'd seen him like that many times when we were young, and for a moment I felt youth returning. Besides, it seemed a safe enough adventure.

"Very well, I'll do it," I said. "Tell your family to expect me three days after my lecture, the twentieth of August. And now that you've thoroughly roused my curiosity, I promise to stay until you arrive, but I'd like to ask a favor."

"Anything, Eddy."

Anything? Put in a good word for me to Elmira, I thought. Better yet, offer to take in my aunt Muddy and save me from that marriage altogether. But of course, I couldn't ask either, and there were more practical matters to consider. "I've been staying at the Swan in Richmond. Could you please stop there on the way upriver and bring me my mail?"

Harry agreed. We spent the next hour discussing trivial matters until Harry said, "My niece, Susan, is visiting from Appomattox and has been anxious to meet you. Would you talk with her and her friends awhile?"

I nodded, and he motioned for the girls to come up to the porch. They came, giggling with embarrassment, falling silent only when I took Susan's hand.

She was a petite girl, no older than Sissy had been when we'd married, with the same youthful fleshiness and dark, expressive eyes. She stammered something about how much she loved my work, and I found myself reciting some of my poems from memory, including "Annabel Lee," which I had finished only months before. She cried as I recited the last lines.

"Why the tears, Miss Ingram?" I asked.

"Because I think that no one will ever love me as you did her," she said.

One of the other girls laughed and told her that she had mistaken the narrator of the poem for myself. I felt a stab of pity for the sensitive child and told the group that the poem's inspiration had come from a love I had felt when I was young. "Old men say that the young cannot love," I said with exaggerated fervor. "Yet their hearts break so easily and the sorrow remains a lifetime."

Then, with a generosity I could ill afford, I signed the volume of poems I'd brought, kissed the girl's hand, and gave it to her. A fleeting, shy smile brushed her lips, and I wished that we were alone so I could sit with her, no more than that, and whisper to her how someday perhaps another poem would come to me and her white dress and dark eyes and innocent tears would be the source of it.

Alas, I never had the chance, and moments later the girls retired for the night, leaving Harry and me to our conversation.

That night, in a soft strange bed, I dreamed again of Pamela. This time she was sitting with schoolgirls on some misty lawn in early evening, their white skirts fanned out around them like bridal trains. They were laughing, oblivious of a dark presence that formed in the sky above them, until it swooped down and plucked Pamela from their midst as if it were a raptor and she its prey. Her screams faded as the dark creature carried her away.

I woke with a start, more terrified by the pleasant part of the dream than by the nightmare, for I realized all too well why I had left that volume of poems with Harry's niece. I had been thinking of the spring social at the Hudson School, and not even realized it.

As I often do, I woke later this morning in Harry's guest room, I looked in the mirror, studying my face as I would a stranger's. As I expected, that feverish light I had seen before and always dreaded was growing in my eyes. At times, when ideas were slowly taking on their fantastic shapes in my mind, I welcomed this glow, for it meant that I would soon be working round the clock, often for days, fueled by coffee, the sharp edges of the mania smoothed by an occasional shot of brandy or port.

Yet now my mind holds no ideas; and I am far away from Muddy, who knows best of all how to nurse me through the terrible attacks of passions beyond any control. I need to find a focus, some compelling reality to hold on to when the madness hits, or I will be left incapable of functioning at anything but the most primitive level.

And all that stands between me and Bedlam is one petite, nervous, and determined woman. For good or ill, I will play my part in solving the puzzle that is her life.

chapter 16

To conserve funds, I did not arrange for a berth on the upriver journey to Richmond. Instead, I spent most of the overnight trip in the common room, surrounded by cigar-smoking farmers, itinerant workers, and a pair of genteel but obviously penniless ladies who noted the lack of a wedding ring on my finger and fawned over me until I excused myself and went out on deck.

The night was chilly, but hardly cold. The new moon shed no light and the stars were thick in the cloudless sky, hanging nearly to the horizon. Unlike others who reported feeling humbled in the presence of such limitless grandeur, I always feel challenged. If I was reborn in some later age, would I fly in some marvelous device to the moon and beyond? Was some strange creature standing on the Earth's silvery satellite, thinking similar thoughts? My mind traveled its own fanciful paths, spinning fragmentary ideas that might one day merge into some whole and fantastic tale. And so I spent the rest of the night with only my imagination for company and thought myself well blessed by the company.

The steamer pulled into Richmond early in the morning. I immediately went to the Swan, but there was no mail for me, though Mrs. Blakely greeted me warmly and noted that she'd been keeping my old room ready for me.

I spent the evening looking over my lecture notes, and the next day I rested. That night, in spite of the sultry heat wave that had gripped the city for the last week or so, I spoke in front of a large audience, fully a third of whom wanted to purchase a subscription to my magazine, *The Stylus.*

I pocketed twenty dollars for the speaking fee and put the rest in an envelope to send to my backer. Of what I kept, I later put half in an envelope addressed to Muddy along with a note telling her that I was certain that a few more weeks in the South would ensure my success, and our financial security. I did not tell her that I was looking into the Montgomery mystery, for I did not want to alarm her.

I barely caught the midmorning coach, and because of my tardiness I found myself sitting between a feuding couple who exchanged insults with the same fervor that drunks exchange blows. I kept my eyes shut and my head bowed, wishing they would shut up so I could stop pretending to sleep and actually do so.

Though it was early morning when the coach pulled into Appomattox, there was a team and single seat buggy waiting for me. The old black driver seemed to recognize me immediately, waving me over and purchasing coffee from the coach house. He insisted that the man fill it nearly to the brim before parting with the two pennies the man asked for. "Master Harry said that you still liked your morning coffee," he explained.

The coffee was far too hot to drink, or even to risk spilling on my hand. I held the mug as steady as I could outside the buggy while the driver turned the team around and headed north out of town on the bumpy dirt road.

"I suppose you don't remember me, Mr. Edgar?" the driver asked.

I looked at him, mentally subtracting some twenty years from his features. "Lloyd?" I asked.

"The same, and happy you recall the name."

Happy! I was amazed it had taken me so long. Lloyd had been responsible for getting Harry back and forth from school every weekend. On my visits to the Ingram plantation, I'd usually ridden in the front with Lloyd. I'd used variations on his language and his superstitions in a half-dozen stories. I wanted to mention that to him, then realized that the poor man would not have been able to read any of them.

"I hears you wants to make a visit to Montgomery House, and maybe get a glimpse of old Montgomery hisself," Lloyd said.

"You heard right."

"Well, there's plenty enough people around here who knew Will Montgomery, grants you that."

"Knew?" I asked. "Has he died?"

"Might as well have. That last anyone saw of him was three years ago when he turned out for his neighbor's funeral. I hear that he didn't stay for the wake."

So much for arranging a chance meeting. "How did he appear then?" I asked.

"Folks say he appeared much older than they remembered," Lloyd replied and began to chuckle; then, deciding he'd been truly witty, to laugh.

I laughed, too. I had been feeling lighthearted for the last few days. The trip to Newport had removed all traces of fever from me, and the unseasonably cool and dry weather the last few days had been perfect for travel. I sat back, sipped my coffee and considered that my memory of the beautiful hills of the area had not been exaggerated with time.

The Ingram plantation was a quick hour's ride from town. I had been there often during short breaks at school. On my first visit it hadn't taken more than a few hours for my envy of Harold's wealth to turn to pity for the way he was mistreated at his father's whim. Even John Allan had been kinder—kind enough at least to send me out of range of his temper and demands and try to pretend that I'd never existed. On the other hand, Harry was required to spend every free period at home.

The house had been expanded since I'd last seen it: the roof raised to create extra bedrooms, a solarium added at the back, and the porch extended along the side to meet it. As the buggy stopped in front of the main doors, a slave came running from the barn to tend to the team while Michael's sons, about eight and five, came running outside to greet me. Their mother followed.

Jane Ingram was perhaps twenty years younger than Harry. She wore her auburn hair parted in the center and gathered at the nape of her neck in a bright green chenille net, which accented her round face and wide-spaced blue eyes.

The Ingram children had lunch with us. Afterward, they went off with their tutor. "Would you like to see our gardens?" Jane asked me.

Sensing that the woman wanted to speak to me in complete privacy, I agreed. We walked past a half a dozen different roses, past the hibiscus and mock orange hedges, to a flagstone-covered clearing where she sat on a painted iron bench and pulled me down beside her. I felt the crinoline underskirt, the thin bone circle that held it out so fashionably when she stood, the heat of her body beneath it.

"Harry wrote to tell us that we are to assist you in researching a story on Will Montgomery," she began. "He seemed deliberately vague about the details."

"That's because I was somewhat vague," I replied, then hastened to add, "Not because I wanted to mislead him, but because I feel uncomfortable sharing another's tragedy without permission. I'm certain you understand."

She took my hand, holding it in both of hers. It was a gesture I knew too well to misinterpret her intent. Looking me directly in the eyes, she went on. "I understand that you are troubled about something. I hope I can help, but to do so I have to understand the full nature of the problem. Mr. Poe, I assure you that I can keep a confidence, even from Harry."

An odd thing to say, yet I believed her. In the next hour I told her Pamela's story, Mary Quinn's strange advice, and my own instinctive belief that the advice was sound.

"So I've come here, though from the information that your husband has already given me, I hardly know what I'll be able to discover," I concluded.

Jane Ingram frowned and considered the matter. "More than you expect, I would think," she replied. "You see, Will Montgomery no longer works his land. Instead, he leases it to neighboring plantations. He leases out his slaves as well, and makes quite a profit on both, so I understand."

"Would that include the woman who raised Pamela, the slave called Emmie?"

Jane shook her head. "But it does include Emmie's daughter, Miriam. She's worked as my mother's cook for the last five years. Mother has become so fond of her that she has tried to buy her and her mother from Will Montgomery at least a dozen times in the hope of eventually freeing them both. Montgomery has refused the offers, even though the last amount was well beyond what they are worth.

"His reasons are his own, and the subject of some speculation on my part. The important thing to you, Mr. Poe, is that Miriam visits her mother every Sunday when my mother comes here for dinner. I see no reason why, if you stay out of sight of the main house, you won't be able to go with her and ask her mother whatever questions you wish."

None whatsoever. And if I pressed one of the five dollars I had left from the money Pamela had given me into her hand, I would certainly start the woman to talking. "Tomorrow is already Saturday," I said. "Will you have time to take me over to your mother's house?"

"We'll go right after breakfast and plan on spending the night there. I'll bring my mother home with me as I always do. Her driver can follow with you on Sunday evening if you're up to the journey."

She stood and smoothed her skirts. The mischievous nature I'd suspected she possessed was more obvious now in her delighted smile, the color in her cheeks, the cheerfulness in her voice. "Now I must go and write a note to Mama telling her to expect us. I do love to solve puzzles. Thank you so much for sharing this one with me, Mr. Poe."

She walked quickly from the garden, leaving me alone with the flowers, and the silence broken only by the somnolent buzzing of honeybees.

I thought I would be spending a quiet morning with a charming woman, but I was terribly mistaken. Jane brought her sons. The boys acted as if they had never ridden in a buggy before—jumping up and down, rocking the buggy on its frame, and demanding that the driver go faster, a demand the driver thankfully ignored. Jane paid little attention to them, and instead pointed out the various landmarks in the area.

The driver set a steady pace for the first two hours until Jane asked him to slow down. She pointed at a weathered fence and wide brick drive. "Montgomery House will be coming into view in just a minute," she said. "When you see it, realize that it was once the grandest house in the area."

Once it would have been as elegant as the house Pamela had described to me, for it held hints of its prior grandeur— in the circular columns of the deep porches on the upper and lower storeys, the wide front stairs, the elegant carvings on the frame of the double doors. And it looked sturdy still, in spite of the exposed weathered wood along most of the south side, the missing sections of porch rail, the untended magnolia bushes in front of it. It reminded me of an old woman, once beautiful and holding hints of that beauty in spite of age, fighting off the death—already glimpsed—and certain to come in a short time.

The house was less than a hundred yards from the road, sheltered from view only by a single huge mimosa tree close to the front door. Yet it had all the isolation of more remote homes, its owners and servants cut off from friends and casual visitors by an iron fence and locked gate. I studied the last and saw rust on the hinges. There had to be another way in, probably closer to the fields and drying barns we'd passed a few minutes before. An hour later—a time that seemed to stretch interminably on after Michael Junior began to torment his easily-frightened little brother by pointing out the presence of a recent spiderweb under my seat—we reached our destination.

Jane Ingram's mother, Martha Pierce Bridger, was descended from and had married into one of the original Virginia families. Her wealth was not evident in the exterior of her square brick house, which was hardly as grand as the Ingram's plantation house or even Montgomery House when it had been in its prime. Instead the Bridger home had been built earlier, at a time when it was both unseemly and dangerous to flaunt great wealth.

Interior comforts were another matter.

The foyer floor was covered in rose marble, the space lit by a delicate crystal chandelier. I sat in a tapestry-covered chair and sipped tea poured by Mrs. Bridger herself from a Limoges porcelain pot into a matching cup. While those of a lesser station might have been put off by my dated and too carefully mended garments, Mrs. Bridger gave no sign of noticing them. Instead, she possessed the gentility I have come to expect from true southern aristocrats.

That gentility extended even to the slaves. After Jane explained the reason for my visit, her mother summoned Miriam. The woman came immediately, with no sign of fear that her mistress might be in a bad temper over some trifling mistake Miriam might have made. She sat at the table, as her mistress ordered, and looked at me with frank curiosity.

Though I was used to thinking of plantation cooks as universally middle-aged and stout, the girl was thin and no older than twenty-five. Her eyes were hazel rather than brown, her hair long and lustrous, her nose and lips straight and narrow, her skin so pale that were she living in someplace other than Virginia, she might have easily passed for Spanish or Italian.

"Miriam, this is Mr. Edgar Poe of New York. He would like to speak in private to your mother. I would like you to take him to see her when you go tomorrow," Mrs. Bridger explained.

"Did my mother do something wrong?" Miriam asked. Her voice was a surprise as well, soft and cultured.

"No, Miriam. Nothing like that," Mrs. Bridger said. "He wants to ask some questions about the Montgomery family."

"About Mister Will? Mama doesn't like to talk about Mister Will."

"No one will force her to, Miriam, I promise you that. But Mr. Poe has a message for your mother that he must deliver in person. Can I count on you?"

Though she did not look pleased by the request, Miriam nodded. "I leave at seven. Can you be ready then?"

"You can leave a little later, Miriam, and ride part way in the buggy," Jane suggested.

"No. Mister Will would see the buggy coming. He watches; I know he does. Besides, it's just as fast to walk overland."

"She may well be right about the owner watching," I interjected. "I don't mind the walk."

"I'll get you up at half past six so we can eat first," Miriam suggested. She glanced toward the back door. "Jade don't know the first thing about managing the stove, and supper's almost ready."

"Of course, Miriam," Mrs. Bridger said. "We don't want to keep you and ruin a masterpiece."

chapter 17

*M*iriam had a light breakfast of biscuits and coffee ready when I came downstairs. We ate together in the kitchen, then she put on thick-soled boots and tied a pair of slippers to her belt.

"Will I need an extra pair of shoes?" I asked.

"Not unless you're worried that the mud won't clean off later. I'll go up to the house and sit with Mister Will awhile so you and Mama can have some privacy. The slippers are to wear then."

She attached the two sides of her skirt to her belt, raising the hem nearly to her knees, then set off in the lead. As I followed, watching her muscular brown legs move confidently through the tobacco and grazing fields, and down the narrow footpaths in the wild strips of woodland that separated them, I began to feel as if I had somehow stepped into another world, one where my tales were real and the mundane daily life I lead a poor and boring fantasy.

The girl set a good pace, one I managed to follow with just a bit of difficulty for the first two miles or so until a sudden fit of coughing reminded me that I was not quite well. Miriam ran back to me and helped me to pull a handkerchief from my jacket pocket, then stood wanting to assist me but uncertain how. As the bout of coughing subsided, my throat seemed to close. I struggled to open it, though there was no air left in my lungs to blow out. Finally, desperate, I forced myself to inhale. After a few more breaths I felt ready to continue on.

"Are you sure you don't want to go back?" Miriam asked.

"Are we more than halfway there?" I asked.

"Well, yes."

"Then I scarcely see the point of turning back."

She shrugged, and continued on but at a slower pace. I wanted to tell her that I was no invalid, but in truth I was thankful for her understanding. Nearly an hour later we reached our destination.

Montgomery House appeared even more dilapidated from the rear. Shutters hung at odd angles from the second-story windows. A section of clapboard was missing beside the rear doors, and weeds sprouted along the stone paths of what had once been the formal gardens beyond them.

The only signs of upkeep were in the slave quarters, where simple huts were kept in repair by their inhabitants, in the vegetable and herb garden beside the outdoor kitchen, and in the kitchen itself, where the floors were well scrubbed, the tables polished, and the pots and pans hung in orderly fashion on the hooks beside the stove.

Miriam walked into the kitchen as if she belonged there and poured me and herself cider before sounding the dinner bell once.

Emmie took her time about responding to the bell. When she came it was with the same quiet dignity I had noted in Miriam. Emmie also had the same tall thin body as her daughter, but there the resemblance ended. Emmie could never have passed for Mediterranean—her features, her hair, her skin were all African. As Miriam introduced her to me, I noted her speech as well. The softening of the consonants which she tried to hide with overly careful enunciation, the occasional dropping of a *g* at the end of a word, and the sometimes odd sentence structure revealed someone who had been raised in the fields and given no education until well into adulthood.

In which case, one thing was certain. From the way she

spoke and looked, Miriam's father had undoubtedly been white, probably well educated, and had taken some part in raising her. Was this why Will Montgomery refused to sell these slaves at any price? Was this why the girl had been raised with such gentility? Miriam was older than Pamela, which meant that she had been conceived before Pamela was born. Did Anna Broussard get wind of her husband's infatuation with a slave, damn him for it, and abandon him and her daughter because of it? There were headstrong women who would do that sort of thing, then wait for the husband to sell their rival and come after them.

"Mama, Mr. Poe has come all the way from Richmond to see you," Miriam said.

"Me? Why?"

"I recently met Pamela Montgomery. She asked me to come and tell you that she thinks of you often, and to give you her love," I said.

I paid close attention to her response, noticing the flicker of interest, the joy, before she hid the emotions behind that guarded facade. "Love? Ah . . . I suppose I understand. No one looked after her the way I did."

"So she told me," I said. "She spoke of you as some women might speak of their mother. She said you were the only person that seemed to care about her here."

"She should not think that her father disliked her. It ain't . . . isn't true. He only found her too much a memory."

"She wants to know if you ever learned more of what happened to her mother?"

"If that's what this is about, it . . . isn't gonna . . . going to do you any good to ask. I won't betray Mister Will by talking of her. I never should have mentioned her name to the child. It would have been better if she'd never known it."

"Pamela married a man from New York State."

Emmie nodded. "I'd prayed she would find someone there. She's better off well away from her father for both their sakes."

"Her husband told her that he was a distant relation of her mother, but he was not certain how. His name was Elliot Donaldson. His family is from Louisiana."

The revelation had only some of the effect I'd hoped to achieve. Emmie frowned, obviously troubled, then asked, "How did he meet Miss Pamela?"

"He went to a social at her school. He told her that he did so at the request of his mother."

"And what was her name?"

"Vivienne Donaldson, née Broussard."

The woman's shock deepened. She seemed about to speak, then thought better of it and stood. "I think you've told me enough, Mr. Poe. I'd like you to leave now."

I am not a forceful man, but I could not let the woman go without telling her exactly why I'd come. I gripped her arm and forced her back into her seat. "You are going to listen to me. I don't care what you tell me, but you must know why I've come so far to learn the truth."

Perhaps Emmie was still accustomed to obedience, or perhaps she was shocked at how my voice had risen, for she did not struggle. I told Pamela's story as briefly as possible, letting go of the woman's arm only when I was certain she would remain where I'd placed her. When I finished, she looked at me and said in a voice so low I had to strain to hear it, "Sometimes, Mister Will cries out in his sleep calling his wife's name with such horror that I have to wake him, even though I know he may harm me before he realizes that it isn't her touching him.

"I don't know what she did to Mister Will, but I do know this—if Pamela is with her mother's family, you must find her and take her away from those evil people before they claim her soul the way they claimed his."

She left me then, walking toward the house, her back straight, the green tweed housedress just brushing the ground. I stood in the doorway and watched her go, then realizing I was too visible from the house, I retreated into the shadows to wait for Miriam to come for me.

On the walk back to Mrs. Bridger's, Miriam kept an easy pace. Once we were some distance from Montgomery House, she paused so I could rest in the shade of the woods. We sat beside a clear, shallow stream. Miriam pulled off her

shoes and bathed her feet in it. I found the gesture more natural than immodest and did the same.

"The woods remind me of those I played in when I was a
boy," I said.

"Pamela and I used to stop at this very spot," Miriam commented.

"You played together often?" I asked.

"Since I was four years older than Pamela, I took care of
her for Mama. I think I was her only real friend."

"Odd that Pamela never mentioned you."

"She may not remember, but I do because I have a reminder." She held out her hand, revealing a small pale scar
just above her thumb. "You see, when she was four or five,
Mama made us both rag dolls. Hers had a blue gingham
dress; mine, pink. Pamela wanted the pink doll. We fought
over them. Since I was bigger, and was supposed to be
watching out for Pamela, all I tried to do was keep her from
hurting me, but she bit me, then started to howl as if I had hit
her.

"Mama rushed into the room. Mister Will followed a moment later. I remember how frightened Mama looked when
she saw him, and I thought she was afraid for me. But Mister
Will only glowered at Pamela, glanced at me, then ordered
Mama never to leave me alone with her again, as if she
were . . . no, as if that little girl could be dangerous. After
that, I did not see her often, and when I did it was not the
same as it had been."

"You recall the moment so well. Why do you think he behaved that way?"

"Mister Will has always been kind to me, do you understand?"

I nodded, understanding, too, why she could not say directly that Will Montgomery was her father and that she perhaps doubted that he was Pamela's

"Are you going after Pamela?" Miriam asked.

"I am. But there is one thing I'd like to know. What did
Pamela's mother look like?"

"Very much like Pamela. Her hair was darker red, though,
and she was thinner, I think. I wish I could describe her bet-

ter, but I was so young when she left. I wouldn't remember her at all if it weren't for the picture."

"The one that was destroyed?"

"No, it was never destroyed. Mister Will keeps it locked away in Anna's room. I saw it once a few years ago when Mama went in to clean the room. Mama says that everything is exactly the way it was when Anna lived there."

"Does Mr. Montgomery want it kept that way?"

She nodded. "Sometimes, when he's been drinking a lot, he'll lock himself in there. Then he talks to her like some men talk at the graves of their dead wives . . . softly, as if she's talking back."

"I want to see that room."

She looked horrified at the idea. "I can't take you back. I won't."

"Are you so afraid of him?"

"It has nothing to do with fear. I will not betray his trust that way."

His trust! It seemed that for all her education, Miriam was a fool. "Did you know that Mrs. Bridger has tried to buy both you and your mother in order to free you?"

"Of course. I discussed it with Mama, and she told me that she has seen Mister Will's own paper that will emancipate us both after his death. In the meantime, she says that if his ownership of us gives him some peace of mind, so be it. He's had little peace so far."

"Does he treat your mother well?"

"As well as he treated his wife before she abandoned him, and with less reason because Mrs. Bridger's polite society would damn them both if they guessed how well."

I gripped her shoulders, aware as I did that I had never touched a woman so roughly. I dismissed my action as necessary. "If you care at all for the woman your friend became, you will help me," I said.

She shook her head, and I knew there was nothing I could do to make her change her mind.

I felt a return of my morbid despair and shook it off. Why did I need her help? The child that had been taken was Will Montgomery's grandson and heir. Even if the man loathed his daughter, he might take the boy's welfare into consideration.

And if he didn't—well, I've been thrown out of houses before.

I let her go and started walking back the way we'd just come, leaving Miriam behind. When she realized that I was serious about returning, she ran after me, begging me to stop.

"I know you can't help me any further, but you can hardly prevent me from pounding on his door and asking to see him, can you?"

With Miriam behind me, silent now, certain she could not alter my plans, I went on through the trees to the cleared fields and up the path to the house.

I hadn't even reached the summer kitchen when I saw a man throw open the rotting back door, stumble down the steps, and head toward me.

Though this was undoubtedly Will Montgomery, he bore little resemblance to the polite plantation owners I had known, nor to the sort of people Mrs. Bridger undoubtedly associated with. Unshaved, black hair unkempt, and dressed in rumpled clothing, he would have been more at home in some squalid saloon. I would have thought him harmless had it not been for the revolver he carried and the fact that he was obviously furious enough to use it.

Miriam moved between me and her father. "Mister Will, please, let him explain."

"Explain? Very well, he can explain. Go to your mother, Miriam, and wait for me." When the girl refused to move, he pointed furiously at the path. "Go!"

With a single anguished glance at me, Miriam obeyed.

"Are you the bastard who was bothering my Emmie?" Montgomery demanded.

"I am," I replied, and without hesitation held out my hand. "I'd like to introduce myself. I'm . . ."

I never finished. At the first sound of my voice, Montgomery lowered the weapon, the shock in his expression gradually softening to a sort of drunken glee. "Edgar Poe! My God, is it really you?"

"I don't believe we've met, sir," I said.

"Met! Of course we haven't met, but I traveled all the way to Richmond to hear you speak not more than a month ago. You wouldn't recognize me. I looked a bit more presentable then."

Some of the man's anger had dissipated, but the revolver remained in his hand. I weighed my words carefully, hoping not to anger the man further. "You don't seem like the usual literary type. What made you travel all those miles just to hear me?"

"A story, Mr. Poe. One I read a hundred times or more until every overblown phrase was committed to my memory if only because I know how much its publication must have irritated the bitch. Even a minor irritation is better than none."

"You're speaking of the Usher story, aren't you?"

"I am."

So the connection between Elliot and Pamela was made clear. I concealed my shock and asked, "After traveling all that way, why didn't you introduce yourself?"

"Since I didn't give a damn about your subject—not a literary type, you know—I stood in the back of the hall for a time, then went outside and lit a cigar. I thought I'd talk to you as you left, but you were part of a group of five men who left together. I followed you to some tavern around the corner from the lecture hall, took a seat near your table, and had a drink while I listened to your conversation.

"After three drinks in less than an hour—yours, not mine—I decided that you were a pompous ass, and that I really had nothing to say to you, so I came home. Now you turn up here. You were hardly invited, and I want you to go."

"Wouldn't you like to know why I came all this way to meet you?"

"If it concerns the Ushers, then no."

"It concerns your daughter."

"My daughter wants nothing to do with me, and I hardly blame her. She married—"

". . . A man from New York state," I continued. Not wanting to try what little patience he seemed to have, I rushed on. "He died in a storm, leaving your daughter and unborn grandson. His mother arrived some time later and kidnapped her grandson. Pamela went after him. Both now reside with Elliot's mother, Vivienne Donaldson, and his grandmother, Madeline Usher."

Montgomery winced. "So the lady Madeline got what she wanted after all. Why am I not surprised?"

"You're not concerned?" I asked.

"Concerned? What good would my concern do? Believe me, they aren't people you want to meddle with; I know that all too well. Now get off my property, Mr. Poe, before I forget that you gave me the only hours of amusement I've had since Anna left me."

"Mr. Montgomery, you hardly understand the situation."

"Oh, I understand all too well. Now, go!" He fired a shot above my head, turned, and went back to the house with such purpose that I knew it would be suicidal to go after him.

I waited in the woods until Miriam joined me. "I can't go back with you," she said. "Mama needs my help with him."

"Is he very drunk?" I asked.

She nodded. "Mama's been drinking with him, encouraging him. If we're lucky we can carry him off to bed soon. If not . . . we'll handle it. We have before."

I understood. When sad old memories press too close, often the only way to obliterate them is to obliterate consciousness itself. "I'll wait for you," I said. "I want to be certain that you're all right."

She insisted that I leave while it was still light, but I had my reasons for refusing. As soon as she'd given up and gone inside to help her mother, I circled behind the kitchen, approaching the house from the east.

According to Pamela, Anna Montgomery's room had been on the east end, the balcony overlooking the kitchen. As I'd hoped, there were outside stairs leading to the second floor, a common design intended to keep slaves from having to cut through the house to do their upstairs chores. I climbed them carefully, keeping close to the wall lest the rotting wood break under my weight. Upstairs were two choices, but one room had open windows and draperies while the other room's windows were closed, the sills dirty and rotted with

age and neglect. This would have been Anna's room. I had
no doubt of it.

The window was unlocked but opened only a few inches.
With no choice but to make some noise, I broke the pane
with my shoe, and carefully removed the broken glass, stacking the pieces on the balcony before climbing inside.

Once inside, I pulled back the heavy curtains to admit
some light and took stock of my surroundings. The room
held hints of the woman yet—in the faint scent of rose sachet
and lilac cologne, in the exquisite cream-colored Belgian
lace coverlet on the bed, in the stacks of pale green pillows
behind them. More lace draped the canopy and sides of the
bed and covered the windows. The dark curtains beneath
them were crudely fashioned, possibly by Montgomery himself to obliterate any sign of the room's grandeur from the
outside. I opened a dresser drawer and the rose scent grew
stronger. Anna's clothes were all neatly folded. I ran my
hands over the delicate laces and satins and embroidery of
her things with the same stab of desire I might have felt had I
touched the woman herself.

Footsteps in the hallway pulled me from my reverie. I
stood still, listening as they passed by the room, entering the
one next door. Reminding myself of my reason for being
here, I made a quick search of the room, finding a covered
canvas behind the huge armoir. Stifling a sneeze from the
dust, I pulled the cover back and got my first look at Montgomery's wife.

My initial impression was disappointment, for she was
hardly the beauty I'd expected to see. Yet there was an almost overt sensuality in the dark eyes, the full slightly parted
lips, and above all in the low-cut gown she'd chosen to wear
for her sittings.

If I had possessed such a woman and lost her, I would
have kept the portrait, too, as a way of holding on to some
small piece of her soul.

I turned and in the shadows of the lace-draped bed I could
almost see her lying naked on the coverlet, her auburn hair
falling over her bare shoulders, her nipples and the tangle of
hair in the cleft of her thighs dark against her ivory skin. The

scent of her cologne seemed to increase, making me dizzy and weak, suddenly in need of fresh air and sunlight. Though I could not hide my break-in completely, I reached for the portrait, intending to return it to its hiding place. As I did, I stumbled, hitting my arm on the dresser and upsetting the wooden jewelry box on it. The contents spilled onto the carpet, but the box glanced off the side of the dresser and broke apart on the wood floor.

I heard heavy footsteps in the hallway, followed by Montgomery's angry bellow, "Emmie! Emmie, did you let that damned scribbler in here!"

Before I made it halfway across the room, Montgomery had the door unlocked and flung open. The revolver, thankfully, had been left somewhere else, but he held an open bottle of whiskey in his hand, holding it out as he advanced on me.

"So now you've seen my Anna's room, Mr. Poe. Now you understand that, even after so many years, I'd welcome her if she chose to come home."

He handed me the bottle. Given the situation, I could hardly refuse to have a drink. I took a small swallow, then, noticing Montgomery glowering at me, a second larger one. I wondered if he intended that I drink it all—a means of killing me just as fatal as any bullet—when Montgomery glanced past me and lost all interest in my presence. Instead, he was staring at the portrait of his wife. Tears came to his eyes and ran down his cheeks. I began to wonder if I'd been forgotten until Montgomery said softly, "If you find her, tell her what I said. Tell her that just being near her would be sufficient. Tell her."

Without another word, he left. I heard his footsteps in the hall, his heavy breathing, his quiet sobs.

I waited until the house was silent, then went downstairs, taking care not to trip on the loose, threadbare carpet. The door to Montgomery's study was open. I glimpsed stacks of books, a cluttered desk, a dusty mantel clock. Montgomery himself was sprawled on a sofa, Emmie sitting beside him holding his hand. When the woman saw me, she motioned for me to go outside.

I did and realized that I was still holding the bottle and that some of its contents had spilled onto my hand. I licked it off, then set the bottle on the stairs. I'd learned as much as I could here, and so I went around to the back of the house and into the woods hoping to find the delightful guide who would take me home.

She wasn't there to meet me, so I sat in the shade, swatting at mosquitoes that buzzed around my bare head, listening to the lower, more insidious droning of the alcohol assaulting my mind and body.

As often happens when I drink any strong liquor, I fell into a sort of waking unconsciousness where time passes unnoticed, where dreams are as real as the solid world around me. In that state I saw Miriam walking toward me across the shaggy lawn, lithe and stately as some fairy princess.

She took my hand, then seeing that I was barely able to stand, let alone walk, she wrapped an arm around my chest and led me down the path.

By the time we reached the little pool where we'd stopped that morning, my clothes were ripped and dirty from my falls, but the buzzing in my head had somewhat subsided.

"I can go on," I insisted.

"Of course you can," she replied. "Now sit here close to the pool." I did as she asked, then watched while she crouched beside the water. With no thought of false modesty, she dipped the hem of her skirt into the narrow stream and used it to wipe my forehead.

Beneath her skirts, her legs were bare. I rested a hand on the inside of her calf, feeling the smooth, damp skin. Under the circumstances, she was probably wise to pretend not to notice, and some minutes later we went on.

chapter 18

*H*arry Ingram arrived at the family plantation three days after I did. As he'd promised, he'd stopped at the Swan and gotten my mail. Among the letters was one from Watkin's Glen.

The speed with which it had reached me was astonishing, and I went to my room to read it in private.

It was from Mary Quinn. The words were printed rather than cursive, giving evidence that the woman had learned to read and write rather late in life. Even so, she had studied meticulously, for her grammar and spelling were nearly perfect.

Dear Mr. Poe,

You cannot imagine how relieved I was to get your letter. I'm happy that you are doing what you can to help my friend.

Madeline Usher's letter to Pamela and the money enclosed in it did arrive in Watkin's Glen two weeks after Pamela left here. The letter from Mr. Grymes to the postmaster, and Pamela's letter to me, arrived in the same mail delivery ten days later. All were given to me. I admit that the Usher woman's kind words made me feel much less concerned about the intentions of Elliot's family.

However, soon after that, a series of strange events here destroyed that sense of security completely.

It began with a storm of an intensity we only experienced once since we settled here—the night Elliot Donaldson died. The storm began in midafternoon, and like the last came with no warning save the odd quiet of the birds all that morning, the sight of a pair of hawks circling widdershins above our house, and the sudden sight of a doe bounding across the edge of a cleared field as if fleeing some unseen enemy.

The actual storm began with darkness and a wind screaming through the trees, bringing down those which were old and weak, and shaking our house. This was followed by rumbling thunder and bolts of lighting so close to the ground that we—Morgan and I—could feel their energy crackling in the damp air. We were so concerned that we wrapped blankets around us and traveled through the downpour out to the barn. We did this partly out of concern for the livestock, and partly to protect ourselves, since the barn was in an open spot rather than surrounded by the high trees. We found our livestock in a frenzy and soon were too busy calming them to be afraid any longer, which was itself a blessing.

After the storm ended, we surveyed the damage. Our wheat field was under water, a portion of the roof of our cottage had blown off, and our two apple trees had been knocked over. We repaired the damage to the house, and some days later journeyed to the Donaldson farm in the hope that the vineyards had fared better.

As we'd hoped, the surrounding hills had protected the Donaldson cottage and lands. Morgan went to the vineyard to prop up some of the trellises while I went to the house to check for damage. I wish I could say that I sensed something amiss, for I have always prided myself on my small powers of precognition, but I was too keyed up to notice anything except that the door had blown off its hinges.

Years ago, when I was a young girl in Germany, my mother and I went on a summer outing to visit her father, who lived alone a few miles from our village. He'd loved the privacy of his lands, and had died in his sleep some days before we arrived for our visit.

As soon as I entered Pamela's cottage, I smelled the same horrible stench of rotting flesh, saw the familiar nightmarish swarm of flies circling not one body, this time, but two, as if trying to find some place untouched by the maggots to lay another thousand eggs. I admit that I ran from the house screaming so loudly that Morgan came rushing from the fields. While I stood outside, fighting nausea, Morgan went in and somehow identified the bodies as those of Colette and Charles Boutte.

They had been dead for some time. We have no idea what killed them.

But the most curious thing was my husband's reaction. While I stood, frozen as much with the horror of the past as the present, my fearless husband was himself becoming unnerved. He bolted from the house as soon as he identified the bodies and dragged me to the horses, leading us out at a dangerously quick pace given the muddy trail we followed.

My horse slipped once but did not fall, but though I called to Morgan to slow down he only did when we were well away from the cottage.

I caught up with him and saw that his hands were shaking. "What happened? Did you see someone there?" I asked.

"No," he replied.

I knew he wasn't telling the truth, but couldn't comprehend why. If he had seen someone, we might be chased, in which case I had to know. "You saw someone," I said, more emphatically.

"No. But I sensed some thing sitting in the shadows watching me. I thought it might be some hungry animal, but I could not comprehend why an animal didn't touch the bodies. Then I felt an invisible hand brush my face, a hand so cold that I began to shiver. I thought that it might be death waiting to claim another victim."

Mr. Poe, my Morgan is a simple man. He never speaks like this, nor does he ever look so terrified. "Well, we don't know why the pair died," I said, trying to calm him. "Sometimes terror can be a natural response to a violent death, nothing more."

Later, we went together to town because Morgan would not leave me alone, though I tried to convince him that death had no interest in me yet.

The commander of the little garrison sent two of his men back to the cabin with us, but because the bodies had been dead for some time, they could not determine how the pair had died. One of the chairs had been broken, clothes were scattered across the floor, and a bowl that had been on the table lay in pieces on the floor. But if the couple had been murdered for money, why was there fifty dollars in Charles Boutte's pockets and another ten in Colette's?

And though even I thought it made him look like a fool, Morgan stuck to his story that something had been in the cabin with him. The sergeant in charge took his statement, then mine. By that time I was sure more than a simple murder had taken place here. While Morgan and the soldiers buried the bodies, I sat on the porch, turned my body due south, and opened my mind to the terror Morgan had sensed.

It came to me almost immediately—as if it knew I would be seeking it and was hungry to respond. It had ancient roots and incredible strength, yet I believe that it came from a human source and that the mind which controlled it would have been able to cross an ocean to work its spells.

I know you are wondering how I know this so clearly. My reasoning is simple. When my mother was teaching me a part of what remained of our family's magical arts, she would have me stay in the house while she went out-side. I would have to travel to her with my mind. We would exchange thoughts in a sort of wordless conversa-tion. I therefore knew the touch of another's power. But while my mother's touch was light, her presence often no more than a whisper in my mind, this was as heavy and obvious as a furious bellow. Then, as its anger subsided, I felt it dig into my mind as it must have dug into Colette's and Charles's. Perhaps it drove them mad and they killed each other. Perhaps it even possesses the power to kill outright. It certainly had the power to bring stabs of agony to my temples. I recited some protective words and felt the pain diminish.

"Who orders you!" I said, my voice a whisper, an echo of the thought I was screaming to the trees and the grass and the air between them.

It sensed me. It sensed that I knew what it was and that I was actively seeking to touch the mind of the one who used it.

Just for a moment I think I did manage to touch the adept. I heard a peal of laughter—a laughter with no au-dible voice, so I do not know if I touched a man or a woman—then the presence left me so abruptly that had I not been sitting I would have certainly fallen.

I tell this story for the most serious of reasons. Mr. Poe, in your letter you told me you were writing because you and Pamela both feared that someone in Watkin's Glen was spying on the Donaldsons and might intercept Pamela's letters to me. I tell you with complete certainty that the person using the power I sensed has no need of human spies.

Pamela has always been a trusting person who sees only the best intentions of those around her. I fear that she may have walked unknowingly into a den of witches who not only have the power to kill, but the inclination to do so.

Realizing this, I took a coach to Albany to post this letter. Hopefully, it will reach you quickly. If you can devise some way of contacting Pamela and warning her, or better yet of getting her away from those people, I will bless you and pray for you for the rest of my days. May God be with you.

—Mary Quinn

I held the letter in my hand for some time, looking down at the paper without really seeing what was written there. Mediums and trance states, channeling and automatic writing had recently become the rage with some of my literary friends. I dismissed the spiritualism as merely another eccentric diversion for those with too much time on their hands.

Mary Quinn's letter was another matter. The reasonable tone, the apology that her powers were not equal to the task of finding the ones responsible for the Boutte deaths, and especially the pious ending convince me that this is not a woman who has turned her back on the religion in which she had been raised, but rather one who has also been trained in an alternate way of reasoning.

And indications were that her way worked. Pamela had noted that she treated the livestock with herbal cures, that she found the well for their farm and her own, and that her advice had been to seek the answer to the child's disappearance in Pamela's past.

Pamela had ignored the advice. I'd followed it, and now possessed information that alarmed me.

In all the years I had written of ghosts and other forces beyond man's control, I had done so as a rational man. Now I had begun to doubt all I'd held as true, to wonder if such things could exist in a world that I had always considered orderly and sane.

I must act before the doubts set in but at the breakneck speed my thoughts often travel, that is already impossible. I coughed, a perfectly normal cough that I could have easily avoided had there been a pitcher of water in the room. No sickness here, no approaching death, though rationally I knew that was a lie as well. Death did approach me, as it approaches everyone, becoming more real with the passing of each year.

More objections followed—that I really possess no power to help her, that the authorities are better able to handle the matter, that the long hard journey (or at least the tropical Louisiana air) will make my fever return.

"No," I whispered audibly. "No. I won't listen any longer."

I left the room, meeting Harry in the hallway. He had apparently thought an hour long enough for me to go through my correspondence and had come to talk with me. "Are you all right?" he asked when he saw my expression.

"Better than I've been, really. My mind's made up. I'm going to Louisiana, Harry."

"Good!" he responded. "I've already said I'm taking a fortnight away from work. I'm going with you."

"Two weeks is hardly long enough for the journey there, let alone the one back," I replied, half convinced that whatever common sense he'd gained late in life was rapidly dwindling.

"Not the way I propose we travel, Eddy," he replied. He took my arm, gripped it actually, and turned me toward the rear staircase. Once outside, he let me go and set a quick pace toward a large shed on the top of a nearby rise of land.

"Is this where you keep your racehorses?" I called as I followed after him, panting from the exertion and wondering how a man as portly as Harry could move so fast.

"You lack imagination, Eddy," he called and pulled open a pair of wide doors.

The interior of the shed was so dark that until I was standing in front of it, I could not see what was inside. When I could, it took me a moment to realize that the neatly folded red and yellow silk in the loosely woven wicker basket were the principal parts of a balloon. Stepping inside, I saw the burner, the bellows, a hooked anchor, bales of straw, and other signs that Harry's balloon was of the montgolfier, or hot-air variety.

Since my well-accepted hoax concerning the first Atlantic crossing in a balloon, many people think me an expert on the subject of flight, or at least an experienced balloonist. In truth, I am neither. I also have a vague suspicion that my usual weak-kneed stance when hiking too close to the top of a cliff would be compounded if I put another few hundred feet between myself and the ground. This is only a theory, of course, but one I wasn't serious about putting to the test.

"Are you suggesting that we travel in that?" I asked incredulously.

"And why not? We need only wait for the wind to be blowing in the right direction, something it often does this time of year. Then we ascend, Eddy. And in the better part of a day, if the wind stays with us, we'll be on the other side of the Blue Ridge, coming down in Knoxville or maybe even as far west as Nashville."

Harry was talking about a flight of two hundred miles or longer. And he was serious! "Have you ever gone that far?" I asked.

"No, but a fellow devotee in Knoxville came here last spring, though it took him two stops to make it. Given that he got here, I see no reason why we can't get there. And once we get across the mountains, the rest of the trip will be easy."

I rested my hands on the basket. It seemed solid, and deep enough that I could cower inside if vertigo took hold of me. "How many times have you flown, Harry?" I asked.

"Ten in the last year. On the last trip I took my nephews. We touched down twice for fuel and stayed aloft a total of ten hours before landing near Richmond. With a little luck we can do this, Eddy. Trust me."

Trust him. If I had more faith in God, or better luck, I might have felt more enthusiastic. And I didn't like the fog that enveloped the Blue Ridge Mountains. My far-too-vivid imagination showed us slamming into the side of a mountain we hadn't been able to see.

But I could not quench Harry's enthusiasm for the venture, his buoyant optimism that everything would go perfectly. After an hour of listening to his exploits, the exploits of his friends and the records for speed and distance being set around the globe (which I suspected were much exaggerated), I began to consider the idea seriously.

I had no doubt that Harry could get us up or down with no real damage. We weren't going across any large bodies of water, so the worst problem would be that we might be forced to land in the mountains. If so, I would lose some days of travel time, nothing more. But if we did manage to cross the range, there were a dozen main roads leading right to the Mississippi and a comfortable journey downriver.

"And you have no idea how marvelous the weather is two thousand feet above us," he said when I'd agreed.

Now that was a piece of information I wish he'd left to himself.

The breezes that have been light and steady and from the northeast for the last few days have increased. We've decided that if they continue in that fashion through the night, we will leave tomorrow morning.

Earlier tonight in the comforting presence of Jane Ingram, I told Harry the rest of the story and shared Mary Quinn's letter with both of them. If Harry is coming with me, he deserves to know the truth. As for Jane, she listened to my account and our plans for the following day with growing uneasiness so that both of us had to reassure her that we would be all right. I think Harry was the more persuasive.

And now I spend my last night in this house, unable to sleep or to find the necessary calm for tomorrow's journey. So I have stayed awake, writing these words for posterity, for Muddy, or for whomever will find my little journal should I not survive tomorrow or the days to follow.

part four

❧

MADELINE

chapter 19

The morning after Judith Donaldson's death, Pamela got out of bed before dawn and padded barefoot down the hall to the library. She walked silently until she was just outside the library door, then entered with no sign of stealth. Though she expected to see Sean drawing, or even Vivienne reading one of her novels, the room was empty save for the shelves of books on all four walls—books with their red and black and brown and yellow bindings. She checked the yellow books, but none of them seemed at all out of the ordinary, and there was no sign of discoloration.

But if the book was precious to Madeline, she might keep it in a more private place. Fortunately, Pamela had been at the plantation long enough to know its routine. Later that morning, while Madeline shut herself in the library to go over the plantation accounts and meet with the overseer, Pamela walked up the hill to her private retreat.

Her perspective on the estate had changed. Suddenly a place that had seemed almost mystical in its beauty evoked a surge of fear in her, and along with it oddly lucid confusion. She had been frightened when she'd come here, intending to leave with her child in a day or two. Instead weeks had passed and she still remained, almost comfortable in the house of her enemies.

No more, she thought, and went inside.

The sudden move from brightly lit courtyard to the dark interior blinded her. Since she didn't want anyone to spy her here, she shut the door behind her and waited just inside the doorway for her eyes to adjust. Like Judith's house, the space seemed devoid of fresh air, but the room was cool and dry. The loose-fitting dress she wore fell away from her body. The sweat on her body dried. She shivered. Though she was certain she was alone here, she wanted to call out, to give the appearance of looking for Madeline before she began her search for the book.

She opened her mouth to do so, then stopped.

The silence of this room was so profound that even her indrawn breath did not break the stillness. Though she could still feel her heart beating, there was no soft internal drumming of blood moving through her veins. She might have died when she stepped over the portal or, more likely, had become suspended in some alien place where time had no hold on her body or her soul.

Could this house be the secret to Madeline Usher's apparent youth? Pamela might have laughed at the absurdity of the thought had she not been terrified of discovering that here even laughter made no sound.

There were a handful of candles and matches on a bench beside the door. She lit one. It barely dispelled the gloom around her, but she saw oil lamps mounted on the walls on either side of the room. She walked forward, brushed her little flame across their wicks, and studied her surroundings.

The walls and floor were made of the same rocks as the outer wall—here split and laid into place in a natural mosaic of swirled tones of gray, slate blue, buff, and brown.

The walls were covered with wildly colored floor-to-ceiling tapestries depicting the same fantastic creatures as on Roddy's blocks. A griffin stared across the room at a glowering centaur; a dragon lay curled in its own cyan universe beside a faun in its sylvan forest. Between each panel was a narrower one. The characters on these were familiar to Pamela because of her reading—one was clearly Brigid, the goddess of healing and industry, known by the snakes that curled around her upraised arms; another Morrigan, goddess of life, death, and procreation, dressed in ritual black with a crow perched on one shoulder; and closer to the far wall was Rhiannon, with one of her steeds beside her. The only male depicted was Mabon, the Celtic god of music and liberation, who inspired the rituals of the ancient priests.

As she neared the alcove on the far wall and the long narrow table inside it, she began to realize the nature of this place. This was not a dwelling, but a shrine, and the table Madeline's altar.

She approached it with respect. The space itself was in shadows that could not be dispelled by the placement of the lamps in the larger room, but there was already a votive candle lit on the altar and more around it. As before, Pamela used the taper she carried to light these so she could get a better look at what Madeline had assembled there.

The legs were made of cypress trunks, matched for size. The edges of its top were carved in a snake motif, here one after another joined head to tail, their bodies arranged in a sort of garland that wound around the entire piece. The serpent theme was repeated in the woven cloth that covered the altar and in the design of the tapestry above it where a naked dark-skinned man sat in a meditative pose. A snake curled around his head like a crown, a second lay across his knees, half hiding his genitals.

Pamela frowned and tried to recall what she'd read. Wasn't there some demigod who could open the portal between this life and the next?

And in a curious scroll above his head was the name Usher.

In the center of the table was a hinged box made of oak, polished to a beautiful sheen but otherwise unadorned. She opened it.

The lamplights dimmed and went out, the taper she held died in a strange gust of wind. She heard a chittering in the darkened room, as if it had suddenly filled with palmetto bugs or hard-shelled beetles. Something walked across her foot, something else flew close to her head, a leathery wing brushed her cheek.

She was afraid to open her mouth to scream, but her hands flew up to protect her face. The noise continued, grew, and with it her terror until it became impossible to breathe—but whether it was from shock or some change in the atmosphere of the room, she did not know. She had no idea how long she stood there, but with some burst of strength she turned and bolted toward the thin cracks of light along with edges of the shut entry door. She'd traveled no more than a few feet when she sensed that something had moved between her and the outer door, moved so silently that she had not heard its footsteps on the slate floor, nor its breathing, nor the slightest sense of a darker shadow in the blackness of the room. She dismissed the concern. What she sensed had to be nothing more than another trick of her terror. She rushed on, colliding with something thick and soft and pliant. It pressed against her arms and body. It filled her nose, her throat. Unable to breathe, barely able to move, she collapsed onto the stone floor, her fall cushioned by the substance. As she lost consciousness, she felt the metal circle of Judith Donaldson's gold pin, a point of warmth against her cold skin. . . .

She opens her eyes to darkness, but also to such a curious absence of terror that she knows she must be dreaming. She pushes herself to her feet and moves confidently through the viscous darkness, as if she could see her destination and know that she will reach it safely.

The decorative panel to the right of the altar has no visible hinges, no sign of a knob, yet she knows that it is a door, knows how to open it. She pushes down on the center of the carved molding. It gives way with a soft click, sliding sideways. Beyond it is light, as blinding as the darkness had been when she first entered it. . . .

Before she could see what was kept there, she truly woke. Whatever had been here had gone as suddenly as the bayou storm on the evening she'd come here.

Mimicking the dream, she stood. Gauging her direction by the slivered light of the outer door, she made her way to the door beside the altar. It opened exactly as she dreamed it, but this time she looked away before the light could blind her and a moment later entered the sun-drenched library.

The room was smaller but more sumptuously furnished than the library in the main house. The walls were orange brocade. A thick bone-colored rug had a border of bright purple wisteria. The reading table was in front of a window covered with delicate ivory lace draperies. There were four peach silk upholstered chairs around it. All of it seemed traditional until Pamela looked closer and saw the salamanders among the vines, the spider and web design of the curtains.

Was there no part of Madeline's life not bound up in her beliefs? Pamela had found the woman's stories fascinating, the books she had lent had opened doors to ancient beliefs, arance wonders. Yet now Pamela began to see Elliot's grandmother as no less a fanatic than an itinerant Bible preacher on a quest for souls.

There were less books on these shelves than in the main house, and they were older. Many were bound in leather, but none of them in the white leather that Judith Donaldson had instructed her to find.

She was about to leave when, through the open library door, she spied a shaft of light. Quickly she pulled one of the titled books from a shelf and sat at the table with it open in front of her. She forced herself to keep looking down at the page until she heard the footsteps just outside the door. She turned in time to see Madeline Usher's momentary look of surprise when she saw Pamela.

"I was looking for you," Pamela said, trying to keep her voice as natural sounding as possible. "I was hoping we could share some tea. When you didn't answer my knock, I remembered that Sean said I could come here anytime. I hope you don't mind?"

"Mind? Not at all. I only ask that you be careful. The stone floor in the main room was my idea, but it's far from even."

"So I noticed, but it's so striking. Whatever made you choose that pattern?"

Madeline seemed to wince at the question but answered immediately. "The way the clouds seem to whirl in the sky just before the great storms hit. I've watched them roll across the lands. I have a vantage point in the house. Would you like to see?"

Pamela had the greatest interest in anything the house had to show. She nodded and followed Madeline through the dark main room, to another door that led to a curved flight of stairs.

They climbed only a dozen stairs before exiting on a south-facing open porch. The floor was painted black and the heat it had absorbed from the noonday sun burned Pamela's feet through the soles of her shoes.

"An aerie designed for less scorching days," Madeline commented. "But look. See what a place I chose for my little home."

Pamela had known that Madeline's retreat was the high point on the Donaldson plantation. Until now, she hadn't realized it was also a high point for miles around. The hill seemed steeper on this side of the house. With no trees to break the view, Pamela could look over the fields to the hazy horizon. She saw a pair of plantation houses in the distance and water shimmering just beyond them.

"In the winter, when the air is clearer, you can see five miles beyond Bayou Lafourche," Madeline told her. "And the houses belong to the Steward and Aubert families. They settled here about the time the Donaldsons did. Judith knew them well."

"Do they know she died?" Pamela asked.

"I sent out an announcement and received only a few polite condolences. The price of being disinterested in society is society's disinterest, or so Judith used to say. We're all reclusives here. If it weren't for Randolph Grymes and the Usher-owned businesses, I wouldn't know even a single soul beyond St. James."

Since she'd come here, Pamela had dug carefully for small scraps of information, absorbing facts from each small conversation, putting them in order in her mind. As naturally as she was able, she asked, "If so, who wrote to tell you I was pregnant?"

"The bank, of course."

"They didn't know how to reach you," Pamela said gently. Adopting Poe's soft tone when he raised the question, she probed with light persistence. "You were worried about El- liot, weren't you? And so you dreamed of him."

Madeline hardly seemed surprised by the question. "That incredible perception, again. If you'd been born centuries ago in my family's village, they would have made you a priestess based on that perception alone."

"Please, answer me. Did you dream of Elliot? Is that how you kept track of him and me?"

A smile flickered over Madeline's face, a smile at odds with her serious expression. "Do you really want me to con- fess it all? Very well. I shall." Madeline turned and disap- peared down the dark staircase. Pamela followed as best she could, feeling her way down the first steep turn.

Madeline waited in the library, sitting in one of the three silk-covered straight-back chairs. She looked older in the yellow-hued light and thinner as well. There were patches of gray hair at her temples and fine lines around her eyes that Pamela had never noticed before.

"My daughter and grandson never got along. I knew it was only a matter of time before he left here to get away from her. Because I did not want him to be without means, I had to give him something. Because I knew how wrong it would be simply to provide him with financial support, I gave him the land. I had an ulterior motive, as well. When I was a child, I stayed in that little cabin for an entire summer.

"When you have been to a place and can picture it in your mind, you can find it with your soul. And when you care for someone as I did for Elliot, the seeking is that much easier. Yes, I spied on him, and on you. No, not often, but at quiet times when you were sleeping. Please, don't blame me for it. I simply wanted to know that you both were well.

"As I often am, I was reading in this room the afternoon Elliot died.

"I felt his panic first, shut my eyes and thought of him. But instead of being an observer on his life, I found myself pulled into his mind. He was so cold, so frightened, yet his thoughts were of you. I stayed with him as he struggled to find a thin spot of ice to break through. I stayed until he died, then I went to you."

"So it was you who helped me? I sensed someone, but thought it was Elliot."

"It was both of us, I think, because just for a moment, I felt him, too. Then, through the pounding of your heart, I heard another frightened soul crying for help and knew you would have a child."

"Must you be born with the power to . . ."

"To ride the wind? Or at least that's what my grandfather called it. Yes, you must be born with power. In my family nearly everyone has it, though Usher blood is not always necessary. You have it, I'm certain of it." She pulled three books off the shelves. "It isn't something I can teach, but I can help you practice it. These books will tell you what you need to know, and once you learn what is written here, you will always be able to find your child. Now, I really must return to the main house. I only came for my book." She pulled open a shallow drawer in the center of the table and removed a ledger book. As she closed it, Pamela glimpsed the corner of a book bound in white.

Pamela made a point of examining the books Madeline had pulled for her. "May I stay here and read?" she asked.

"Of course you may. If you have any questions, we can talk after dinner."

Pamela walked to the outer door with Madeline and watched her leave, then returned to the little library. She opened one of the books Madeline had given her and laid the other aside. With her ruse prepared, she lifted the white book from the drawer. It was a thin book of perhaps fifty pages, an account set down in an elegant, easily-read writing. There would be no problem in reading it all in a single afternoon, she thought, as she began.

chapter 20

1803. Now that I am utterly alone in this world save for what remains of my little family, I will write down this account of my life and let this serve as both a family history for the generations who will follow me and a reminder of the tragic effects of greed.

The earliest advice my grandfather gave me and my brother Roderick was always to remember that real power lies in the blood and that the bloodline must be kept pure. I was too young to know what he meant when he said that the family constantly folded in on itself, with cousins marrying cousins, half brothers their half sisters, and always the most powerful to the most powerful, as if we were race horses or hunting dogs bred for the chase.

As a result of this practice, the family has always been small. There are the Ushers and their cousins—the Donaldsons of Louisiana and the Montgomerys of Virginia and the Carolinas—but we are the branch with the powers of the old Druids in our veins. Even Father, who had no belief in the old ways, married a first cousin with the same family name so that we were Ushers on both sides and bragged about it to relations who understood what our breeding meant.

My parents and maternal grandfather came from Wales some years before the American revolution. Father had been involved in a trading company in Chester and wanted to continue that work in the new world. He and Mother settled in New Orleans. She was a country girl, a healer, and by all accounts a sensitive who could read the feelings, and sometimes the thoughts, of those around her. It was no wonder that she hated the city. Many times when I was young, Roderick would tell me how she despised the socialites, the filthy streets that bred so many fevers, the terrible gap between rich and poor.

Fortunately, she did not have to live there long. By the time Roderick was born, father's business had become so prosperous that he could build the family a house across the river, on the edge of a bayou some twenty miles southwest of New Orleans.

And what a house it was! Even when I was a little girl, I thought of it as a castle, with its stone walls so deep that I could open an inner window and lie full length with my feet at the inside and my head at the outside of the wall. It had a parlor and ballroom on the main floor, both with tall windows that opened in the direction of the sea. It had a half-dozen bedrooms and library on the second floor, and a private suite for Mother. Every room was lavishly furnished, with lush carpets, silk chairs and divans, and a mahogany dining set with lions carved in the arms. There was a walled garden in the back and a little gate that opened onto the bayou.

In spite of all this wealth, most people would not have found the house a pleasant place to live. Though it was set on a rise of land with four live oaks to shade it, there were swamps all around it giving off vapors. Even before the house was finished, the foundation had begun to settle so that the builders were constantly plastering in cracks in the walls and foundation. Rather than try to lift such a massive structure, they settled to having the main floor of the house two steps below ground level, a compromise that made the stones of the house so damp that the lower layers of bricks wept from the winter damp and the main floor carpets were all covered with black mildew on the bottom. In time the water level in the bayou rose and father had to hire men to come and build a levy to keep the first floor of the house from flooding and to connect what had now become a narrow isthmus of land to the main road.

Father had designed our estate to resemble a Welsh manor house. He'd intended to use the house as a place to entertain his business associates but instead found himself the laughingstock of his neighbors for creating a house so out of character with the climate. I think he might have torn it down had Mother not loved it so. She declared that she would catch the next ship back to England if he dared touch even a single stone of it.

So he left her and her aging father to their stubborn folly and retreated to New Orleans, visiting the house only occasionally. He and Mother were compatible enough, though, that he fathered Roderick in 1778 and me five years later. Mother died as I was born. Grandfather blamed the dampness of the house, but I know better. She died giving birth to herself, for like her I had a love for the strange house, the desolate swampland around it, and the dark deep bayou waters.

By then Father had established bachelor quarters in Veaux Carre and had a mulatto mistress who lived a few blocks away. He hardly needed the complication of two children in his comfortable arrangement, so he left us in the swamp with Grandfather and sent money every month to support us.

Since I knew of no other way of life, the one I had suited me. I cherished my lessons in literature and history with Grandfather, and the more arcane knowledge he imparted when he thought I was ready. I loved the loneliness and the danger of the swamps. I loved to watch the sun rise and set, coloring the water and the bare black arms of the decaying trees reaching up through it. I would sit for hours on the bank, practicing some new discipline grandfather had taught me.

In those early years Roderick shared my life and we learned together. We could lay in our separate beds, in separate wings of the house, move out of our bodies, and converse while servants and teacher slept. We could float over the waters of the bayou, bodiless, impervious to harm. We learned the uses of healing herbs and foods, and the secrets of special blends to assure health and youth well beyond middle age.

The work fascinated me, and I had a natural ability for it. Grandfather said that in the Wales of a century ago I would have been a healer and a leader in spite of my sex. I took no greater delight than in expanding my knowledge, my craft, my mind.

Things were different for Roderick. Like our father, he was a practical man, whose early education could not dispel his need for money and a life of luxury that our castle in the swamp could not give him. Recognizing his inclinations, Grandfather eventually gave him the responsibility of managing the house—such as it was—so that he could spend his time preparing lessons for the two of us.

"Nothing we learn is worth a damn outside this house," Roderick used to tell me outside of Grandfather's presence. "Superstitious nonsense."

Nonsense! He once saw Grandfather change the direction of a slow-moving cloud. I reminded him of that and of how we had come together in our dreams. "Dreams," he mumbled, but with a bit more affection, though his voice was sly.

That night, when I went to Roderick in my dreams, I found him lying in his bed awake and naked, one hand moving slowly over his erect penis. He felt my presence, for he smiled, but his motions continued—blatant, challenging. "Little girl," he whispered. "Little girl." The two words continued as his hand moved until he came to climax and spurted over his bare stomach and hand.

I retreated to waking, got up from my bed, and locked the door to my room, shivering from fear and some emotion I did not completely understand. I was twelve years old. What little I knew of emotional love was for Grandfather, some vague memory of the woman whose body had carried me before my birth, and Roderick. Was it no wonder that I would look to Roderick to teach me about physical love as well?

"Little girl," he called me after that, by day as well as night, his voice taunting, as if the taunt could force me to mature. But though his acts and his attitude frightened me, I locked my door and sent my soul to him every night. I watched him for months.

And finally, I hungered for him.

That was the night I stopped going to him. That was the night I, too, disrobed and lay naked on my bed, with the door unlocked, waiting for his soul or his body—for whichever he chose—to come and claim me.

He came to me that night, body and soul, and every night for weeks thereafter. I would have undoubtedly conceived, but I already knew what herbs to take to keep that from occurring, and which to take if I made a mistake and needed to rid myself of something unwanted.

I suppose I could say that we matured together, but it was a divergent maturity. I loved my reclusive existence, the blend of loneliness and fantasy that comprised our world. Roderick, on the other hand, despised it. As the months passed, he grew even more restless. One morning he was gone.

Grandfather said he'd gone to New Orleans. He did not sound concerned, but rather sad, as if he knew that Roderick would be home soon, though his note indicated otherwise. "Do you think your father will let him stay and upset his life?" he asked.

I thought of how rarely Father visited us and understood his point. Nonetheless, it took three weeks for Father to tire of his son's presence, three weeks that felt like months to me while I waited for him.

He returned as unexpectedly as he'd gone, bringing a dozen packages for me and Grandfather. I had new silk stockings, lace shawls, hats with bright blue feathers, pearls, and tiny gold shoes no thicker than slippers. Grandfather received spices, books, coffee, and a broad-brimmed hat to replace the one he'd lost in the last storm. "So, was the trip worth it?" Grandfather asked.

"I learned what I had to learn," Roderick replied.

Later, while I stood in my room, clothed only in the shawl, slippers and pearls, I asked, "Did you buy all this finery for me to wear just for you?"

"Someday you'll be the belle of New Orleans," he replied.

"When I take you there, I'll hold a ball for you and introduce you to everyone."

I looked at him in shock, but he was serious. He really meant that we would leave this house and go to the city, and live among others.

As brother and sister? As lovers? As husband and wife?

I was well read, isolated but hardly a fool. I knew what the world would think of us.

For the next few weeks Roderick seemed to be constantly in the library always studying, learning. I think he rued the need to sleep and eat and even to breathe. I tried to discern what he was studying, but he was too aware of me to make it possible for me to spy either in person or with my mind. I finally gave up trying, half convinced that he had found someone else to love. But that was far from the truth, for he loved me yet, almost as much as he loved the city and the family's wealth.

One night I went down the hall to the library and demanded to come inside. He could hardly avoid letting me in, and when he did, I saw an open bottle of brandy on the desk. He'd undoubtedly brought his own stores when he returned to us. "You would put such poison in you?" I asked, for Grandfather had always told me that poison it was.

"You'd like it yourself if you only tried it," he replied.

Since I was not about to let him have an experience without me, I had him pour me a glass. We sat on the carpeted floor where I matched him drink for drink. Of course, he'd had quite a head start and with a bit of careful prompting the entire tale of his weeks in New Orleans came spilling out. His words were slurred. I thought he was sick. Now I know better and realize that he was drunk, drunk enough to dull the pain when he told me what Father had done in their weeks together.

Father had been surprised to see him, and proud of Roderick's initiative as if he were a boy of twelve, not a young man of seventeen. Gradually he began to realize that years had passed since he'd seen his son's face and tried to make amends.

He'd taken Roderick to the best tailors, paying extra to have suits finished overnight. He took him to the offices of his half-dozen firms, and the employees had treated him with the same respect they showed to Father. Later, he'd shown him the town—the excesses of food and drink, and of women.

Father's established mistress, Yvonne, was ten years older than Roderick, which meant that she'd already passed her prime in that sorry profession. So I suppose that she would do whatever Father asked in order to stay in his favor, and be thankful for the money that he still gave her and his roof above her head.

One evening Father took Roderick to the woman's house. The three of them shared a bottle of wine. Roderick could remember little about it save that it was sweet and strong and that he'd been the one drinking most of it. After it was gone, Father left him there.

Yvonne may have been coached in what to do, or perhaps being an intelligent woman, she guessed what Father wanted. No matter, Roderick soon found himself naked and in bed with a woman of experience.

"And what did she do that was so different?" I asked him.

"She demanded. She told me to put my hands on her breasts, to rub the nipples in a certain way. She placed my hand over her sex, guiding my fingers to the most sensitive places, showing me exactly how hard to rub to drive her to ecstasy."

So Father had thought him a virgin. In a sense he'd been right because in all our nights together I had never thought to instruct Roderick in what was most pleasurable for me. He was older, male. It was hardly my place to do so. Yet now he'd come home with some new knowledge. I hardly felt jealous. Instead, tipsy as I was, I leaned against him and placed my hand in his lap.

He pushed it off. "There's more," he said.

"Tell it all," I replied, fell backward with my arms and legs splayed, and giggled. "When you're done telling, show me."

"I'll show you, if you still want me to when I'm done," he replied, then continued. "Only after I had satisfied her did she begin to satisfy me. She did things with her mouth that I had never imagined, then asked me to do the same to her. But always, when I was ready to come, she stopped and held my penis tightly at the base until finally, when I swore I couldn't stand it any longer, she sat me down on the narrow bench in front of her dressing table and lowered herself onto me.

"As she moved above me, she instructed me how to thrust up from below. I have never felt such penetration before and never felt you close so tightly around me. Madeline, it was wonderful and I was losing myself in her, half swooning with pleasure when I said, 'I can't hold back any longer, I'm sorry, Madeline.'

"I will never forget the look of horror on her face when she heard your name. She broke away from me and grabbed her robe from the floor, covering her body with it, then backing away from me as if I had some terrible disease. 'Put your clothes on and get out,' she said, her voice full of loathing.

"What right did a whore have to condemn me? I jerked the robe out of her hand, grabbed her by the hair, and pushed her down onto her bed. She tried to kick me away, but she was hardly strong enough. I had my way with her, but when I was done, I wanted her again. Even that wasn't enough.

"I don't know how many times I raped her, for rape it was by then, but when I was done her hair hung in damp ringlets around her face and her makeup was all smudged so that she looked like some parody of a whore rather than a whore herself.

" 'I'll tell your father what you did,' she said through her tears. 'I'll tell it all to him. He'll know what to do.'

"For both our sakes, I couldn't take the chance that this was more than an idle threat. I don't know if she or I was more surprised when my hands closed around her throat and stayed there in spite of her struggles and the way she actually managed to soften her features near the end as if she hadn't meant the threat at all.

"I hid the few signs of our struggle. I covered her body with the sheet. I even disguised the single bruise I saw on her neck by sucking on the spot until it looked like a mark of lust rather than violence. I found a half-full bottle of laudanum in her dresser and put it open, on her bedtable beside the empty wine bottle. Then, with nothing more that could be done, I put on my clothes and went home.

"Father wasn't there when I arrived. I bathed and went to bed. In the morning when I finally saw him, he winked at me and said nothing. By evening his entire countenance had changed to one of silent grief, but he still said nothing.

"I finally forced myself to ask about Yvonne, for I knew that would be the natural thing for me to do. I did so with feigned embarrassment, for he would expect that as well.

"He told me that she died, but he never asked if she'd appeared ill or upset to me, or if someone else had visited her that night. Two days later he demanded that I return home. Do you understand what that means?"

I started to shake my head, then hesitated. "He knows how she died?" I suggested.

"Or at least he guesses. Either way is disaster."

"What can we do, Roderick?"

"It's my problem. Let me deal with it," he said.

"How?"

"My problem," he repeated more emphatically and kissed me.

I confess that to me the end of his story was as arousing as the beginning. Whatever loathing I felt was directed at Father, not Roderick, and I kissed him back with as much enthusiasm as ever. We lay together there on the soft musty carpet of the library. It was, in some ways, the last truly happy hour of my life.

Roderick continued his studies with the same frantic pace. Knowing what need drove him, I left him alone, asking no questions when he sometimes shut himself away for a day or two, or departed without saying where he was going. Indeed, I had other problems to contend with.

A wave of early summer heat brought the usual summer sicknesses, and extras the area had not faced in years. Until now I have not described how we lived. In spite of its simplicity we had livestock—chickens for food and eggs, two cows, horses, and servants to care for them and us. These were not slaves, but free men. Grandfather, who had told us often enough that there was a time when our own people were enslaved, would have it no other way. Though Father had little respect for the man, he valued Grandfather's services and humored him. So the farmhand, the two maids, and the cook were all hired hands. We valued them, and when first one, then another became ill, it was our responsibility to see that they recovered and to take over their duties until they did. It is a tribute to both our skills that no one died, and that all recovered within weeks.

Yellow fever is a disease of swamps. We were used to the epidemics. Not so New Orleans. Though we had no way of knowing, the city was also gripped by the same pestilence. It took its toll among the poor and malnourished then, having wiped out the young, the old and the infirm among them, moved into the houses of the wealthy. Father was among those who succumbed.

Roderick had just returned from one of his extended absences. His clothes were torn and muddy, his eyes bright. I thought he might be getting the fever, but he denied being ill and went to claim Father's body. After we laid it to rest in the family crypt beside Mother's, I thought that everything would be the same as it had been before. Of course I was naive. I should have known that Roderick would have his way, no matter what.

I returned from a graveside vigil to find Roderick and one of the maids packing my belongings. I stood in the doorway to my room, too astonished to say a word in spite of my anger.

"I promised Father's valet a bonus if he would stay at the house until the end of the month," Roderick said. "We have to get there before he realizes that the contents of the house are far more valuable than my money."

"But what about Grandfather?" I asked.

"The old man has been half alive for years. He'll remain that way for years more with or without your presence. But this is no place for a woman like you. Come with me. Let me show you the world, Madeline."

When he talked like that, it was impossible not to listen, And so, with terrible misgivings, and misguided trust, I left my grandfather—the only parent I had ever known—and went to live in New Orleans with my brother.

chapter 21

The city's poverty sickened me. The epidemic was slowly losing its grip on the town, but there were bodies piled up on empty land, rotting until there were enough to make it worthwhile to burn them. Some areas had been so hard hit that workers would not even go into the hovels to bring out the dead, and so entire blocks reeked of rotting flesh and crawled with the vermin that feasted on it. Even worse was the sight of those who still lived, picking through the piles of corpses, looking for anything of value.

"Don't look at it," Roderick said as our hired carriage passed the poor areas near the river, moving to the richer areas northwest of the landing. But how could I not? It is not my nature to avoid the truth, and if this was to be my home, I wanted to know everything I could about it.

By the time the carriage reached Father's house, I was trembling from anger and disgust. "How could you have brought me to such a dismal place?" I screamed at him as soon as we were alone.

"Dismal?" He actually smiled and poured us both a glass of sherry. I wanted to fling it—glass and all—into his face, but I admit there was something far too beautiful in the cut of the crystal and in the smoky scent and sweet taste of the wine to waste it on such a useless gesture. Besides, I thought my anger would be lost on him. So I did as he asked, drank the wine, then followed him from one magnificently appointed room to another—the parlor, the den, the solarium on the main floor; the two ornate bedrooms and smaller maid's room on the second floor. But of course we had no live-in maid for an obvious reason. In the year we lived together in that house, Roderick's bed was rarely used. Instead he shared mine in the spacious room with the balcony overlooking the private courtyard. Beyond its high stone wall the boats went up and down the river, their whistles calling to one another like lost children in the night.

I wrote to Grandfather every week and missed him terribly at first. But in the months which followed, the call of my past fell to a whisper, then to an inaudible memory. The city in all its splendor had seduced me.

All of Father's wealth was ours now, and as Roderick had promised, he clothed me like a princess in lace and satin. He took me from one elegant drawing room to another, introducing me to society as Father had done for him some months before. In those places we were brother and sister, for there was no way we could deny the relationship. Everyone knew that Father had left two heirs, and with our oddly colored eyes and closely matched features we looked too much alike to pass for husband and wife under the circumstance. Far better for me to flirt with prospective beaus while Roderick did the same with the ladies, then go home together and live as we chose.

We were not always together, of course. Roderick had the family businesses to run, and in his absence I amused myself as best I could. Having been raised in solitude, my greatest pleasure in the first few weeks was to walk through the city, observing its life, and the countless little dramas that seemed to unfold on every street corner.

"Could you at least take a carriage?" Roderick demanded when he first learned of my excursions. "Wandering the streets alone hardly fits your status. It's common."

"Common! Roderick what makes us any more than common? Grandfather said—"

"Blast that old man! Go back to him if it will make you happy."

Of course I wouldn't. I may have missed that life, but I loved Roderick more. So I did my best to fit in, but I still sometimes disobeyed him. When I left the house, though, I did so by the back gate, through the little alley to a side street, and I kept my face covered.

Yellow fever had been the epidemic of spring. Cholera began claiming victims in the fall. The poor went to their voodoo priests for health charms. The wealthy consulted physicians whose skills often seemed no more scientific. I knew better solutions and I brewed them—first for Roderick and me and the servants, later for the servants' families and their friends. Understand that I did not do this simply out of love for total strangers, or out of any kindred with the humanity swarming around me. No, I did it out of boredom, as a way to be useful to someone now that I seemed to be of no use to my brother save as a plaything, and another possession to show off to his rich friends. I began to hear rumors of his lovers, of a bastard child he was supporting, of his drunken escapades, his losses at gambling, all conveyed by the good matrons of New Orleans with an openness they would never have displayed to Roderick's wife. And I of course had to laugh, to remind everyone that he was too much like his father, all the while hiding my fury that he would treat me so much like a wife of many years and not at all like the equals we had once been.

Then, one afternoon while I sat at a social, so like all the other socials that I could only with difficulty recall the name of my hostess and the reason for the event, I saw a man watching me from across the room. He was hardly a handsome man, not nearly as tall or muscular as my Roderick, yet there was an intelligence and intensity in his dark eyes that made me look more than once in his direction. Finally he found someone to introduce him to me. We sat together for hours, and the flirting I had only practiced with others became a bit more sincere.

His name was Adrien Broussard. In the first ten minutes that I spoke to him, I learned that he was an artist of Acadian descent and that his portraits allowed him a comfortable though hardly lavish lifestyle, that he was nearly thirty and never married and, of course, that I was the most fascinating woman he had ever met.

I waited for him to tell me that he wanted me to pose for him, but he didn't. I waited to hear some stories about his famous clients, but he didn't do that, either. Instead after a rush of words about himself, he fell silent for some minutes, then asked if I would like to go for a drive with him. Once we were alone, he asked why I'd seemed so out of place in that parlor.

I was far more careful in what I didn't tell him than in what I did, and he found my account of how I had lived and been educated fascinating. After an hour in his company I let him escort me home. I've never understood whether or not that was an error on my part, but I knew that I needed at least one friend I could count on in the city, even if I could not be honest with him about the reason for my loneliness.

I'd known he was attracted to me, but I'd never guessed the intensity of his attraction. He began calling on me, taking me riding or to the theater. Roderick was often away. I didn't think he'd noticed, and if he had I actually thought he might approve.

Women are such petty, romantic creatures. How we delude ourselves.

The night I told Roderick about my suitor, he raped me. I say this honestly because there is no other way to look at our argument and the act that followed as anything but rape. After, when he lay above me exhausted by his fury and his passion, I placed his hands around my neck and said a single word: "Yvonne."

I expected sorrow or fury. Instead I saw no reaction at all, not even a slight tremor in his hands before he pulled them away. "You gave me no reason to harm you," he said, though there was neither regret nor apology in his voice. I knew then that he had killed more than once.

"What are we to one another?" I asked.

He didn't answer immediately. Instead he moved away from me and stood at the window, a pale shadow in the dim candlelight. "I don't know, but I love you, and I cannot survive without you," he finally said.

That was the confession I'd hoped to hear. I moved behind him and wrapped my arms around his waist. "Sell the businesses, Roderick. Sell the house and Father's castle as well. We can take Grandfather and go back to Wales. You can be the lord of some remote manor and I its lady, and we can live as we please with no one to condemn us."

He shook his head. "We have each other here," he said.

"That isn't enough," I whispered, knowing that any more protest was useless and things would go on as they always had unless I forced some change.

I have never been a coward. I did what I had to do.

The next day I stopped taking the drug that made me infertile. I also made it clear to my persistent Mr. Broussard that while I cared a great deal for his friendship, marriage was far from my mind. He called on me less frequently after that, but he still did and I valued our time together.

Some weeks later I told Roderick that I was pregnant.

I hadn't expected him to take the news well, but I thought he would have some mixed feelings for it, enough to realize that the future I envisioned for us was the right one. Instead, he looked at me coldly and asked, "How far along?"

"A few weeks," I answered, though it was hardly that long at all.

"Get rid of it," he said.

With perfectly calculated fury, I began flinging every breakable item in our parlor at him. He avoided the hits but did nothing to stop me until, with nothing left to throw, I stood defenseless.

He gripped my shoulders hard enough to bruise them, then kissed me. "Get rid of the monster," he repeated.

I didn't answer. Instead, I left the room to pack my bags and go. I didn't bother with a note. He would have known where I had gone.

Grandfather welcomed me back. He listened to my story as if he had always known what Roderick and I did in the privacy of our rooms, as if he had expected it, almost as if he approved.

The bloodlines, of course, could not have been more pure.

In the year that I'd been gone, the old man had become even more of a recluse. Though we ate our noonday meal together, he rarely responded when I tried to draw him into conversation, and when he did he'd often tell me something he'd said the day or week before or forget what he was saying in the middle of a sentence. As Roderick had noted, he'd seemed perpetually middle-aged. Now I recalled that he had married late in life and Mother had been his youngest. He had to be nearly eighty. Though the tonics he drank had kept his body looking at least twenty years younger, the years were beginning to destroy his mind.

I stopped conversing with him, except for a few loving words to let him know that I was not angry with him, or to reply to his questions about my health. He seemed relieved.

I spent the remainder of the summer in welcome solitude, and the first of the cold, damp months in misery. Even my healthful tonics could not alleviate my shivering, the constant ache in my back, and all the other unpleasantness that comes with carrying a child.

Roderick never wrote me. He did not come to see me. It was as if I had never been his lover, or even someone he cared about. The only letters I received were from Adrien, who begged for a chance to come and visit me in the old castle I had described so vividly to him.

I wrote and told him I was unwell and not up to a visit, then downplayed my symptoms so that he would not rush to my bedside to console me. We wrote each other through the months of my pregnancy. I kept that a secret from him, filling my letter instead with things I had learned, and thoughts on my life of solitude. Our letters grew less frequent, then finally stopped.

Roderick arrived with no notice just before Christmas.

I was sitting in my room wrapped in a blanket and reading. My hair was dirty and uncombed. I hadn't washed it or bathed in days because in the cold weather, I would start to shiver as soon as I left the warm tub. The fire on the hearth barely kept the dampness from the room, and I had a cough that Grandfather feared to treat until after the baby came.

I sensed rather than heard Roderick come into my room and greeted him without looking up. "You look as terrible as Mother did before she gave birth to you," he said.

I sat motionless, ignoring his presence until he wearied of the game and left me. Then, though my heart was pounding, I followed him with my mind as he walked down the hall to his old rooms, unpacked his bag, and settled in. Perhaps his defenses were down, perhaps he wanted me to know his thoughts, or perhaps he had just forgotten that I had this power. In any case, I discerned why he had come and I was terrified.

He meant to kill our child.

I could not imagine a more terrible deed, or a sin more likely to condemn the sinner to an eternity of torment by the gods. I could not allow him to do such a thing, for his sake as well as the child's and my own.

That afternoon I went down to the kitchen and had the cook heat me a bath. I washed. I did my hair as he liked it. I dressed in one of the few gowns that still fit me. I put a drop of perfume behind each ear. Looking as desirable as I could, I went to him.

The door to his room was open. He was sitting at his desk with his back to me absorbed in writing a letter. I stood in the doorway and called his name. When he looked up I saw his cold expression soften to one I knew so intimately. Nothing had changed between us. After so many years, it never could.

"Is this more like the old Madeline?" I asked.

He stood and walked toward me, arms outstretched.

I backed up a step, a strange almost mad smile deliberately playing across my lips. "Do you still desire me?" I asked.

He didn't have to speak. His expression had already made that clear enough.

"If you ever wish to possess me again, you must promise not to harm our child in any way. If you think that I would ever forgive such a thing, you do not know the depth of my resolve. If you think that you can force yourself on me, know that I will kill myself as soon as you leave me alone and my

ghost will haunt your waking hours and your dreams forever."

He swore that he had never planned such a thing. That he
had only come home to be with me when the child was born.
He sounded so sincere that I even began to doubt my own
power, and to think of myself as a foolish, pregnant woman
and nothing more.

Foolish. Yes, I was that, because I promised that if he did
not harm our child, we would go on as before. Foolish, because I let him kiss me and run his hands over my swollen
belly as if he desired the child as much as I did. Foolish because I loved him still, not because he deserved it then but
because of what he had been.

Our son was born three days later; not the two-headed
three-eyed monster I think Roderick expected to see but a
perfectly normal, beautiful boy. After I drank the opium
tonic Grandfather had prepared for me, I began drifting off to
sleep with my child in my arms and Roderick sitting beside
me staring down at the infant with wonder, looking exactly
like the proud father he should have been.

"He looks so much like you it's as if she's her own mother
giving birth to you," Grandfather said to Roderick.

"Your memory may be failing," Roderick commented.

"Old memories are the only ones that stay the same,"
Grandfather replied.

I fell asleep listening to that good-natured banter and
thinking that some good had already come out of the child's
birth.

Even before I opened my eyes the following day, I sensed
my loss. There was no warmth of a child in my arms, no soft
sounds of infant breaths coming from the cradle beside my
bed. My breasts ached for him, and as soon as I was able I
stood. With one hand on the wall to steady me, I made my
way slowly from the bed to the door and down the hall to
Roderick's room.

His clothes were gone, and in the center of the bed Roderick had left a note. *Madeline,* it read. *Any thoughts I'd had of
ending the life of what I viewed as an abomination vanished
not with my promise but rather when I saw that perfect child*

in your arms. But this crumbling old house is no place to raise my son, so I have exercised my right as his father and taken him away to a happier place. He will be safe there, and loved. It is better for you that I do it now than later.

I sat down on the bed. Too weak to stand, or even to cry, I stared dumbly at the note, concentrating on turning my grief and anger into strength. "Marie!" I screamed to my servant. "Marie! Come quickly."

When she did not answer, I lay back on the bed, angry tears seeping from the corners of my eyes. Some time later I heard a slow shuffling in the hall. "Who's coming?" I called and heard the nearly inaudible reply, my grandfather's voice.

He made his way through the room to sit at the foot of the bed. One of his arms rested in a makeshift sling and there was a bruise on the side of his face.

"I'm no match for a young man. You'll have to go after him," he said ruefully before I could ask what had happened.

Yes, I would have gone after him, but Roderick had taken care of that as well. All the servants had been dismissed. Roderick had given them severance equal to half a year's wages and the pick of any of the horses in our barn if they would leave immediately.

Weak though I was, of the two of us, I was the stronger. I helped Grandfather to bed, fed him the same poppy tonic he'd given me to kill his pain, set his arm, then tended his other wounds. They were too severe for me to leave him alone. There was no way I could pursue my brother and son.

So that night after Grandfather had been fed and was sleeping soundly from the drugs I had given him, I sought Roderick with my mind. But he had not gone to his house. Over the next three weeks I tried to find him with no success. Then, when I had nearly given up hope, he returned to his house alone. I tried to discover where he had taken the boy, but now that he knew that I had not lost my powers, his defenses were always up. He rarely slept at home, and when he did he was rarely alone. I took some comfort in the fact that his usual bedding choice resembled me, and that from what I could discern his note had been no lie. The child was being cared for and loved.

Was that enough? I tried to convince myself that it was and nearly succeeded until Grandfather died. No, the wounds did not kill him, but I think the struggle with Roderick and the despair he felt in knowing that he failed me had gnawed at his soul.

When he died, I wrapped him in his blankets and dragged the body from the house to the crypt behind it. Once the crypt had been white marble, but the years and the damp had worn and mildewed the stone, making dark streaks across it. It seemed more beautiful that way, its tall pillars ancient like the huge live oak beside it, the land around it. The rusty hinges of its rotting iron outer gates and marble inner door screamed in protest at being moved, and it was only with great effort that I managed to pull them open enough to admit me and the body.

If there had been some servant to help me, I might have ordered Mother's casket opened and the body laid there. I was not loathe to disturb her, but the casket was of the same white marble as the crypt and rested on a wide marble slab with scarcely a hand's breadth between the lid and the ceiling. As a result, I would have had to slide the heavy marble lid off the casket, move the casket as least part way off the shelf, then lift my grandfather's body into it. This would have been a difficult procedure for two men. For one weak woman it was impossible. So, with no other choice left me, I laid Grandfather's wrapped body on a slab below Mother's, then shut and locked the doors. Afterward, exhausted by the work and finally able to say a proper goodbye to the man who had raised me, I sat beside the crypt and prayed that his time in the afterlife would be peaceful and that his next life would be filled with the things he loved—his books, his comforts, and a family that respected him as I had.

chapter 22

Soon after Grandfather's death a trio of servants chosen and paid by Roderick came to live in the house. Their instructions seemed to be to tend to my every need, to watch me constantly, and to see that I did not wander far from the house. The first time I tested this theory, the man shadowing me caught up with me and carried me back to the house, holding me tightly but gently, careful not to hurt me.

They were Acadians. Their culture was not mine. Their language was unknown to me. What a fool Roderick was. Did he not realize that I would learn to speak to them?

From my months in New Orleans I'd already picked up a few French phrases. Now I set about mastering the language. I already spoke Welsh as well as English, and I read Celtic, so adding French to the mix was hardly difficult. The servants helped in my education, and within a month we were conversing easily. I learned that though Roderick paid them well, they had never liked him and soon after coming here had decided that his instructions were a lie.

He had told them that I was unbalanced and that I would harm myself if left alone for any length of time. I told them that he had locked me away here because he did not approve of the man I had wanted to marry because he was Acadian like themselves. After making them promise never to reveal

the name of my intended, I told them it was Adrien Broussard. They were proud and sensitive people. Which lie do
you suppose they believed? The woman, Caroline, even
cried when I'd finished.

So with his own paid servants allied against him, I set out
not for revenge—the only vow that kills its maker—but to
restore the life I had lost.

My request to the three was a simple one. All they had to
do was leave me alone when my door was shut, for as long
as my door was shut, and to interrupt me only in the most
dire emergency.

The first few times I made them promise they of course
broke it, but all they saw was a woman seemingly asleep on
her bed, and finally they left me as I asked even if more than
a day had passed without my stirring.

And so I went to Roderick with my mind. I watched him
sleeping and awake, viewing him like a spider from above.

At first I wanted only to cause him some pain and make
him understand what he had done to Grandfather. But in
some things I am not a strong woman. As I watched him, the
memories came flooding back. I loved him still. I wanted
him still.

And I would have him.

Carefully, so he would not know that it was me who had
done it, I began to insinuate myself into his dreams. At first I
just gave hint of my presence—a glimpse of my face, a whisper, the touch of my hand. When I knew he was convinced
that these were his own thoughts spilling over into dreams
while he slept, I became bolder. He dreamed of kissing my
lips, my breasts, the soft sensitive places between my thighs.
He dreamed of mounting me, pounding into me.

Then, finally, he woke with his sheets wet, having spent
himself like a boy not quite a man. I remembered how he had
led me on while he lay alone in his room. I thought of the
irony of his shame now that he was grown, and just for a moment I lost control and began to laugh.

"Witch!" he screamed to the darkness. "Witch! Will I
never be rid of you?"

Come to me, Brother, I whispered in his mind. Lay with

me. I want you still. In spite of everything, I want you still. Then I touched him with my mind, as expertly as I had with my body. In spite of his wet dream, his penis hardened at my command. With a scream of rage Roderick rolled over and pounded his fist into his pillow like the angry little boy he still was.

I went to him day and night, sleeping only in those few hours that I let him sleep, unwilling to let his soul go, fearful that he might flee his house, abandon his businesses and his usual haunts and move beyond me forever. I tormented him for weeks before he finally gave in and began packing to come home to the crumbling house of Usher.

As soon as I knew that he had given in, I got my first real sleep in weeks. When I woke, I prepared for his arrival.

His favorite foods were cooked, his favorite wine was decanted and ready. I wore the first gown he had bought me in New Orleans—a cream-colored satin and lace creation so low cut that it barely covered the tips of my breasts. Thanks to the healthful teas Grandfather had taught me to brew, I was still the young and lithe and beautiful Madeline he remembered from our youth.

I was somewhat prepared to find him changed, but no amount of mental observation could equal the changes I saw when I finally beheld him with my eyes. The last few months had been hard on him. Though he walked into the dining room with the same masculine swagger as before, his lean body had filled out around the middle and his face, while still handsome, was puffy and had an unnatural pallor.

Drink was poison, Grandfather had said. Here was proof of it.

I sat across from him, my eyes fixed on his face. Even if I'd wanted to, I doubt that I could have hidden my shock.

"That's right. Look what you've done to me. Gloat," he said.

What I'd done? Yes, he would think it was my fault. That was how his choices in life had affected him. There was no way to convince him of this, he was beyond understanding, his logic corrupted by the world of possessions and material power.

We ate in silence. Afterward, we each had a glass of wine. I vowed that while it might not be his last, I would never allow him the excesses he'd pursued in the city. He seemed astonished at my serenity, even more at my willingness to let him kiss me. I went with him down the hall to his room where the fresh sheets had been pulled back, where a warm bath was waiting for him. I sensed his weariness and helped him undress, sitting on the edge of his bed while he bathed. After, when he joined me, I pulled the covers up around him, tucked him in, and kissed his forehead. "Stay with me," he whispered.

I shook my head. "When you're rested. When you're stronger." I pointed to a teapot on his bedside table. "Drink a glass tonight and another in the morning. It will cleanse your system and bring back your strength."

"I've forgotten so much of what we learned," he said.

"It will come back to you." I blew out his candle and left him to spend his first night in weeks in a lonely dreamless sleep.

He recovered quickly, and soon our life returned to some semblance of what it had been before, though Roderick stubbornly clung to two impossible ideas—that the child he had spirited away from me was better off in his new home and that he and I would return to New Orleans to live the same sort of life we had before.

When I refused, he went without me. I gave him a few days to get his businesses in order, then forced him back as I had the first time. He tried to leave again. This time he settled in a different part of the city, hoping no doubt to elude my presence. Though it took me some days, I knew the pattern of his mind so well that I did eventually find him. He tried again, then again. At last he seemed resigned to his fate, almost cheerful as he settled in to our crumbling home.

On his last trip to the city, he returned with a case of my favorite wine—a late-harvested sauternes. Each night after dinner, while he sipped his brandy, I would have a glass of the sweet wine before we retired together to his room.

Ah, he was so passionate then, so marvelously passionate,

so willing to do whatever I asked. I let down all my defenses and loved him as unconditionally as I had in the past.

So gradually that I never realized when it began, I felt a change in me. It began with insomnia, a problem I had never experienced. It progressed to nightmares in which I would wake screaming and trembling. On those nights Roderick would draw me into his arms and stroke my hair until I quieted. I had never had trouble with food or drink before, but suddenly nothing would remain in my stomach for more than a few hours, so that the teas and tonics that might have aided me in recovering were nearly useless. I administered them as best I could, in small concentrated drops that I held beneath my tongue, but they seemed to do no good.

My skin acquired an incredible sensitivity, so that even the brush of thin clothing against it held a kind of agony. I began wearing nothing but a thin silk robe when I walked through the house, and in my chambers or in the locked library I would strip it off to find some relief from my illness.

Yet in spite of it, I felt an incredible passion, a need so strong it seemed a symptom of my illness itself. For when Roderick touched me, I felt not only his hands on my skin but the pressure in the tissues beneath it, in the organs beneath those. I would go to him every night and lay with him, demanding that he love me in spite of my illness.

My hearing became unbearably acute, until the sound of Caroline's footsteps outside my chambers would boom in my mind like some huge drum. I began to speak in whispers because the sound of my voice gave me a headache. Roderick and the servants replied in the same low tone.

Then, late one morning, after I woke from a blessed few hours of restful sleep, I heard Roderick coming down the hallway toward my room. I wanted to call to him to come and join me, but I knew the pain my voice would bring and I lay silent. He walked past my door and down the stairs. I heard the dining room door open and close. I held my breath lest the sound of it in my ears would distract me and listened. The stopper clinked against the lip of the wine decanter. I heard the distinct sound of liquid falling one drop at a time into the bottle, of the wine being swirled in its decanter, of the stopper being replaced.

That night I did not have a glass of wine after dinner. Roderick did not seem concerned but gladly poured me some of his brandy instead. It did not agree with me and I slept even worse than usual. The following night, at Roderick's urging, I poured myself some wine but only pretended to drink it, letting the liquid fall into the stones beneath my chair. That night I woke screaming, every muscle in my body convulsing with pain. Roderick rushed down to the kitchen and brought back a drink—poppy and chamomile. I downed it thankfully and fell asleep in his arms.

Roderick and the servants often spoke together of my nervous condition. I knew they thought me mad and until I realized what Roderick was doing to me, I didn't blame them. Nonetheless, since I was unable to travel far from my bed, I needed to trust them. I wrote a letter and sent for Caroline. "I need to have this sent to New Orleans," I said in my usual whisper.

"Your brother could do it, Mademoiselle," she suggested.

I shook my head. I could not tell her what my heightened senses had revealed, so I merely said, "I've been studying some of Grandfather's old books. I believe that I've been poisoned. I hope my brother is not the cause, but since I cannot be certain, I cannot trust him. This letter is to Mr. Broussard, asking him to come and take me away from this place. I'm not as certain of his house number as I am of the street. Can you find someone to deliver it?"

She nodded, staring sadly at my face. I knew there were dark circles under my eyes and that my cheeks were hollow, giving my features a cadaverous look, but even so, I thought myself still beautiful. "Do you think he'll take me away after he sees what has been done to me?" I asked.

I won her over completely with that. "Of course he will. I'll take the note to him myself and guide him back here," she said and squeezed my hand gently so as not to bruise it.

Before she left, I made her go down to the kitchen and bring up a pot of hot water. After first smelling the blend of healthful herbs and roots I'd harvested so many months before, I had her throw all of them into the pot and set it and a cup at my bedside.

Then, with that healthful, marvelous smell filling the room, I closed my eyes so that I could not be compelled to watch Caroline go and remind myself how small she was, how timid and how easily the city would confuse her.

I waited an hour until the water was cool then drank the last of the tea. It seemed to have little effect on my condition. By that evening, I could not leave my bed and the exhaustion my body had fought for so long finally claimed me. I shut my eyes, and beyond caring if this was a healing sleep or the unconsciousness preceding death, I let the world slowly slip away.

I woke to total darkness, a musty smell not noxious but hardly pleasant under the circumstances, and an atmosphere so thick that every breath I took seemed to make me weaker rather than more strong. I tried to move my hands, but the sides of whatever contained me made motion nearly impossible. I fought down my growing terror as best I could and ran my fingers along my prison, feeling the damp smooth stone. I turned my palms upright and raised them. A few inches above my head, they hit the same smooth stone. I shifted in my prison and felt something crackle beneath me, though I feared what I would find, I let my hands explore there, too. I felt pieces of old rotting cloth, dust, and then, with horror, my fingers closed around what could only be the crumbling bones of a human hand.

Roderick had put me still alive into my mother's coffin.

chapter 23

*W*ell *after the* actual events themselves, I learned everything that had happened.

Roderick had come into my room some hours after I'd lost consciousness. He screamed for Caroline, but of course she had already left for New Orleans to deliver my letter. Marcus and Louis, the two men he had also hired, answered his summons instead.

"My sister is finally out of her misery," Roderick said. "Tell Caroline to come and help me prepare the body for burial."

Whether he lied or thought me dead is irrelevant. The effect on the men, however, was undoubtedly what Roderick had expected. Thinking of their future employment, they confessed where Caroline had gone and why.

Roderick's face grew white. "Well, he can visit her grave, then," he said.

"We can help you with the work," Marcus volunteered.

Roderick seemed to explode at the suggestion. "No!" he screamed. "No one will touch her but me. I will do it all. Now bring me water and towels and fresh sheets for the grave cloths." As they rushed to obey, he went to the cupboard and pulled out the green brocade dress I had worn for him so many times.

And so he undressed me and bathed me, touching my body for the last time, he thought. He brushed out my tangled hair. When I lay pale and motionless, with whatever beauty his endeavors had managed to impart, on the fresh linen of my bed, he lit candles at the head and foot of my body and invited Marcus and Louis into the room.

"Say prayers for her. I have none to give," he said and left them.

If I had only moved one finger, had only drawn in a single audible breath, none of the tragedy which followed would have needed to take place. But I was dead to them, and to Roderick, and to the world.

But even so, the poison in my system was slowly being fought by my own healing drugs. I can only be thankful that my state made it impossible for me to have known what was happening. If I had, I would have undoubtedly despaired long before I was capable of moving, breathing, thinking as rationally as I could under the circumstances.

From what I could recall, my mother's coffin had not been sealed but had relied on the close-fitting lid to keep the vermin away from the body. The lack of a seal was undoubtedly the only reason that I had not suffocated, though now that I was awake and stirring, my body needed more air.

I bent my knees until they touched the lid. I did the same with my arms and managed to raise the heavy stone the smallest fraction of an inch enough to feel a sudden influx of cool dank air before my strength gave out and I was forced to drop the stone once more.

Strengthened as much by my accomplishment as I was by the fresh air, I planned my next move. Reaching beneath me, I found another small bone, which I tried to wedge between the coffin and its lid. I managed it, but the bone immediately crumbled. I tried again, this time with a rolled-up corner of my grave wrapping. It held.

With the immediate danger of death gone, I closed my eyes and sought some aid.

In the hours since my interment, Roderick had been busy. Everything of value had been stripped from the house. Marcus and Louis were gone, undoubtedly taking the goods to

New Orleans for storage or sale. I was hardly surprised to discover that the books Grandfather had so carefully preserved were not deemed valuable enough to transport.

Roderick alone remained, sitting at the table in his room and reading. There was an open bottle of brandy beside his book, and he seemed more than a little bit drunk. In my disembodied state I took all of this in, then entered his mind as I could so easily do.

Roderick? I called, my thoughts soft, barely a whisper among his own. I expected that even this would be alarming. I expected him to jump from the chair, perhaps overturning the brandy in the process, and rush to the crypt to rescue me.

But in the saddest, most terrible revelation of all in a day filled with them, he began to laugh and said aloud, "So it's come to pass that the woman who made me a prisoner for so many years is now a prisoner herself. I half hoped you were alive when we interred you. You're going to die there. Probably by nightfall. You've been in there for some time, you know."

My ghost, Roderick, I reminded him.

"Your ghost can be no more intrusive than your living mind has been," he replied and lifted his glass. "To my sister's ghost," he said before downing the contents, then pouring another.

I could have begged him for aid. I could have sworn that I would never use my mental powers on him again. In short, I could have made a fool of myself and died anyway. If death was what the gods had decreed for me, it was better to face it with my pride intact.

I considered the possibilities of survival. Caroline might have already reached the city and found Adrien Broussard, but I could not count on it. I did not wish to expend my powers looking for her or him. Better to assume that I was entirely on my own and concentrate on saving myself.

I began to slide the casket lid sideways. With each exertion it moved another fraction of an inch. Eventually I was able to hook my fingers along its edge and push. Even that was slow going, and it must have been hours before the lid finally fell to the floor of the crypt with a heavy boom. The weight of its impact shook the structure. Dust rained from the ceiling, blinding me for a moment. As I blinked my eyes to clear them, I saw a thin shaft of light appear along the opposite wall. Could the crypt itself be ready to come apart? The marble had certainly become weathered and mildewed. Could it be crumbling as well?

I pressed my knees against the ceiling and pushed. But though more dust fell on me, neither the ceiling nor the stone slab on which I lay seemed to budge.

But in the dim light now leaking into the crypt I saw numerous handholds in the ceiling. I positioned myself as best I could and began to try to slide the casket as I had its lid, but though I put every bit of strength I had into the attempt, I could not budge it. I tried a different maneuver—pushing against the wall, but it was just as ineffective.

The ceiling dust continued to fall into my nose and mouth, and I swallowed with difficulty, the grit sticking in my dry throat. Was this how my life was going to end—so friendless that there would be no one to mark my passing?

As I lay, in the midst of my most crushing despair, sobbing for the first time since the terrible ordeal had begun, I heard the distant sound of thunder.

With some difficulty due to my emotional state, I focused my mind on the world beyond my stone prison and saw the dark clouds moving up from the south like some avenging army advancing on our little rise of land. The topmost branches of the oak beside the crypt began to move in the wind. It reminded me how Grandfather had been able to control the clouds, and how he had often made the worst of them bypass our area so that we did not flood quite as often as our neighbors.

If I only had the power to do the same, then perhaps I could use it to harness the force of the wind or the awesome power of the lightning I detected through the crack in the side of the crypt. But, alas, Grandfather had downplayed his gift, calling it nothing more than a trick to frighten unbelievers into accepting the old religion and the family's hereditary claim to wielding the power of it.

"Of what use is such a trifle now?" he'd asked me. "No

one believes. No one cares. Life is short, Madeline. Far better that I take what time I have to show you how to heal the family's ills, to make the crops more productive and the livestock healthier."

"But you keep the land from flooding. Isn't that valuable as well?"

He'd looked at me strangely then, and replied, "Nature is a power man was not meant to toy with. You see how I am after I control the storms—exhausted, feeling a generation older than my years. No, it's not something you'll ever need to know. I'm sure of it."

So much for his powers of precognition.

I listened as the storm moved closer. The wind increased, howling through the trees, and the clouds broke into a heavy downpour that beat against the roof of the crypt. I felt moisture on my hand and licked the dirty water from it.

The gods were providing. Perhaps, if I could survive for a few days, then Adrien would come, or someone else would wander onto our land, or Roderick would . . .

That is the kind of madness that gripped me, the kind that renders the victim impotent, catatonic, waiting for some savior that will never come.

I formed an image of my grandfather in my mind—a taller, younger figure than the old man I'd interred. I saw him standing at an upper-floor window that faced the oncoming wind. One arm was raised, pointing toward the storm. The other arm pointed in the direction he wanted the storm to move. His eyes were shut, his body tensed with concentration.

I did the same, pointing toward what seemed to be the center of the storm, the other raised as high as possible directly above me.

But he had mumbled some words and I did not know them. Then, though my concentration had no effect on the storm, something unplanned and wonderful happened. As I fixed my mind on my grandfather's memory, I felt his presence in me with as much surety as I had felt his mind in mine so often when I was young and learning his secrets.

He'd died with only me to tend him. Did I have so little

faith in him that I would think he would leave me alone with only the books for company?

He told me the words to say. No, I will not set them down, not here or ever, for he was right about that power. It is sufficient to report only that I spoke them, repeating them over and over and over as the sound of the rain and the thunder deafened me, repeating them as the old stone walls shook from the power I was concentrating on that little rise of land.

The oak that had stood beside the crypt for a century or more was no match for the bolts of lightning that struck its base, or for the wind that tore at it, twisting it, pulling even its roots from the soggy delta soil.

So it fell. Thankfully, it did not fall on me, but rather beside the crypt. But its size was such that one branch tore a huge hole through the roof while a second crashed through the side of the crypt in which I lay.

The slab supporting me crashed down onto the one below me and that to the ground. The casket cracked beneath me, spilling Mother's remains onto Father's more recent ones. But the heavy stone sides held and what had been my prison became my protection as pieces of the roof and wall fell on top of me.

I instinctively rolled sideways, pressing my face against the side of the casket and covering my head with my arm. I tried to stand and found I did not have the strength. So I lay where I was, too exhausted even to be concerned whether Roderick had seen what had happened, and would come out to find me defenseless.

I had no idea how many hours passed before I managed to push myself to my feet and stumble toward the house. By then the bayou had risen enough that water was flowing over the low points in the levy and sections were threatening to give way altogether.

Though the storm was no longer concentrated on the rise, it had not moved on but was instead venting its fury on the house itself. Water poured down the stone walls, pulling bits of crumbling brick from widening cracks.

I was hardly concerned with the fate of the house, but only of that of my brother still within it, and with the rare books in my grandfather's library. Quickening my pace as best I could, I made my way down the hill to the open doors.

The beautiful chandelier in the foyer was gone, as were the paintings of my parents, and the oil lamps that had once lit the stairs. Only the mildewed oriental rug and tall mirror remained. In the flashes of lightning I saw myself. One eye was an angry shade of red surrounded by a bruised socket. My lip was swollen and a single line of blood ran down my cheek from a cut on my temple. My arms were bruised and bloody. The tips of my fingers were raw from clawing against the stone ceiling. My beautiful gown was ripped and covered with blood and dirt. Worse, all the carefully applied makeup had been washed off, and my sunken eyes gave me the look of one already dead.

And of course I had to smell of the grave.

I confess that the horror I felt at seeing this reflection lasted only a moment. Then I began to laugh. What a marvelous spectacle I would present to my brother! With that pleasant thought in mind, I made my way through the water pouring through the open door and up the stairs to Roderick's chambers.

In the hours since I touched his mind, he'd managed to finish the bottle of brandy and now lay sprawled on his bed, oblivious to the storm and the flood that had followed. His steamer trunk was filled with clothing, and he intended no doubt to follow his cartful of treasures to New Orleans once he woke.

I stood in the doorway and watched him sleep. I took great pleasure in seeing how his whole body trembled with every thunderbolt, and how just once he cried out my name.

"Roderick," I called.

He came partly round. "Go away," he mumbled.

I moved to his bedside and laid a cold hand on his bare ankle.

He opened his eyes then, and as he realized who stood before him, he gave a terrified cry and jumped off the bed, putting it between himself and me. Though he'd moved quickly, he stumbled when he stood and had to grab the bedpost for support. So he was as drunk as I was weak. We made a well-matched pair. "How?" he whispered, his expression so perfectly filled with fear and surprise.

"My ghost, Roderick. I've come for you just as I said I would. Did you really think that my death could keep us apart?" I whispered, moving toward him like the terrible specter he thought me to be. I don't know what I intended to do to him, but the sight of his terror filled me with such joy that I wanted to laugh out loud.

I could see that he did not quite believe me, but even so he backed down the length of the bed, glancing toward the fireplace where a pair of old dueling swords were mounted on the wall. Since I hadn't fought so hard to live only to have him kill me after all, I placed myself between him and the weapons.

I held out my arms to him. Blood dripped from my ravaged fingertips. "Come to me," I repeated.

"Never!" he cried and rushed past me. I clutched at his sleeve. He jerked his arm away and ran into the upper hallway.

"You cannot escape me. You cannot hide," I called and went after him.

So many things happened in the next moments that it is hard to separate one part from another and put them in any order.

The bayou broke through the levy. A wave of brackish water beat against the side of the house and through the open front doors lifting the huge oriental carpet from the floor. The water carried with it some of the cypress poles that had been used to strengthen the fortification. These hit the rotting stairs with such force that the structure broke and fell into the rising tide below.

Roderick had been partway down the staircase when the flood hit. He might have a chance to turn, run upstairs, and save himself but the sight of me standing on the landing above him made him freeze where he was. When the stairs gave way, he fell into swirling muddy water below. The pilings beat against him, and the stone banister came down hard against his back. He let out a single scream. His legs and arms went limp, and he sank below the floating carpet. He didn't struggle and I knew that he was already gone.

I sought him with my mind, but he had moved beyond me, into the darkness of the afterlife that undoubtedly waited for one such as him, a place where he would be tormented until his rebirth.

And so I was alone, trapped on the second floor. The storm continued through the night, the incessant lightning reflected in the flooded land around me. The water rose another foot or so, then began to slowly recede. When it seemed shallow enough to be safe, I used the servants' stairs to reach the ground. I found my brother's body, beaten and bloody, wedged among the pilings and boards in the deep puddle that remained beneath the stairs.

There was no crypt to place him in save the stone walls of the house itself. So I left his body where it lay and brought my grandfather and parents to lie beside Roderick in what remained of the house of Usher.

Thankfully, much of our larder had not been damaged, so I had food and more than enough fresh rainwater from the cistern on the roof. I bathed. I slept. Later when I was strong enough, I began the long and difficult task of sorting my grandfather's books. Some were too old and brittle to withstand a journey of any length. These I read through once more, making notes on sections that might one day prove useful. The others I separated into piles—from those which must be taken with me to those I could easily leave behind.

That I would have to abandon the house soon was all too clear. At times I would feel the foundation shifting under me as the huge cypress supports settled into some new pattern. I had to leave my chambers because the widening cracks in the wall made me wonder if that section of the house would give way next. I began sleeping in Roderick's room, which was nearly as familiar to me as my own.

Caroline, bless her, did persist and finally found Adrien Broussard. As I had feared, he had moved but had not found another woman to replace me in his life. He read my note, and listened intently as Caroline described the sudden illness that had stricken me.

He was no fool. He recognized the signs of poisoning.

Ten days after I freed myself from the crypt, he came for me.

He had not known how strong I would be, so he brought a cart, which he was forced to leave beside the main road. Most of the road leading to the house had been washed out so he made his way carefully, often dismounting to lead his horse through the mud.

Long before he reached the house, I saw him coming and ran outside to meet him.

He stood beside me some distance from the structure and looked at the oaks with their wilted, dying leaves; at the house with the cracks in its side; at the ruined landscape, at the crumbling timbers of the barn.

"If I try, I can see the house as you described it, and the beautiful structure it must have once been. What a terrible tragedy that it should be destroyed so utterly." He looked lovingly at me and took my hand. "But something did survive."

I smiled. I led him up the servants' stairs for I did not want to take him through the front and see the rotting sepulcher the foyer had become. It seemed better that he be sitting in the library, perhaps with an amply-poured glass of my brother's brandy in his hand, when I told him the rest.

I think he had already guessed the relationship between Roderick and me, for he did not seem shocked or revolted by my story. Instead, he took my wounded hands and kissed them, then kissed my closed eyes, my lips.

And that night, in the ruins of the house of Usher, I found a kind of peace in his arms.

We returned to New Orleans the following day. Though I had a house that I could claim, businesses which were now in my name, and given my austere lifestyle, seemingly limitless funds I could draw on, I moved into Adrien's more modest dwelling and went into seclusion. I left the security of Adrien's little house only twice in the following month.

The first time was after a local newspaper printed a lurid account of the destruction of the house and the death of my brother and, so they thought, of me. I went before a magistrate who was a close friend of Adrien's. With Adrien and one of my brother's business associates as witnesses, I proved that I was not dead and more than able to handle the Usher fortune and affairs.

The second time, again in the presence of witnesses, was to marry Adrien.

But, in spite of the year we've spent as husband and wife, in spite of the little girl I bore, a child of uncertain parentage to whom he has given his name and his love, in spite even of the deep love I have for my husband, I cannot escape the loneliness I will always feel now that Roderick is gone. Half of me passed from the world with his death and will always be missing until Roderick and I are reborn together into a happier life.

chapter 24

The account ended. Pamela turned to the front of the book, noting the date it had been written, then put it back in the desk drawer and buried her face in her hands.

The events Madeline had described had been unspeakable, monstrous, unnatural, and yet Pamela could not bring herself to condemn the woman for her part in them, nor pity her for the tragedies that had been beyond her control. Instead, her feeling for Madeline was one of profound respect—as a survivor like herself, as a woman who refused to be the victim and who in spite of tremendous odds managed to find peace in a world she despised.

Apparently, Madeline had also managed to locate her brother's bastard son and to marry her daughter to him, thereby restoring some of the precious family blood. Pamela wondered if the woman had ever managed to locate her own son. Judith had spoken of more than one journal. Perhaps others would continue the account. She checked the drawers, the shelves, and found nothing.

She made her way to the front door and through the dimly lit outer room, walking a wide circle around the altar. She refused even to look at the smooth wooden box, certain that if she did she would be tempted to touch it again and feel the same horrible effect.

There are more powers in heaven and earth, Judith had written.

She considered a logical explanation for the box. Perhaps it was covered with some exotic oil that was absorbed through the skin and induced hallucinations in its victims.

Logical enough, but what of the strange aftermath when she felt cleansed of all fear? No, she couldn't come up with an explanation for that. Best to keep her faith in reason and not think of the box at all.

She stepped outside into the dazzling afternoon sun. Though the heat was damp and oppressive as she made her way back to the main house, her mind was fixed on snow and an ice-covered river.

No, Elliot had said that sudden storms were common in western New York. Nor could she believe that Madeline had actually focused the storm that eventually caused her brother's death. Perhaps the god of all gods had answered Madeline's prayers and seen that justice was done, but it was far more likely a happy coincidence, rather than an event over which Madeline had any control.

The house was silent. Pamela made her way to her room, thankful that she met no one on the way. Roddy's blocks were scattered across the floor, the crib sheets hung over the side of it to air. Happy that he was awake, Pamela stepped through the outer doors and saw Abeille coming toward her. There was no child in her arms.

Could Madeline have known that she had read the book, expected to be condemned for what she'd done, and spirited the boy away? Could Vivienne's fragile grip on reality have broken completely so that . . .

No! Pamela thought, fighting the moment of panic. It's nothing like that. "Where's Roddy?" she asked.

"He was getting a rash from the heat. Missus Madeline took him to the pool to swim. I wish I'd thought of it first." Abeille wiped her forehead with the hem of her apron. "Would've cured the sun pain," she mumbled half to herself.

"Does it get this hot often?"

"A few times every summer. We might be in for a long

spell of it. You can always tell it's going to go on and on when the frogs get too worn out to croak at night. If you're hot, Missus Madeline says you should join her."

Pamela grabbed what she needed and walked down to the little pool. She paused in a patch of shade just outside the gate, smiling as she listened to Roddy's happy squeals.

"See, my little Roddy. The water is good for you." Sounds of splashing followed. Roddy squealed louder. "That's it, Roddy. Pretty soon you'll remember how to swim. Then you'll remember all the rest, but this time, I promise you, your parents will love you and care for you as mine never did."

The words were almost innocent, yet Pamela could hardly interpret them that way. Madeline believed them as totally as a Christian believed that baptism was the only means of reaching heaven.

Now that Elliot was dead, was Sean supposed to take over the role of father? Given his actions, it seemed likely. Given her own, she could hardly claim that she disliked the arrangement.

She decided to return to the house and sort out her feelings before facing the woman who was clearly the mistress of the estate. However, as she started to leave, she heard Madeline call, "Who's there?"

No way to run now. "It's Pamela," she replied.

"Marvelous! Come in and see what your boy has learned to do."

With no way to avoid speaking to Madeline, Pamela went inside.

Madeline was kneeling near the edge, her long hair braided and curled around the top of her head like a crown. Apparently nude bathing was the norm here, and the tops of Madeline's bare breasts were just above the water. As soon as Pamela stepped inside, the woman moved to the center of the pool. She held the boy at arm's length, positioned him so he was floating on his stomach, and let him go.

Roddy floated a moment, then began kicking toward Madeline in a sort of froglike stroke. He made it nearly to the side before his legs began to sink. Madeline caught him before he could panic, splashing him up and down. "More!" he demanded whenever she stopped, more being the only one of a dozen or so words he knew which he used regularly.

"A smart, strong boy! You should be proud!" Madeline exclaimed. "And I see that you came to swim as well. Join us."

Pamela undressed with less difficulty than on her first trip to the pool, probably because Madeline was already unclothed. Apparently standards of dress were lax here, something the freethinking Mrs. Lowell would heartily approve of especially in the tropical heat.

They passed Roddy back and forth for a time, then Madeline kicked to the far end of the pool where she'd left her clothes and stepped out of the water. Pamela glanced at her, intending to modestly look away. However, her attention was caught by something as unexpected and alien as the unnatural events in Madeline's little house.

Madeline's breasts were not the sagging breasts of an old woman, but still high and firm as those of a woman her own age who had never given birth. Her stomach was flat and firm, her legs lean and shapely. Whatever effect her tonic had on her face and energy had been more than superficial; it had included her body as well. Pamela tried not to stare.

"Are you going riding today?" Madeline asked.

"I don't think so. It's too late and I feel a bit tired."

Madeline smiled. "All that reading. Well, come up to my little retreat later if you wish."

"Tomorrow. I want to devote the rest of the day to my son."

"Bring him along."

Not there, Pamela thought. Never there. A pleasant hour alone with her son wiped out some of the uneasiness she felt, but when Roddy started fussing, she decided they'd both had enough. By the time she'd dressed him, he was already nodding off. As she started back to the house, she saw Sean coming down the path toward them. He'd carved a little boat for Roddy with a red hull and yellow silk sail. A string of tiny fishes were attached at the back so they would follow the boat in the water.

"I'd hoped to get it to you before you were done," he said.

Would Sean have knocked or simply walked inside and joined her? Oddly, the knocking seemed more unlikely in this place.

"You could come and watch me launch it," he suggested.

"Let's do it tomorrow. Roddy is too tired to notice anything now."

Sean laid a hand on the boy's head. Roddy didn't stir. "You're right about that," he said and walked beside her down the path. She was prepared to say she was tired, and needed time alone, but he left her before she could. The only indication that he recalled last night at all came from how intently he looked at her, how long his lips stayed pressed against her forehead before he turned and left.

That evening she went to the dining room and found Vivienne sitting alone. As usual, the woman did not look directly at Pamela, though Pamela sensed that Vivienne was staring at her the moment her back was turned. Since she'd read Madeline's journal, she had managed to find some sympathy for her mother-in-law, whose fragile nerves may have been caused by the attempted murder of her mother when she was still in the womb. Nonetheless, the thought of sitting at the same table with the woman was still distasteful, so she carried a plate back to her room and chatted awhile with Abeille before the girl left for the night.

Once the house was silent, she took out her writing box and began her letters. To Estelle Braud and Mrs. Lowell she wrote only that she had succeeded in finding her husband's family and that everything was well. To Mary Quinn, she added some information on Madeline Usher's Celtic beliefs. With Poe, she was more candid, describing much of what she had discovered since her arrival. She left out only the information on Madeline's background. This was her son's family and she was reluctant to pass on a tale which a writer, known to drink, might one day repeat. Worse, she could imagine him writing a sequel to his story, something she doubted the reclusive Madeline Usher would ever forgive.

Tomorrow she would ride into St. James and post the letters herself. Sometime during the journey, she would also take the opportunity to pay a call on Lacey Stelley and sit and gossip for a while.

She left the letters on the table, drank her tea, and prepared for bed. She didn't worry about someone stealing them in the middle of the night. If Madeline had any desire to know what Pamela had written, she had easier means to discover the information.

Pamela had just blown out the lamp when she heard someone knocking on her door. Sean stood outside it, holding the little boat he'd made, the colorful sails jiggling in the lamplight. "I thought that you might like to go swimming with me," he said. "The moon is nearly full and the night clear. We'll have plenty of light."

"Is it safe?"

"Am I?" He grinned and she could not help but grin back and agree.

She'd never done anything so wicked before, she decided as she and Sean floated together in the center of the pool, both in the same state of total undress, with the little boat bobbing between them. "Do you ever visit your neighbors?" she asked.

"Why do you ask?"

"Because I'd like to meet them. I don't want to live in total isolation. I had my fill of it. I think you have, too."

"It won't be pleasant, you'll see."

"I think you misjudge your neighbors."

"You don't know what you're talking about. People around here can't abide any of us. Given our beliefs, that's hardly surprising."

"I talked to the Stelleys and they apparently saw a great deal of Elliot. I don't think they'd treat you any differently than they treated him."

"Cajun trash," he mumbled.

"They're poor. That's not the same thing as being trash at all. Elliot and I were poor and our neighbors were poorer. I didn't take you for a snob, Sean. And I'm sure Madeline would agree with me."

"Madeline is less democratic than I am. She thinks everyone who isn't family is trash."

Pamela laughed, then sank and came up sputtering. Sean had already moved beside her, as if ready to rescue her from the waist-deep water. He smoothed back her hair and held her tightly. She felt the heat of his body, as astonished as the first time by her sudden arousal. He nuzzled her breasts; his hands, slick from the water, moved down her sides, lifting her, laying her back in the water so that his hands could touch her where they would.

Yes, she thought as he kissed her, caressed her until she was past ready when he lowered her down onto his waiting erection. Yes, if she decided to go, she'd give him a choice and pray that he decided to leave with her.

She kept her distance as they walked back to the house, pleading exhaustion when he asked if he could stay the night. "I'll sleep better alone in this heat," she said and kissed him before saying good night.

Once she was alone in her room, she checked the writing box where she'd left the letters. They were still there, Poe's on top just as it had been before. Satisfied that nothing had been moved, she went to bed.

That night, as she had twice before, she dreamed of Elliot. When she woke it was with a wistful sort of sadness, as if she mourned the dream more than she had the man.

The stablehands had become used to her presence and to obeying her orders. So when she told them she would be riding most of the day and asked them to provide her with a horse faster and younger than Cooley, they saddled a brown long-legged mare. After some advice on how to handle the animal, they sent her on her way. She breathed a sigh of relief, yet her anxiety stayed with her, as if she expected to be stopped and her letters taken from her.

She traveled northeast from the barn, paralleling the main road until she was well out of sight of both barn and house. Then she cut over to the main road, quickened her pace and headed directly for the ferry on Bayou Lafourche. The horse, sensing a long run, settled into a smooth quick pace.

She occasionally glanced over her shoulder, but no one seemed to be following her. The weather was beautiful, unusually cool and dry. When she reached the crossing, she saw Lacey Stelley working in her kitchen garden. She waved to the woman, rode to the edge of the garden, and asked if she needed anything from town.

"I just used the last of my tea." Lacey wiped her hands on her apron. "I'll get you the money."

"Keep working," Pamela replied. "You can pay me on my way back. Will you be here?"

" 'Course. Weather's too fine not to be working."

If she were home, she'd be doing the same, Pamela thought. Instead, here she was, dressed in cotton and lace pantaloons on a Thoroughbred horse, sitting above the ferryman's wife with nothing to do but make calls and lord it over the poorer folks. At least she was doing the woman a favor, she thought as she led her horse onto a smaller raft than the one she'd crossed on before. "Can you go it alone?" Lacey asked.

"I think so. The horse seems calm enough."

"All right. Blaine will help you off, he." She fired a shot into the air, and a moment later the raft started to move.

chapter 25

The little town seemed huge after so many days of isolation. After posting her letters and arranging for her horse to be tended to, Pamela decided to do a bit of shopping. She began by going into the general store to buy Lacey's tea. She put a box on the counter, then wandered down the store's aisles looking for nothing in particular. She finally settled on gifts for Roddy and Lacey's son; a pair of brightly painted wooden mobiles; Roddy's was of different kinds of birds; Jamie's with fish. She also bought bags of oranges and lemons, which the owner told her had come in from downriver just the day before.

The temperature had risen by the time she started back, and the persistent tropical dampness had returned to the air. Lacey had abandoned her gardening and changed into a fresh cotton dress. She was sitting on her front porch with her child in her arms. Beside her sat the old woman whom Lacey introduced as her mother-in-law.

Pamela took the woman's hand. Her skin was thin and dry and overly warm as if she had a high fever. Her lined face was flushed as well and her eyes seemed red. Pamela would have guessed the woman to be Blaine's grandmother. She wondered if she'd given birth to Blaine late in her life, or if hard work and the sun had prematurely aged her.

"I brought a gift for Jamie and something for you as well," Pamela said and handed Lacey the mobile and some of the fruit.

Lacey put her son on the floor, unwrapped the mobile, and held it above him. "Look, Jamie, a pretty," she said and hung it from a hook on the porch ceiling. The boy lay on his back and watched the fish, swimming it seemed a few feet beyond his reach.

"That'll keep him occupied while we talk," Lacey said and went inside, returning with three glasses of cold tea, each with a lemon wedge floating in it. She handed one to the old woman, a second to Pamela, then suggested that they move to the far end of the porch to talk.

"How's your boy? Still sick?" Lacey asked after they'd settled into a pair of old whitewashed chairs with homespun cushions.

"Well. Madeline Usher took care of him. Whatever she gave him seems to have worked."

"She has that gift, I hear. What do you think of the family?"

"They're polite. They've welcomed me like a family member, but . . ." How could she explain to a stranger? She'd had trouble enough writing about them to Mr. Poe.

"But they got strange beliefs, them, is that it?" Lacey asked.

"In a way. Did you know Judith Donaldson?"

"My ma did. I hear the woman died, and afterward they set fire to her house. Don't surprise me none. They're the sort who would do something like that, they are."

"Why didn't you warn me about them?"

"Ma Stelley wanted me to, but I couldn't then, not with Bill skulking around. Besides, if I'd warned you, would you have stayed away with your child still in their house?" Lacey retorted. "Then they'd see your fear right away, smell it out right away like the wild things they are. It's better you didn't know it all when you first went there, believe me."

"You said you knew my husband. Could I ask a question that's been troubling me for some time?"

Lacey stared across the flat lands toward the west. "Ask

away. I'll answer what I can," she said without looking at Pamela.

"Why did Elliot leave Petite Terre?"

"He left for the same reason you should. He left so that he could be in charge of his life without his grandmother telling him what he had to read, what he had to eat, and who he had to marry."

So his marriage had been arranged. Apparently he'd gone along with one part of his family's plan. "Do you know who the girl was?" Pamela asked, hoping that it wasn't her.

"Some little tart from New Orleans, or at least that's what Elliot called her, he did. Apparently she was family in some manner that Madeline never made clear to him, maybe one of his uncle's bastards. He tried to find some affection for the girl, he was dutiful enough to do that, but he finally refused to go through with the wedding. That's when the fighting started, the kind of feuding that can rip a family apart.

"They finally reached some kind of agreement, and a year later his grandmother let him take over some property she owned in New York."

"What kind of agreement?"

Lacey shook her head. "No, you don't want to hear about that. What's done is done. No use stirring up the cream. Keep your happy memories."

"I need to know it all, Lacey."

The woman didn't answer. Her hands gripped the arms of her wooden chair. Her eyes were still focused on the western horizon where a line of storm clouds were forming. The breeze had increased and a dust devil skittered across the road. Lacey noticed that with more agitation than she did the clouds, as if she were seeing a ghost rather than some aberration caused by the wind. "Angry weather," Lacey muttered.

Pamela ignored the comment. Her thoughts were miles and years away, fixed on her wedding night and the skill Elliot had shown for lovemaking. "He lived with the woman, didn't he? She had his child, which is probably all Madeline ever wanted. Was that his bargain?" she asked.

"So you guessed that part of it, you did. What's the point

of me putting myself at risk and telling you the rest?" Lacey replied angrily.

"Risk? What are you talking about?" Pamela asked, certain that she had offended the woman though she had no inkling why.

"That's her storm. She's already here, she," Lacey said.

"Do you mean Madeline?"

Lacey stood, both hands on her chest, her thin hair blowing in the rising wind. "She's here," Lacey whispered. Her arms hugged her chest.

"Your husband told me that sudden storms were common in these parts. You said as much yourself when I first came here."

"Not like this one. Besides, I feel her in my heart. It's beating too fast. Too fast."

"You're going to scare yourself into a faint over nothing," Pamela insisted. "Here, let me help you." Pamela rushed to Lacey's side, arms outstretched to support her.

As she did, they heard a soft thud followed by the sound of breaking glass, then the sort of angry wail Pamela knew all too well. She looked across the porch and saw the old woman slumped sideways in her chair, one hand dangling at her side and just touching the wood floor. The glass of tea had fallen and broken, and the infant was reaching for one of the larger pieces of it.

"Jamie don't!" Lacey cried. She rushed across the porch and plucked her child off the floor. Holding him tightly, she knelt in front of her mother-in-law and called to her, but softly, as if she knew the woman was dead even before she saw the open, sightless eyes, the thin line of blood flowing from one nostril.

Lacey shut the eyes and began to sob softly. Pamela moved close to her, resting a hand on her shoulder.

Lacey shrugged it away, stood, and backed toward the far end of the porch. She held her child tightly with one arm while her free hand, index and little fingers extended, were pointed to the west and Petite Terre. "She told me to talk to you. Look what my talk got her. Now you go back there and you take your son and you get away from those people before they make you one of them. You listen. You don't let them sense what you're thinking, don't let them into your thoughts, your dreams. If you have any of their power, you can beat them. Do you understand?"

Pamela nodded, not only to placate Lacey. She'd felt the heat of the old woman's hands, and seen the signs of a stroke coming on. Lacey was overwrought, rightfully so, and superstitious. "I'd like to stay and help you," she said, reaching tentatively for the child.

"No! Blaine will be crossing over before the storm hits, and he can be a hothead even when there's no reason for it. Better he not know why or how his ma died, or he'll go after the Donaldsons and I'll likely lose him, too." She pulled the mobile down from the hook and handed it to Pamela. "Best take this just in case he asks about it. Now go!"

Pamela left quickly, riding against a steady wind, keeping an eye on the gray clouds hanging close above her. But though the clouds were dark and rain-swollen, their fury never touched her. Instead, as if it had been directed to do so, the storm broke over the lake.

She turned and watched the bolts of lightning striking like arrows over Lake Verret, the dark cloud of a deluge. Thunder deafened her. Though her first instinct was to ride as quickly as possible for the Donaldson land, she stayed where she was until the storm spent itself, then headed back for the crossing, spurring the horse on so that in a few minutes changing her mind would be ridiculous.

The air was chilly and damp and unnaturally still, as if nature had exhausted all her energy in the storm. The storm had brought hail as well as rain. It covered the land, giving off vapor in the warmer air that lay like a thick blanket on the road and marsh. The horse grew skittish. She forced it to go on.

The road leading to the crossing had been washed out in places, the missing sections growing wider as she approached the Stelley house. She passed the pair of willow trees that marked the boundary of the property. One was missing several branches. The other had been split in two,

the pale pulpy wood half submersed in a pool of brackish
water the swollen earth could not claim.

Pamela passed the barn first. Its doors and part of its roof
had blown off. The mule used to pull the rafts was wandering the corral while Stelley's single workhorse cowered
close to the barn wall, sniffing the wind as if it expected another storm. From the side the house appeared intact, though
one of the porch chairs lay in pieces at the foot of the stairs.

"Lacey?" Pamela called, then listened.

There was silence at first, followed a soft and terrible
keening. Lacey sat at the far end of the porch beside the old
woman's body cradling her son in her arms. She had a deep
cut on the side of her head. Blood dripped from it onto her
child's bare arm and from there to the soggy porch floor.

"Lacey?" Pamela repeated.

The woman looked at her, seeing her, comprehending her
presence, but long past caring if Pamela stayed or went.
Without a word, she pointed toward the lake where the larger
raft floated, its boards smoking.

"Blaine?" Pamela asked.

Lacey nodded and went back to her keening.

"Is he dead?"

"I don't know," Lacey replied. "I couldn't go down to see.
If I'd left Jamie, she would have taken him, too. She leaves
the ones who wronged her and takes the rest. She always
does. Remember that if you ever cross her."

Pamela tied the horse to the porch rail and went down the
path and onto the dock. "Blaine Stelley!" she called, held her
breath, and listened. To the slow lapping of water against the
side of the dock.

To drops of water hitting water as a soft breeze shook the
rain from the trees.

To Lacey's muffled sounds of grief.

There was nothing Pamela could do here, no comfort she
could offer that the woman would accept. She'd go and collect her wits on the ride back to Petite Terre. Once there, she
would devise some subterfuge for getting her son off the
land, and be far away before anyone noticed they were gone.
She'd come for the truth. Now she knew at least a part of it.

She started down the dock toward land when a slow shifting in the motion of the water near the shore made her pause. An alligator climbed onto the bank and disappeared into the rushes beside the dock. A second followed, pausing to stare at her with unblinking eyes before it went on its way.

The water continued to move in small twirling eddys. But the shape that surfaced was pale instead of dark. Even before she made out the human form, she saw a tattered brown shirt and guessed this was Stelley.

He floated facedown, one arm reaching toward the land, as if even in death he were still trying to save himself.

She wanted to scream for Lacey to come and help her, or to ignore the sight and simply leave as Lacey had asked her to. Overriding both of these was her feeling that she had to do something to help the woman, to atone for her part in the tragedy.

Keeping part of her attention on the rushes, she reached for the body. As she did, some shift in the slow current caused it to roll sideways. One cheek had been torn off by the alligators, revealing part of the skull. The rest had been burned beyond recognition by the lightning, yet it seemed to Pamela that the features reformed into a face she knew all too well.

"Elliot!" she whispered, horrified at the vision but unable to look away, frozen where she stood and wishing that she could find the strength to run.

Someone gripped her arm. She turned and saw the living image of Elliot, alive, concerned. She wanted to explain what had happened, but something in Sean's stance told her that there was no need.

"Let me take you home," Sean said.

"You knew Madeline sent the storm, didn't you?" she asked.

He said nothing, shutting his eyes as if he were unwilling to face her anger.

"How can you live with someone like that?"

He shrugged as if he had never considered the matter, or as if he had no choice.

"The day you met me, you said that I could take Roddy

and go and no one would stop me. I want you to take me back to Petite Terre, then drive Roddy and me to St. Joe's. When we leave, I want you to leave with us."

"And go where?"

"To New Orleans and from there anywhere you want to go. Roddy and I will go with you if you wish. We needn't live together if you don't want us to, but we can live close together and support one another as families do."

She couldn't tell if her words were making any impression on him until he shook his head.

"Sean, you don't belong here," she continued.

"Do you really think that she'll let us go? We're family."

"Family! I'm some distant cousin, that's all."

"You're family." He pulled her toward the horses. "And you can't leave, at least not until Madeline gives you permission to go, even if you wanted to go without your son. There's too damned few of us to spare you."

Sean dragged Blaine's body onto the shore, then took her arm and led her toward the horses, insistently but gently, as if afraid that she would break.

Lacey still sat in the same place on the porch, hugging the child. She seemed not to notice either of them. "Your husband's body is at the edge of the dock," Sean said. His voice held no sympathy, no triumph.

Lacey nodded, still without looking at either of them; humbled finally. Contrite.

Pamela wanted to add something, some words of apology for her part in the tragedy. Before she could think of what to say, Sean helped her mount, then got onto his own horse and started back for Petite Terre.

Pamela followed in apparent obedience until they reached the main road, then swung her horse north. If she rode far enough, there'd have to be another crossing. She'd go back to New Orleans and find the help she needed to get her son back. Mrs. Braud would help her. Mr. Grymes might also, once he knew the facts.

Facts! Did she really expect anyone to take her seriously if she gave them her facts?

Well, if she had to, she could always lie. She dug her heels into the horse's sides, spurring him on.

"Halt," Sean called.

The horse stopped so suddenly that Pamela was nearly thrown over the front of it.

"Follow," Sean said.

The horse did as Sean commanded. Pamela jerked on the reins, trying frantically to make the horse obey her rather than Sean. She continued to try long after she knew it was hopeless, until Sean took pity on the beast and took the reins from her hands.

chapter 26

In one of the rare times he'd spoken to Pamela on their journey back to Petite Terre, Sean had warned her that Madeline showed anger through nervousness. If so, she had to be furious now as she paced the private library in her little house, traveling from one corner to the next and the next. Pamela sat at the desk, her hands folded to hide her own anxiety, her eyes straight ahead lest she start following the woman's movement and become dizzy.

"Do you understand what you have done?" Madeline asked. "Two people are dead because of you."

Because of her? Pamela could not believe the words she'd just heard, or comprehend the justification behind them. She began to suspect that the ordeal Madeline had endured so many years before had left her not quite sane, and astonished that this suspicion came so belatedly and as such a surprise.

"Am I still free to leave this place?" she asked.

Madeline did not answer, at least not directly. "It would have been so much better for you if you had simply looked at everything logically. We care for you. We love your son. You can have a life of luxury here, the kind of life you were raised to have. You still can. I'll teach you. I'll arrange to educate your son so that when the time comes for him to be master here, he'll understand his duties."

"Am I to understand that I still have a choice? Very well, I will go up to the main house and pack my things." Pamela stood and walked toward the door. Her steps were slow and even. It astonished her that she had the strength to stand at all.

"No!" Madeline cried. The air seemed filled with her anger, charged and oppressive as before a storm.

Pamela stopped a few feet from the door, certain that if she were to continue toward it, it would slam in her face without anyone touching it. "Am I a prisoner then?" she asked.

"If that's what you wish to call it," Madeline replied. "You may go anywhere you like in my house or the main house. You may continue your studies with or without my assistance. I think you will find them a solace while you become accustomed to our life here. Perhaps in time you will even learn to care for us as we do you—as family."

Madeline opened the desk drawer and pulled out the white journal. "You read this, did you not?"

"Judith told me to look for it."

"I thought she would. She tells everyone that and expects them to be as revolted by the story of my life as she was after she finished it."

"Is it true?"

"Every word of it, and I have suffered every night since I killed him. But someday when I am reborn, I'll be a different person, one who won't wake every night screaming, caught up in the terrible tragedies of my past, the memories that refuse to show mercy and die."

Someone will rescue me, Pamela thought, then realized that she had only been honest with Poe. But he would come, she knew it with as much certainty as Madeline possessed about her own short future.

But since she likewise knew that the feeling could be false, she remained in the library long after Madeline left her. If she wanted to free herself from the woman's grasp, she would not do it through logic or an act of will. No, she would have to learn to wield Madeline's power.

She fixed her mind on this fact, and reminded herself of it

when her head began to pound and her attention to wander from the texts she devoured as quickly as her mind could absorb them.

In the week following Blaine Stelley's death, Pamela kept up the frantic pace of her studies. In the beginning understanding was difficult, but within a few days, she started to absorb the knowledge with such speed that she began to share Madeline's belief in reincarnation.

"It is as if this knowledge had opened a door to some secret room in my soul, a room closed and forgotten before I was born," she told Sean as they and Roddy took their usual twilight swim.

"It was that way with me and animals," he responded. "The first time I rode a horse, I felt some power rise inside of me. By the end of an hour I was controlling the animal as if I'd had years of experience at it. Madeline says her great uncle Etienne was said to have been like that. She says that if she'd known who I was, I'd have been named after him."

"Why do you call her Madeline?" Pamela asked.

"She insists on it. She believes that kinship is unimportant since it changes within the family from generation to generation. But if you can identify the soul and call it by name . . ."

". . . you give it back its power," she said, finishing for him.

"Exactly." He smiled tenderly, one of his hands brushing the side of her face. She flinched as he touched her but did not pull away. His smile broadened, the grin of a little boy almost forgiven for some serious prank.

She wondered how long it would be before his charm caused her to give in to him completely and again allow him into her bed. She'd certainly found it impossible to break off her friendship with Sean. She continued it partly because she had noted the anguish in his expression as he took her back to Petite Terre and knew that he did indeed love her. Also, to treat him as an enemy would deprive her of the one true friend she had found at Petite Terre, and why not admit it, someone who had quickly replaced Elliot in her life.

She knew that he often spoke of her to his grandmother,

but at least she could count on him to convey her thoughts and actions to Madeline without any distortion. She doubted that she would get the same justice from Vivienne or one of the slaves. Even Abeille, for all her good-natured company and the sincere devotion she showed to Roddy, owed her loyalty to her mistress. Sean was at least independent.

She moved to the far end of the pool and let Roddy go. "Swim to Sean," she told him, laughing as he paddled with clumsy enthusiasm in that direction.

"In a year or so you'll think he has the soul of a fish," Sean commented as he caught the boy, lifted him high in the air, and let him fall into the cool water.

Roddy sank, then surfaced, paddling back to Sean. "More," he said and giggled.

"Not for me," Pamela said and left them, slipping on a robe over her wet chemise before leaving the enclosure. She walked back to the house alone, aware all the time that if she turned she would see Harvey following some distance behind. He was a huge slave, well muscled as field hands usually were, the dark skin of his back crisscrossed with old scars. His previous master had been a cruel man, and Harvey a stubborn one. Abeille told her that Harvey had nearly died before his master decided to sell him to Madeline five years earlier. Madeline had recognized Harvey's worth, given him responsibility, and eventually allowed him to marry and live with his wife in a private cottage. In return, he did whatever Madeline asked with perfect obedience. That now included shadowing Pamela, letting her do what she wanted so long as she remained on plantation land.

The arrangement frustrated Pamela, because she was never quite sure if she dared to test it, and what the consequences would be if she did. She often thought a locked room would be preferable.

As she walked toward the house her attention was drawn to the front gates. A man stood beside them. From the cut of his light-colored shirt and pants and the floppy hat he wore, he must have been Cajun, and she wondered what he was doing there. "Harvey, do you know who that is?" she called to her shadow. As she expected, he didn't answer.

She stopped, moved into the shadows of the trees, and observed the stranger until he started up the walk. Whatever business he had with the family hardly concerned her, she decided, and went through the open doors of her room.

There she sat in front of her mirror, combing out her wet hair, lifting it off her shoulders, then letting it fall until it had dried somewhat in the cool evening air. That accomplished, she sat at the table, picked through the books she'd chosen from the library, and began to read.

Sean arrived with Roddy some time later. As had been his custom for the last few days, he tried to kiss her before he left. She turned her head away.

"It was better that I brought you back than that you should face her power," he said.

"It would have been better had you stood with me. Perhaps together we might have fought her hold on us," Pamela countered.

"Will you ever forgive me?" he asked.

"When you find the courage to do what is right."

He fingered a strand of her hair and looked at her with the same devotion as before, only now the love in those dark eyes did not have the same exhilarating effect on her.

After he left, she went to bed, lifting the little case from her bedside table, smelling the white and red roses in it. They were open, the petals ready to fall. Tomorrow morning when she woke, they would have been taken away and replaced by two fresh ones. She never knew who stole into her room to leave the blooms, only that they brought her a strange sort of comfort as if someone were watching over her.

chapter 27

(taken from the journal of Edgar Poe)

I have just passed through four days of such incredible terrors and exhilarations that it is a wonder I am capable of setting pen to paper to write this. A rock serves as my desk chair, Harry's flight log as my writing table. I am alone in the wilderness. Though last night I believed I was close to my destination, this morning I must admit that in truth I am lost.

The adventure began nearly a week ago in the most boring fashion as I sat beside Harry in the fields above his plantation observing the heavens, or more precisely the cirrus, nimbus, and cumulus clouds and the directions in which they were heading.

"The wind is coming from the east," I said, wishing we could get started immediately. Once the early stages of the journey were over, I decided that I would grow used to the height and the manner of travel and find it almost pleasant if only because it is my nature to grow accustomed to unpleasant things beyond my control.

In addition, as soon as I accepted Harry's idea on how we should move ourselves from Charlottesville to Louisiana, Harry made plans to assure that we would travel like gods above the earth. He laid in three bottles of French burgundy, another of brandy ("to chase away the chills," he told me), four of fresh water, plus cheese, dried meat, crackers, and preserves.

He added a pair of feather pillows and a blanket. It was his thought that one of us could curl up in the basket and sleep while the other navigated. For the last he provided a set of beautifully detailed maps with added notations by himself and his fellow balloonist to the west.

Then we waited. And waited. "The wind near the ground is out of the east, but the clouds farther up are heading northeast and the cirrus clouds higher still are nearly stationary. We'll need a good southeast wind to cross the mountains," Harry explained.

Three days passed before Harry saw the right signs in the sky and ordered that the balloon be inflated and that if the weather held we would take off at dawn. I confess that no one had any trouble waking me in the morning for I didn't sleep at all that night.

"Just feel how cool the air is, Eddy," Harry said as we rode up to the launch spot on a rise behind the plantation house. "We're going to get tremendous lift because of it. Exactly what we need with the mountains."

Tremendous lift. Mountains. Ah, yes! No fool like one who ought to know better.

The balloon was half inflated, lying on its side on the ground. Harry dismounted and handed the reins to one of the attendant slaves. As I watched somewhat incredulously, he walked up to the billowy mass of silk, already far larger than my little cottage in Fordham. The men working the fire and bellows moved aside so Harry could step into the half-inflated balloon. I followed behind, standing near the opening, watching him inspect from within every inch of seams and feeling far more relaxed when I saw his caution.

He emerged some minutes later, his face dripping sweat, and took the same care in examining the anchor ropes and the harness that connected the basket to the balloon. "We're off within the hour, Eddy!" he exclaimed, and walked upwind of the fire where our breakfast table had been arranged. As we ate, I watched the balloon slowly increase in dimension until it righted itself and strained, like a nervous racehorse, against its tethers. I confess that I did not eat very much.

Jane herself untied the last of the anchor ropes. As she did, the rope whipped from her hand and we rose at such an incredible speed that my weight seemed to increase tenfold. My knees buckled, less from the weight than from the burst of fear I felt as the ground seemed to spring away. I fell into the bottom of the basket, too stunned for a moment to do anything but pray to some unknown power to spare my wretched life.

I looked up at Harry's massive bulk. He was standing with one hand on a support rope, leaning out of the basket and waving to those on the ground. Not wishing to appear a coward, I forced myself to stand, but as I started to move to his side, the basket began to slant downward. Realizing what this meant, I grabbed onto the frame opposite Harry and forced myself to look over the opposing side.

Everyone below was waving, the boys their kerchiefs and Jane her blue scarf. I waved back, though after a moment of watching the ground sway and fall away from me, I shut my eyes and waited for the vertigo to pass.

As soon as we were too high to see anyone on the ground clearly, I sat in the bottom again, swallowing hard. Harry looked down at me with gleeful sympathy. "You're missing the best part, Eddy!" he said.

"I'll have plenty of time to view it all. Let me get used to the motion gradually," I responded.

He opened the biscuit tin and handed me two, along with the jug of water. "Take it," he said. "You'll feel better."

He was right. Within a half hour I was able to stand up and watch the mountains approaching more quickly than I had ever imagined. Harry began feeding handfuls of straw and wood chips into the burner. "We need at least another thousand feet," he explained. Understanding what he meant, I began to help him, and together we gave the burner enough heat to raise the balloon level with the lowest clouds.

There was something about the sight of them floating so peacefully around us that erased all fear from me. I felt one with the gulls and the hawks, those long-winged birds that soar so effortlessly on pockets of air.

It is one thing to imagine flying, another to experience it. I admit that for the next hour or so I felt true awe.

All of which vanished with a sudden lurch of the entire

structure. As the balloon increased its westward speed, the basket swung to the east so that I found myself at a precarious angle, staring nearly straight down at the earth and gripping the basket frame with every bit of strength I possessed. "Harry!" I bleated.

He maneuvered his girth to the upward side of the basket, and everything righted itself once again. "Perfect, absolutely perfect. If this keeps up we'll be in Knoxville by suppertime! Better to spend the night in a comfortable bed than surrounded by wilderness."

I could only agree.

"And tomorrow we can continue. The land gets fairly flat west of these mountains. As long as the wind direction is with us, we can go all the way to Louisiana. Imagine coming down on the front lawn of . . . what did you call it?"

"Petite Terre."

"That's it. Coming down on the lawn. A fine rescue, don't you think?"

I nodded, then recalled the storm Mary Quinn described in her letter, imagining our little balloon blown apart by lightning, the basket crashed to pieces in the swamps, the two of us lying unconscious, easy prey for the alligators.

Ah, well, they'd probably eat Harry first.

We continued the strange journey, buffeted by the updrafts of the mountain range and swaying in the increasing wind until both of us were too exhausted to hang on. We threw our entire supply of oak chips onto the burner, generating enough heat under the envelope (as Harry called the balloon proper) to raise it well above the highest peaks. With nothing more to do but see that the burner remained lit, we crouched down in the basket to eat and drink as best we could.

So we passed most of the first day. As we approached Knoxville, Harry decided that the wind was too high to attempt a landing. Knowing how much Harry valued a good dinner, I could only yield to his judgment.

We came down west of Knoxville. What had seemed like a gentle breeze while we were in the air was treacherous near the ground. The basket bumped along the field as the envelope slowly deflated.

We'd just begun to fold the balloon when a man rode up on a solid-looking gray mare. He was hardly a gentleman planter, or even a gentleman at all if his clothes were any indication. "I thought Fitz went and got himself a new balloon," he commented.

"Not Fitz, though I know him," Harry said. "We came over from Appomattox." Harry introduced us both.

"I'm Bob Smythe. You're on my land." He paused to scratch his wiry sideburns and considered what to do. "Fitz would surely say that as a result I'm obligated to put you both up. Besides, the wife would be cold for a week or more if she heard I passed up guests. We don't get many visitors out here."

Here was somewhere west of Chattanooga. When Harry heard this, he let out a whoop of joy and announced that he had set a distance record. I didn't doubt it, though I thought it would be simple enough for balloonists to act like fishermen and lie.

We spent the night, entertaining Smythe, his wife, and three young children with the tale of our mountain crossing. Harry provided the concrete information while I handled the embellishments, relishing how the children sat with rapt attention as they listened to the tale. I doubted that they ever had a chance to hear such a story, so I lowered my voice at appropriate times, I howled like the wind, I demonstrated how the rising balloon had thrown me to my knees.

"Mr. Poe is famous for his tales and poems," Harry said when I'd finished, and told them who I was. As I suspected, they'd never heard of me, but were more than willing to take Harry's word about my reputation and listen to some of my fiction.

I considered the age and education of my audience and told them an abbreviated version of "The Pit and the Pendulum." At Harry's request I recited "The Raven."

I think they would have listened for hours, but it was time to eat. Mrs. Smythe served us smoked ham stewed in apple cider, fresh peas, and biscuits. Harry added one of our bottles of wine, uncorking it with a flourish, pouring a little for all of us. After, he raised his glass and toasted the cook, declaring that he'd never had a better meal.

Knowing what I did of Harry, I likewise doubted that he'd had a worse one since he came into his fortune.

Before the children went to bed, they asked to hear one final recitation. With that small bit of Harry's wine I'd dared to drink energizing me, I began "The Bells." My voice rose and fell. My gestures were wild. I doubt that I had ever given a better performance. When I finished, they applauded. The youngest, a boy not more than five or six, came shyly up to me and shook my hand. It was one of those spontaneous gestures that only children are capable of, and its sincerity touched me.

We slept on the cottage floor that night, with only a pair of thin blankets as cushions. I pressed my back against Harry's listening to him snore and wondering if I would ever join him in slumber. Eventually, however, my restlessness the previous night, my exhaustion, and the small bit of wine I'd drunk all did their part to send me off to sleep.

That night I dreamed of storms, of our balloon looking small, then smaller, then rising into the dark clouds and disappearing from this world altogether.

I woke to the feel of a damp air on my face, and the sound of rain on the cottage roof. Harry stood in the open door, looking at the trees, the sky. "Will we be able to travel today?" I asked.

"The wind is from the northeast. If we can get enough lift, our next landing could easily be somewhere in Louisiana. Let's inflate the balloon. If the wind is still slow when we're ready, we can take off. If not, well, we'll have to start over the next day."

And so the laborious procedure to inflate our vessel began anew. Smythe brought a load of wood to what Harry deemed the best launch site, and we all took turns tending the fire and working the bellows. Again, I felt a moment of near ecstasy as the partly inflated balloon, already hooked to its basket and tethered to the ground, rose upright in front of us.

We refilled our water bottles. Harry accepted some fresh bread and meat pies from Mrs. Smythe and insisted on leaving a second bottle of wine in payment. We said goodbye to them and took off. Though I felt a rush of the same disabling fear, it quickly passed and I leaned over the side of the basket and waved, determined to enjoy the rest of our journey.

We put down twice more over the day which followed, using the anchor rather than deflating the balloon. On the first landing, we bought straw and wood chips from a farmer. On the second we were forced to touch down in a remote area where it seemed that no civilized man had ever walked before—a wild, overgrown savannah of twisted vines and stunted trees. A fit setting for one of my stories, I thought, as I watched Harry loading the revolver. He guarded the balloon and our supplies while I foraged for dry wood. Fortunately, the area must not have seen rain for some time, so I found more than we needed with little difficulty. We broke the sticks into manageable pieces and set off without delay. Though meeting some of the Apalache Indians would have added to the adventure, Harry and I thought it better to eat in the security of the air, than to risk losing everything we carried due to savages' hunger, anger, or superstitious fear.

We spent the next hours of our steady journey southwest, scanning the empty terrain below, seeking some landmarks. All we saw were a few isolated farms and a wide river that Harry thought might be the Tennessee in northern Alabama. If so we were about two hundred miles from the Mississippi and had traveled nearly four hundred miles in two days' time.

For the remainder of the day we saw nothing but the same empty land whose vegetation seemed to grow denser and greener as the hours passed. We were evidently moving into the tropics. Even at a thousand feet, I could smell the damp earth beneath us, feel the heat of it rising around our little craft.

We dared not spend the night on the ground. Instead, we put down in late afternoon in as clear a spot as we could find and foraged for fuel, moving as quickly as we could through a thick growth of vines and moss that seemed to cover anything living. If this was what the Spaniards encountered when they first landed in the South, it was surprising that they hadn't simply turned around and gone home without laying claim to it, for I had never been in such an inhospitable place. We found only a few pieces of dry wood and used these and some of the embers from our burner to start a ground fire to dry additional fuel.

By the time we were ready to lift off again, the wind had increased and the eastern sky was dark with more than approaching night. I didn't ask Harry if it was safe to leave; anything less than a typhoon would have seemed safer than remaining where we were.

This time we barely cleared the scrubby trees before the wind began to buffet our craft, swinging the basket to dangerous angles. More than once I thought we would be thrown to the spongy ground, but we hung on, sometimes to the basket ropes, sometimes to each other, until we rose above the ground winds and the balloon found a haven in a pocket of relatively calm air.

The rains were a more serious matter. Though we rigged a canvas tent around our burner to protect it from the water, the wood we had collected soon became damper than when we'd gathered it. The smoky fire shed little heat and the balloon began bobbing, rising and falling as the wind dictated, often falling nearly to the ground before taking off again.

We emptied our water jugs over the side, and threw additional fuel on the burner, angling the bellows beneath the envelope to push every bit of heat upward. The maneuver worked for a time, giving us some respite until the wind increased.

"Can we put down?" I asked Harry.

"In this wind we'd certainly lose the balloon, and likely the use of one or two limbs if we tried."

"We could deflate it completely."

"It would still be dangerous, and we'd likely be forced to remain where we landed," Harry countered.

I looked at the ground too close beneath us. It was swampland, as thick as that where we'd stopped to take on fuel. Harry was right; we had to go on for at least a little while.

An hour passed. Two. In the waning evening light we began to notice cleared patches of land beneath us, an occasional rustic hut, and one larger house in the center of a whitewashed fence. The wind slacked off a bit, enough that Harry decided we should try to land. We let off on the heat, and the balloon began its slow descent. When we were near the ground, Harry let down the anchor, and we held tight to the basket and waited.

The anchor hooked a tree limb almost immediately. The anchor rope was connected to a simple pulley, allowing us to haul ourselves down. As we did, I saw that we had snagged a limb over a dozen feet above the ground. We pulled as far in as we dared until our balloon floated just above the tree, where it was tossed to and fro by gusts of wind.

Harry let out a second rope, and climbed over the side of the basket. "I have to anchor us to the ground," he explained before he began his descent.

His idea was a sound one, but we would have fared better if he'd sent me instead because as soon as he set foot on the ground, the absence of his considerable weight caused our little craft to rise quickly to the end of the anchor rope, snapping it. Harry managed to grab hold of the second rope, but now that the thirty pounds of cast iron in the anchor was no longer part of our total weight, the balloon continued to rise, though at a far slower pace. Harry apparently decided that he didn't have the strength to pull himself into the basket, so he let go and fell before the balloon climbed too far. The balloon immediately shot upward to perhaps two hundred feet. Harry lay stunned for a moment, then picked himself up.

"Harry!" I called down, though at the height I had already reached, I doubted he could hear me. "What should I do?"

He looked at the anchor, then up at me already so far above him. His response was no more or less than I expected of him. He pantomimed something that undoubtedly meant that I must record where I landed, took off his white straw hat, and waved goodbye.

"Go that way! That way!" I called to him, waving my arm in the direction of another cleared field. "I'll meet you at Petite Terre." Then he faded from my view, and I traveled alone toward the dwindling sunset with the broken anchor rope swaying below.

Darkness came quickly. I fed some of the remaining fuel into the burner and prayed that when I set down it would be on dry and civilized land. I kept my eyes fixed on the west, hoping to see the broad shining ribbon of the Mississippi River where there would be settlers and aid.

If I had managed to stay awake for a few more hours, I might have been able to save the balloon. Instead, though I arduously kept feeding the burner, I finally passed out from exhaustion. I woke when I landed, if such a passive term could be applied to slamming into the side of a tree, some time after midnight. The balloon net broke and the envelope split, spilling the remaining hot air. The fine yellow silk fell over me and I lay beneath its gentle folds until daybreak, gauging my injuries, which seem to be nothing more than a sprained wrist and some bruises, and collecting my strength before pushing it off me to observe where I had fallen.

I had landed beside a pecan tree. I climbed it and viewed the land around me. What I discovered startled me. I had apparently blown into a small stand of trees on a high spot of land. Around me as far as the horizon were wild fields of scrubby bushes and palmettos, as the dwarf pines are called. Dispersed among them were stands of reeds signifying low spots, and open pools of water dotted with lily pads. To the east I saw three large stands of trees, similar to the copse in which I stood.

It seemed meaningless to leave where I was until I had some idea of how far I had traveled, so I returned to the basket and ate my breakfast while I waited for full daylight. As I spread jam on the last of Mrs. Smythe's bread, I listened for some signs of life other than the birds above me and the flies that seemed far more interested in my meal than in their usual fare. Two hours have passed. During that time, I've added the last few pages to this journal. I've also climbed the tree a number of times but have detected no sign of life.

I've decided to take what I can of the food, my journal, and a few small sundries in a bag made of canvas, and leave this place. I'll travel first to the stands of trees in the hopes that a house is being shaded by them. If I don't find anyone there, I will go in the only logical direction—south. Eventually I will reach either help or the Gulf, in which case I will know that I've traveled too far.

chapter 28

The hike proved far more difficult than I'd expected due to the dangerous earth over which I traveled. At best it felt spongy beneath my feet. At worst I sank into mud that came past the top of my boots. More than once I stumbled and fell. Soon I was filthy but dared not try to wash myself in the open pools of water, for the ground bordering them was so unstable that I thought I might sink altogether as in quicksand.

Finally, when I was so covered with mud that I decided to take a running leap into the next available pool of water, a storm came up out of the south, drenching me with a deluge of warm water. I moved to the highest bit of land I could find and sat, wringing mud and water from my hair, not certain whether I should curse or thank nature for this new development. Though the rain stopped quickly and the sun shone once more, my clothing remained wet. As I continued on my journey, I began to cough, first from the damp, later as my heart began to race from exertion and hunger.

Then, when I had just about given up hope of surviving another day, I heard a sound so alien to my location that at first I thought I was hallucinating. A man was singing. The language was not English, and though it bore similarities to French, it was not French. I considered all I knew and let out a whoop of joy. The language could only be Cajun, which meant that I was close to my destination.

The man answered my calls, and we moved toward each other—I on land and he in a small boat hewn out of a log some twenty-five inches or so in diameter. He maneuvered it with a pole, which he pushed along the bottom of the bayou. In spite of the weeds near the shore, he made good time, probably because the boat was so narrow.

He looked me up and down, noted my clothing and the pathetic state of it, and invited me to sit in his *pirogue,* as he called the craft. We introduced ourselves. He was called Pierre Debreaux. I first tried communicating in French and he in Cajun French but to little avail. Finally we agreed on English. I managed to explain through words and gestures how I'd come to be there alone, and the story quite naturally impressed him. I learned that I had landed twenty miles west of the Mississippi River and approximately forty miles north of my destination.

The maps we'd used during our journey had been in Harry's pocket, but I had half the traveling money, more than enough to pay for a riverboat ride to St. James. "How much to guide me to the Mississippi?" I asked.

"Mississippi!" He spat into the water in a contemptuous Gallic manner. "What you want to go pay some dandy captain for?"

"To reach Lake Verret," I replied.

"Lake Verret miles west of the Mississippi. Better south from here, hein?"

Hein, I'd already discovered, was a sort of prompt for me to agree with him, as if any fool would see the logic of his position. However, I could not. "Cross country?" I asked incredulously.

"On the Atchafalaya, she goes to the Gulf. If you have paper, I draw a map for you."

I opened my journal to the back page and watched in amazement as he drew a maze of intersecting waterways and lakes. He pointed out how the Atchafalaya ran only a few miles west of Lake Verret, merging finally at the lake's southern tip, and heading southward to the Gulf. Though he was undoubtedly motivated by greed, I could see the wisdom of his plan. Even given the slower travel time in a boat such as this, I'd shorten the journey by a day or more. "Hein," I said. "But you have to get me all the way to my destination—a plantation called Petite Terre."

A veil seemed to descend over his features, making it impossible to recognize the exact emotions the plantation name aroused. "There is a road that goes from St. James all the way to the Atchafalaya. I put you on it and tell you the way. You walk the last two miles. Hein?"

I doubted he would take me any farther if it wasn't enough. "Hein," I said.

We negotiated a fee to include Pierre's brother, Martin, as a second oarsman. And because I would not walk onto the Donaldson plantation without someone other than Harry knowing of it, I paid the man extra to post a letter to Mrs. Braud for me.

So began the final days of the strangest journey of my life. We traveled the shallow tributary down to the Atchafalaya proper. On the way Pierre told me that he was thirty-four and had lived alone since his wife and three of his children had died when their cottage caught fire two years before. His two older boys were living upriver with their uncle, helping him bring in a cotton crop.

Pierre's cabin was built where the two rivers joined, protected by a high levee. I could not imagine him maintaining such a structure on his own and asked about it. He pointed out cottages across the river, at the most some two hundred feet apart, then the ones up and down river on his bank. "My mother and father there. My cousin there. My uncle there," he explained. "Every farm a hundred acres straight back from the river. The land is ours as long as we keep the levee high."

Such a logical idea, and far less work than other plans might have been.

Pierre started a fire in a pit behind his house, adjusted a tripod over it, and started a pot of water heating. The beginnings of our meal underway, he walked to the edge of the water and gave two beats on a gong at the end of a pier. When someone upriver answered with a similar sound, he wrapped his hands around his mouth and yelled. I heard his brother's name, and something about dinner. A moment later it seemed that the phrase echoed to the north of us, and echoed again, each time in a different voice. "I tell Martin to come to dinner. I tell him we have business, Mr. Poe," Pierre explained.

By the time Martin arrived, dinner was nearly ready. Pierre had added potatoes, onions, and spices to the pot, then when they were almost cooked through, he pulled a wire mesh trap from the water and added the contents—a wiggling mass of crustaceans—to the stewpot. Though they looked most unappetizing, the brothers watched them cook with the same relish Harry had applied to Mrs. Smythes's biscuits and ham.

That evening, while the two men planned the journey, I ate my first crayfish and understood that in this part of the country a man, no matter how penniless, would never need to go hungry.

Or unclothed, at least if the community was as helpful to one another as to strangers. Though I was paying them only for the trip, Martin and Pierre furnished me with a pair of loose-fitting undyed cotton trousers, a similarly made shirt, and a broad-brimmed straw hat to keep the sun off my face. "We get you there alive and white, Monsieur Poe," Martin said, then placed his sun-darkened hand against my pale one and laughed.

We are worlds apart in temperament and background, yet Pierre gave me his own bed in which to sleep while he bedded down on a pile of blankets on the floor in the main room. And a moment ago, seeing the candle still burning in the bedroom hours after we retired, he came to the door to ask if I was well and comfortable.

Since this journey began, I have often been moved by the generosity of strangers but never so much as today. If I am ever reborn, as so many philosophers believe, I would like to be a part of a community such as this with a huge and jovial family all within range of my voice.

I suspect that if Harry and I had taken a ship around the Florida coast, or a train west to the Mississippi and a steamer from there, we would have reached Petite Terre together only a few days later than I expect to reach it alone. However, the journey would have been far less interesting.

We are traveling downriver on what seems as much a raft as a boat. Wide and flat bottomed, it measures some eight by twenty feet, with a hull that slopes nearly to the waterline at the center. Martin, who has a better command of the English language than his brother, tells me that the boat can be used for fishing, trapping, catching shrimp and crayfish, as well as for travel. I find the canvas tarp that shades the center of it a particularly welcome feature since it protects me from the sun that in this sultry climate seems to steam rather than scorch the body.

Pierre assures me that in spring and early summer there is a definite current in the Atchafalaya, but in this unusually dry autumn the river is muddy, buggy, and so shallow that there are times when instead of rowing, Pierre and Martin use poles to push us along. I tried to help, but they laughed at my efforts. "This is pole for you!" Pierre declared and thrust a fishing pole into my hands. So it has become my duty to catch us dinner, something I assured them that I have some experience at. I think of my happier days at our cottage in Fordham when I would spend afternoons with hook and line pursuing our evening meal along with my next piece of verse or fiction. I am sure there are a dozen or more stories that will be inspired by this murky brown water and the moss-covered cypress whose roots seem to clutch the muddy banks like the talons of some ancient bird of prey. For now, however, I am content to sit with my hook and line, breathe the country into my soul, and record some few details of the journey.

I shall begin this section of my narrative by reporting that I hooked five large catfish for dinner, something Pierre found particularly amusing. "Edgar, he don't even spit on his bait, him, and he catch five," he said to Martin. Since it was more than we needed, Pierre put ashore at the hut of a distant uncle. The man must have been something of an eccentric or a recluse, for he looked at his nephews with dull ambivalence, keeping silent while they started a blaze in his firepit and borrowed his skillet to cook. We cooked. We ate and shared with him. We left and still he said nothing, not even goodbye.

During the first day on the river, Pierre and Martin were jovial, waving often to friends and relatives working along the shore. The following day the land became more wild and they grew silent and watchful, their shotguns loaded and always in reach to defend us should we be attacked. They did not have to tell me what they feared. The thick growth of the untended lands around us would make it an ideal refuge for gangs of runaway slaves and outlaws, desperate for a boat and weapons. I also said little and studied the shadows beneath the trees, the dark pools of quiet water near the banks.

Pierre has decided that we must anchor in the center of the river tonight and take turns standing watch. Though there is an hour or so until sunset, he has stopped at a wide deep point and let down the anchor. We eat stale biscuits and some sort of dried meat, washing it down with cider that has already started to ferment in the tropical sun. I drink little, but after so many days of travel my constitution has weakened, and what I drink affects me. My heart begins to pound, setting a staccato rhythm I can feel in my temples and the backs of my hands. Sweat beads on my already damp forehead and remains there, for though there is a steady breeze blowing from the south, the air is so sultry that it does me no good.

A moment ago, seeing my misery, Martin pulled the scarf from around my neck, dipped it in the water, wrung it out and handed it to me so I could wipe my face. This, like so many of the brothers' small acts of kindness on the journey, was done without a word being spoken by either of us, save for my sincere, whispered *"Merci."*

Night was falling by the time we finished our evening meal, turning the brackish river water from brown to silver to indigo. The brothers seemed exhausted from their hours of work, so I volunteered to keep the first watch. Though my overtaxed mind will undoubtedly conjure up a score of nightmarish visions, I'll likewise be awake and able to spot any actual danger. Pierre unrolled a pair of thin straw-stuffed mattresses and spread them on the deck. Before lying down, he handed me a shotgun and a hunting knife and told me to be alert for anything odd.

I try to imagine what that might be as I strain to see in the fading light. A wild cat screeches somewhere nearby. I jump and stifle a cry, looking sheepishly at Pierre, who smiles but does not laugh. My heart is racing. I fight for calm.

So ends the second day of my journey through the heart of Louisiana. . . .

Soon after the brothers went to sleep, my guard duty became useless because I could see nothing in the darkness. Even listening did no good, for I could hear little but the bellows and chirps of frogs and insects, the repetitive ghostly cry of an owl, and the occasional splashing of fish in the water. Then, as my eyes began to grow accustomed to seeing by only the light of the distant stars, I began to imagine that I saw shapes moving beneath the surface of the water, savages peering at our boat through the bushes on the shore.

As the air cooled, a fog rose from the water, its tendrils winding toward the shore. It thickened until the sounds from shore grew muted, remote. I felt strangely comforted by its pressing, lacy isolation. My vision shifted to the area immediately around the boat, for I could see no farther. But then, at the very time the blackness should have been complete, the fog began to glow first gray, then white, then silver. Long dark shadows of the gloomy cypress trees fell across the still water, and a moment later I saw the moon rise above the earthbound cloud, its light covering the world in a silvery mist.

Tears came to my eyes, tears of thanks for this magical place, this moment of peace more infinite and perfect than any I have felt in my life. I held my breath until something splashed in the water near the boat and broke the spell.

I was supposed to wake Martin when I grew tired, but I never had the desire to rest. I let them both sleep as the moon arched across the sky, as the sky lightened with approaching dawn.

The birds, not I, woke them, but I paid them no heed. Instead, I stood in the back of the boat staring at the mists on the water, glowing golden until they dissolved at the warm touch of the sun.

Pierre started a coal fire in our little stove. Last night before retiring he had filled a gallon jar with a few handfuls of crushed peach pits and the muddy bayou water. This morning, the water seemed quite clear, and he poured it carefully into a metal pot so he could heat water for coffee. I lay back on the mattress he had abandoned and watched him work until my eyes shut.

In the few hours I slept, the land vanished, replaced by tall swamp grasses that seemed to extend to the horizon in every direction and waved in the slightest breeze. Though we were still on water, the swamp bore little sign to a river and I wondered what landmarks the brothers used for navigation.

Martin handed me a cup of tepid coffee and pointed to our supply sack. "Best eat what's left of the biscuits and cheese, Edgar. Your landing come soon, just past the swamp."

"Are we still on the river?"

He shook his head. "We go across the swamp. Pierre is not certain you can make the long walk, he. He wants to leave you closer to the house. Three miles you walk, no more, hein?"

"Merci," I said, loud enough to include both of them.

By the time I finished my second cup of coffee, I could see a line of trees in the distance, and the huge oak that dominated them and marked the landing spot where Martin said the fisherman kept a communal dock.

From that time until I left them, the brothers' carefree demeanor changed. They worked with ruthless efficiency while Martin gave me careful directions on how to reach my destination. They are exuberant people and I expected Pierre to embrace me when I left, but he only took my hand and pressed a penny into it. *"Por chance,"* he whispered and turned back to the boat.

By the time I reached the land's end of the old cypress dock, the brothers had shoved off. By the time I walked to the narrow road that ended beside the oak tree, the boat was already some distance from shore. I turned and waved. Pierre nodded to me but did not wave back.

Though Pierre and Martin did their best to hide their feelings, I have aroused the emotion in others often enough to recognize true fear. I am thankful that I have come here, but dread what I will discover when I reach my destination.

part five

THE WEBS OF DREAM

chapter 29

(from the journal of Edgar Poe)

*W*hile *Petite Terre* would hardly be considered more than a large farm by the plantation owners in Virginia, it holds a charm of its own—a cool tranquility in the lush green lawn, the ancient trees and the sprawling house beneath them.

Harry knew where I was going. Mrs. Braud would receive a letter stating my concerns about the family and asking her to contact the authorities should she not hear from me in a week's time. I had no other plan, though my earlier notion of sweeping into Petite Terre, rescuing Pamela and her son, and escaping with them seemed both overly romantic and pessimistic given the isolation and apparent peacefulness of the estate. Pamela might not need or want to be rescued.

With that in mind, I followed my instincts, abandoned my observation spot, and walked down the path to the door.

Of course, I assumed I was being watched from the time I stopped in front of the gate. I anticipated the door might open before I reached it. However, I expected a Negro servant to be standing there, not a petite fashionably dressed woman whose bearing indicated that she was mistress of this house.

From her appearance, I assumed that this was Elliot's mother. "Mrs. Donaldson," I began. "I am a friend of your daughter-in-law's. I've traveled from Virginia to see her. May I come in?"

I saw a faint smile dance across her lips as she studied me. I thought she might be wondering why a stranger with a northern accent would be standing in front of her wearing Cajun-spun clothing not in the best of repair or cleanliness. However, instead of inquiring about that, she put down the lamp she carried and held out her hand. When I took it, she drew me inside and shut the door. "I am Madeline Usher, Mr. Poe," she said. "I see that you are surprised that I know you. In truth, I think I would have recognized you the moment I met you even if I had never seen your picture in my daughter's magazines or learned from Pamela that you were expected. You have no idea how many years I've hoped for the pleasure of knowing you."

The last words could have countless meanings depending on the tone in which they were spoken. She said them simply, without a hint of rancor or infatuation. "There have been opportunities, surely," I replied in a similar tone.

"Not for someone who rarely travels, even as far as St. James."

"You could have written my publishers. They would have forwarded your letter."

"Written and told you what? That your story was passed around the county? That it gave my neighbors one more reason to whisper about me? I'm a private person. The damage had already been done before I thought of contacting you."

"I'm sorry," I said, hoping my voice conveyed my sincerity. "As I told Pamela, I thought you were dead. I would not have used your name otherwise."

After studying me a moment, she seemed to decide that I spoke the truth and gave a quick nod. "Someday you must explain to me what powers inspire you, for in truth your account of my death and resurrection was remarkably accurate." She paused, then added, "You must have had a hard journey. You seem unwell."

Without asking, she took my hand once more and studied it from all sides, observing the skin on the palm and fingertips, the color and shape of the nails, then she went further and rested her fingers on my wrist and the side of my neck. Her touch was light, her hands cool, but the unexpected gesture set my heart to racing. "Did you have a difficult journey?" she asked.

"A long walk, nothing more. I'm used to them," I replied.

"I'd read that you were ill some years ago. I see that you still are. Unless you get some help, you haven't long to live," she said.

How could she have guessed the truth from just the briefest examination? "I've been told by a friend's physician that there is some weakness in my heart and that nothing can be done for it," I replied.

"Told by a fool who has no idea how to help you. I can," she replied. "And I will, if you make me a promise."

There was something strange about the conversation, as if she and I had been together for some time and this hardly the first time we'd spoken to each other.

No one had ever offered me any hope before, yet she did it with such calm conviction that I believed her. "I came here because I am concerned about Pamela Donaldson. I can make no promises until after I've spoken to her and know for certain that she is content to remain here."

"Content. Yes, I think you will find Pamela that." She said this as she had the rest, with good-natured calm, yet I sensed a ripple of droll amusement in her voice, a suppressed smile on her lips, as if she believed we were playing a game and that I had already lost. I've seen that sort of expression on women before in the New York and Baltimore drawing rooms where the literati hold court. Now, as then, it made me more than a little uneasy.

"But the promise I request imposes a different sort of burden," she went on, after a pause. "I value my privacy. I have already read your far-too-accurate account of my brother's demise and do not care to read another concerning my family. So I ask that you forget about us when you leave here."

"I have no desire to do otherwise."

"That may change."

"Then, yes, if you wish it, I will keep our meeting secret, though I doubt I will ever truly forget it," I replied.

Her eyes were fixed on mine. Through them, I could see her intelligence, a serenity more willed than innate, and something else—an intensity that was hardly natural, scarcely sane. I knew it all too well, for I'd seen the emotion in my own eyes far too often, and the effects of it were always unpredictable.

I knew then that while I might take the medicine she gave me, I would do so only because I knew the future would be short without some aid. But I would never trust her, and never leave Pamela in this house until she told me herself that she wanted to remain, and I was certain that the words she spoke were not forced from her through threats or drugs.

"Now that we understand each other, you may stay here as our guest." She picked up the lamp and motioned for me to follow her. We went straight back through the vestibule, past the parlor and dining room to a long hallway branching left and right. We turned to the right. She stopped at the next door, unlocked it, and lit a lamp inside from the one she carried. I followed her in.

"Do you have clean clothes?" she asked.

I held out the canvas bag that had managed to survive a flight, a crash, and a wade through the swamp relatively intact.

"If you like, you can wear some things from the cupboard. This was Elliot's room, and he took little with him when he left. I understand that you are a fastidious man. If you had arrived earlier I would have offered you a bath. Perhaps in the morning. Sleep well, Mr. Poe." She backed through the door and closed it behind her.

As soon as I was alone, I studied my surroundings. The room was large. The magnificently carved bedposts, the cupboard, the writing desk and chair, and the floors were all dusted and polished. The air seemed fresh, but there was a lack of personal possessions, and a feeling of emptiness to it that made me certain that it had not been in use for some time.

Nonetheless, the bed linens were fresh, and the netting

hanging around it free of dust and spiderwebs. The water in the pitcher was cool as if only recently drawn from the well. There was even a light supper of biscuits and sliced cheese and a pot of tepid herbal tea on the desk along with a stack of clean paper, pen, and ink.

This had not been done in the few minutes since I'd entered the house. Therefore, I could only assume that this room had been prepared days ago and kept ready for me. Perhaps Pamela had told them to expect me. For her sake, I hoped she'd done so willingly, though I could not dismiss the feeling that I was being overly optimistic. However, Madeline Usher had provided me with the few comforts I needed to maintain my sanity, and that in itself made me feel somewhat less anxious.

I pulled back the heavy draperies covering the window and saw the wide spaced bars across it. Flakes of rust broke off against my wrist when I reached through them to push open the window and let in the night air.

This had been Elliot's room. Had he caused so much trouble that he'd deserved this?

I went to the door. As I expected, it was unlocked. Yet when I tried to step through it, a curious sort of dread came over me, a certainty that if I stole through the house, prying into the woman's affairs, I would be punished in a way that would be singularly unpleasant to me, possibly even fatal. My hands trembled. My breathing quickened and my heart responded. Signs of fear, yet there was no reason for any of it save perhaps my own overworked imagination.

I thought of Mary Quinn's letter and hastily shut the door. No sooner had I done so than the feeling diminished and I began to rationalize what I had felt. I was famished and exhausted. Better to play the polite guest for the moment and explore later when I was rested and my mind sharper, more up to the task.

So, convincing myself that I should be thankful for the hospitality, I sat at the table and devoured the little meal, then sampled the tea. It tasted ordinary enough—lemon grass, perhaps, definitely some chamomile and rose hips, the last undoubtedly to ward off the fever in this inhospitable clime. I'd just relaxed enough to set aside the paper provided for me, pull out my journal and pen, and begin to update my account of the journey when I grew uneasy. I understood the feeling at once; I was not alone.

Someone was standing in the shadows just outside my barred window. I could feel eyes fixed on my body, the mind behind them agitated and curious. "Who's there?" I called, and the figure, no more than a darker shadow against the indigo curtain of the night, retreated.

"It's all right," I called in a soothing tone. "Come forward. Let me see you."

I'd expected to see a slave standing there, some poor wretch pulled from sleep and given the unpleasant task of standing guard outside my window. Instead, a woman stepped into my lamp's dim light. She kept her head lowered so that I could not see her face, but I easily recognized the magazines she carried—*Godeys* and *Grahams*. "Would you sign these for me, Mr. Poe?" she asked. Her voice shook from nervousness, but it was a cultured voice with an accent similar to Madeline's.

I was a prisoner in this house, and I had no idea if I would be alive in the morning. Yet this woman was asking for my autograph. Perhaps she didn't realize my situation. Or perhaps she had merely taken my most macabre work too much to heart, as had other of my more ardent devotees, mixed my reality with my fiction, and assumed I usually lived in just such a precarious state. No matter, I needed an ally in this house, and her adulation might serve some use. "Of course," I said, and went back to the desk for my pen.

When I returned to the window, the woman had disappeared into the shadows once more. "It's all right." I whispered in case someone had startled her, but I heard nothing, not even the rustle of her skirts as she left me.

She would be back, I decided. I was about to return to my journal when I heard a faint tapping at my door. "Edgar Poe, may I come in?" a woman, the same woman I'd spoken to at the window, asked.

"Of course," I replied and opened my door.

At first all I could see in the lamplight was the pale green skirt and cream lace trim of her gown. But as she stepped inside and looked at me, I realized that I had seen her face before. Once she had been striking and unforgettable. Now the brilliant brown eyes were bright and unsteady as they looked into mine. The mouth that must have kissed with such greedy passion was trembling so much that I suspected she was about to cry from some overflow of emotion. Yet it was a beautiful face still, one filled with incredible animation as if her expressions had an independent life of their own. And Pamela's words came to me, with almost droll humor.

She was not a beautiful woman.

"Anna Montgomery," I whispered.

She stared at me, her expression suddenly slack, her eyes wide with fear. The magazines she'd been clutching so tightly fell from her arms, but she did not seem to notice. Instead, she turned and ran from the room, bolting so rapidly that some shift of the breeze made the door slam shut behind her.

I fell into the desk chair, my legs suddenly weak, my mind reeling from what I had discovered. Then, inexplicably, I began to laugh, softly and without humor.

Why should I be so surprised to find her here? Hadn't I known most of the truth since Will Montgomery leveled his revolver at me only days before?

Knowing what my conscience demanded that I do, I took off the light-colored homespun clothes and put on a dark jacket and pants that I found in the cupboard. Prepared to face all the demons in hell if need be, I lit one of the bedside candles and with it in hand, walked to the bedroom door and threw it open. That terrible sense of dread returned. I fought it, and felt it lessen as I stepped in to the hall. I took a deep breath and started toward the foyer, stopping at each closed door. Listening. Hoping to hear Pamela's voice and wondering if I dared to whisper her name.

chapter 30

Darkness has a way of making even small spaces seem cavernous. So it was with that my journey down a hall that seemed endless, and the foyer felt as broad as the universe, my part in it limited to the pool of light shed by the candle I carried.

As I traveled, I tried some of the doors, opening the unlocked ones slowly, retreating if a rusted hinge began to grate or groan. Each time I entered a room, I shaded my little light with my hand until I made certain the room was empty. Since I doubted that any explanation I devised for my actions would be accepted, I decided to tell the truth if I were caught. Indeed, I would blurt it out, scream Pamela's name. In that fashion I would convince my captors that I was half insane—a part I know all too well how to play—and let Pamela know through the sheer volume of my voice that I had come for her.

Fortunately, I encountered no one, but did manage to explore a library, the dining room and parlor, and an empty bedroom whose rose scent and delicate lace curtains made me certain the chamber was used by Anna Montgomery. I paused finally outside an open door at the end of a second hall, on the opposite end of the house from my room. As I'd done before, I hesitated and listened, then hearing no one breathing, I stepped inside. Here I didn't have to use my light to know where I was, for I recognized the space by its smell. Linseed oil, turpentine, the earthy scent of drying clay, the equally natural smell of cedar and southern pine meant this had to be a space used by artists and craftsmen. I held up my light.

And marveled at the skill of the one who had created a wolf so lifelike that I backed up a step and caught my breath as the candlelight reflected off its menacing green glass eyes. Suffice it to say, the room was filled with such creations, and paintings as well. The easel was turned away from me, and I eagerly crossed the room to see what the subject might be.

It was a man, not old in the sense of age, but aged through dissipation. He held a naked child in outstretched arms. The infant's features were similar to those of the man, but if the man were the child's father, there was no love in the eyes. Instead they were dull and glazed as if the person were already dead. But that alone was not enough to cause this feeling of dread inside me. I looked closer at the man's expression and saw a hunger so ravenous that were this scene real I would expect the man to pull the flesh from the infant's bones, and when they were stripped, suck even the marrow from them.

And as I stood there, horrified less by the painting than by my interpretation of it, I heard a sound coming from behind the closed door across the hall, a soft whisper that grew into the angry, high-pitched wail of a toddler. Roddy, no doubt. Where Roddy was, Pamela would also be unless she was a prisoner or long since dead. Not certain who would come to aid the child, I remained in the studio, hoping that no one would notice my little light.

The crying continued but no one came. Eventually, I ventured from my hiding place and went to the door across the hall. I listened, but though the cries softened somewhat, I heard no crooning from an adult, no footsteps of someone going to assist the boy. I tried the door, found it unlocked, and slowly pushed it open. As I had at the other rooms, I paused while I was still outside it and listened.

The child's cries had lost their urgency, replaced by an occasional whimper. This allowed me to hear other sounds—

rustlings and breathing, a soft cry, and an answering murmur. A candle flickered somewhere inside, making my own unnecessary. I blew it out and stepped into the room.

From where I stood, I could see a door slightly ajar, leading no doubt to the nursery. I might have gone to the child even then, but there was a couple in the bed positioned between me and the nursery door. I could make out forms but no features beyond the thick curtain of mosquito netting, so I stepped back into the narrow corner space between the windows and the cupboard where it was less likely I would be seen.

In truth, the man and woman were so occupied with each other that they could scarcely have been expected to notice me even it I'd been in plain sight. The white cloud of netting around the bed made it impossible to see the features of the pair. The woman could have been Anna, but in this proximity to Roddy, I could only assume it was Pamela.

Now I understood Madeline Usher's enigmatic smile. Of course Pamela was content. She had found a lover here. My journey had been for nothing, and I felt like a sentimental fool for making it. I wanted to retreat from the room, and go back to my own and think up some words of apology to use the following morning. At the same time I knew there was something wrong with this scene. Pamela had abandoned her home and undertaken a long and uncertain journey alone. She would hardly let her child cry to remain in the arms of any lover—no matter how passionately she cared for him.

With all thoughts of retreat gone, I remained where I was, thankful in a way that the netting was so thickly gathered along the bed that I could see them only indistinctly, though there were enough signs to convince me that the woman welcomed the presence of the man with her.

He straddled her, taking a few deep thrusts before withdrawing so that his hands and lips could move her to a greater height of ecstasy. Each time he would mount her, then withdraw as soon as she relaxed and begin to caress her again. So their lovemaking continued until they were both spent. I expected him to fall asleep beside her, but instead he rolled off and pushed back the netting. As he stood, I had a clear view of them both. I watched him pull on his nightshirt. I saw her, her body sheened with sweat, her white gown pushed up above her breasts. Her hands were still gripping the headboard posts and she seemed to be asleep.

He went to the washstand for pitcher and basin. Returning to the bed, he moistened the corner of a towel and washed her—her breasts, her stomach, her thighs, then between her legs. His ministrations done, he lifted her and carefully pulled the nightshirt down, then spread the sheet over her. At the end, he paused to study her face, sliding his hand beneath the gown, to caress the tips of her breasts one final time. "Pamela," he whispered. She murmured something back, but the words were too soft to be distinct. Satisfied, the man sat beside her on the bed and fumbled with something on the headboard. Pamela lowered her hands and rubbed her wrists.

For an instant my mind refused to accept the horror of the situation I had witnessed. When it did, I wanted to spring from my hiding place and beat the man senseless. But of course, I would likely lose, and in the rare event that I didn't, the struggle would bring any other residents running, hardly what I wanted.

To leave the room, he had to pass close to me. I hid my bare fists in my pockets, and turned my face to the wall lest my pale complexion make my presence known. I stayed that way until I heard him close the door across the hall.

By now the child had returned to sleep. Nonetheless, Pamela pushed herself to her feet and walked unsteadily into the adjoining room to check on him. I remained where I was until she returned alone to her bed.

I opened the outside door and shut it softly. "Pamela, it's Edgar Poe," I called, hoping the low tone would keep her from being too startled.

She turned her head toward me, slowly and without surprise as if she were drugged or exhausted. "Edgar? Is it really you?" she asked.

I lit my candle and sat beside her. She made no move to cover herself, and I saw one bare breast sticking out of the open bodice of her gown, its nipple dark, still hard from passion. I kissed her forehead. "It's all right," I said, though she hardly seemed in need of consoling so much as of a strong pot of coffee or some other stimulant.

"Did you see him?" she asked, her eyes dull, her voice expressionless.

"Who?"

"The ghost of my Elliot. He comes to me every night."

I replied as gently as I could given my lingering anger at the abomination I'd unwittingly witnessed. "I saw a man, not a spirit. When he left you, he went into the room across the hall."

"That's Sean's room. But he would not do that," she said, but there was doubt in her voice. In this house she had probably come to doubt everything, her sanity most of all. "Besides, it has to be a dream. Elliot only comes to me when I am sleeping. I can't move to push him away. But it's so pleasant, I don't want him to leave. I tell him every night that he should stay and come back to the waking world. But he tells me that he can't."

"Here." I moved the candle close to the head of her bed and showed her the worn spots on the posts. "The man binds your wrists so of course you cannot move," I said.

She looked at the posts, then at her wrists, wincing when she saw the red marks that would have undoubtedly faded by morning. "It always seems like a dream when he touches me," she said.

I dipped my finger into an empty teacup on the bedside table. The herbal blend seemed pleasant, but as I expected, there was an underlying taste I knew well. "It seems like a dream because you've been given opium, not strong I think, but strong enough to make dreams and reality merge in someone who is unaccustomed to the drug. By morning the effects would probably have worn off. You'd wake to a pleasant sort of languor, and recall only half of what happened."

The revelation had the effect I'd hoped it would. Pamela sat up straighter. Her eyes became more focused. Anger was a potent stimulant, and she had every right to be furious, and hurt, and probably hysterical, though I would not expect her to give in to the last. She shuddered. Her eyes became bright, but as she had done in my little room at the Swan, she fought back the tears. Some sense of propriety returned, enough so that she sat up straight in bed and pulled her nightgown closed. When she spoke her voice was strong. "Soon after I came here, I invited Sean into my bed. He seemed to suit me more than his brother ever did."

"He's Elliot's brother?"

"Yes. You must understand how right he seemed at first." She frowned and went on. "Later, after I realized that his loyalty would never be to me, I refused to let him touch me.

"I cannot blame him completely for tonight's act, though. Madeline undoubtedly ordered it, and he will do whatever Madeline asks. They fear her. They have every right to. The penalties for disloyalty are, I know, most unpleasant."

She paused and took my hands in hers, then impetuously let them go, threw her arms around my neck, and hugged me. I felt the warmth of her breasts, smelled the perfume in her damp hair. As I held her, my resolve melted. I would not tell her the relationship between her and Sean. Better to give Vivienne Donaldson a chance to do it herself.

"I'm sorry you came for me," Pamela said. "Now you're a prisoner here as well, Mr. Poe."

"Edgar, please. If I've come so far for you, it should put us on a first-name basis, don't you think?"

She did not smile. "How were you able to find my room?" she asked.

"I walked through the door of my own. It wasn't locked." Anxious to put some distance between us, I went to the door and tried the handle. As I expected, it was also unlocked. "Then I wandered the dark halls until I heard Roddy crying."

"You didn't feel it . . . the creature that walks the house at night?"

In truth, I had, but I was used to more horrible things—my Sissy drowning in blood, fighting for each small breath of life, my mother with her tiny delicate hands and huge eyes made all the more beautiful by the fever that consumed her, my stepfather with his face all bloated from disease, and the creature that I sometimes see in the mirror—a creature ancient and despised—looking back at me through my eyes. "I felt it, but I'm accustomed to such things. It's my occupation," I said and added a short, soft laugh.

"I'm not. I tried to leave more than once, but from the time I retire until morning, I can't find the courage to cross the portal."

"Does anyone come to make sure of that?" I asked.

"Not anymore. We won't be disturbed unless Sean . . ."

Unless Sean possessed some superhuman strength, he would be sleeping soundly by now; well-spent, as the younger Harry used to say, always with the hint of a leer. I said as much to her, though far more diplomatically.

For the next hour I told her about Mary Quinn's letter and how concerned it had made me, and a bit about my journey in the balloon and pirogue. I added what details I could recall, because the story seemed to interest her so. During the time I related it, the drug began to leave her system, and by the end she seemed quite awake and concerned about everything that had happened.

When I'd finished, she spent the better part of the night telling me of her own journey, of meeting Mr. Grymes and the Usher family. Then, after making me pledge on my honor never to use the information she gave me in any way that would make the characters identifiable, she told me what she had read in Madeline Usher's journal.

"At first I didn't believe it. I thought Madeline exaggerated her power, and that the storm had been no more than coincidence. Something changed all that. She unleashed that power and killed a man."

"You saw this?" I asked, astounded.

"I saw the storm. I saw the man's body." She went on to tell the story of Blaine Stelley's death. "Even then I would not have believed it, had it not been for the wife's terrible fear. Since the hour when Sean forced me to return here, I have been a prisoner on this estate. Every move I make is noted. Even at night when I sleep she sends her spirit to me to spy on my dreams and read my thoughts. She'll do the same to you, so she'll know soon enough that we've talked."

"Pamela, do you think that Madeline caused the storms in New York?" I asked.

She thought a moment, weighing what she had learned. "I do," she said. "At first, I couldn't believe it of her, but the storm was too similar to the one that killed Blaine Stelley. I don't think that she intended to kill Elliot, though. She values her little family far too much for that. I think she wanted to frighten him and force him to return home with me. As for the Bouttes, after seeing what she did to Blaine Stelley merely because his wife told me some stories about Elliot, I can well imagine her killing them. She would think it justice for the theft of her money, and how they left me to die."

"You still believe that she wanted you here, even after everything that's happened to you?"

She nodded. "Madeline might punish me, or even arrange to have my lover rape me, but she won't try to kill me. As for the storm, I think she can focus it and unleash it, but then she has no real control over it. It's like her anger, buried and waiting to explode."

"You sense that, too?" I asked.

"How could she not be angry? Consider what was done to her, how she was used and betrayed. Yet she writes that she mourns Roderick still. I can't believe that even a saint could be so forgiving."

"Can't you? I can see that you are already forgiving Sean for his transgressions, and they are hardly minor."

"I don't forgive, I merely understand," she replied. "It won't take many days among these people before you'll come to appreciate the difference."

"Did you ever find the other journals Judith Donaldson mentioned?"

"No. I looked through Madeline's private library and the larger one in this house, but nothing resembles the first one I found in the drawer. She must have them hidden somewhere, though I cannot fathom why the first wasn't with them."

"I can. I think you were meant to read it," I replied. She frowned, and I went on. "Even if Judith Donaldson hadn't told you what to look for, you would have checked that desk drawer. You would have found it and once you started reading, from what you tell me, it would have been hard to put it away without finishing. What I can't comprehend is why Madeline doesn't simply give them all to you."

"I know the answer," Pamela said. "I've already read things most people would consider unnatural or worse. She wanted to see if I would accept what I read, or if I would be revolted by it.

"I have accepted it. And the more I learn, the more I believe, the more willing I'll be to accept whatever else she's done. I've been doing what she wants and giving her every indication that I am more than sympathetic to her beliefs."

"Then why don't you simply ask for the journals?" I suggested.

"I thought of that, but I think it's too soon. Better to wait until she believes that I have provided the other thing she expects of me. She wants me and Sean to conceive a child together, another Usher to carry on their power. I considered telling her that I already have, but I don't dare. She may well have a way of divining the truth."

We spoke a bit longer, until the birds announced the dawn, whose dim light we had not noticed. "I'd better go," I said, and started to stand.

"Just a moment, Edgar. I haven't said a proper thank you." She reached for my hand, pulled me back down beside her, and kissed me. Her touch was light and fleeting, but enough to make me realize once more how much I was drawn to her. "Thank you for coming. I can face whatever she has planned for me much more easily with you here," she said, her breath soft against my face, her body warm against mine.

"After meeting you, how could I have possibly stayed away," I replied. I wanted to kiss her again, and more, but after what I'd witnessed and what she'd endured it would hardly have been the time. Later, perhaps, when the ordeal is over and I can allow myself the luxury of ego once more, I will think of her youth, her pleasant temperament, and yes, her wealth, and tell her how I feel. I held her close a moment longer, then left her.

The dim light that leaked through the window at the end of the hall made the retreat to my room that much easier. As I expected after the night's revelations, my sleep was unsettled. I felt the uneasiness which follows nightmares into the waking world, though I could not recall the dreams which led to it.

While I slept, someone had removed the offered books and replaced them with a new stack and a breakfast tray containing a pot of lukewarm coffee and a plate of biscuits with sliced ham.

Until I saw the food, I had no idea how ravenous I'd become. I devoured what had been left for me before even glancing at the reading matter that had been provided with my breakfast.

Among the offerings of indifferent novels were three old copies of *Punch*. These were more to my liking. I pulled a chair close to the barred window, and with a breeze refreshing me, I began to read.

Some time later I looked up from the magazine and saw a figure standing in a shadowed corner. She might have tiptoed into the room while I was absorbed in my reading. She might have been there since the beginning, standing quietly, observing me.

"Anna," I whispered.

She shook her head, placed a finger to her lips. I understood.

"Vivienne," I said. "Is that better?"

She nodded, let out the deep breath she'd been holding, and shut her eyes. A small smile played across her lips. It seemed almost mischievous, as if she were part of an innocent game played by children. "Don't you like my books?" she asked.

"So it was you who brought them. I thought so!" I said. "I've read these, though there are others I would like to see."

I reached for her hand. Her smile grew wider as she touched me. It seemed to fill her face, and for a time the anxiousness left her expression, leaving in its wake an incredible, fragile beauty, not unlike that of her daughter. Though it pained me to break the moment of peace, I said, "I would like you to bring me Madeline's journals, the ones bound in white leather."

"No!" she said and pulled away from me. "No one should read them. Never!"

"Pamela has already read the first one Madeline wrote. Doesn't she have the right to see the rest?"

"I can't get them. Even if I could, I wouldn't. She'll hate me once she reads them, just as her father does."

"I've met Will," I said. "He asked me to deliver a message to you."

"Message?"

I sensed such terrible fear in her tone that I quickly conveyed it, lest I pause long enough for her to bolt from the room. "He said to tell you that he loves you still, and that he would gladly live with you however you wished if he could only have the pleasure of your presence."

"Pretty words, but then you would know many," she said.

"If you really think I'm lying, why don't you make certain? Write him. Tell him where you are."

She shook her head. "He knows where I am, Mr. Poe. He traveled here to take me back to Virginia. A one-hour discussion with Mother changed all that. We met only for a moment as he was leaving. I wanted him to say those pretty words to me then. I wanted him to take my hand and drag me from this house, this prison. Instead . . ." Her voice broke. She pulled a kerchief from her pocket, covered her mouth and nose with it, and took a deep breath. The shifting emotions in her overwrought expression lessened, her voice grew dreamy as she went on. "Instead, he slapped me. He called me an abomination. He cursed this house and everyone in it. Then he was gone."

"Anger has a way of turning into regret," I said. "Is anger why he keeps your room exactly as it was when you lived there—a shrine to your presence? Is anger why he drinks so much, then locks himself in it and cries?"

"No! You must not lie to me! You must not say these things!" she cried.

"I'm not the one who lies to you, Vivienne," I said calmly.

"Please! You must not say those things! Especially not to Pamela."

"She'd understand if you go to her and tell her the truth," I replied. "But the truth should come from you before she hears it from me or someone else."

She looked at me with those same frightened doe's eyes. "Not *her* truth," she blurted, then turned and fled the room.

chapter 31

The better part of my first full day in the house passed before I saw Pamela or her mother again. During it, I was treated with all the deference one shows to a guest. A servant came and helped me unpack my bag, then handed me one of Elliot's robes so I could undress. After, she took my torn and soiled clothing to be cleaned. While she was gone, a second servant led me to a little enclosed pool where I could bathe.

Well fed and well tended, I returned to the house some time later to discover clean pants and shirt and cravat laid across the bed for me. They weren't mine, but they fit well enough. While the cut of the jacket wasn't fashionable any longer, I looked far better in them than I had in my own things for many years. They were also cut from a thinner cloth, something I was thankful for given the sultry heat and absence of any breeze.

Though the issues of *Punch* remained, a new stack of books had replaced the first. As I was reading over the titles, I noticed an envelope sticking out of one.

I pulled it out and saw that it was addressed to Pamela, with a note for me on the back.

Mr. Poe,

I pray that you are right. The time has come for truth. I am sorry, but I cannot see my daughter's face when she reads this. But you are right, it must be my truth she learns first. Read this. I don't think I can face her, and I certainly have no luck with speaking my mind, but if you think I've set down what is in my heart well, give it to her.

Vivienne.

The writing was tiny, the words written quickly. I wondered if she thought that someone was reading over her shoulder as she composed the account or afraid that her sudden courage would fail her.

I'd already gotten the feeling that I was watched. Reasoning that the spy would have to be outside my window or looking through some peephole in the outer wall, I pulled the curtains nearly shut, then moved the desk chair close to them where the light leaking through them would make it easier to read. Even then, I found it difficult, for in her anxiousness to explain her life to her daughter, Vivienne had edited her sentences until the account resembled the initial draft of one of my poems, with scarcely a paragraph that did not have at least a half-dozen words crossed out.

Dearest Pamela,

I know you must despise me for all the sorrows I have brought to your life but they were never intentional. I love you, child. I always have, and I never wished any evil on you.

I should begin by saying that my given name is Vivienne, but I never liked it, for it always sounded harsh and overly proper. My father, that same Adrien Broussard who rescued Madeline from what Mr. Poe aptly calls "The House of Usher," took to calling me Anna. I loved him all the more for it.

Though I did not visit that house until I was fifteen, it was always a part of my life. As an infant, I would sleep in the room next to my parents' room. I would hear their conversations, their quickened breathing and soft cries as they made love, then later, inevitably, my mother's terrified scream as she dreamed of the most horrible moments of her past.

You may wonder how I can recall things so far back. Mother tells me that it is because my soul is trying to remember the life before my birth. In this, she says that she cannot help me, for she does not know who I once was.

I was as nervous as a child as I am now. The condition—not unlike Mr. Poe's Roderick and his heightened senses—gives me terrible headaches, sleeplessness, and an indecision that often makes it impossible for me to think rationally for myself. So, I have always needed someone close to me—to guide me, to protect me, to use their strength to make me strong. That person, for good or ill, has usually been my mother.

I grew up in New Orleans, in a little house west of Canal Street, and well north of the river. We lived simply in a neighborhood that seemed to be composed of artists and writers and craftsmen, many of whom were gens de colour, as free Negroes are called there. Father painted and displayed his work in a number of galleries throughout the South. Mother had her books and manuscripts to keep her occupied. Once a week a number of men would come to the house and go into mother's study. The door would be closed for hours while she met with them.

Later I learned that these were the heads of the businesses my mother had inherited from Uncle Roderick. Later still, I realized that we were wealthy. Tutors taught me English and French, music and deportment. I had little skill at any of it, and the more I tried to overcome my stupidity, the worse I did, though no one condemned me for my lack of intellect. However, I was always surprised that my parents never had another child—one who would be less of a disappointment to them.

My life might have passed uneventfully. I would have

matured, been introduced to society, and in spite of my nervous condition eventually married. When I was younger, I despaired of any of this ever happening. I would cry and confess my worthlessness to Mother. She would laugh at me and remind me that we were wealthy and I her only heir. "Besides," she said, "women in society aren't expected to do anything but look beautiful and gay. You have the beauty in plenty. When you realize that, the gayness will surely follow."

But of course, the gayness did not follow, for Father died when I was fourteen, taking all chance of normalcy to the grave with him.

On the day after the funeral, when my eyes were still red from crying, Mother sat beside me in the parlor, took my hand, and in a simple, adult way told me the story of what my uncle did to her and how she killed him for it. Of course, I believed none of it, but in the weeks that followed she made me believe. Then she made me study, but I was no better at that sort of work than I had been at the more mundane subjects and the thought of being a practicing witch terrified me.

"We Ushers are hardly witches," Mother insisted. "We were once the healers, and the protectors of our clan. The skill is already in your blood, you only have to remember it all."

"But I'm only half an Usher!" I retorted. "The memories are in the part that is missing."

Eventually she stopped trying to educate me and left me to my own devices. Her only demand was that once a year, on the anniversary of Roderick's death, we would travel together to the ruins of the house of Usher. Needless to say, I never wanted to go, but she forced me to, and made me look at the pile of old bones, half hidden in the mud, to stand before the cypress casket she had requested that Father make for Roderick's corpse, and to pray with her in that cursed language. After we went, she would leave me alone.

Of course, I became a wild creature. I took lovers, discreetly at first, then openly, daring her to discipline me. She ignored the matter, until I went to her sobbing that I was carrying a child. She went into the little upstairs room where she kept her herbs and seeds and molds and brewed me a tea. Within an hour I was cramping, then bleeding, expelling the tiny innocent life, the victim of my sin. She sat beside me, holding my hand, a remote expression on her face. "It's time you settled down with a husband, I think," she said as she handed me a second cup of tea to drink. As I swallowed this, she rubbed her hands together and laid them on my belly. Their warmth seemed to flow into me, healing and comforting.

"Whatever you wish," I said, until the sleeping drug claimed me, relieving for a time both pain and guilt.

I had, of course, ruined my reputation in New Orleans, if such a thing as a reputation can exist in that city. So it came as no surprise that Mother would seek me a husband well upriver, even less of one that she would pick a man somehow related to me through her brother.

Phillip Donaldson was a steady and sensible man, handsome in a rugged sort of way. He loved his mother, his land, his animals, even his slaves, who in turn adored him. He managed a good living from what he owned, but he had for some years coveted a parcel of his neighbor's property. The money that came to him through our marriage made him able to meet the price. However, I don't think that was the only reason he married me. Rather, my mother's proposal, in which she reminded him of the family ties and responsibility, allowed him to find a wife without having to take any time away from his work to go and court me. The money she offered only made the arrangement that much more tempting.

So we were married and had our wedding night in the room we shared until his death. He was quick and so inexperienced that I don't think he ever realized that I wasn't a virgin. He even thanked me when we were done, then rolled over and went to sleep.

It was a fitting beginning for our marriage, for in the years we lived together, I never really knew him, or even felt close to him in any way except physically.

At the time Mother did not live with us. I felt lost without her, and would write her long letters detailing my misery and begging her to come. She did, finally, when she heard that I was expecting another child.

Pregnancy only heightened my nervous disposition. I would laugh at something hardly worth a smile, and moments later be crying over something as foolish as a spilled glass of cider. Mother brewed me some teas to steady my nerves and help me sleep. She gave me tonics to assure a healthy child. My mother-in-law, Judith, thought it all no more than witchcraft, but Phillip wisely refused to listen to her, especially since Mother had already given him some simple herbs to add to the cattle feed which had kept the beasts healthy through the worst of summer's heat.

Elliot was born in late October, and through his birth I managed to make both Mother and Phillip and even dour Judith ecstatic. They brought in a wet nurse to tend to Elliot and treated me like a child in need of recovery. For a time all the differences between us were forgotten, and we lived together with only the disagreements which an ordinary family must have.

I don't know when that changed, or even why, but it seemed that Mother was at the center of it. I would see her watching Elliot, a hint of disapproval showing in a frown, a slight narrowing of the eyes. I knew the expression all too well, for it was the way she used to look at me, with never a word of reproach for my backwardness.

"How has my child failed you, Mother?" I finally asked one day when we were alone.

She looked completely astonished, more I think at my perception than the accusation. That she didn't deny, at least not directly, though I can't recall exactly what she said. The next morning I found her packing to go home to New Orleans. "Everything seems so much better here now. You don't need me anymore," she said.

She was wrong about that, but I was stubborn and still angry over her displeasure with my child, so I refused to say so. Though we wrote each other every week, I did not see her again for nearly a year.

During that time, Phillip added another thousand acres to what we already owned. He rebuilt the summer kitchen and the slaves' quarters. He had plans drawn to add a second floor to our house, with separate wings for each of our mothers. I think it was all the work he did which finally made him ill.

It began with sleeplessness, and complaints of terrible dreams. He would stay awake well into the night, drawing new plans for the house or the fields, throwing himself into his work, as if through work he could vanquish the disease which plagued him.

Of course, this only served to allow his illness to take a stronger hold on him. Finally he was too weak to do anything but remain in bed. Even there he fought the rest he needed. A physician finally prescribed sedatives on which he overdosed, so that his rest was more unconsciousness than actual sleep. Judith and I took turns sitting with him. Once I came in to relieve her and found two slaves walking him from one end of the room to the other. He had taken so much of his sleep tonic that he had managed to stop breathing for a time.

"The Donaldson men all die young," Judith confessed to me that evening. "I had hoped Phillip would be spared the curse."

"Will I be left a widow so young?" I whispered, half to myself.

Those were the first words to come to my lips. Yes, they were self-centered and certainly inappropriate to say to a woman about to lose her only child. I think Judith should have understood my concern for myself and my child, but she refused to accept the apology which immediately followed them, even refused to speak to me outside of Phillip's presence.

For his sake, we maintained the facade of a truce which lasted even after Mother answered my hysterical summons and returned to Petite Terre. With the physicians able to do nothing, Judith finally asked Mother to help. Mother could only manage to make Phillip's last days peaceful. He died a week later.

"It wasn't the same weakness of the heart that killed Edward and his father," Judith said to Mother, then looked at me as she went on. "Perhaps it was the nervous condition from your family. For my grandson's sake, I should never have agreed to let first cousins wed."

So it was that after Phillip's death I learned that I had married Uncle Roderick's bastard and my first cousin. In truth, I am glad I did not know before, for there were parallels in the way Phillip treated me and Roderick my mother, enough that I might have despised him for habits that I learned to ignore, and that others had seen as virtues.

But the revelation was one more shock to a system already overburdened by them. I went to my room, stripped off my dress, and lay on my bed. I remained there, alternately sobbing and sleeping, through Phillip's wake and burial. For weeks afterward I spoke to no one, and when others spoke to me the words seemed muffled, their meaning obscure as if we were all trapped in some thick, unnatural fog. I ate nothing and drank only water. I'm sure that to the family it must have seemed that I was determined to follow Phillip to his grave. Even Judith, for all her spitefulness toward me, would come and sit at my side telling me that I was being selfish, that my child needed me, and that I should put the past behind me before I killed myself from grief.

In truth, I didn't care if I lived or died. But Mother did.

Soon she was forcing me to eat, to drink water and the teas she prepared for me. They lifted my spirits enough that I would get out of bed, sit in a chair, speak when spoken to. But it still seemed that this was a dream of life rather than life itself until one became confused with the other and I sank completely into a sort of madness.

Then, without ever recalling how it came to pass, I found myself in my sumptuous bedchamber in the house in New Orleans. "Let Judith take care of the child," Madeline said. "You're my child and I must take care of you."

She had the seamstresses come and make me new dresses. She took me to the finest restaurants and shows. I lost my name, and my immediate past. I became Anna Broussard again, a gay young woman so unlike the tragic Vivienne Donaldson, widow and mother of a child she had no idea how to raise. Then, when I seemed quite well, Mother suggested a trip east.

We visited many places—New York, Philadelphia, Baltimore, and Richmond, then finally Appomattox. Now I know that was our destination all along. Then it only seemed like one more stop on a grand tour of the new republic.

There was an opera that evening. Mother made me rest until an hour before, then suggested that I wear my most beautiful gown. We sat together in a private box belonging to some absent business associate of the Usher firms. "So many eligible men. Do you think I should marry again?" she asked me.

"If you think that suits you," I replied.

"Well, if I should, I would like . . . that one, if only he were a few years older. Tell me, have you ever seen anyone so handsome?" She held up her fan and pointed discreetly from behind it at a young man in the third row. The man was, of course, William Montgomery. Later, she arranged for us to meet, first between acts at the opera, then at a private party after it. She, not I, pursued him. She, not I, persuaded me to choose him. She, not I, arranged the marriage contract. But it was I who fell in love—hopelessly, perfectly, completely in love. What was more wonderful was that, though our marriage had been arranged, he loved me as well.

Everything was so different from the time before—from the romantic courtship to the ornate wedding to a wedding night I would blush to describe, to an extended honeymoon on the Continent where he lavished me with every luxury he could afford. When we returned home, his attention to me did not alter, and we lived as harmoniously and as passionately as any couple could ever hope to.

Mother had left the day after the wedding. She went home, not to New Orleans but to Petite Terre, where she began to look to the education of her grandson with the same concern she had looked to mine. The results were, I learned through her frequent letters, far better in his case.

Pamela, you may think it was wrong of me to keep so much of my past from your father. You are right, I should have been candid, but once I realized that I loved him, I was so afraid of what he would think of me, that I kept silent. When Mother wrote of Elliot, she always identified him only as her grandson. I finally told Will that Elliot's parents were both deceased and that Mother was helping raise the orphan until he was old enough to claim his inheritance.

We lived this idyllic existence for nearly two years. The portrait that Mr. Poe discovered was painted during that time. I recall posing for it in the rose garden, sitting so still, trying to ignore an occasional bee drawn to the color of my dress and hair. Then the thing I feared and hoped for most happened—I became pregnant, and as I expected, the nervousness that marred my first pregnancy returned. I wrote an urgent letter to my mother, and while I waited for a reply, I did my best to function on my own.

Will was so understanding—a saint in his patience. He

would sit by my side for hours on end while I alternately cried and apologized for my tears. He would hold me when I trembled. Then, finally, when I thought my mania would cause me to reveal too much of my past, I would send him away, bury my head in my pillow and mumble Elliot's name. I was being punished by God, I thought, punished for abandoning my firstborn.

Mother's letters were of little help. She suggested that perhaps I was not meant to have children, and that I should be thankful that Elliot was born so healthy. I always listened to her. I always believed her, and I wondered what my passionate Will would think if we had to sleep apart.

Along with advice, Mother also sent me a packet of tea to drink each night before bed, still others for morning and noon. These did help me sleep more soundly and to function with some normalcy through the day, but they could do nothing to alleviate the strong and horrible feeling that my time of happiness with my husband was nearly over.

That was, of course, a most accurate case of precognition and the only sign I've ever gotten that I possess any of the coveted Usher powers at all.

But after you, my Pamela, were born, I managed to put my fears behind me. I suppose you were told that I refused to hold you, to nurse you, to love you. I did, but not for the reason the servants suspected. I did not reject you, I was only afraid that my condition would somehow infect you, make you weak as I am weak, vacillating, dependent. But I did love you, and I often sat in your room at night watching you while you slept, and praying that your future would be steadier than my past.

Gradually I came to see that you were nothing like me, and I began to take more of an interest in you. Perhaps if you can think back to the time before your thoughts were expressed in words, you can remember sitting with me on the lawn and playing with the lace on my skirts, or crawling over me to grab the buttons on my bodice. I only wish there had been more memories like these for both of us.

Then as suddenly as before, I had a bout of the same old nervousness. Fortunately, Mother had sent me far more tea than I had needed to see me through my pregnancy with you. I began taking it again, and hiding how I felt. I still wasn't certain that I was pregnant, but thought I might be and I feared the effect another child would have on me. I did not confess this to Will. Instead I wrote Mother and asked her advice. She wrote back immediately, telling me that she was coming to Charlottesville to visit friends she had met on the journey before my marriage. She asked that I meet her there in two weeks' time and discuss my difficulties in private.

I had no idea what her plans would be for us, so I took all my best gowns, my jewels, and some of the prettier things Will had given me. I could show them to her, to tell her how marvelous my marriage still felt, and how thankful I was that she had arranged it. When I arrived at the house, I learned that the couple who owned it were abroad and my mother had rented it for the month.

There, in an elegant drawing room beneath the oval portrait of a girl with raven locks and a teal-green gown, I learned that Will was my half-brother, the product of my mother's and Roderick's horrible sin. "How could you have made such a mistake!" I screamed.

Then she said the most horrible words I have ever heard from anyone. "Not a mistake, Vivienne. I wed you to him on purpose. What's more, he will never believe you when you say you didn't know."

The revelation had all the effect I believe she intended it to have. I screamed. I cried. I swore that she was lying, then when presented with papers that proved it all true, I turned on her, focusing all my wrath on her.

"What did all this scheming give you besides certain damnation!" I screamed.

"A pure bloodline to keep our powers intact, and to give us vessels to receive the Usher souls."

I knew then that my madness was minor compared to hers, but that it made no difference. She ruined my life. She ruined Will's. I can only say that I am thankful that you were not also damned by your bloodline, that you were born beautiful, serene, intelligent—in a word, normal, for we Ushers are hardly a normal people.

What could I do, Pamela? Should I have returned to your father and told him of my mother's scheme and our unwitting sins? I did more than love him, I worshipped him. And he was such a devoted father, everything that Phillip hadn't been. What effect would the revelation have on his relationship with you?

All these thoughts were tumbling around in my mind as I sat and listened to my mother calmly tell me what I must do. If I left Virginia with her, and went back to Petite Terre, Will need never know where I had gone or why. He would be left with a mystery, but she was right. The mystery would be better than the truth.

So I left you and Will and returned to a place I despised and a son who at six hardly knew me. When my condition became obvious, Mother said the child was by a lover. Judith swore she would never speak to me again and moved into the old house where she lived the rest of her life in isolation. I found some peace in my loneliness, and the knowledge that my sacrifice had been for the best.

I had not counted on your father's persistence. Months after I thought he had forgotten me, he arrived at Petite Terre. Mr. Poe already knows how he met with Mother, how she finally told him the truth (though I believe she left out how innocently I was drawn into her plans), and how all the love he had felt for me and for you vanished in the scope of an hour's conversation when he slapped me and called me an abomination.

That last was, perhaps, the final blow of far too many. I

don't think I was sane for years afterward, for the only memories I have of my boys are when they were very young or nearly grown—far less memories than I have of our few short years together. By the time I returned, they looked to Madeline as their mother, their teacher, and in Sean's case at least, their priestess. I think they saw me as some sort of eccentric, distant relation, to be tolerated and ignored. I functioned in my own way, thanks to Mother's dubious aid, and as the years passed, my hold on reality increased until I was ready to challenge my mother for the sake of my children.

After he refused to marry a descendant of one of Roderick's bastard children, it was I who advised Elliot to leave Petite Terre for good. He tried, but as Uncle Roderick learned decades ago, Mother gets what she wants. The dreams brought him back, but in his rebelliousness, he did manage to win some concessions, agreeing to her compromise that he take over some land she owned in New York while she ran the plantation for him.

But his revolt was far from over. As part of their bargain, he was supposed to become your friend and confidant, to bring you to Petite Terre to be with the family. She undoubtedly wanted you to marry Sean and maintain those precious bloodlines, though her reason for this has never been clear. Instead, Elliot went against her dreams and wrote that he intended to marry you.

I don't know if he loved you so dearly, or only wanted to use you as a means of showing his independence. In any case, he was of age and Mother could not stop him. Of course, he underestimated her power.

Mother was more furious than I had ever seen her, but as quickly as it surfaced, it died. I thought her power would not extend as far as that little cabin, but then I learned how Elliot died.

Mother intended to travel north to see you through your pregnancy, but I convinced her that it would be better if I went instead. I made a promise—that I would bring you and the child back here—but once I saw you, I couldn't subject you to this place, though I didn't know what to do instead. She sensed the indecision in my letters and reminded me of my promise through my dreams. Still I held out, becoming more anxious with each passing night. Then, when you and Roddy both became ill, I knew she was taking her revenge on me, forcing me to do what she wanted. Thinking the child was the one she really desired, I left with Roddy deliberately making certain you did not know where we had gone.

You cannot imagine her rage when I returned here without you. She punished me in ways too painful to describe, then took steps to make certain you knew where to come to find the boy. You showed how resourceful you were, though. You managed to arrive early, but as I feared, all your wrath was directed at me.

Yes, she can be such a charming woman when it suits her—so full of honey that most people cannot see past it to the sting. You were different, though. You've decided to fight her. For that you have my respect, and my sympathy. Would that you could also have my support, but I am still too much a coward to do anything but, belatedly, tell the truth.

So believe me when I tell you one final thing—you have always had my love.

> Your mother,
> Anna Broussard Donaldson Montgomery

chapter 32

I folded the letter and put it in my pocket, then considered how the words had aroused so many emotions in me that, like poor manipulated Vivienne, I scarcely knew which one to trust.

So I sat and waited. As I expected, Vivienne could not stay away from me. She had to know what I thought of what she had written.

She came to me soon after a servant brought me a late lunch—an opulent meal formally presented on an ornate black lacquer tray. I'd just lifted the fresh gardenia that rested on my napkin when she stepped through the open door and stopped just inside it. Her head was cocked. The anxious smile I had misinterpreted and seen as mischievous still played on her lips. "Do you pity me?" she asked.

"A bit," I replied.

"Despise me for my weakness?"

"You could have shown more strength," I admitted. "But no, I don't despise you."

"Do you at least understand?"

Her voice broke at the last, and as I looked at her, I saw tears come to her eyes and roll down her cheeks. "I do understand," I said, and instinctively held out my arms.

She rushed into them. I pulled her down to sit on my lap,

where she sobbed like an overgrown child while I stroked her auburn hair.

It seems so odd to me that I who have always taken such comfort in the solace and understanding of women, should find myself in their role, first with the daughter, now with the mother. I rocked her back and forth, murmuring, "She'll understand, Anna. Now that she's been here and seen what sort of place this is, she'll have no choice but to understand."

Her sobs diminished to an occasional shudder. She played with a lock of my hair, a gesture that seemed either childlike or erotic, though there was no mistaking her intent when she nuzzled the side of my neck and kissed it. "I've loved you ever since the day that Sean brought me a copy of 'The Raven.' I read it and thought of my father and cried."

She stayed where she was for a time, then asked in the small voice a young child might use to his tutor or parent, "Do you really think she should know the truth?"

I nodded. "And if it's time for the truth, shouldn't you know all of it as well?"

"I do know it. I wrote all of it down for Pamela."

"That's only part of it. Your nervous condition wasn't caused by any hereditary weakness, but by the drugs your mother was given when Roderick tried to kill her."

Vivienne's sorrowful facade shattered with a cry of fury. She pulled away from my grasp and retreated to the door. "It isn't true! I was Adrien's daughter!" she screamed. "I have his name. My son even inherited his talent. Don't try to confuse me. Please, not you."

Though I half expected her to bolt again, I would not feed her delusions any longer. "It's in Madeline's white journal where she calls you a child of uncertain parentage," I said.

"She lies! Ooooh, she is so good at it!"

"No, Vivienne . . . Anna, believe me. In her journals I am certain that she does not lie. You have to find the first one, and though you think you know the story of your mother and uncle, read it. When you're finished, find the others and share them with me and your daughter before it's too late."

"What are you saying?"

"That Madeline intends to narrow the bloodlines further

still. I came here for Pamela. Last night I went looking for her. I found her, but she wasn't alone. Sean was in her bed. Do you think Madeline sent him there?"

"No. Mother wouldn't make him do that!"

"She wouldn't have to make him, Anna, not if you're right and he thinks of her as both priestess and mother."

She bit her lower lip. Her body trembled even more than before. She seemed ready to speak but could not find the words, so I continued. "You said it yourself, Anna. She is insane. But delusions have their own innate logic. We need to know the logic of hers."

With a look of terrible anguish, Vivienne ran out the door and down the hallway. I followed her as far as the door and watched her disappear into a room that had been locked the night before. When she did not reappear, I went to the window and flung open the drapes just in time to see her running across the oak-shaded lawn, past the kitchen, to a thick stand of trees on a rise beyond it.

She's going to find her mother and when she does, she'll confess everything that she's done, I thought. Whatever chance I had of gaining the poor woman's allegiance and freedom for Pamela and me had just ended.

Later that afternoon my worst suspicions were confirmed. I answered a soft knock on my door and found Pamela standing alone outside it. "Mr. Poe! I'd heard that you'd come to see me. Madeline said that you were ill and thought you should rest before we met. Would you like to join the two of us for tea in the parlor?"

She spoke naturally, with just a hint of embarrassment that I had traveled so far on her behalf. I wondered if she recalled anything of our conversation the night before, but she never gave me an opportunity to question her.

I followed her down the hall, to a pleasant little room where Madeline was waiting for us. We sat on floral-covered chairs in front of a bright north-facing window, drinking tea. Pamela spoke glowingly of the opportunities for her son, of her studies in Celtic lore with Madeline, of her desire to remain at Petite Terre. She hinted that she might even marry again. Her tone was polite and alert, with not a trace of the drugged confusion she'd shown the night before.

"I love her as much as I do my own," Madeline told me. "And Roddy, of course."

"I hear he is a charming child, one worth traveling across the country to find," I commented.

"Pamela has accepted my apology for my part in that unfortunate incident. I hope you will eventually be so understanding."

"If Pamela has forgiven you, that is enough," I replied. Under other, better, circumstances I would have meant the words.

When we were through, the women walked me back to my bedroom.

Then, just as Pamela was following Madeline out the door, she paused to take my hand. "Thank you so much for coming all this way out of concern for me," she said. "But as you can plainly see, I am quite well. I do hope that you'll stay a few days, though. I'd like to share something of what I've learned and see what you think of it."

As she said the last, she winked. I responded by dipping my hand into my pocket and passing Vivienne's letter to her. I admit that I felt a pang of sadness that I would not be able to witness her immediate reaction to Vivienne's confession, but my writer's inclination toward voyeurism has enough to be satisfied with in this house without having to witness that as well.

And so I spent the rest of my second day at Petite Terre updating this journal while I waited for either Pamela or Vivienne to appear once more. When no one came, I again stayed awake reading until the house was quiet, then attempted to leave the room as I had the night before. But now the dread feeling was stronger than my will, making it impossible for me even to touch the doorknob, let alone pass over its threshold.

Well, Pamela had been alerted to both the drugs and the ravishment. It was up to her to decide what she must do. I suspected that she could handle the matter well enough on her own.

Holding on to that optimistic thought, I changed into Elliot's nightshirt, opened the window to let in the cool night
air, and went to bed. I quickly drifted off into the kind of
dream that can so easily lead to insanity.

As always, it began innocuously, as if I were an ordinary
man with ordinary nightmares. Muddy and I were in the
cemetery in Fordham, where we buried our Virginia in another's vault for lack of money to purchase a resting place
for her. I stood beside the handful of mourners, the tattered
army cloak that had covered her through her last days heavy
across my shoulders. Too exhausted for tears, I listened as a
minister, a stranger who had never known my Sissy's sweet
uncomplaining nature, spoke words that brought me no comfort.

A cold, dry snow began to fall, the flakes swirling in the
air so that the vault, the minister, even the mourners closest
to me vanished in the frosty haze. I was alone with snow that
whirled in a vortex around me, the wind increasing as night
fell, a night so cold that I lost all feeling in my hands and
feet. I tried to speak, to pray, but my lips were frozen as well
and refused to obey my mind's command.

When the snow cleared, I saw that the location had
changed and I was in the secluded copse behind our little
cottage where Sissy and I had spent so many happy hours
when she was well enough to join me there. With what
strength I could manage, I lowered my body onto the little
stone ledge where she had so often sat and thought that of all
the women I have ever known, she alone had the gift of raising me out of the worst despondency with a sweet smile or a
cheerful word.

The tears I had not shed earlier welled in my eyes and
froze on my cheeks. If I was willing, I could remain in that
isolated spot, my lifeless body a frozen monument to her, my
soul and hers joined. I tried to shake my head, to deny that
thought, but even that simple gesture was impossible.

Yet, in spite of this, her spirit knew my intent and came to
me. I saw her standing before me, her body draped in the
white linen funeral clothes, delicately embroidered in the
days before her death. Though it was far too soon, and far

too cold for decay, in the vision decay had already claimed her. Her eyes were dull, fallen back into her skull. Her cheeks that had maintained some of their youthful fleshiness even in the last hours of life, were sunken and so thin and drawn that the cheekbones seemed sharp enough to cut through her skin. Only her tiny hands had become bloated, the fingertips darkened. She pointed at me, then opened her mouth as if to speak but no words came from her. As I tried to stand, or at least to hold up my arms and reach for her, her body began to fade from my sight, and I knew that even after death I had failed her.

Just before she vanished altogether, she ran her fingertips lightly over the side of my face. I wanted to pull away but fought the urge. This hideous glimpse into the future that waits for us all was nearly unbearable, but since the creature that conveyed it had once been my darling little wife, I would not recoil. I did not know the extent of Madeline Usher's power. This could be a genuine apparition, not another of my nightmares, and this spirit really the ghost of my Sissy. If so, I would not have her think that I was anything less than pleasantly astonished to see her.

Then she touched me again, and her hand seemed far warmer than my own cold cheeks. So the worst was true! I had died and she had come to claim my soul. "Not yet, Eddy, but soon," she whispered and was gone.

There is little sense of the passing of time in the dream world. Moments, minutes, hours flow by without notice. So when I woke, my heart pounding in an unsteady beat, my hands clenched into tight fists, at first I knew only that it was still night. Moonlight fell through the uncovered window remaking the carpet pattern into the silver and black stripes of light and prison bars. I'd started toward the window to gauge the time by the position of the moon, when I saw my wife again, standing now at the foot of the bed, her arms outstretched, ready to embrace me.

"How dare you!" I shouted to the one who ordered the dreadful vision. "How dare you manipulate her soul this way!"

Someone screamed, the sound growing louder as I surfaced to reality. I woke to total darkness, in bed with the sheets all tangled around me.

I heard voices in the hall, someone calling out my name.

In spite of how hard my heart was pounding, I rushed to the door, intending to fight my way past the portal as I had last night. Before I reached it, I heard the outside bolt slide into place, locking me in far more effectively than the witch's spell had done the previous night.

With no better choice left me, I allowed my overwrought body to resume its convulsive trembling. I fell slowly to the floor, then pressed the side of my head against the door and tried to hear some hints of what was going on outside.

It was Pamela's voice, I was certain of that even before she cried my name a second time. She was farther away now, probably near her room. I wanted to yell something back, though I doubted that she would be able to hear me. Besides, what good was there in doing so? Even if the door had been open, the dream and the fear it conveyed had sapped most of my strength.

I crawled back to the bed and lay there, too overwrought to sleep, fighting to recover my calm and the semblance of energy that calm would bring. The room seemed to whirl around me as the snowflakes had done in my dream. The memory of the storm pressed close as a lover once again. I heard the tinkle of my Sissy's girlish laughter, felt her hands holding mine, her lips brushing my cheek. In spite of the horrors that would undoubtedly follow, I smiled at the memory of her.

On the edge of true sleep a sharp crack of thunder jarred me awake. Lightning flickered beyond my closed curtains, the darkness between its flashes muted by approaching dawn. I heard a distant cry of rage, a ringing bell, then the bolt on my door sliding back.

I rushed to the door as quickly as I was able, but when I opened it, there was no one in the hall.

chapter 33

When Pamela woke the morning after Edgar's visit to her room, the memory of Sean's rape and that visit were all jumbled in her mind. She stayed in bed, cuddling Roddy in her arms and feeding him bits of biscuit from the tray that Abeille had brought her, trying to separate dream from reality with no success until Madeline came to talk to her.

Pamela immediately sensed the woman's nervousness, evident now in how controlled her voice sounded, and how overly kind. "You have a visitor," she said.

Reality, Pamela thought. "Visitor?" she asked.

"Mr. Edgar Poe has come to ascertain that you are well and happy here. I would think he was more than a little worried about you to have traveled so far given his condition."

"Is he ill?"

"Weak. Exhausted. The wisest thing we can do is let him stay a few days. If we put his mind at ease about your situation, then send him on his way with enough money to make his journey home as restful as possible, he'll make it to New York well enough."

Madeline didn't say what the unwise thing to do might be. She didn't have to.

So, sensing that the author's life was in the balance, Pamela played her role of contented mother as best she could. As she expected, Edgar realized the charade and followed her lead perfectly. He later slipped a letter to her only when certain the exchange would not be noted. After, she walked down the hall with Madeline. "Would you mind if I shared some of your books with Mr. Poe?" she asked when they stopped outside her room.

"I think he'd find them fascinating," Madeline replied. "His are the only fiction in Vivienne's lurid collection that I have taken the time to read. At first, I did so because of his story about my brother and me. Later, because I found him to be a believer in the old gods and their powers."

"A believer?"

"He sees the truth, child, and so he is one of us. He sees it deep within his soul, so instinctively that he would deny its existence because he cannot examine it with the logic that he pretends to love so well. Who else could speak of honeyed tresses changing to raven's black? Of lovers returning from the dead solely through strength of will? Of conversations with those long dead?"

"An overzealous imagination is not a sign of belief," Pamela countered.

"In his case, I think it is. We'll see who is right tomorrow."

Pamela hugged her. "Thank you," she said.

Madeline held her at arm's length, studying her face as she asked, "Have you given any further thought to Sean's proposal?"

Pamela held her gaze. "Often it's all I think of," she replied. "Now I'm going to the pool to bathe. Would you like to join me?"

As Pamela expected, Madeline declined.

Though Pamela would have preferred to wait until after dark to bathe, she did not want to risk reading the letter Edgar had given her anywhere else. The pool seemed to be the best place to take it, for she doubted that Harvey would be allowed to spy on her bath, and anyone who might join her would knock before entering. So, with her bare feet dangling in the cool water, Pamela opened the letter.

She scanned it once, quickly, then when no one came to rip it out of her hands, she read it again. By the time she had finished, her body was shaking with so many conflicting emotions, it would take days to sort them all out. But the greatest of these was fury . . . and rightfully so.

There should be some sort of repellent carried through the blood of siblings that would somehow have made it obvious to her and her mother that they and their lovers were related and any erotic element to their relationship a perversion. Instead, even now when she knew the truth about Sean, nothing had changed between them. She felt her body responding to the thought of kissing Sean again, of allowing her will to weaken from his touch.

The night before when Poe told her she'd just been bound and raped, she'd even smiled at the thought of what Sean had done, as if the two had just been discovered playing some wicked sexual game. When Edgar told her that she'd been drugged into compliance, she hadn't argued, but she knew he was not entirely right. There was more depth to her feelings for Sean than could ever be found in a drugged cup of tea, no matter how potent.

While she'd absorbed the contents of the books in Madeline's library, she'd learned a dozen love spells, each reputed to be stronger than the others. She'd skipped over them in her first reading, convinced that they held no more power than a gypsy's deck of cards. Now she was less certain of that.

She washed quickly, then with the robe tied loosely around her body, the letter thrust deep in its pocket, she returned to the house, joining Madeline in the library. "It's late, child. Aren't you tired?" Madeline asked.

The woman would have to see through her strained voice, her forced calm. 'I just want to study for a bit. I haven't been in here all day."

"Why not take a book or two to your room?" Madeline suggested, as if Pamela had any real choice and could return one book to exchange for another any time during the night that she wished.

In the same indirect manner Pamela said, "I'll concentrate better in here."

"Stay for just a little while. These halls always seem so frightening after dark," Madeline replied smoothly as if she weren't the cause of that fear.

Pamela paged through three of the books she'd read most recently, settling finally on the simplest and oldest of the spells, hopefully the right collection of words to uncross another's spell.

"The Lady Brigit is my protection, long may she reign and give me strength against my enemies," she thought to herself, accompanying the words with a complex gesture as the fear of the darkness, and the things she sensed moving through it, threatened to send her rushing to the safety of her room.

Yes, these spells worked, enough that hours later when she looked up and saw Sean standing in the doorway, she did not feel the usual thrill at the sight of him, the almost uncontrollable desire to forget how he had wronged her and run to him. "What is it?" she asked.

He missed the intentional chill in her tone. "It's nearly dawn. I saw the light. Are you going to stay awake all night?" he asked with a bit of surliness.

"If I choose to."

He moved behind her and began to rub her shoulders. Even now, she had to admit that the touch felt wonderful. "So tense you are. You need something to relax you." He kissed the side of her neck. She shuddered and pulled away, standing and placing the desk between them. "Please, Sean, I've already made my feelings for you clear."

"Have I committed some additional wrong that I am not even allowed to touch you?" he asked, frowning as he said the words.

Could he be as ignorant of their relationship as she had been? Saying one of Madeline's little invocations for luck, she decided on the truth: "Who do you think I am?"

He grinned. "The woman I want to marry and spend the rest of this life with."

"Because Madeline orders you to?"

"Ah, so that's it. I admit it was that way in the beginning, but then I realized so pleasantly that perhaps for the first time in the history of the Usher family, a family match was perfectly made."

"Did she put you under a spell, too? Did she make you love me?"

"After I met you, a spell was hardly necessary."

"Do you know that I am your sister?"

He only looked amused. "How else does the power stay pure?"

"Power! There's all this talk of power, yet you seem to possess little and poor Vivienne even less."

"But you do. Look at you now, managing to speak to me with such anger while you recite words in your mind to force us apart."

He moved before she could flee, grabbing her wrists and pinning them behind her, forcing her to kiss him. "Tell me it isn't pleasant even when you're not half asleep," he demanded.

"Of course it seems pleasant. She made it so."

"Only a little spell, one that was already almost gone when you consulted the book for a way to break it." He tried to kiss her again, his intent interrupted by the sound of thunder. She broke away from him and fled the room, running in the direction of Edgar's.

Sean caught her before she'd gone halfway. When she could not free herself, she screamed for help . . . to Poe, to the slaves, to the self-professed coward that was her mother. He let her go only long enough to bolt the door to Poe's room. She ran but did not even reach the foyer before Sean caught her, dragging her down the hallway to her room.

"Sean, you mustn't!" she begged.

"You don't understand. I have to give her what she wants."

Holding both her hands in one of his, he dragged her to the bed and pinned her down. He was not gentle about it, but then she was hardly cooperative. She only wished she'd worn her walking shoes instead of her slippers, so that her kicks would have caused greater pain. Instead, he appeared to ignore them, pulling off her robe, then cuffing her hands as he had on previous nights. He worked methodically and skillfully, checking the bonds after he'd finished to be certain he hadn't fastened them too tightly.

"What kind of a woman would want to see her granddaughter bound and raped?" Pamela demanded. "What kind of a woman would make slaves of her descendants? I'll hate you when you've done with me. I won't be able to help myself."

"Nor can I. Now since you can't stop the act, stop the little litany you're reciting in your mind and let me finish this," he responded.

She ignored him. He poured a cup of the drugged tea and forced the tepid liquid past her lips.

She spit it back in his face. "I'll hate you for this," she repeated.

"Not for long," he replied. "Madeline will see to that."

Exhausted by the struggle, she lay quietly. Thinking from her sudden pliancy that she was his slave once more—he unlaced the front of her chemise and, laying back the folds, began to stroke her body as gently as he had so many times before.

It was that consideration for her pleasure, her comfort in spite of everything else he'd done, that made her give up the fight.

Though she condemned her weakness, there was nothing she could do to prevent him for using her as he would. Better to let Madeline's spell, and Madeline's drug, and Sean's skillful hands turn rape into ravishment, helplessness into pleasure. So she followed Sean's suggestion. Immediately she felt her nipples harden from the lightest touch of his lips, her womb tighten with anticipation as he ran his hands down her body, her legs part willingly when he pressed against the inside of her thighs.

She had no idea how long she lay there, more helpless in her passion than she was from her bonds. "I love you," he murmured as he entered her. "The reason makes no difference. I love you."

She didn't reply. She didn't have to. He knew her response from the way her legs wrapped around his thighs, in the way her hips rose to meet his downward thrusts.

Had Roderick welcomed Madeline with the same sort of passion and loathing? Had she made certain of that as well?

Lightning flashed beyond the half-drawn draperies, followed by a crack of thunder so sharp and close that she and Sean cried out in the same moment as the intensity of the coming storm brought them both to climax. He rolled off her, but unlike the previous nights, he left the cuffs in place and began to touch her again. "Sean, I can't," she whispered with no real conviction.

"Ah, love, you can, for tonight is the night you conceive our daughter," he replied and kissed her. She felt her passion growing swiftly, as his grew, as the power of the storm increased. Rain beat against the draperies. Lightning struck close to the house, but she paid little notice to any of it, until she heard a distant, furious scream that broke her ordered passion.

And Sean's. "That was Madeline," he said. Pulling away from her, he ran to the draperies, throwing them back, looking beyond the lawn to the distant copse of massive oak trees where Madeline kept her private abode. Pamela saw his body, chalk-white in the bright flashes, no more than a shadow in the darkness between them. She heard the harsh clang of the plantation's fire bell, his cry of anger. "Sean, what is it?" she asked when he returned to her side.

"Madeline's house is on fire." He released her arms. "I have to go and help put it out. You see to Roddy."

"What can you do that the downpour and the slaves can't?" she asked.

"I can help her save her library. There's not a slave on the plantation that will voluntarily set foot in that house no matter what the threat." He held her for a moment, then pulled on his clothes and left her.

She forced herself to stagger to the window and watched him run across the lawn, his gait made staccato by the flashing sky. The trees whipped so fiercely in the deadly wind that she expected to see them uprooted. Instead, bolts of lightning began striking the tallest oaks, the cracks so deafening that she instinctively flinched and covered her face. When she looked again, she saw that a glowing haze seemed to hover over the lawn and that Sean had disappeared.

Oblivious to the danger, she put on her robe, lit a covered lamp, and went after him, racing across the slick grass toward the last place she had seen him. A thin hard rain, whipped by the wind, stung her face and bare arms, and the strange luminescence was all around her; both made it hard to see the ground until she stumbled over Sean's body.

She set down the lamp, and knelt beside him. He had no apparent damage. She decided that the blast had knocked him unconscious. She called his name as she shook him, but he did not respond. When she tried to lift him, his head fell sideways, revealing a burn on his left shoulder. Looking more closely, she noted others on his feet.

She began to cry—for the brother she had never known, for the lover she had lost, for herself because in spite of everything he'd done to her, she mourned him.

The rain subsided, and though the lightning continued, it was not as deadly as before. In the calm, Pamela heard footsteps on the path that led to Madeline's house. She looked up and saw Vivienne picking her way around the fallen limbs, a stack of books in her arms. A mad grin distorted her face, remaining as she looked at Pamela, shifting quickly to horror as she noticed her son. "Is he all right?" she asked.

"He's dead," Pamela replied. "She killed him."

Vivienne took a step backward, shaking her head. "No!" she said, and let the books fall from her arms. The spines of the older ones broke, their pages scattering in the wind.

As Pamela reached for her, Vivienne ran the way she had come, in the direction of the house where Madeline had stored her secrets.

"Vivienne!" Pamela called after her. "Mother!"

Pamela's use of the word *mother* had been deliberate, and the result was almost what she expected. Vivienne faced her again, her features softening for a moment. "Mother?" Vivienne said and paused long enough for Pamela to reach her.

"Yes. You still have a child, one who wants nothing more than to know you."

As Pamela reached for her, Vivienne backed away. "When you do know me, you'll hate me even more than before."

"Hate you? Why?"

"Because it wasn't her. It was never her! And there's more. Read it if you wish, after we are both gone. Now stand away from me, and let me end this life before I kill someone else I love."

"Now that I know you, I won't give you up," Pamela said and stayed close to her, not touching but ready to restrain Vivienne if she had to.

"So be it," Vivienne said. "You've been warned. At least your death won't be on my conscience." She raised her arms to the sky and began a chant in the same ancient language Madeline had used to bless Pamela only weeks before. The clouds thickened overhead. The lightning increased.

Pamela wanted to run and find Roddy, then keep on running, away from this terrible place, and the woman responsible for so much misery. Instead she backed up a few steps, then began to speak, yelling above the rising wind and downpour. "I do have a memory of you. I was wearing a green cotton dress trimmed in cream lace, made to match yours. We were sitting in the parlor and you were laughing at something I had done. Sometimes I dream of that laugh. It's all I have and that's not enough. Don't leave me. Please."

"Sean died. Elliot died. I won't see you and Roddy meet the same fate. I used her own witchcraft. Now I fear nothing, not even death." Vivienne turned and ran toward her mother's private abode.

Pamela thought of her son being raised only by Madeline, being trained in her deadly ancient arts. With her loyalty clear, she stayed where she was, turning her attention to the scattered books, on whose exposed pages the ink was already starting to run in the steady driving rain.

chapter 34

Throwing open the door had been an instinctive act. When I realized my mistake, it was too late. But the invisible creatures, real or imagined, that had guarded it for so many hours had departed, no doubt to the black pit from which they had come.

I moved quickly down the long hall to Pamela's room, not trying to listen for anyone following me—as if I could hear footsteps above the clamor of the storm. Then, as I approached her room, I heard Roddy's terrified screams.

Whatever hurt the family inflicted on Pamela, they at least had the mercy to make it seem pleasant. But only a beast would let a child shriek that way. I threw open her door, intending to beat Pamela's seducer senseless if need be in order to reach and comfort that child.

The room was empty, the outer doors flung open. The curtains which covered them were soaked and blowing inward from the force of the storm. I paid little mind to any of it, going to the nursery and lifting Roddy from his crib. Though I was a stranger to him, he clung to me. His screams subsided as I crooned to him and carried him to his mother's bedroom so I could stand at the window and look out at the lawn.

In the near darkness I saw what at first seemed another

ghostly apparition with outstretched arms and flowing robes. But as I squinted against the wind and rain, I realized that it was Pamela and that she was speaking to someone impossible for me to see from the angle of her window.

"I need to leave you for a little bit," I whispered to Roddy as I returned him to his crib. He began to cry but now that the storm had quieted, the terror that had aroused such fury in him had gone.

Keeping low to the ground, I ran across the soaked grass, slipping more than once but managing to keep my footing. When I reached Pamela, I saw that she was collecting pages of books that were strewn across the lawn. Sean lay nearby. I pulled her to her feet and held her in a brief comforting embrace. "Who was just here?" I asked.

"Vivienne. She means to kill herself."

"Suicide? Why?"

"This is her storm, not Madeline's. She told me that they were all her storms. I think she intends to make certain that this is her last."

"Take the books and go back to the house," I said. "I'm going after her."

"Then I will, too," she replied, and clutching the pages, she ran ahead of me, showing me the way.

I followed her through a thick stand of oaks, to the clearing where one corner of Madeline's house was still smoldering in the downpour. "She destroyed the library," Pamela said.

I was hardly surprised since so much of the misery in this family had come from those books and the beliefs they represented. We were near the front gate, where a pair of cypress statues holding aloft an arch of carved twined snakes guarded the entrance. I could hear distant shouts. I recognized Madeline's voice, and the deep soft male voices, undoubtedly of her slaves.

"Stay here," I said to Pamela and moved to the side of the house. The fire seemed to have been confined to a small wooden addition, leaving the larger stone-walled section intact. The roof still smoldered, giving off a dense smoke. A huge ebony-skinned man was ordering the other slaves forward toward the open window. Only one, a young girl, obeyed him, darting quickly through the broken window to carry out stacks of Madeline's most precious books—undoubtedly the ones Madeline would not risk losing should the fire flare up again. I could not see Madeline at all, but since the library was not on fire, she was most likely inside collecting the volumes the girl carried out. I saw no sign of Vivienne.

I hadn't been spied and did not wish to be, so I stayed close to the ground and began a slow retreat. I hadn't gone more than a few feet before I heard a soft cry of surprise. Turning, I saw Vivienne standing between me and her daughter. Her body was rigid and trembling, her eyes wide. As I walked toward her, I saw Pamela coming up behind. We both moved slowly, as if Vivienne were some wild creature who would bolt at human contact.

"You never should have come here," she said. "This house was built on lies. You've brought us the truth and destroyed it."

"Anna, please stop and think about what you're doing," I said and held out my arms.

This time she didn't rush into them. Instead, looking like the spectral figure of death itself, she pointed at me. "I've killed another of my children, Edgar Poe. You think about your own future before you stand between me and that devil disguised as my mother."

She walked toward me and began to chant, the words spoken with deliberate softness I think, so that I would not be able to make them out and set them down, as if I would dare to remember them and unleash such a power on the world. The acrid scent of ozone filled the air, and the charge to it made my skin tingle. "Anna! Stop it!" I ordered.

"Will you be the sacrifice that stands in the witch's place, Edgar Poe?" Vivienne screamed above the wind.

"Edgar, please!" Pamela called. "She means it. Let her go to Madeline and end this."

I looked incredulously at Pamela, then again at her mother. Vivienne's face was colorless. Her beautiful auburn hair, soaked with rain, lay in dank strings over her shoulders.

She stood only through whatever scraps of feeble will remained in her. I, who have often seen my own death approaching, who have often felt like welcoming its endless embrace, have never looked as full of despair as she did in that moment. Pity more than anything else made me do as the women asked. I stepped aside and let Vivienne pass, as did the slaves holding Madeline's precious books.

Vivienne stopped in front of the broken library window. "Mother!" she called.

Madeline stepped through it. "Idiot child! Haven't you destroyed enough today?" she said in a derisive tone.

"Sean is dead. He was coming to your aid and the storm killed him."

I could not see Madeline's face, but I heard her sudden cry of grief.

"It's over, Mother," Vivienne said and began that soft chanting. A believer now, I wasn't surprised when the rain fell with sudden vigor and the lightning increased. When Vivienne lifted her hands—one pointing at the sky, the second at her mother—a deafening volley of thunder made the slaves drop the books and scatter.

As I watched, in astonishment, in horror, the lightning began to coalesce and pulse above Vivienne's upraised arm. Bolts of it streaked out from that central source. The sound they made was deafening, and I was astonished that both women were able to stand so implacably beneath such a potent and terrible force. Like the poor slaves—undoubtedly less ignorant of the spectacle than I—I felt like running as fast and far as I could before the climax of this scene. Instead, some perfidious curiosity made me stay where I was and see the terrible confrontation to its tragic end.

Vivienne's chanting grew louder as the wind rose, ending with a high-pitched shriek to the sky. I saw the lightning fall, but it seemed to do her little harm at first. It appeared to pass through her and out her outstretched arm as if she were directing it toward her mother.

Just for a moment it seemed that Madeline decided that it was time to leave this life. Whether she had a sudden change of heart, or merely an instinctive reaction to her daughter's attack, was never clear. But as the lightning flew from Vivienne's hand, Madeline held out her hands, the gesture deflecting the bolt back toward her daughter.

The bolt hit, and this time it grounded. Vivienne's hair flared first in a glowing cloud around her face. Her clothes followed, and as they burned away they revealed emaciated limbs, long and white and already skeletal as if her nervous disease had devoured her flesh. No wonder, that in spite of her mature beauty, she had seemed no heavier than a child when she lay in the comforting embrace of my arms.

She stood a moment longer, as if the force that destroyed her also held her upright. Then she folded slowly to the ground. Her death seemed all the more terrible because, though the pain must have been unbearable, she never made a sound after that last shrill cry. Rather, the scream came from my lips, an instinctive reaction to the horror I witnessed.

The involuntary scream brought Pamela rushing to aid me. She threw her arms around me, comforting me at first until she saw the sight which had aroused such emotion in me. As she cried out in horror and grief, Madeline focused her attention on me.

"You brought this tragedy to us!" she screamed. "Now you will feel the pain you have caused. Let's see what's left of your precious sanity and lofty reason when I'm done with you, Edgar Poe!"

A word. A gesture. Darkness surrounded me, a darkness more profound because I could still feel Pamela's arms wrapped around me, the rain falling on my unturned face, the damp grass beneath my hands as I crouched, motionless, waiting for the next mental blow.

How had she known that I feared blindness more than anything? That I knew too well that in such permanent darkness, only demons and the visions of demons hold sway?

I heard her laughter, soundless and sinister deep within my mind, then for a time, nothing at all.

chapter 35

Later, when I was sane again, or nearly so, Pamela told me how I clung to her so tightly and pitifully that she had to fight to break away from me. With little strength of her own left, she stood and dragged my shivering body through the carved front gate into the great room of Madeline's private retreat.

The fire that had caused such destruction to the library had not burned through the thick stone wall or heavy oak door. Because of this, the air was breathable, though the scent of smoke seemed to permeate every stone.

Fire scent brought me fire dream.

. . . a terrible dream in which my own precious retreat, my little cottage at Fordham, was the victim. I'd been working in my second-floor study, my knees pressed against the warm chimney which abutted the opposite side of my narrow desk. One minute I felt a pleasant warmth, the next it seemed that my skin was on fire, my eyes blinded by a dense and acrid smoke.

I grabbed the pages I'd been writing and fought my way down the narrow stairs. In the front room I saw Muddy kneeling beside the shrouded body of Virginia, Muddy in her grief as heedless as my dead wife of the flames creeping toward them across the matting on the floor. As the flames touched them both, Muddy, like Vivienne, made not a sound.

But from the corpse laid out on a table between the windows came a shriek of such excruciating intensity that I could do nothing but stand unnerved by it. Virginia got up from the table, her white linen burial clothes flaring around her, as Vivienne's clothing had done, and pointed a spectral hand at me. "This is your doing," she said in a voice more stern and implacable than I had ever heard her use in life. "Now sit and see what you've done to us all."

I did as she asked, lowering my body into the rocker in the center of the rising, hungry flames. I felt the agony of their touch, but still I stayed as Muddy stayed, while they devoured what remained of my reason, my will. . . .

"Who did this thing? Who?" I mumbled, afraid to open my mouth to speak clearly lest I lose my ability to speak at all.

"Shhh," a woman whispered. "Edgar, everything will be all right."

And in truth, someone's arms did hold me, someone's breath on my cheek cooled the fire, while the voice continued to softly whisper my name.

Pamela told me that I began to twitch and jerk in frightful agitation. She said that it took every bit of her strength to keep me from jumping up and running off as the slaves had done, fleeing blindly into the swamps where I would be sucked into the mud or drowned in one of the murky ponds that dotted the land.

I remember none of this. My only memory is of her voice, her breath, her strong arms.

. . . The brilliance of the flames died slowly. When I was able to see again, I was standing in the garden behind a house in Albany where I spent so many of my happiest hours in the company of a man I admired, his wife whom I adored, and their children. What I sensed here was the peace, the comfort that has forever been denied me as if my critics were inexplicably correct and I already had one foot in hell. As I stood there, smiling at the tranquil scene (a woman I will not name even in these notes lest they fall into the hands of our enemies) stepped through the door. She carried an infant in her arms, a child whose face I could not see, whose hands moved weakly beneath the knitted blanket. I walked toward the woman, invisible

to her until I was close enough to touch them both. As I
reached for the infant, the woman gave a startled cry, dropped
the child, then fell forward herself. As I caught her, I stepped
on the helpless child. The tiny body broke apart under my
weight, crumbling into the powdery ash of one long dead. Only
the face remained . . . my face, as clear to me as in a reflection
until it, too, crumbled. . . .

"Lies! All lies!" I raved, repeating the words again and yet
again while someone held me.

. . . The little girls came and skipped around me. "Ulalume.
Ulalume. 'Tis the corpse of thy lost Ulalume!" they chanted in
a singsong voice, their golden curls and red hair ribbons bobbing in time to their music. . . .

"Lies!" I repeated. Yet, were they? In truth on so many of
the nights that I had found solace in this house, in the embrace
of that woman, I had been raving, unable to remember what
had transpired between us. Could she out of mercy have been
so generous, yet discreet enough never to confess even to me
what we had done?

As if I were deserving of her trust. As if I would have been
able to keep such a secret. "I wanted a child," I mumbled.

"Hush, Edgar. There's years enough for that," someone said.
Hair brushed my face. Lips touched my lips and for a time, a
blissful time, I sensed nothing at all save the pleasure of the reality—more unreal than the nightmares—of that caring human
contact.

"She's inside me," I whispered and felt her arms begin to
tremble.

So started a dark contrived night of phantasms culled first
from my past, then from my most lurid stories—of ravens
plucking out my eyes; of rats emerging from their stinking
holes to skitter across my bare chest, my motionless arms, my
laden legs useless save for their suddenly heightened sense of
touch.

These and the others like them were horrible, yes, but they
were designed to wear down my will and invade my past. I
could feel Madeline's mind in my own, seeking out and clutching at the greatest tragedies of my life. I tried to fight her, to
keep my mind empty of the past, but the memories were too

strong, the melancholy of them sifted through her into the most exquisitely pure horror.

. . . I knelt beside the grave of a woman I had loved more than the mother I had never known. As I thought of her, I saw the gravestone shift, the earth move in front of me, her hands claw their way through the lush grass. I wanted to flee but was as frozen to that spot as one of the dead, while the corpse fought its way from the grave. The death, so long ago, should have made her unrecognizable from decay, but she looked the same as she had in life. I waited for her to speak, but she said nothing, just as she had said nothing through the last days I had seen her.

I never learned how Jane died.

. . . I again saw my Virginia lying near the cold hearth in the front room of our cottage, my thick army coat and the hands that held hers so lovingly her only source of warmth. In life, she had never reproached me. In death, she was more honest, though no less kind. "A fire, my dearest," she suggested, a smile playing across her lips as if its flickering loveliness were the reason for the request rather than the terrible chill invading her weakened body. "Ah, Eddy, if you had only truly loved any of us," she whispered. . . .

"Make this stop!" I screamed and flailed my arms, an impotent attack on the creature ordering these waking nightmares.

I hit something solid in the strange darkness and felt someone holding me even tighter than before. "Can't breathe," I mumbled.

"It will be all right, Edgar," the woman repeated. She sounded less certain than before. The dreams came quicker now, often no more than a flip book of one terrible scene after another pulled from my now disjointed mind with nary a breath's break between them.

On the edge of consciousness I heard a low and terrible moan. I knew that it came from my throat, my breath, yet I could not feel myself making the sound. This is the ultimate insanity, I thought, the body alive and tormented by the soul already trapped in hell.

*   *   *

Through most of the following morning, Pamela listened to me rave. More than once she thought I was going to die. Finally hunger and a need to see what happened to her son became more important than my welfare. She waited until I had quieted somewhat, then left me lying on the cold stone floor.

The morning was quiet and bright, but evidence of dawn's destruction covered the land. On the way to the house she stepped over huge branches torn from the trees and made her way around a pair of ancient oaks that, rotted at their heart, were unable to stand against the fury of the storm. Even the fields, high with sugarcane the day before, were beaten down by the force of the wind.

The kitchen stove was cold, the larder nearly empty, stripped no doubt by the slaves who had fled the plantation along with their children.

The outside doors to her room were locked, so Pamela made her way to the front of the house, pausing in the foyer to listen. She heard nothing but the sounds of a breeze through the trees, the rustle of fallen, dying leaves. Until then she'd been frightened of meeting Madeline. Now her fear of the silence was deeper and far more terrible.

She ran down the hall to her room, and through it to the nursery. The crib was empty, the blankets gone. "Roddy!" she screamed, then desperate she called another name. "Madeline!"

No reply. Pamela searched the house and found no one. Guessing what had happened, she ran out to the barn. Cooley and the faster mount she'd ridden to St. Joe's were missing. Every other horse had been shot. Sean's dog stopped lapping at a bloody puddle on the floor and bounded over to her, nuzzling her hand. She backed away from him in horror and surveyed the scene one final time before running through the ravaged trees to the stone shelter where I lay, still blind, still trembling, still trapped in my past.

"Edgar!" I heard her scream. She began shaking me. I could feel that well enough, as I did the sunlight warm on my body, but though my eyes were open, I could not see.

I reached for her, clutching at air, then at her dress. She held me again, brushing the damp hair off my forehead. "She's taken Roddy away with her, Edgar. Everyone's gone."

"She's here," I said with growing horror at what her absence meant. "She has to be here."

"Are you certain? Try to feel her inside you."

Though the thought of actually seeking out my tormentor unnerved me, I tried to feel her presence inside my mind and detected nothing at all.

"Then she's gone," Pamela said after I told her.

The trembling that had subsided at Pamela's touch increased. As I considered the dark future that lay before me, I heard her whispering in a language I had never encountered before. The sable curtain that had descended on me began to thin, enough that I could make out light and shadow. Nothing more, but it gave me hope that one day I might recover completely.

"Edgar, I believe that you possess the strength to end this. Try."

I did as she asked, but the harder I fought to see, the less vision I seemed to have. The hysteria that I had managed to control threatened to surface again. "I can't," I said.

We sat in silence for a time, her breathing becoming deeper, calmer. Finally she helped me to my feet. "Edgar, this is Madeline's retreat," she said. "The room has an altar at the far end of it. I am going to leave you standing in front of it. When you hear the outside doors close, step forward and pick up a smooth wooden box. Open it. What will follow will be worse than any of Madeline's visions, I think, but it will pass and, I hope, take your blindness with it."

"What is it?" I asked.

"I don't know," she replied. "Just remember—what transpires will pass."

We took a few steps forward, then she left me. "Listen for the doors," she repeated and was gone. As they shut behind her, my blindness became complete.

What could be worse than what I had gone through? I considered this as I held out my hands, groping on the carved wooden table until I felt the smooth edges of the box. Something worse than those nightmares was likely to kill me, but death was preferable to this. With that far from comforting thought uppermost in my mind, I lifted the lid.

For the first time in my life, words fail me. The force of the mental assault that struck me was stronger than any physical blow. The box fell from my hand as creatures I cannot describe roared into me. I screamed and kept on screaming until what strength I had for breath left me and I fell, sobbing, to the cold stone floor. With my will vanquished, they tore at my soul with all the ravenous ardor that a pack of starving wolves would have shown to my helpless body.

My fear nourished them! Though I'd assumed that what was to come could not be more intense than what had already been, as they fed they found the strength and the means to make it grow. My heart raced at an impossible beat, then fell into the impotent, deadly flutter I knew too well.

As I lost consciousness, I found more than a little irony in the cause of my incipient death.

But of course, I survived to write these words. I don't know precisely what saved me. Perhaps it was my very weakness, my sudden loss of consciousness which made the creatures from the box lose interest in me as my body calmed. Perhaps the fear Madeline had already aroused, had sated them quickly. Perhaps, and I like to believe this more than any, it was my will, for as I believed my life to be ending, I saw Madeline's face, scornful and triumphant. It was a vision, an ironic kiss of hope that resided in that perfidious polished box, but it was enough to rouse my anger and the truculent determination that has seen me through the worst setbacks of my life.

No, I did not die.

It seemed that I lay there for days before the doors opened and a shaft of brilliant afternoon sunlight sliced through the center of the room. I woke and looked through my tears at the space that Madeline had claimed for her own, at the pictures, the tapestries. Last, I studied the magnificently carved altar where the box sat closed and waiting to tempt another victim.

"Edgar, how do you feel?" Pamela asked.

I got to my feet. I ran my hands over the carved snakes edging the altar. I fingered the tapestry. I saw it all with a sense of wonder, of awe, and yes, of belief.

She repeated the question twice more before I thought of an answer.

"Cleansed," I replied.

chapter 36

Without horses, or any idea which way Madeline had gone, Pamela and I could never catch up to her. We therefore decided to remain at the house until morning, using the time for rest—as if sleep were possible after what we'd both been through!—and to glean what we were able from what could still be read in Madeline's journals.

While Pamela went to find us something to eat, I carried the sodden books to the library in the main house and carefully separated the pages. Of the four, the journal that Pamela had already read was almost entirely intact, possibly because of the type of ink used, or because it had been set down so many years ago that the ink had merged with the paper.

The most recent of the books had been started when Roddy arrived here. It had been in the center of a stack and so had received some protection. It also had only a handful of its pages filled, so there had been far less ink to run. Because of this, it also had nearly all of its pages intact. Since this was the one that concerned Pamela most directly, I decided to wait until she returned so we could read it together. In the meantime, I carefully blotted it and set it open on the sunny window ledge to dry. In the two remaining journals, only a few pages from each were completely readable, and the other isolated paragraphs gave little information out of context.

Fortunately, what I could make out seemed less the revelations of an admitted witch than the infrequent and far more mundane day-to-day journaling of a contented mother and wife. Madeline discussed friends of the family, Vivienne's childhood illnesses. I saw a reference to the child's fear of storms—little wonder, I suppose. And then, this interesting revelation:

. . . and though she was not much hurt from the fall, the storms came again last night. I fixed her a cup of chamomile and catnip tea. After she drank it, Adrien sat with her, holding her hand until she returned to sleep. He is so much more patient with these bursts of ill temper and the result of them than I am, just as he is so much more inclined to forgive her backwardness. I vow to be like him if only because there is nothing I can do to change her nature. Perhaps he is right and someday we can train her to control this terrible power.

Perhaps not, I thought. Perhaps someday the storms she'd learned to summon while still in the womb would be strong enough to kill. I scanned further. There was more on Vivienne's nervous condition, concern about it uppermost in Madeline's mind. I also saw occasional mentions of her business dealings, two references to Mr. Grymes, and frequent observations about her husband, whose virtues she, like any good wife, seemed to extol overly much.

I'd just started deciphering another page when Pamela returned. She'd managed to find us some day-old bread, a bit of smoked ham, and a jar of honey. She'd also recalled my habits and brewed pots of both coffee and tea.

"And I found these," she said and handed me little packets of herbs each labeled with someone's name. There were blends for every family member, as well as some of the slaves and Pamela. One even had my name. I looked down at it, wondering if it was the treatment Madeline had mentioned or merely another form of torture. Someday I might brew a pot and try to determine exactly what it contained. Now, with more pressing concerns, I slipped it into my pocket.

"I just started reading a section of some interest," I said.

She laid the dinner tray within reach, poured us both coffee, then pulled a chair beside me. With her looking over my shoulder, I read the words about Vivienne aloud, then continued in a new section some pages later. . . .

. . . everything I have used to try to calm her, the attacks grow stronger. She is not rational then. Often she does not even recognize me. It's grief, I suppose, and natural, but I am so frightened for her.

I have decided to try one more treatment, one I use on myself when the nightmares of my past grow too strong and threaten my own sanity. Today, while Adrien is gone, I will say the words to seal her room, then I will set Grandfather's little box on the table beside her bed. She will open it—indeed, she will have no choice, for the alluring spell on it is too strong for a child to resist—and I hope the creatures inside will devour her fears and let her face the future with some semblance of peace.

I wish I knew more about the creatures. Grandfather often hinted that they are some sort of bodiless sprites, creatures who prefer darkness and the company of one another, so once collected are easy to control.

I used to view them more romantically—thinking them like the djinnis in the magic lamps of Arab sultans. When I was a girl just beginning to learn from my grandfather, I disobeyed him, crept into the cupboard where he kept the box, closed the door, and pulled off the lid. My screams brought Grandfather running, but because the room was not sealed he was not able to let me out. Instead he stood outside the cupboard door and in a commanding tone told me to yield to the terror as I would to laughter or tears, to give it to the creatures who demanded it. I tried, and as my screams subsided, I felt a most incredible absence of fear.

I pray that Vivienne will feel the same when she is done, but I also fear that their voracious strength may permanently

harm a girl as sensitive as she. Tomorrow when she wakes,
I'll see how she behaves and decide.

The narrative ended abruptly halfway down the page and
continued at the top of the next.

Morning.
All night I listened to her screams, audible even above the
claps of thunder from one of her storms. They stopped just
before dawn. I went into her room. She was sleeping soundly
for the first time in months. As I reached for the box, I
paused to study her face, to marvel at how beautiful she is
with her delicate features and auburn hair.

The second page ended. The next few were indecipherable,
the occasional readable section of little interest, save that
they revealed that Vivienne would have been about six years
old when the last words were written.

"She gave her daughter to those things?" Pamela asked.

"Apparently, she also used them on herself to some benefit just as you instinctively did on me." I turned the pages
and found another reference to Vivienne's strange treatment
some months later. "Vivienne may have needed it," I added.

Pamela considered this. "I still feel its effects, a sense of
calm most unlike my usual self. Vivienne may have let those
things cleanse her just before she came north to find me.
That would explain why she seemed so calm at first and why
the Stelleys said she was hysterical by the time she returned
here." She paused, added, "Poor creature."

I saw her wipe away a tear, but she didn't cry. I expected
that. Now that we had a new difficulty to overcome, she
would force herself to be strong. I rested a hand over hers
and began slowly to turn the ruined pages, searching for another legible entry.

"How much of this do you think Vivienne read?" Pamela
asked.

"Enough to lose all hope," I said. "Enough that she would
fear ever becoming close to you or to Roddy, lest a sudden
fit of temper end your lives, too."

Pamela covered her face with her hands. "God bless you, Mother," she whispered.

I found only a few more readable entries in that journal, even less in the third. While I'd hoped to learn more about Elliot's rebellious nature and Pamela's marriage to him, the entries yielded no useful information. We turned our attention to the last book that had been drying in the sun. I will ignore the frequent consultations between us over an occasional illegible word and set down the account as we believe it was written.

chapter 37

June 28, 1849. Vivienne returned home this morning, holding my great-grandson too tightly in her arms. The poor child had been wrapped in so many blankets, one would think Vivienne was trying to get him through one of those fierce northern winters. I could feel the heat of Roderick's fever as I unwrapped him. He had a rash over most of his body, and fever blisters on his lips. "How could you travel with him this way?" I asked Vivienne, trying to control my temper by reminding myself that slaves and servants have always cared for her children so that she had no concept of how to treat the boy.

She told me that she had no choice. "Pamela will never come here except to retrieve her son. She despises me. Were I to tell the truth about myself, she would hate me as well. She'll follow, though. I made sure of it."

I didn't know if she was right, but it was clear that if I didn't deal with the child's fever quickly, I would likely lose him and that would be a far worse tragedy. So I carried him to the pool and bathed him in the cool water. This set him to shivering, but I was prepared for that with a thin cotton blanket and some drops to bring down the fever. While I labored to restore his health, Vivienne worked with Abeille to set up a nursery in the little room adjacent to hers. By the

*time I returned to the house with my precious burden, the
room was ready. Vivienne calmed considerably when she
learned that the infant's fever was markedly diminished. I
laid him in the bed, then paused to study him closely for the
first time. "It is my Roderick come back to me," I said, kissing his cheek, then Vivienne's. I led her into her room and
made her sit beside me on the bed. "Now tell me everything
that happened," I said.*

*She spoke of a bond that immediately formed between her
and Pamela and how her own growing nervousness made it
weaken. This in turn made her more anxious, creating a spi-
ral that moved them even further apart. She spoke of the
strange illness that struck mother and child—an illness that
after so many years of watching my daughter's unwitting use
of her power, I cannot help but believe came from within her.
"When I had to go into town alone with Roddy, I understood
that the fever gave me the chance to bring him here," she
said.*

"And Pamela will follow?"

*"If she survives, she will. She was far more ill than the
boy. Unfortunately I don't have your gifts. I could do nothing." She described the message and money she had left with
the hired help.*

*I have never trusted French Canadians, not because they
are more dishonest than the rest of us, but because politics
and war have left them poor and so more easily tempted. The
money Vivienne left with Charles Boutte would have seemed
like a fortune to him, and from what Vivienne said about
him, he had little loyalty to Pamela.*

*That afternoon I sent my soul to the house I had given my
grandson. Pamela was gone, but the Bouttes had returned.
From their actions I knew that they had stolen the money and
thrown away the note.*

*How dare they gloat over what they had done! How dare
the woman go through even Pamela's clothing, the intimate
garments she'd worn for my grandson! I let my rage grow. I
let the storm grow. I killed them both, and I am no more contrite about my deed than they were about theirs, less so since*

Charles Boutte had actually been surprised not to see Pamela's body rotting in the bed.

June 30. My soul returned to the cottage again. This time there was a young woman there—an adept, I was surprised to discover—who had helped send Pamela on her way south. This was what I had hoped to discover. I've begun making plans for her arrival.

The narrative broke off, resuming on the following page.

July 10. Two nights ago, Pamela arrived. As I held the lamp up to get a good look at her face, I had the feeling that I was looking at a ghost, and that the ghost was of a woman I had never known—my own mother. Mother was always the recluse. There are no daguerreotypes of her, no paintings, nor even any sketches, yet Roderick told me often that our eyes were the same strange color, our figures similar, our hair the same rich shade of reddish brown.

"I should have known!" Pamela exclaimed. "I should have looked at her face and seen the truth of our relationship in the color of her eyes if no where else!"

"You were hardly in a position to be logical," I responded and began to read again.

As she stood in the foyer, exhausted by her journey, I could feel her hatred for me and I rejoiced. By coming here on her own, she's also revealed a marvelous protective instinct for her child, and when they were reunited, the relationship between her and Roddy was delightful to see. What a perfect mother she will be, and what an ideal wife for Sean!

Ah, she makes my decision so easy!

"Decision?" I asked, then glanced at Pamela. Her hands were folded as if in prayer, but the knuckles were white, her expression one of controlled hysteria.

She stood and walked to the window, looking out at the ruined trees. "Please finish," she said.

I did as she asked, my confusion changing to urgency as I began to understand what she feared.

July 25. After nearly three weeks here, Pamela has settled into the contemplative rhythm I'd hoped to see. She reads voraciously and retains so much. Her questions reveal that she is hardly a believer (yet), but she shows respect for our beliefs and a willingness to learn some of the simple rituals, and though this is merely intellectual curiosity, I find her attitude encouraging. Sometimes we study together. On the night of the full moon I showed her how to make and consecrate a scrying box for divination and to help her ride the wind. I told her how to hunt for a spot for her altar, a place where she can feel her own sacred link to the earth. She decided on flatrock spring—a place the slaves had determined possessed real power even before I discovered it. It was a choice which hardly surprised me after she described the potent dream she'd had there. She sometimes goes there in late afternoon and takes the little box with her, staring into its convex crystal. She has no success, and I doubt that she will until she truly believes. Then her power may be stronger even than my own.

When she truly dreams, it is often of the stories I've told her or others that she's read. When she wakes, I feel her sense of wonder, as if she had not been dreaming at all, but had found herself in another, better reality.

Best of all, Pamela seems to truly love Sean. After so short a time here, she is already welcoming him, almost willingly, into her arms. I've already begun to weaken the spell on her with no change in her ardor. Sean is enamored with her as well. Sometimes my soul watches them together. Sometimes it moves into her while she is so absorbed in her lover's caresses that she cannot feel my presence. I think of Roderick then and how passionately we loved.

Soon. Soon one life will end and another begin.

I grow weary of waiting. Fortunately, I have the means to make certain that Pamela conceives quickly. And she is so dependable, never forgetting to drink the tea that restored her completely to health. I doubt she'll notice the change in taste, it's so strong already.

I paused and looked at Pamela, standing with her back to me. She said nothing, but I could hear a deep indrawn breath. As she fought for calm, I went on.

August 2. Judith died last night following one of those sudden fevers she always seemed to acquire in late summer. She died clutching her prayer book and crucifix. There is no minister to perform a service, and she would not want me to say any words over her. So we laid her in the family crypt without any service.

I doubt that she will be mourned by anyone except by Selma, who sat beside her mistress's bed, holding her hand and crying more than enough tears for an entire wake. Her sorrow did not surprise me, but her honesty at showing it did. Not wishing to anger the dead, I followed Judith's last request and gave Selma her freedom and enough money to live the rest of her days in comfort. May she make the best of them.

After we interred Judith, I stood in front of her house. I seemed to see it for the first time. Something in its seclusion, its despairing disrepair reminded me of my own ruined home. We both live with ghosts, I thought, then in a sudden burst of uncontrollable fury I gave Sean the torch and told him to burn the house. I did not expect the rotted wood to catch so quickly, but it flared immediately, the fire spreading even to the trees surrounding it.

Goodbye, Judith. May your bitterness remain in the grave when you are reborn.

As I was leaving the fire, Pamela came running up, demanding to know what had happened. I told her the truth, and I think she accepted it, but it has raised more questions about us. I know that she will shake off her lethargy now, and then seek the answers. I shall begin to lay them out for her, slowly, to give her time to absorb the strangeness of each of them.

*   *   *

August 5. Pamela found the courage to enter my little house in search of the journals. I realized that she had gone there when she opened the box Grandfather had used to protect his altar. I heard her terrified screams in my mind and went to rescue her. I expected to find her unconscious on the floor in front of my altar. Instead, the girl was rummaging around in my library and actually had the cheek to try to fake interest in some of my more ordinary books. I find her recovery fascinating. It indicates that behind the insecure exterior is a true survivor, and the potential for real power. Someday she will recognize her talents for what they are.

Yes, Elliot found the perfect match for his disposition. Pity, he wasn't the husband I had chosen for the girl.

After I'd gone, she found the journal I had left for her and read it. In spite of what the Christian world would call our abomination, I felt no revulsion in her. That afternoon I sensed little change in our relationship. If anything, in the hour we spent together, it seems closer than ever.

Someone raised her to be tolerant. I doubt it was Will with his Christian prejudices. While I can, I should write the headmistress of that northern school and thank her.

August 7. In a single day's time every plan I had made for a happier future has come undone.

My problems began innocently enough two night's ago. I'd paused in the shadows outside Pamela's room and saw her writing something. I immediately went to my own room, hung the white knotted rope on the doorknob as a sign that I did not wish to be disturbed, and sent my soul into her room. As I'd hoped, she was writing letters to friends. They were innocuous enough, and I sense no fear in them. The only thing that struck me as odd was that one of them was to Edgar Poe, whose story of my family had so unnerved me when I read it a few years ago. I reminded myself that New England is a small area and that Pamela is a well-schooled woman, so their knowing each other was hardly surprising.

Later, because I knew how much Vivienne enjoyed the man's horrific works, I mentioned the letter to her. She became excited—with delight I thought. I should have paid

*closer attention to what really aroused her—the incredible
fear that Pamela might stop and speak with Lacey Stelley
and somehow learn the truth about their relationship, as if
the woman had ever discovered anything of real importance.*

Pamela left before breakfast and headed for St. James to
post what she'd written last night. She didn't say where she
was going, and I didn't ask. I suppose that was a test of us,
too, one I would not have us fail. I went about my work as
usual, hardly noticing that Vivienne was absent for both
breakfast and lunch.

It was Sean who alerted me to what she had done, running
into the library. "It's Mother," he said. He didn't have to
say anything more. He rarely calls her Mother in my presence save in times of crisis. I followed him to Vivienne's
room and saw her lying on her bed, her eyes open, sightless.
But she was hardly dead or unconscious, because a soft
whimper came from her lips, as if she were caught in a
nightmare so strong that she was afraid to scream. I've seen
these fits before, and I knew what to do. I shook her, and
when I got no response, I slapped her. Still she lay limp in
my arms, that near-silent whimper of hysteria filling me with
fear.

I'd already noted the storm clouds gathering on the eastern horizon, so I didn't have to guess where her mind had
gone. "Sean, saddle a horse and ride to the Stelleys. If
Pamela is there, escort her home," I said.

He did as I asked while I sat beside Vivienne. For the first
time in my life, I was too frightened of her power to force her
back to me. And I thought of all the grief sudden storms have
caused our family, and how I had never admitted until now
that Vivienne may have been at the root of many of them.

I sat silently, holding her until she blinked and focused her
eyes on my face. As soon as she saw me there, she pulled
away from me, retreating into the corner, wrapping her arms
around her knees and watching me warily.

"What have you done?" I asked.

She looked confused, honestly so.

"You were crying out in your sleep," I said.

"I had a nightmare. About the Stelleys and Pamela."

I nodded and said nothing. She is still so much a child—my child—and I cannot bear to see her suffer.

Fortunately, our conversation was interrupted by Sean and Pamela. I could hear them arguing on the path that linked the house with the barn and went to her room to meet them.

Whatever hopes I'd had for her total acceptance of our family has been ruined by Vivienne's act. Pamela knew the storm had been summoned, but logically enough decided that it had come from me. I let her believe what she would. I let her rave on about leaving, then told her quite simply that it was impossible and that she might as well accept the hospitality we would not allow her to refuse. She was a strong enough person to find my honesty comforting. I left her with Harvey standing guard outside and one of my strongest spells keeping her locked in her room.

Sean's relationship with Pamela is a more troublesome matter. She refuses to speak to him, let alone allow him to touch her. I'm sure that her anger will subside in time, but meanwhile there is the matter of the child she must conceive. Her body is ripe for it and that leaves me no choice. Tonight I will make certain that she drinks her tea, then I will force her to dream of Elliot once more, to keep on dreaming of him while Sean is in her arms. . . .

August 9. As I expected, Sean did not relish the idea of playing the role of his brother's ghost to his drugged lover. I told him that it was only for a little while, and that after she is with child and I am gone, she will have no choice but to focus all her anger on me and forgive him.

For the first time in his life, I saw past his affection to how much he truly fears me. "Just do as I tell you," I said. "Blame me, but do it. Then I'll be out of your life and you can do as you please."

"I don't wish you dead," he replied. He even believed that he meant the words, for I know how much he cares for me. . . .

*   *   *

*August 10. Last night, after a few sleepless hours, Pamela fi-
nally drank the tea I left for her and soon fell into a deep
drug-induced sleep. She dreamed of Elliot—I made certain
of that—and kept on dreaming of him while Sean lay with
her. But at the end, when her arms wrapped around a body
that was warm and solid, she woke, recognized Sean, and
tried to push him away.*

*I forced her back to the dream. I stayed with her until
Sean had finished and left her. I stayed with her even then,
dreaming of her life in New York, sharing all the sadness of
her losses.*

*I woke in tears. Nothing moves me like her memories.
Tonight, I will make certain that her desire and her confusion are both heightened. I do not ever want to have to stay
inside her mind for so long again.*

*This morning Pamela seemed calm. She spent the day in
the library, reading one book after another with the same
sort of urgency I displayed while the water pressed close
around my first home. This gives me hope that she may one
day accept my reason for keeping her here.*

*August 15. In the last few nights I've found the proper mix of
herbs and drugs—and, I confess, restraints—to convince
Pamela that her lover exists only in her dreams. Her ardor is
so strong that Sean is half-convinced that she is on to us, and
playing along with our charade because she desires him.*

By the time I'd finished, Pamela was crying softly. "It
wasn't your fault. There's comfort in that," I said.

"I wasn't thinking of me, Edgar. I was thinking of Sean
and how easily she destroyed his soul. Do you think he is
damned for what he did to me?"

"You told me once that you weren't a believer," I reminded her.

"This place has made me one. Now please finish."

I read on, skipping nothing, though I am certain that
Madeline's detailed account was not pleasant to hear. Then, I
saw my name for the first time.

*   *   *

*September 3. Today Pamela's letters brought her first visi-
tor, the one I had least expected to see—Edgar Poe. He wore
a brown cotton shirt and trousers and an old straw hat, all of
which made him look like a middle-aged Cajun of little
means. But as soon as I looked into those intelligent gray
eyes and heard his melodic voice with its pleasant Virginia
accent, I knew who had come to call.*

*But he is ill . . . his face so puffy, his complexion so sallow,
his pulse so uneven and weak. I could almost rejoice in his
illness because his untimely demise would make it far less
likely that he will cause trouble for my family. Yet I cannot
help but think of him as a kindred spirit, and as such I will
mix something to help him.*

*Since Vivienne killed Blaine Stelley, she has been in a
state of nervous exhaustion. Sometimes a stern word can restore some sense of balance to her, but not when she is so
overwrought. Knowing the danger that her condition poses,
I've been sitting with her at night, holding her hand until she
sleeps, sleeping beside her in case she wakes, which she
often does. Tonight she seems much better, but I feel my actual age and more. I sent Sean to Pamela, gave Vivienne a
tea to calm her nerves, then took my usual precautions to
make certain that our visitor and Pamela both remain in
their rooms. Tonight I will get the sleep I need so that I am
ready to face what comes tomorrow.*

*September 4. This morning when I told Pamela about her
visitor, she seemed surprised that he came so far for her. I'm
not, if only because I've always expected that our paths
would one day cross. After his terrible tale was printed, I
even rehearsed what I would say to him to make him understand the hurt he caused me. But he diffused all my anger
with an apology so swift and sincere that I cannot help but
believe it. Hopefully, Pamela will be sensible about her future and say nothing to alarm him, so that I will not be
forced to do him harm.*

*We—Pamela, myself, and Edgar Poe—met together for
the first time late this afternoon. Pamela appeared charming
and quite at ease, and I could see that by the end the poor*

man felt a bit embarrassed for coming so far without an invitation or any reason to be concerned about her.

Sean is keeping his distance from Poe (out of jealousy, I think) while poor Vivienne has positioned herself on the lawn outside his window, adoring him from afar because she is too shy to approach him. The emotional turmoil makes her seem so young, so innocent. Her excitement makes me consider what sort of match he'd make for her. Dreamers both of them, not quite of this world. From what I've read of him, Poe has not led an easy life. I wonder what sort of work he would produce if he could remain in the comfort of our little retreat.

Now Mr. Grymes would say that I am thinking even more like a recluse—picking brides for my children from wanderers on the road.

chapter 38

"*That's all,*" I said, and laid the book on the table. I felt an incredible weariness, not unlike Madeline's own despair with life.

"But there must be more," Pamela said, echoing my thoughts. For a moment we were both silent, overcome by the woman's desperate madness. Then Pamela went to the desk and began opening drawers, seeking some scrap of paper to give her some directions as to where Madeline might have gone.

"Which room was hers?" I asked.

"On the opposite end of the hall, on the right next to Sean's.'

While she searched the library, I went there. I'd expected a challenge, some artfully concealed scrap of paper, but instead her writing box sat on the bedside table, and inside it an envelope addressed to Pamela.

After I gave it to Pamela, she held it a moment, handed it back. "Please," she said.

I opened it. I read.

Dear Pamela,
    What little remains of the Usher family is almost com-

pletely destroyed, and for this my overconfidence is much to blame. Had I known all the work Edgar Poe had done to unearth your past, I would have locked him in his room instead of assuming that my spell would be enough to keep him safely away from you. Instead you met, you exchanged information, and that information has cost two lives.

I spent last night in my retreat, reading until late, then sleeping on the sofa in the little room on the second floor. I woke sometime before dawn with a painful sense of uneasiness. I lay there for a moment with my eyes shut trying to find the source of my disquiet, realizing finally that I wasn't alone.

No slave would dare to enter that house. You should have been in Sean's arms. Vivienne has never set foot in that house except for the few times I dragged her, half-hysterical, into the main room. That left only one.

Poe! I thought and ran down the curving staircase to the main room, where Vivienne lay in front of my altar, the closed box on the floor beside her.

She had never touched that box willingly before. I dragged her from the room into the library and saw my journals on the table. When she opened her eyes, they focused on me, first in surprise, then in hate.

"When Father died, you told me it was an accident," she began.

"It was."

"He died in a flood caused by a storm."

"So did a half dozen other people," I replied.

"And why? Because he didn't compliment me on a dress or a change of hair style? For what foolish reason did he die, Mother?"

"There was a storm," I said. "I'm telling the truth. You were not angry with him that night. You had nothing to do with his death."

"And Elliot?"

"Do you think your power goes so far?" As I spoke the

words, I heard a distant roll of thunder but dismissed it. Storms come up so quickly in this area, and if it were caused by her, I'd be able to deal with it, just as I always have.

"I'll never be certain, will I?" she said.

Anger kept me from telling her the truth. I also thought that guilt might make her more pliable. In that I was wrong. She gathered the journals up and walked toward the open window. "Where are you going?" I asked.

"To save my soul," she replied, with all the melodrama I've come to expect from her.

I went after her, but before I could grab her arm, I saw the storm's full force gathering over my retreat, felt the charge just before the lightning struck. I covered my face. When I looked up, Vivienne was gone and the ceiling of the library had begun to smolder.

You and your poet know the rest. Now my hope for rebirth with Roderick is nearly ended.

Yet there is one course open to me. There is an old Celtic saying that those who die together return together. And those who die young return swiftly. I am sorry. This must be.

Madeline

If ever there was a moment when I expected Pamela to break down completely, it was then. Instead, she only whispered, "We lost half a day, but at least we know where she's gone—back to her old home." She opened Madeline's earliest journal, finding what she sought on the first page. " 'Some twenty miles southwest of New Orleans,' " she read. "Madeline told me that a woman with power can always find her child. She insists that I possess that power. Edgar, I finally believe her and I'm going to use it to find both of them."

Without Madeline's powerful controlling presence the isolated plantation did not seem peaceful any longer. I thought of the slaves who had escaped—irrationally I suppose since they were undoubtedly well away from here by now. I thought of the alligators I'd seen and the wildcats I'd heard screeching in the night. I thought of Madeline herself, and how easily her mind could travel. I found a revolver and shells in a library cabinet. Though it's been years since I held a gun, military training, unlike soldiers, never dies. I loaded it. Some time later I followed Pamela across the sodden lawn and down the riding trail between the useless lowland swamps and the ruined fields.

The late afternoon shadows obscured the rock and spring, but I heard the water bubbling up from the earth as it undoubtedly had for centuries. I started to follow her into the trees, but she motioned me back. "I've claimed this place," she said as solemnly as Madeline Usher would have. "I need to do this alone."

So I stood outside the grove until after dark. In all that time I saw nothing unusual, and heard only the cacophony of natural sounds I have come to associate with this sultry climate rising from the land around me, in sharp contrast to the total silence of Pamela's chosen retreat.

While I waited for her, I prayed as I haven't prayed since my Virginia was dying. When there was nothing more to say to the Almighty, I sat with my back to one of the trees and began to set down Pamela's adventures, sticking the loose pages into the appropriate sections of my bound journal, creating a sort of whole that one day Pamela's children and grandchildren will read. What they will make of such an incredible account I cannot imagine.

As I was leafing through my later entries, I dropped the journal. It fell facedown. I picked it up carefully so I would not lose any of the loose pages to the breeze, turned it over, and saw that it had opened to Pierre Debreaux's map.

As I stared at it, astonished that I had forgotten I possessed it, I thought I heard the soft tinkle of a woman's laughter, thought I felt the brief touch of a ghostly hand. It could have been my imagination; considering what I'd been through, it probably was. Nonetheless, I murmured, "Thank you, Vivienne," before I set to studying it.

*   *   *

Inside the woods Pamela climbed to the top of the rocky table, stripped off her clothing, and lay facedown, hugging the cold stone, feeling it warm—first from the touch of her body, later from the energy she drew from the earth. When she had tried this before, she'd thought the pronounced heat some strange natural occurrence, perhaps from a warm spring below ground or from her overworked imagination.

Now, knowing better, she lay and waited until she felt she had drawn all the energy she could from the earth beneath her, then sat up and opened the little box she'd carried there.

In Celtic, she knew from her reading, it is called a keek stane, and consists of little more than a dark felt lining on which rests a convex piece of glass. One with power could use it, much as a gypsy would use a crystal ball, looking into its distorted center and, depending on need, seeing either the future or events happening some distance away.

Pamela tried, focusing all her attention on her child's face, but saw nothing. A great weariness came over her as it had on her first visit. Acting on her newly discovered faith, she stretched out on her back and stared up at the swaying branches and pale night sky. Her thoughts were still on Roddy when she closed her eyes.

And soared—first above the stone where she looked at herself, then far above the earth.

She saw the plantation, the thin ribbons of water cutting across the lowlands to both the east and west, the brown strip of road running to Lake Verret and beyond. And there, some miles east of the crossing, she saw a lone rider in a dark cloak carrying a child. She focused on the scene, finally seeing Madeline balancing Roddy in front of her on the saddle.

Madeline's long braid was over one shoulder. Roddy gripped it, as if it were the reins. His laughter contrasted sharply to Madeline's remote expression, to the tears in her eyes. Pamela tried to touch the woman's thoughts, but as soon as she tried, Madeline sensed her attempt and thrust her away.

For a time Pamela was content to observe her son, to be thankful for his laughter, to be thankful that so many people had cared gently for him so that he did not fear being away from her.

Pamela woke—for that is as close a word as she could think of to describe her returning to her body and to consciousness—well after sunset with the complete certainty that she had indeed reached her son.

Pamela came out of the grove and told me what had transpired. "I even know they're on the road to St. James," she said.

"Do the riverboats run at night?" I asked.

She shook her head, then frowned. "With such a long walk ahead of us, we'll likely have to spend tomorrow night in St. James."

"We may not have to go so far." In the dim light I showed her the map in the back of my journal and explained where it had come from. "These people seem to know one another as well as they know this land. As you can see, Lake Verret becomes part of a bayou at its southern tip. One of the Cajun guides may be able to show us a faster way from here to our destination. And possibly the destination itself."

"How would they know it?"

"Because Roderick Usher once hired Cajun servants to guard Madeline, and from what I can tell, they all seem to know one another. Also because in this desolate land, a British manor house—even the ruins of one—would be an oddity."

I watched her expression brighten until she actually dared to smile, to hug me, to whisper, "My Monsieur Dupin."

We walked back to the house, saying nothing, alert instead for some sign of danger. As we approached the house, we saw a candle burning in Pamela's bedroom. "Stay close behind me," I whispered. We entered the house and crept softly up the stairs. Gripping the revolver, and staying out of the soft light the candle threw, we reached the open outer doors and stepped through them. The room seemed empty, though the flame made it clear that someone was nearby.

Though it was too much to hope for, Pamela motioned toward the nursery. As we expected, Roddy was not there, but a thin black woman sat beside the crib, her head resting on the foot of the bed, sound asleep.

I cleared my throat. She woke, startled, and grabbed an old pistol from the floor. Seeing me, and Pamela behind me, she put it down as if she'd never really meant to touch it let alone point it at us, stood and nervously smoothed her skirts.

I was about to ask who she was, when Pamela rushed past me and hugged the woman. "Abeille!" she exclaimed. "I am so glad to see that you're all right!"

"The others ran away, but I had to make certain that you were not hurt, Mrs. Donaldson," she said.

"She took Roddy," I said.

Abeille nodded. "I knew she would. I saw her riding east with the child. I wanted to tell you before I left."

"Abeille, did anyone else stay nearby?"

"Bill because he's so old that he has no idea where else to go. And Harvey, but only because he hopes that Madeline Usher will return and set him free as she promised."

"She doesn't have that power, Abeille. None of you belong to her, but to the Donaldson family. If you promise me that you will bury Sean and his mother, then stand guard over this property until I send word that you may leave, I will give you your freedom now and pay you well for your help."

"What about Bill and Harvey?"

"I'll do the same for them. Indeed, I would feel much better knowing that someone else was here with you."

Abeille took the candle to the window and ran her hand in front of the flame three times. A moment later a huge black-skinned man stepped out of the shadows followed by an older, far smaller man who must have been Bill. We had passed by them in the night and never knew they were there. So much for our powers of observation, as well as the slaves' skill.

I wrote the statements that freed them. Pamela signed them, and I witnessed. Harvey and Bill made their marks, then Abeille stepped forward and triumphantly signed her name.

chapter 39

Whatever rural charm the Stelley land had once held had been stolen by Vivienne's irrational rage. The garden that had been so well tended now held only dying plants, beaten down and coated with mud from the storm that had claimed Blaine Stelley's life. The fallen trees had been pulled out of the road and left to rot. The barn had been only partially repaired and two swaybacked horses nibbled on grass growing along the edge of their muddy corral.

Only the house still stood as it once had, save that its hospitality had also died. The doors and windows were shut, barred from the inside we discovered after we knocked, and getting no reply, tried to enter.

"Lacey!" Pamela called. "Sean and his mother are dead. Madeline is gone and took my son with her. They can't hurt you anymore."

Still no reply, but I thought I heard a child's giggle, cut off as soon as it had begun.

"Lacey, you have to help me. Please! She's never coming back, believe me."

The shutter swung open just far enough so I could see the woman. She clutched her child, as if she used him as a reminder of what she would lose were she to find the courage to help us. "She says that she'll kill us both if I let you cross, and I believe her," Lacey said. "So I promised her I wouldn't. I can't break my word. You'll have to go north another ten miles for the next assistance."

Pamela ran her hand through her hair. I could sense her searching for the right words to change the woman's mind. However, while they had been speaking, I thought of how quickly I had traveled through less conventional routes. I stepped in front of Pamela and asked, "If I show you a map of where we're going, can you tell me if we have to cross?"

The woman's expression became both wary and puzzled. The way she stared first at me, then at Pamela, made me realize that she might be frightened, but she was far from broken. "I suppose that sending you off in a different direction would be all right," she finally replied, as if Madeline were listening to her words, not her intent.

I wasted no time in pulling out my journal and handing the map to her. She studied it a moment and nodded. "You don't want to cross. Go back to the wooden gate and head south about four miles on the narrow road just beyond it. You'll know you're at the south end of the lake when you reach a town called Mochen, though with no more than four or five ugly buildings, it should hardly be called any name at all let alone one so pretty."

"Do you suppose that we can find a boat and guide there?" I asked.

"Maybe. There's fools all through these swamps who are poor enough to take the job."

Pamela took ten dollars from her bag and held it out to the woman.

"I don't take charity," Lacey said before Pamela could explain.

"I'm not offering charity. I'd like to buy one of your mounts."

To me the money still seemed mostly charity, since that amount should have easily bought five such sorry beasts, but Lacey seemed reluctant to agree. "If I sell you Blaine's old horse, it might not be able to carry you both, and I kind of like having the old guy around. If I sell you the mule, I won't have any way of pulling the larger raft."

Pamela doubled the amount. "Then let me rent the mule with this. I promise to get him back to you in a few days' time, or send one better."

"You sure she's gone?"

"She is. And Vivienne is dead. So is her son."

"Vivienne? Well, that I always expected. But Sean?"

"The storm killed him."

"Storms." Lacey repeated and shook her head. She seemed about to cry, but fought the tears back and started toward the barn.

A half hour later we were off. Rather than ride together, we decided to alternate, a method that let us set a good pace through the rest of the day so that we reached Mochen, which meant "my dear" in the local dialect, by evening.

Every house looked much the same as the next, with the peak parallel to the front, and the roof gently pitched over both house and broad front porch. Fathers and mothers, along with their parents and children, were seated on them. While they had undoubtedly not been sitting silently before we arrived, they were as we rode in, eyeing us warily, until someone called out "Ferme!" which was the name of our mule. We were immediately surrounded by the men of the town. They seemed to be demanding to know how we had come by the beast, but they spoke so quickly in the Cajun dialect so that it took me some time to sort the question from the noise.

Their suspicions quieted somewhat after I explained how we had rented the mule and hoped to hire one of them to take it back to Lacey Stelley, and someone else with a boat and knowledge of the area to take us southeast through the swamps. Afterward, the women and older children joined the men so that we were surrounded by everyone who mattered in Mochen.

"Where you go?" one of the men asked.

"To a ruined mansion owned by a family called Usher," I replied.

"House?"

"Castle, actually." I began describing the building with as

much detail as I could recall from Madeline's journal. I was met with blank stares until someone understood.

"Maison de la femme," the man said. The others nodded.

"De la morte," a woman added. "Why you go to such a terrible place and take the poor woman, you?"

I glanced around, then whispered to Pamela, "There are so many children here." She understood, and speaking slowly and simply so they would understand her English, she told them how Madeline Usher had stolen her child and how she and I intended to rescue him.

Madeline's reputation was known to them. The men were suspicious of our request. Some even appeared frightened, but our tale had an effect on the wives. "He'll take you," one of the women said, pushing an older man forward. "And our boy will take Ferme home."

The man looked from his wife to us, then shrugged, as if she'd only spoken first, and he'd intended to volunteer all along. "My name is Victor Bucher, and yes, I will guide you," he said and held out his hand.

"Wait!" Pamela said. "How long will the journey take?"

"One full day, and half the next. From tomorrow morning to the next afternoon."

"Yes, Edgar!" she said with the first real animation I'd seen in her face since she'd read Madeline's parting letter. I took the man's hand, consummating the agreement.

All that remained were the details. We retreated to the man's house to negotiate a fee. In similar fashion to Pierre Debreaux's arrangements, it included both meals and shelter for the night, the latter given us in a narrow room on the second floor belonging from the look of the hand-carved toys and stuffed dolls, to the younger Bucher children.

I wish I could say that Pamela and I talked long and earnestly into the night, that I managed finally to confess to her that my concern for her safety stemmed most for the affection I'd felt for her since she first entered my life, that she confessed she felt it, too. Instead, emotionally as well as physically spent, we removed our heavier outer garments and lay beside each other in the broad straw bed.

"Edgar," she whispered. "Madeline lost a full night waiting for the riverboat. And the boats stop at almost every plantation. Do you suppose we might arrive at the house first?"

"Possibly."

"Then everything is going to turn out right?"

"I'm sure of it," I replied.

She slipped her hand into mine and kept it there. Soon after, we were both asleep. Perhaps I dreamed, but if so I didn't remember any of it this morning. That in itself is enough to convince me that Madeline has lost interest in us.

We will leave Mochen in an hour. Pamela is assisting Mademe Bucher in packing food for our trip. Victor refused my help with readying the boat, so I've been sitting on one of the rockers on their front porch, updating this journal. Victor has just started back to the house. It is undoubtedly time for us to leave this peaceful place.

During our first day navigating the intricate maze of delta waterways, Pamela sat in the front of the boat with her head raised, her eyes fixed on the southwestern horizon as if she should already be able to see her destination. In a way, I think she did, because when I moved beside her and rested a hand on her shoulder, she did not move or acknowedge me in any way.

So she observed the woman. I hoped Madeline was so absorbed in her own journey that she did not realize that we had also started our own.

Though we made excellent time until midafternoon, traveling down what I was surprised to learn was once more the Atchafalaya, since the turnoff onto a quieter bayou, there was no sign of a current. The water appeared so murky, and the land so monotonous that we hardly seemed to be moving at all. I doubted that we would be able to reach our destination by water only and hoped the land we would cross on foot would be stable and dry. I wanted to ask Victor Bucher how much farther we had to go, but he was utterly unlike the jovial Debreaux brothers. At times he seemed perversely sullen, at others merely taciturn, and I had no desire to try to initiate a conversation with him, no matter how brief it might be.

"Will we sleep on land tonight or in the boat?" Pamela asked.

"You will sleep in the boat, both of you. I go on. When the moon rises, he sends enough light to travel, him," Victor replied.

The moon, when he did rise, him, might have been fuller than on my earlier night on this river, but he provided not even half the awe of my earlier experience. I dozed off to the sound of the leaves brushing against the side of our little boat, and one of Victor's occasional grunts as he poled the vessel along.

Through most of the following morning, the land actually managed to grow flatter and less interesting, so that by the time Victor told us we would have to continue on foot, I had no idea what landmarks he used to determine where we were.

The marshland is wild and empty, the oppressive swaying grasses covering the lowland, invading even the creveys—as the people here call the ponds and lakes too small and shallow and ephemeral to name. Often I see signs of the shifting waters of the delta—the occasional patches of rotting brush or lone dead oaks, draped in dun-colored robes of Spanish moss, as if they mourned their lost leaves, their lost lives.

The marsh's feeling is one of exquisite, almost painful loneliness. A man could get lost here and, once lost, could die. Within days all traces of his passing would be gone, swallowed by the swaying grasses.

Pamela and I traveled cautiously, trudging along behind Victor, trying to step exactly where he stepped and to avoid his occasional mistakes. Muskrats had tunneled through the damp spongy earth, and the few times when I had moved to what I thought was safer, dryer ground, I sank knee deep in a burrow Victor had skillfully avoided.

"He try his own way, him," Victor said with an unsympathetic laugh. I believe those were the only words he spoke for the better part of two hours save for those times when, solicitous of Pamela's welfare, he would ask if she wished to stop and rest. She was always in favor of pressing on, and kept a grueling pace, fueled no doubt by her fear for the safety of her child.

Victor never asked that question of me, assuming no doubt that a man had the stamina to keep up. I reflected sadly that I did not. Indeed, the walk through the pressing heat was beginning to make me feel more than tired. The buzzing of the gnats and mosquitoes seemed painfully intense, irritating further the quick painful throbbing of my pulse.

Finally, thankfully, Victor chose to stop. He waited until we were settled for a midday meal, then pointed to a pair of cypress trees some half mile away. "The land is higher there, the walk easier. The house, it is visible soon." He stopped and waited for some reply.

I knew that though he was reluctant to admit it, he did not want to go the rest of the way with us. "There was once a road from the house to New Orleans. Is it still there?" I asked.

He nodded, and looked hopeful.

"Shall we go on alone?" I asked Pamela.

She agreed and pulled out the money she had promised our guide—ten dollars for his services, another three for that of his son. At the time we arrived at the amount, it seemed exorbitant to me, but Pamela had been right. The man thought he was risking his life to help us. That alone demanded some extra compensation.

He left us just before we reached the trees. By then it was midafternoon, and we had pushed ourselves almost to the limits of our endurance to catch a glimpse of our destination. So, from the cool shadows beneath the pair of trees, I first laid eyes on the house of Usher. It seemed much as I had pictured it near the end of my story, frozen in the storm of my imagination. A portion of its walls were standing, that was true, but though they were made of stone, they seemed fragile and weak, like the shell of some great beast well past its prime, on its feet only through what remained of its feeble dwindling will.

And as my imagination had revealed, the storm lay about it, the clouds a whirlwind of lowering silence, building strength, waiting for the command to strike. So Madeline intended that she and Roddy would die as her brother had died, one final coincidence to assure their proximate rebirth.

Pamela stood beside me, her hands clenched into fists and pressed hard against her chin. Her eyes were wild, but unfocused. "She knows we're coming," she whispered fiercely, and ran toward the house.

I followed as quickly as I was able, my heart pounding from exertion, from fear, and in response to the strange charge that seemed to rise from the earth, an electric fog, as unnatural as it was strong.

"Hurry, Edgar!" Pamela called from halfway up a winding stone staircase on the outer wall of the house. These would have been the stairs that Madeline led Adrien up, so that he would be spared the sight of the dank tomb the front of the house had become. If so, in a moment she would be facing the worst view the house had to offer. I tried to hurry, hoping to spare her the sight of facing it alone.

I reached the outer stairs just as Pamela disappeared into an upstairs hall. I was halfway up them when the storm broke.

I paused, and though I wish now that I hadn't, I turned and looked at the land around us.

The water fell with such intensity and speed that each heavy droplet seemed to form a straight line between clouds and earth. And when they hit the ground, they did not soak into it but remained like piles of gray string on the ground. A moment later these began writhing snakelike across the desolate land. They were forming on the stairs as well, curling around my ankles. I could see slitted eyes, fangs, glistening scales. A vision of hell! I thought, no more than one of Madeline's final defenses. Had they caught us while we were still in the swamps, we might have been completely unnerved. Now, with only a little way to go to escape them, I shook them loose of me, then kicked each step bare of them as I ascended. Only when I'd reached the doorway to the ruins, and shut it behind me, did I dare to allow myself to give in to the terror that vision had evoked.

My breath was quick, my heart pounding, but it seemed

the only sound in that structure, as if by shutting the door I managed to shut out the world as well.

I whispered Pamela's name, but heard nothing. Soon it seemed that my ears grew accustomed to the silence as my eyes did to the darkness of the hallway, a darkness broken only by small slits of light leaking from the dilapidated frames of closed doors and an occasional crack in the walls. From the far end I thought I heard a low, almost whispered chanting. Thinking that the floor might be as unstable as the outer walls, I kept close to the side of the hallway as I made my way toward the sound. As I approached it, the darkness seemed to lift and I saw a dim light, most likely coming through an open door just out of sight.

Now that I could see a little better I quickened my pace, heading no doubt for the front of the house, and the sepulcher Madeline had created in its ruins. The hall ended, for such a term has never been more aptly used than to describe the place where the floor fell away. I stood over what had once been the foyer, at the top of what had once been a wide stone staircase curving in a slow, long drop to the main floor. Now its stairs were partially eroded and ended some dozen steps from the top, and some half-dozen feet above ground level. Pamela stood near the end of them, swaying slightly, one hand gripping a narrow chink in the wall. "Pamela," I whispered. Again, no reply.

From my angle I could not see what held Pamela's attention. I followed her down and looked beyond her to the drama taking place below.

A pair of cypress boxes, no doubt the caskets of Madeline's mother and grandfather, flanked either side of a carved marble sarcophagus. Had I any doubts that this was the resting place of Roderick Usher, they would have vanished by the sight of the glass-cased candles burning on either side of its wide flat top, the brazier of incense smoking between them. The person who stood before the altar was covered in a black hooded cloak that hid everything but the upraised hands which gripped a straight short knife. I knew this was Madeline only because Roddy sat in front of her on the cold stone, his face puckered up from the incense smell, his eyes tearing from the smoke. But he wasn't crying. Instead he stared at Madeline, with such curious solemnity that it seemed he must understand and approve of her course.

A portion of the roof was still standing and the house had been built on slightly higher ground, so that the water falling outside had not yet invaded this space. But the snakes I had thought a vision were piled outside. Some of the boldest had already wriggled through the ruined wall and slithered along the floor of the foyer toward the pagan altar and the woman who had summoned them here. Roddy spied them. He saw them as some new plaything. He clapped his hands, laughed, and tried to climb off the stone to chase after them. Madeline picked him up and placed him in the center of her altar, holding him so tightly that he cried out from pain.

I lay a supportive hand on Pamela's shoulder. My presence gave her strength, enough that she called out, "Madeline! Let him go."

Madeline ignored her. The chanting continued, punctuated by Roddy's angry wails.

"Let him go!" Pamela repeated, adding a second sentence in Celtic, her free hand moving gracefully through the air.

The rain stopped. Roddy quieted and fell silent. Even the snakes seemed to cease their movement as air and earth lay waiting.

Madeline pushed back the hood of her cloak and looked up at us. I have never seen a creature more changed. The long chestnut hair had thinned and grayed until it seemed the same shade as the moss on the trees. All traces of her haunting beauty had vanished, the cadaverous pallor and sunken cheeks accentuated by the flickering lamplight.

"Madeline, you don't have to do this."

"I do. You'll never reach him in time. So make this less painful for the child. Take that man you've chosen and leave us."

"Not until you hear me out. You wanted a second child from me. I will give you one."

"It's too late."

"Is it? Look at me, Madeline. Look inside of me. It's already done."

Something brushed against me, intangible yet painfully cold. I shivered. Pamela cried out but stood without protest until the presence retreated. "So there's a female child coming. Whose child, Pamela!"

"Sean's. Conceived the night he died. You have ways of knowing if I lie. Use them now."

There was a hush, a sigh as if God Himself had exhaled and waited with the rest of us inside the ancient, crumbling walls. Then a roar grew in the silence, an angry drawn-out sound, painfully loud.

The storm that had been held in check so long had only grown stronger. Now no power on earth could control it. The ground beneath us trembled, as if hell were opening its gates to swallow us all.

"Madeline!" Pamela screamed above the storm's ferocious din. "Roddy will have known you in both your lives, and loved you in both. What could make for a more perfect future for both of you? Now bring him to me!"

Madeline stared up at her, her expression one of perfectly controlled hysteria. "You will see to my books, my property?"

"I promise."

By now the water was curling around Madeline's legs. She took a hesitant step toward us. Another. Pamela crouched down and held out her arms while I gripped her waist so she would not fall.

Madeline paused, kissed the child on his forehead, and lifted him up to his mother.

Pamela would have tumbled forward had I not been holding her. As it was, it took all my strength to pull her backward on top of me. Clutching Roddy, she moved above me.

"Come," I said and held out an arm to Madeline.

She shook her head, mouthed some Celtic words. Above the cacophony of the storm, I heard an even louder roar. Through the open space where the tall front doors had once hung, a wave of sickening brown water rolled toward us. It washed into the narrow foyer, its force cracking the wooden caskets to bits, pushing the marble one upright. The top fell off, and the corpse, little more than calcified bones, washed free of its container.

As the skeleton touched the water, it created a turbulence that merged and grew into a maelstrom of mud and debris. Madeline did not struggle as the whirlpool sucked her to the center of it. Her long skirts twisted round her body, her hair around her face, as if the water, like some huge aqueous spider, enclosed her in its web. She clutched the pile of bones and tattered scraps of cloth close to her breast, murmuring as if Roderick were dying, not long dead, and still in need of comfort. As she sank, I saw on her face a look such as a martyr might have displayed—she had stood firm in her beliefs, even to death itself.

There have always been moments of delusion in my life, even hallucinations that seemed to last for days or weeks. But I had deluded myself, I had thought myself a rational man, one given to all the rational virtues of self-preservation. Yet I was mesmerized by the sight of Madeline's frenzy, frozen by the horror of the death she had chosen, even more the all-too-real horror I felt when seeing some of my most terrible visions made real.

The water had risen over the bottom two steps when Pamela gave a strangled cry and grabbed me with her free arm, pulling me upward, to safety, to reality.

chapter 40

I don't know how long we sat at the top of those stairs, Pamela rocking back and forth cradling her son, I with my arm over her shoulders, both of us shivering in our damp muddy clothes. The storm gradually subsided. The flood began to recede so quickly I feared that Madeline's body, wedged beneath the coffin or the rocks that had crumbled under the force of the water, might rise through the opaque brown water, might through some witchcraft live still.

Better that than to think of Roderick's ghost, or Vivienne's making an appearance. No, best not to speculate at all of matters beyond the grave in this macabre and crumbling house.

"Come," I whispered to Pamela and helped her stand. Leaning against each other—for emotional as well as physical support—we made our way down the hall to the one intact room where Madeline had stayed after her ordeal so many years before.

It seemed that the room had been used not long ago. The linens were musty, their hems mildewed, but they were hardly ancient. The table and washstand had only a thin layer of dust.

Roddy had long since fallen asleep in Pamela's arms. We arranged some of the cleaner linens in a lower drawer.

Pamela laid him gently into it, then began to strip off her soaked and muddy garments. With no where else to go, I stayed, not certain of her intent until she came and unbuttoned my shirt, pressing her breasts against my chest. " 'And there in the crumbling ruins of the House of Usher, I found a kind of peace in his arms,' " she said, reciting the words from Madeline's journal, tilting her face toward mine so I could kiss her.

My passion surprised me as much as her, I think, for once I began kissing her with all the promise of where that kiss would lead, I realized what I had known since our first meeting. She was the one, the child-woman I had sought to replace my Sissy—to breathe life into me when I grow cold, to steady me when my emotions run too fast for my poor body to endure. And I will be there for her as well, ready to hold her when the memories of this ordeal press too close.

I will not speak of the women I have loved save to say that there were others. Pamela gave me more, far more than any of them, as if her passion and the passion she aroused in me would absolve her of the sin she had unwittingly committed with her brother.

Later, as I lay beside her, my heart racing from an all too common reason, I brushed the damp hair from her cheek and asked, "Why didn't you tell me you were having a second child?"

"I was hardly certain. Only Madeline made me so."

"Do you want me with you when you leave this place?"

"For always, my Edgar, if you will have me and my children," she replied.

So it was that in one night I broke my engagement to the love of my childhood and made a promise to another. When I tell Elmira the reason, I doubt that she will protest overly much.

"Where do you want to go when we leave here?" I asked.

"As soon as we've settled our business in New Orleans, I want to take Roddy home to my father. I want him to read Mother's letter. I hope her words will give him some peace."

Or a lifetime of guilt, I thought. "We'll leave as soon as the road is above water," I said.

So we slept. When I woke again, moonlight was streaming through the window. I went and looked at it, painting the muddy ruined land with streaks of silver. Pamela came up behind me. She wrapped her arms around my chest until I turned and led her back to the bed.

We left the house the following afternoon, traveling on foot, leading Madeline's horses. Once we left the island, the road became less treacherous, and we rode, letting the animals set the pace. In midafternoon two days later, mud coating our feet, our clothing soiled and torn, we reached New Orleans.

We had scarcely three dollars between us. I suggested that we go to Mr. Grymes's office before it closed for the day, but Pamela objected. "I will not have us arriving there looking a pair of beggars," she said and directed me down the narrow gilded streets to Estelle Braud's house.

The lady herself answered the door. After she'd rung for a valet to see to our mounts, she led us inside and looked us up and down. "A hard journey?" she asked. The hint of a smile on her lips and the amused glitter in her eyes revealed that she was one of those lucky women who had not lost the marvelous spirit of her youth and who eagerly awaited a chance to hear our account.

"Not so hard," Pamela replied. "I didn't mention him before, but this is my son."

"So this is Roddy!" Mrs. Braud exclaimed. Ignoring Pamela's surprised expression, she took the child from Pamela, holding him up to the light so she could see his face. "A beautiful boy," she said.

"And this is Edgar Poe," Pamela continued.

"I thought it might be," she said as she took my hand. "But I had not expected to find you or my dear friend here so . . . disheveled."

"We have so much to tell you," Pamela said.

"Tell me over dinner. In the meantime, leave your son with me and go upstairs. I'll send Sally up with towels and soap."

By the time we'd washed away the last traces of the bayou

mud, Sally had managed to acquire a full change of clothing for each of us. By the time we'd dressed, dinner was ready.

We've spent a pleasant evening in the house. I was elated to hear Pamela's laughter as I told our hostess of the balloon trip, and later to see Pamela sitting with a composure I hadn't glimpsed in her before.

I left the two women in the courtyard and went upstairs. Now I sit near the open window listening to their distant voices while I set down the details of the final days of our journey. It is a story that will never be published, but one that our descendants or Roddy's have a right to know.

My last thought is of Madeline—intelligent, serene, powerful. If she had only shrugged off the past, she might have been happy. Yet who am I to condemn her?

I hear Pamela saying good night to our hostess. It is time to blot the ink on these last words, then sit and wait to hear her step on the stairs, to feel her hands on my shoulders, to allow her kisses to drive away my own potent memories of a haunted past.

We remained in New Orleans for three days, partly to settle our affairs with Mr. Grymes but also in the hope of hearing from Harry Ingram before we started back to Virginia. His letter arrived the day before we were to catch one of the faster ships sailing the coast. Not surprisingly, he had decided to abandon the journey and the *cursed tropical heat* and had hired a guide to take him as far as his fellow balloonist's farm. *I did inform the authorities about what was happening at Petite Terre, and they in turn promised to get in touch with the militia in Natchez to look into the matter. I wait to hear from you and learn what sort of record we set. If the balloon is still intact—and hopefully it is if you receive this—please arrange to have it shipped at my expense. Best wishes to you, Mrs. Donaldson, and her child. Harry.*

"Is there a Celtic god whose earthly manifestation includes a wicker basket and a thousand yards of yellow silk?" I asked.

Mrs. Braud laughed. Pamela smiled but only out of politeness. In truth I had made a jest about a religion she had more right to believe in than any good Christian one. "I have a tendency to be irreverent. It's gotten me into trouble more than once in my life, but never with someone I cared so much about," I said to her when we were alone.

"I'll try to understand, but not now when everything seems so new."

"What sort of a wedding would Madeline approve of?" I asked.

"None. She would say that we are already married because we chose to be."

"You could have picked a less sorry husband."

"I've seen you at your sorriest, I think. You'll do."

Then she smiled, calmly, radiantly. I tried to do the same, though it was difficult. What I have found in Pamela is too precious, too perfect to last. Madeline will take it from me out of vengeance. If she has moved beyond that capability, the ill luck that has plagued me through my life will likely do it for her.

chapter 41

O_n *the journey* back to the Montgomery plantation, we stopped briefly in Richmond so I could retrieve my mail from the Swan. The only letters of real interest were from my aunt, who chastized me for not writing her, from Harry who had made it back to Appomattox in still another record flight, and from a local literati reminding me of my promise to do a public lecture and reading on the twenty-fourth of September. The last correspondence the woman received from me had been a note telling her I would be visiting friends in Appomattox, so she'd hardly been surprised when I had not contacted her.

And the function was a mere four days away! Though it had already been publicized, I would still have time to contact the Richmond paper and cancel. I wanted to do so, but Pamela seemed so excited at the idea of hearing me speak that I accepted for her sake.

"Think of it, Eddy. For the first time I can sit in the audience and listen to the adulation you'll receive."

Adulation! Given my exhaustion, the audience would likely throw tomatoes or worse. Nonetheless, I agreed and wrote a note to my sponsor. That brief business completed, we set out for Pamela's home.

Pamela had wanted to meet with her father alone, but after

the reception I'd received only weeks ago, I refused to allow it. We hired a private coach in Appomattox. Roddy, who had enjoyed the gentle rocking of the clipper and river steamer, hated the confinement of the coach, the heat, and the dust as much as we did, but being hardly more than an infant, gave greater voice to his dislike, his howls alternating with an occasional deliberate "No!" Even our singsong rhymes that usually make him giggle had no effect on his temper, and by the time we reached our destination, the driver seemed relieved when he learned that only I would be returning to town.

I had tried to explain the state of the house to Pamela, but no description could prepare her for the sight of it. She looked in dull shock at the rusted entry gates, the lawn given over to weeds and vines, the rotting front porch, and the doors and windows pathetically in need of repair. Even Roddy fell silent, attuned no doubt to his mother's sudden shift in mood.

"Good Lord, how could Emmie have let it get so bad?" Pamela asked.

"I think he refuses to let her repair it. He wants it to crumble, as if he can forget his bride when the house he brought her to is gone."

"Father will listen to me. Once he understands why Mother left him, things will be better," she said, sounding confident though she gripped my hand tightly for support.

I knocked, half expecting Will Montgomery to shoot through the door rather than answer it. Instead, no one came. I was about to knock again, when Pamela handed Roddy to me and tried the door.

It swung inward, revealing a dusty parquet floor, a broken spiderweb, and the spider who'd built it skittering up the faded painted wall. The breeze that entered with us raised a cloud of dust. Roddy sneezed and let out another piercing howl.

At least the boy knew how to attract someone's attention. I heard footsteps on the second floor, and a moment later Emmie came down the stairs to meet us.

I recognized the woman only by her features, for everything else about her had changed. The woman I had previously met was as well groomed as any Virginia matron, outwardly calm, and as cultured as a late-life education would allow. This woman's hair was loose around her shoulders, and so kinky and oily I doubted that she'd washed or even combed it in days. Her stockings were ripped. I was aware of that because her skirt was as well. Though her skin was too dark and the light too dim in the hallway for me to see the full extent of her injuries, one cheek was swollen and her hands were bruised.

"Emmie?" Pamela asked.

Emmie reached for Pamela, swinging her around to face the light. "My God, you look more like Anna now than you ever did!" she exclaimed.

"I met her, Emmie. I have a letter from her that Father must read." Something in the woman's features made Pamela pause, then ask, "Is he well?"

"He was . . . but then, some two weeks ago, something changed. He—"

"Changed?" Pamela interrupted. "What was the date?"

"September fifth. It was early in the morning. I'd just awakened when I heard him crying out in his room. I ran to him. He didn't recognize me. He seemed to be looking at someone only he could see. His eyes were focused near the foot of his bed. . . ."

But Pamela had stopped listening and started for the stairs. "Is he in his old room?" she asked.

"Your mother's. Let me go up with you."

But Pamela was beyond patience. I expected her to be rebuffed, but I could hardly call her back, for I knew all too well the emotions that excited her. As I had confessed so recently to Harry, I'd once been in her position myself.

So I handed the boy to Emmie and followed Pamela up the stairs, growing far more concerned when I reached the second floor. It was the smell I think. After Virginia died, I went insane with grief. Seeing my state, a friend who thought to frighten me into lucidity took me to an asylum in New York. The memory of much of what I saw there has thankfully faded, but the scent, the stench of alcohol and excrement that accompanied the inmates' madness and despair, is fixed forever in my mind.

Pamela stood at the far end of the hallway outside what had been her mother's room. She glanced my way, held out her palm toward me to warn me away, and entered it.

I expected to hear Montgomery shouting, perhaps even to meet Pamela in the hallway as she fled from his anger. Instead there was silence. I slowed my pace and stopped just outside the door, where I could see what transpired inside without disturbing their meeting.

Pamela had her back to me, facing her father, who lay sleeping in a bed close to the window. The lace curtains and the velvet ones that had blocked out the light had both been pulled from their rods and lay in a heap in one corner. Books were piled on the floor beside the bed, and magazines atop them, all arranged so neatly that it was clear they had not been touched. Anna's portrait covered the mirror above the bureau. I saw a half-empty bottle and a glass on the table, a second broken glass on the floor.

Pamela seemed reluctant to approach her father, hardly surprising given Emmie's recent bruises, or the state of the once-beautiful lace bedcovers, now ripped and stained with alcohol and worse. I wondered when the man had last left that room.

"Father?" Pamela called.

He woke as if from a dream and stared at her. The moment extended for some time, she too overcome with emotion to speak, he . . . well, it was clear a moment later what he thought.

He rolled up on one elbow and held out a hand to her. "I've dreamed about you," he said. "I've dreamed of you every night for so long, and now you've come back to me."

I could see Pamela's shoulders shaking and knew she'd begun to cry. "I have so much to tell you. So much," she said and went to him.

They embraced. He held her at arm's length for a moment, then said softly. "It's you in the flesh. Anna. I always knew you'd come back to me."

Ah, that must have hurt, but Pamela took it well. "Not Anna," she replied. "It's Pamela, Father."

He did not seem to understand. "I'm your daughter," she repeated and I saw his expression shift to despair. "But I have seen her," Pamela went on, motioning me to come into the room. "Eddy . . . Mr. Poe . . . made sure she received your message."

He glanced up at me. His expression did not change, nor did he acknowledge our earlier meeting. "I have a letter from her I want to read to you," Pamela went on.

"Letter?"

She pulled it from her pocket and held it out to him. "It explains so much," she said.

He stared at the envelope and shook his head."Give me a bit of time to get used to what you've told me. Later, after dinner, I'll read it and we can talk."

"I brought your grandson home."

"Grandson?" For a moment his despair seemed to lift, then he lay back once more, staring desolately at the lace canopy above him as if he had already absorbed more than his mind could bear. "Later," he repeated and waved her away.

She walked me downstairs and outside. "Everything will be better now. Three days more and I'll be with you again." She kissed me goodbye with almost childish playfulness.

I got into the coach. As we pulled away, I looked over my shoulder at her standing in front of her father's ruined house. I raised my hand, in farewell and in acknowledgment that we had both been through enough. Surely luck would be kinder to us now. Even that hope made me shiver, as if optimism were a sickness and I its sudden victim.

In Richmond there was more than enough to do to keep my mind off Pamela at least part of the time. At her insistence I took the money remaining from our travel funds and purchased a new coat and pants and shoes to replace the ones ruined on the journey to Louisiana. I unearthed my lecture notes from the bottom of the trunk that had been stored at the Swan. Since I wanted to make the best possible impression on my future bride, I read them over at least a dozen times, though I had given the same speech often enough before. Then, in what I almost thought was bravado, I decided to speak from memory and not consult them at all.

I put off my most important obligation until it was impossible to avoid any longer. The evening before the lecture, I paid a formal call on Elmira.

We sat in her drawing room, in those uncomfortable straight-back tapestry chairs, drinking tea from blue china cups. The handles were far too delicate to be easily held, and the tea had a faintly chemical perfume. I thought almost wistfully of the sturdy Cajun mugs and thick boiled coffee Pierre had served me. I described the balloon trip, the journey downriver, and the arrival at Petite Terre. Through this entire, almost wondrous, account, Elmira's expression remained stoic and calculating. It was then that I realized that Pamela and I might one day live near Richmond, and in polite society. Because of this, I could not trust Elmira with any knowledge of what had transpired within the walls of that lush plantation or in the crumbling house of Usher.

"Did you find Pamela Donaldson and her child well?" she asked me.

"Well enough, but troubled by the climate and isolation," I replied, pleased I could answer with that much of the truth. "We traveled back to Virginia together. She is with her father now."

"And during that journey you came to love her, didn't you?" she asked. The teacup in her hand was steady. The only discernable emotion in her tone was mild disapproval.

"I did," I replied. I wanted to set aside the cup and saucer, to take her hands, to make her understand what a terrible mistake our marriage would have been.

"So it's settled." She looked away from me, as if she had already dismissed me, then asked, "Will I get to meet her?"

"She'll be at my lecture tomorrow night," I said.

"Very well. We'll dine here afterward."

I supposed that I owed Elmira at least that.

It rained the morning of the lecture, the rain continuing through the afternoon. I was scarcely surprised that Pamela had been delayed, but as the hour of the lecture approached, I became concerned. If it hadn't been for the crowd which gathered around me at the hall, I would have paced the floor. Instead, I shook hands. I feigned interest in those to whom I was introduced. I said a few vague words to Elmira and greeted my landlady, who looked woefully out of place among Richmond's literary elite. My attention was fixed all the while on the open doors, and the strangers filing in. At any other time, I would have been astonished at the size of the crowd.

I watched for Pamela as the lamps were dimmed through the room and the others lit around the stage. Then, at the last possible moment, she entered the room. Even after the darkness took her from me, I still seemed to see her standing in the back of the room, her nervous hands clasped tightly below her chin, her eyes bright with love.

Enraptured by her presence, I never spoke so eloquently or so spontaneously. My recitations of "The Raven" and "Annabel Lee" were exquisite because she was listening.

When the applause had died and lights had been turned up, I motioned to Pamela to come forward. She shook her head and remained where she was until I had accepted the accolades of my sponsors and the crowd in the room had thinned.

Pamela came forward then, a bit shyly it seemed, and I introduced her to Elmira. I'm sure I felt the most awkward of the three of us, positioned as I was between my previous betrothed and my future bride.

By the time we reached Elmira's home, the tone of the evening had been set. I was silent, Elmira her usual stoic calm, while Pamela, with all the innocent charm of a kitten, chatted on about her hopes for her father's eventual recovery and for our future together. She asked Elmira's advice often on everything from the hiring of free servants to the renovation of the Montgomery house and grounds. Pamela wasn't flattering Elmira, but took everything she said most seriously and thanked her sincerely when the evening ended.

As we were leaving for the night, Elmira took Pamela aside and said a few words to her privately. I heard Pamela's bright laugh, the hint of a whispered reply. Then Pamela was beside me and linked her arm with mine. "Walk me home, Eddy," she said.

"For evermore," I croaked as I had when I recited "The Raven." The sound seemed too harsh, too much a reminder of the family Pamela had so recently lost. I shuddered as from a sudden draft.

"What did she tell you?" I asked as we walked to the Swan, where I had already arranged a room for her.

"That your aunt will be of the greatest value to me. Elmira said she has never corresponded with a more sensible and frugal woman."

"Her reminder, no doubt, of my poverty," I grumbled.

"Perhaps, but I told her that the Montgomery plantation faces a number of lean years and that I will welcome anyone with common sense and thrift."

We walked silently, arm in arm, the cares of the past forgotten. "Do you suppose she can travel here soon?" Pamela asked after a time.

"As soon as I go to fetch her," I replied. "And I must say my goodbyes to all those who have been so kind to my family. You would like them all, I'm sure of it, if only . . ."

Dare I suggest what my mind was already set on?

". . . if only you would come north with me," I went on, the words gaining speed as I uttered them. "I can introduce you to my Helen, my savior after Virginia died and the inspiration for so many of my poems. We can visit my friends in New York. They'll all love you as I do. We only have to stay in Fordham for a few days, then we can bring Muddy back with us."

"But Father, and Roddy . . ." she began.

"You told me your father is better. And we'll only be gone three weeks at most. Bring Roddy if you wish. He takes to travel well enough, doesn't he?"

"He does, but I think he's traveled enough." Nonetheless, she considered my proposal. I managed to keep silent, though I wanted to beg her to come, to confess to her my fear—irrational though it might be—that any separation of more then a day or two would mean we would never see

•

each other again. "I could leave Roddy with Emmie, I suppose," she added, though she didn't sound convinced.

"Please," I begged. "We could even marry in Fordham, or better yet on the steamer if the captain is willing and you agree to it. It would be fitting, don't you think? We fell in love on a journey. What better way to marry?"

She stopped in the shadows thrown by the oaks in front of the Swan and took my trembling hands in her own. "Shhh, Eddy," she said calmly. "We've already said our vows to each other and God. We can formalize them whenever you wish."

"Then you'll come with me?"

She nodded. I kissed her then, and as I did, I took off her hat and pulled the pins from her hair. It tumbled over her shoulders in a dark cascade. I ran my fingers through it, then kissed her again. Laughing quietly, like a pair of young lovers on our first secret tryst, we stole into the Swan and up to her room.

"Soon we won't have to be so discreet," she whispered, kissing me again, her body pressing close to mine.

Now she sleeps peacefully in her bed—her brown hair dark against the white skin of her shoulders; her tiny, delicate hand resting on the deep blue quilt. Mrs. Blakely will be up soon. I should go to my own room, lest I sully our reputations so close to our future home. But I cannot bear to leave her yet. Instead, I look at her often as I sit at the window, letting a patch of morning sun warm my hands and dry the ink on this page. I think of that last time I saw her so in the morning, lying in the crumbling house of Usher, exhausted from our terrible ordeal.

Dare I hope that it is over now, completely? Dare I hope that my own life, so full of tragedy, will change for the better? Dare I assume that God will let me stay with her?

chapter 42

Our goodbyes were far less emotional than they would have been if I was going on to Fordham without her. Instead, anticipating only a short separation, Pamela and I spent a lighthearted morning together before I saw her off on the noon coach.

We were leaving Virginia together in less than three days, and there was so much to do! I made a round of calls to those who were kind to me in the weeks I had been in the city. I wrote a letter to Mrs. Ingram and another, longer, one to Harry (making certain to give the most liberal figures for both distance and landing time). Then, with over a day left before Pamela's return, I visited a jeweler, looking for the perfect wedding ring for my bride.

I chose one made of two thin strips of gold twisted together in a delicate pattern. It had some similarities to my own ring—a gold band formed from Muddy's and Virginia's wedding rings—and, happily, it was not overly expensive. I paid for it with some of the money I'd received for speaking, then used a bit more to buy a velvet-lined wooden box to hold it.

A gift for my bride. My bride. My bride!

Those delightful words went round and round in my head, keeping me awake that night and the next, and preoccupied by day. Energy seemed to fill me—not the creative mania I used for my work, or the strange restlessness that gripped me in the dry times—no, this was perfect happiness, an unfamiliar but marvelous emotion.

The evening before Pamela was to return, I dined once more with Elmira. Now that all thoughts of a match between us were over, we seemed easier with each other, almost as if we were young again and our futures lay before us, uncharted territories full of riches waiting for discovery. I told her that as we were saying good night. Then, as I turned to go, a wave of fear hit me so hard and unexpectedly that I grabbed the porch rail for support.

Elmira saw me stumble, try to right myself, then nearly fall again. She rushed to my side and took my arm. "Is everything all right, Edgar?" she asked.

How could I explain what I could not understand myself? "I feel a bit ill, that's all," I replied. My heart was racing, my mind confused.

She rested a hand on my forehead. "You're too warm. You must have a fever. I think I'd best take you to see a physician, especially since you'll be traveling again soon. And across that cold Atlantic water, too."

Had a premonition caused my dizziness, or only the belief that given my tragic luck, something must be wrong? Probably the latter, I thought, though that rationalization didn't make the feeling any less real. "You're right," I said, with the appearance of calm that I usually managed to achieve even when my mind was nearly incapacitated by emotion or drink.

Elmira's doctor suggested a sedative, something my system cannot abide. To put Elmira at ease, I took the bottle the doctor gave me, intending to dispose of it later. Elmira took me to the Swan in her carriage, holding my hand all the while. "Wait a bit," she called to the driver as we pulled up to the boardinghouse. She kissed my cheek. "If there is anything you need, Edgar, you have only to ask," she said.

I considered pressing my luck by asking for her coach, team, and driver to take me immediately to Montgomery House and make certain that the fear which I felt was only my usual pessimism, nothing more. Instead I thanked her and left. She waited until I was safely inside before leaving, as if there were anywhere else I could go at that late hour.

A light shone from the public room. I went inside and saw Mrs. Blakely sitting at one of the tables, a cup of tea in front of her. I'd been so busy the last two days that this was the first time I'd seen her since we met briefly the morning after my lecture. "You gave an interesting talk, Mr. Poe," she said. "Though I'm not certain I understand it. Perhaps you could explain it to me over a cup of tea?"

"I can try," I responded, though of course we discussed the matter only a little before the woman, always an early riser, began nodding off. "Is there anything else you need tonight?" she asked.

"Nothing I can't get myself," I replied.

She left me, sitting in front of a full cup of tea. My mind was so preoccupied with that strange feeling of fear and my happy plans for the next day that I scarcely realized what I was doing when I walked behind the bar and opened a bottle of ale.

I hadn't done this without thinking. I had simply willed my reason to stop. How could I be so foolish? I stared at the deep amber liquid with regret—for the illness that made me so intolerant of it, and the weakness of soul that made me desire it so much, then carried the bottle outside and dumped the contents between the wide floorboards of the porch.

That night I forced myself to lie in bed, though I slept but little. When I did I was caught up in nightmares that left only the emotion of their content. I rose with the birds and packed my steamer trunk. I arranged for a porter to convey it to the dock and store it. Then, with nothing more to occupy my time, I waited for my love. My bride.

Two daily coaches connect Richmond and Appomattox. Pamela wasn't on the midafternoon one. The next would come late, just before the steamer was to leave. I had worked myself into an agitated frenzy by that evening. Though it had begun to rain at sunset and my fever seemed higher, I went to the coach house early and waited under its awning with the collar of my coat raised high against the chilly wind.

When the coach pulled in I stood as calmly as I could and watched the weary load of passengers exit.

Pamela wasn't among them.

The fear that had never completely left me intensified. I rushed forward to question the driver. As soon as he saw me coming toward him, he called out, "Are you Mr. Poe?"

I nodded. The sudden panic of the evening before returned. I was unable to speak, watching fatalistically as he reached into his jacket and pulled out an envelope.

I carried it to the shelter of the awning and opened it. Inside was a brief, almost cryptic, note from Mrs. Bridger. *There has been an accident here,* she wrote. *Pamela and her son will be unable to travel north with you at this time. Please go on ahead. She will write to you in Fordham when she is able.*

Able! Did that fool of a Virginia matron really think I would leave my love now? "What time does the next coach leave for Appomattox?" I asked the driver.

"This coach goes back at five in the morning. You'd best get some rest till then."

Rest! How could I sleep after such news? Ah, but I should try. Pamela and Roddy were all right. Mrs. Bridger would have undoubtedly told me if they were not, but then why hadn't Pamela herself written? "Could I sit in the coach until it's time to go?" I asked.

"Sleep if you can. There's blankets and pillows in there."

I tried to take his advice, but it is impossible. I doubt I will close my eyes again until I know that Pamela is well.

So ends another scrap of this journal, written in the dim light of the carriage lantern in a shaking script.

By the time the coach pulled into Appomattox, I realized that the damp air and the tiring journey was rapidly making my fever worse. Nonetheless, I pressed on in a rig hired in town. The same driver who had taken the three of us to Montgomery House just days before drove again, this time a small two-seater. Though the ride was less comfortable in the spot beside the driver, I'd get there more quickly. "You've missed the wake," the driver said to me.

My heart skipped a beat, the internal blow against my chest making me cough. "I didn't know someone died," I whispered.

"Old Montgomery's finally out of his misery. I don't have no details except that they buried him this morning."

So it was Will, not Pamela or Roddy. I'd seen how sick the old man had been, so I was only surprised that I had not guessed the truth earlier and saved myself hours of frantic worry. "When did it happen?" I asked.

"Day before yesterday. Mrs. Bridger's been over there helping the family. It's good that the daughter got to see him before the end," he said, echoing my thoughts.

We said nothing else on the hour's drive. I paid the man and sent him on his way, then walked up the uneven cobblestone path to the house. The ruined porch was draped in black crepe, the faded whitewash of the door covered in more of the same dismal fabric.

Emmie answered my knock. Though she was dressed in mourning, her grooming was once more elegant, and her bruises had begun to fade. Nonetheless, her eyes were red and she held a linen handkerchief in one hand. "You heard?" she asked.

"On the journey here. I came because Pamela did not meet me as she promised. But that's hardly surprising."

She looked at me with sympathy.

"What is it?" I asked.

She was a strong woman. She should have answered me. Instead she looked away and wiped tears from her eyes.

"Please," I whispered. "Tell me."

A door shut upstairs. I heard footsteps and looked up hopefully, nodding a greeting when Mrs. Bridger came down to join us. She was not, of course, expected to dress in mourning, but instead wore a deep brown dress and a black lace veil over her hair as a sign of respect to the family. "Mr. Poe, I'm so glad you came. Perhaps later you can be a comfort to Pamela."

"I'd like to see her now," I said.

"In time. Did Emmie explain matters to you?"

Some tragedy more than old Will's death had taken place

here, that much was certain, yet Mrs. Bridger referred to it only as "matters." "Emmie scarcely seems capable of it," I replied.

Mrs. Bridger seemed to notice the poor woman's distress for the first time. "Go up to your mistress," she ordered. I wondered if Mrs. Bridger was aware that Emmie was no one's servant, or if she only chose to ignore that truth. Nonetheless, Emmie did as the woman asked.

"Negroes can be so emotional," Mrs. Bridger commented, long before Emmie was beyond hearing the words. Though I have never been an Abolitionist, the cruelty of that remark, directed to a woman who had lost her lover, made me clear my throat of the sharp retort that threatened to surface.

We went into the parlor, where a buffet of sandwiches, sweets, wine, and cider had been arranged for visitors paying their respects. Only a small bit of the food had been taken, making me wonder if the supply had been replenished or if poor Will's wake had been largely unattended. When I reached for something, I saw a roach making its way across the fringed edge of the runner. Though I'd eaten nothing since the night before, I pulled my hand back, taking only the cider the woman poured for me.

"Is Pamela ill?" I asked.

Mrs. Bridger waited until we were seated to answer. "The situation is enough to have me believing in spiritualism," she said. "From what I understand, Will had been raving for weeks before Pamela's return, talking to his wife and her mother as if they were both in his room. Just before Pamela's arrival, Emmie become convinced that he meant to shoot himself. She refused to leave him alone. He beat her, showing no remorse even when she bled."

"I saw her bruises. However, he seemed calmer after Pamela spoke to him."

"Emmie tells me that was indeed true. He started washing and dressing and taking his meals at the table with his daughter. He seemed to enjoy the company of his grandson a great deal."

"Then he had a relapse?"

"More than that. I'll tell you all of it. I understand that you

and Pamela intend to wed, and so you have a right to know."
She walked to the sideboard and poured herself a glass of
sherry. The simple act seemed full of portent, for I would
hardly have expected to see a woman like her take a glass of
wine so early in the day.

She returned to her chair and continued. "The night after
Pamela returned from her visit with you in Richmond, she
woke to the sound of her father's cries. She ran into his room
and found him standing in the center of it, apparently
screaming at some apparition only he could see.

"Pamela ran to him intending to comfort him. As he had
with Emmie, he became violent. He shouted his wife's name,
and attacked her."

"He beat her?"

"Worse, Mr. Poe. You see, he thought she was his wife.
There is a startling similarity in features between mother and
daughter, and in his insanity he tried to have his—" These
were words the old matron could not speak. She stopped,
then added, "Do you understand?"

I nodded, feeling less anger than pity for the man. "Go
on," I said.

"Pamela fought. She managed to get away and ran down
the hall. He chased her, catching her at the top of the stairs
and ripping off one sleeve of her gown. Rage gave him
strength, but she was still the stronger. She pushed him away
and he broke through the railing, hit the floor below, and
died. She told me this story herself. Emmie, who had arrived
just in time to watch Will fall, corroborated it. No one questions the facts, and no one would dare place any blame on
Pamela for defending herself. But she must have blamed herself, that much was evident in her hysteria and the strange
state which followed it."

Strange state. I could well imagine. "I wish to see her
now," I said.

"I don't think it would be wise just yet," Mrs. Bridger
said. I began to realize that there were other facts she hadn't
the heart to tell me, facts of far greater importance. I stood
and in a sudden wave of dizziness stumbled to the stairs and

gripped the rail. "She is my fiancée. I have a right to see her!" I insisted.

"You must not, not yet," Mrs. Bridger called after me.

I was beyond heeding her advice. I steadied myself, then ran up the stairs so quickly that I was panting by the time I reached the top. I did not pause to catch my breath, but rushed down the dark hallway to Pamela's room.

Emmie was inside. Miriam was there as well, also dressed in mourning. Mother and daughter sat side by side, holding hands. I must have been a wild apparition—my hair mussed, my gait uneven, and my body trembling from weakness and fear. Emmie started to rise to come to me, then changed her mind and watched Pamela intently as I approached the bed.

My bride sat propped up by a pile of lace-trimmed pillows. The blue dressing gown set off her hair and coloring, the soft glow in her cheeks and lips. Roddy sat beside her on the bed. As soon as he saw me, he laughed and held out his hands. "Eddy!" he cried.

I lifted him up slowly, took his place beside his mother, and set him on my knee.

Pamela smiled at me. Her expression was sweet and oddly vague, so at odds with the passionate way she usually greeted me—her Eddy, her betrothed. I began to guess that the shock of her father's death had affected her with more than the expected sorrow. I did not dare try to kiss her. Instead, I took her hand and waited. "Are you a friend of Will's?" she finally asked.

"Don't you remember?" I asked gently. "It's me, Eddy." I looked into her eyes, begging God to let her please remember some shreds of the adventure we'd been through together, some hint of what we meant to each other.

"Eddy?" she questioned, as if my name meant nothing to her.

"Edgar Poe," Miriam prompted. "You remember him, of course."

"Poe?" Pamela's expression changed rapidly from remote politeness to confusion to anger. She jerked her hand out of my grasp so quickly that I lost my balance. Roddy would have fallen had Miriam not rushed forward to take him.

Pamela sat up straighter, her hands clenched into fists. "How dare you come here after what you've done?" she demanded.

"What do you mean?" I asked.

"You penning those terrible words about my Roderick and myself. Your calumnies have pursued me all my life. And now, now when I'd almost forgotten about them, you have the gall to come here and remind me."

Her tone was so fierce, so cold. My Pamela at her angriest had never sounded like this. I tried to understand that she was confused, probably half insane with grief. Yet the words stung just the same. "To apologize. To set things right," I replied, not wishing to cater to her delusions, but desperately wanting to have her look at me with some shred of affection.

"I don't need your apologies. Not now or ever."

"Pamela. Please, I beg you to—"

"Pamela?" she interrupted, frowning through her anger as if I had just revealed myself as less bold than mad.

The sound of that beautiful name spoken in such a remote tone made me even more frantic. I had to make her see the truth. If she did, then perhaps all would be well again. I took Pamela's hands. She tried to pull away, but I held them tightly. I didn't care if I bruised her if I could somehow make her understand. "You are Pamela Donaldson," I said. "That child is your son. We are to be married. Remember. Please, remember."

"Son?" She stared at Roddy and smiled so beautifully that I let her go and motioned for Miriam to place the boy in her arms. Pamela brushed back his hair and kissed his forehead. "He is my Roderick come back to me," she said. Her eyes narrowed as she looked at me once more. "Do not try to confuse me with your lies, Mr. Poe. I've always been on to them. Whatever you sought to gain by coming here will not be given. Now leave my house, or I'll have my servants throw you out."

Emmie touched my shoulder and motioned toward the door. I shook my head. "Who are you?" I whispered to Pamela.

She laughed. She did not have to say a name, for I knew that laugh far too well, had heard it in the damp halls of Petite Terre and in the hollow nights of my uneasy rest on our journey south.

Madeline Usher had died, but her will had been too strong to let her rest.

The woman smiled in triumph as she saw the horror in my expression, the way I stood too quickly so that I had to lean against the bedpost for support. And I'm certain she was smiling still as I left her, though I did not dare to look back and see the face of the one I loved so altered. My Pamela has been lost to me, and I have no way of knowing if I will ever be allowed to have her back. I was conscious of nothing as I went down the stairs, not even of Emmie at my side, supporting me. Without her, I would have fallen. Perhaps I would have died then as Will had died, half mad with despair. Even that small blessing eluded me.

"Mrs. Bridger said no one doubted Pamela's story. She must have been lucid then," I said to Emmie, looking for some hope.

Emmie didn't answer until we were in the parlor. She poured us each a glass of brandy. This time I drank it, for the madness it would bring would be welcome. "When did she—" Die? Lose her soul? Become possessed? Even words failed me.

"I was with her every minute after Will died. She was herself at first, but sometime when I wasn't watching closely, I lost her."

Emmie began to cry, looking away as if her grief were an embarrassment.

I might have joined her, but my despair was too deep for tears. So I went to the sideboard. I poured another glass of brandy. I pulled the journal out of my traveling bag and began to write.

So our journey ends, my beloved. In the last hour since I left your room, I have sat at the table in the parlor, recording the final details of it. I've eaten nothing, but have drunk a great deal. It's already begun to make me ill, but my mind finds comfort in that. Forgive me for my weakness; it will pass as it always does and then I will be forced to rest. If the mania grips me too tightly, I have the doctor's sedative to help the drink along.

I have only one thin shred of hope remaining—that belief that Madeline will have pity on you and release you, perhaps when I am gone or when the baby is born. I can only pray that God will demand this and show me the mercy that He has denied me all my life.

I wish I had the fortitude to stay here with you, but I think it would drive me mad to spend even one night so close to your body and so far from your sweet soul. I've explained my decision to Emmie and Mrs. Bridger and made them promise to write me often and tell me how you and Roddy are faring. Emmie has packed me a huge supper to take along, though at the moment only the bottle of brandy she included holds any interest for me. Miriam is going to drive me into town in the one buggy that Will Montgomery kept in some state of repair. She wants to leave soon. There is another storm coming.

Before I go, I will leave a door to your recent past with Emmie—this journal for you to read when you are well enough to do so. I pray that the account will help you remember all of our adventure and that you will still love me as I love you, and desire me as I desire you. Write me then in Fordham, and if I am still alive I promise that I will come to you, for I will only be complete in the blessed comfort of your love.

Your Eddy.

epilogue

A letter to Maria Clemm,
August 14, 1850

Dear Mrs. Clemm,

I can well understand your reasons for not answering my previous letters. Months have passed since our Eddy died, and I had not even sent condolences, so of course you have reason to doubt that we intended to wed. But in truth, I did not learn of his death until recently, and I confess that I would not have cared if I had. Until the birth of my child in early June, I was caught up in some strange illness—a possession, Eddy called it—in which another soul seemed to inhabit my body. As Eddy surmised in his last journal entry, this illness seemed to have been associated with my pregnancy, for as the time for my daughter's birth approached, I had hours of lucidity, then days. After my child was born, I was nearly myself again. And when I looked down at her beautiful face, a name came to me, and with it the memory of all that Eddy and I had been through.

I called her Virginia after your daughter and Eddy's wife. The following day after I had recovered from the delivery, I asked Emmie for my writing desk so that I could send Eddy a letter and tell him that I was well. The expression on her face told me the worst had happened, even before she sat beside me to take my hand and tell me what she knew of his death. So of course, I wrote you instead, though with my grief and the ordeal I had been through, I may not have been completely coherent.

Between the second letter, where I told you some of what Eddy and I had been through, and this one, I sold the Montgomery plantation to the Bridgers. The repairs to the house would have been costly, and when done I would have been living in a place that held too many tragic memories for me. Emmie, Miriam, and I have traveled south to my second inheritance, Petite Terre. Since coming to this remote section of Louisiana, I have lived a quiet existence, caring for my children and studying the books in the library. Here I have finally made a full recovery.

My children are happy here. Virginia is well, and Roderick is a doting older brother. I am amazed at the similarity in their features. I only hope that I can raise them with more affection than they had in their previous life and through love alone end the curse that has plagued the Usher line.

I often read from the journal Eddy kept on our travels. If I were to send it to you, you would have to believe what I have told you. But I cannot part with the last bit of Eddy that I still possess. If you can find it in your heart to believe at least some of my tale, and of the heroic part your Eddy played in it, come to Louisiana. I will welcome you as my own kin, something you will easily understand after you read his words. I will caution you that it is a difficult journey, one best made in autumn or spring when the air is cooler and the storms less intense.

All my love,
Pamela

historical note

On September 24, 1849, Edgar Allan Poe gave the final public lecture of his life at the Exchange Hotel in Richmond, Virginia. On the evening of the twenty-sixth, he stopped briefly at a doctor's office in Richmond for treatment of a fever. On the twenty-seventh, he was to leave on the three A.M. steamer for his home in Fordham, New York. He checked out of his boardinghouse, then disappeared until October 3, when he appeared on a street in Baltimore, sick and incoherent. He was admitted to a local hospital, where, delirious, he continuously called out a name no one could understand.

He died there on October 7. No one ever discovered where he spent the last week of his life, save that he seemed to be speaking to people no one could see, and that he raved about having been married and abandoning his wife. His last words were "God help my poor soul."

The source of Poe's final illness is unknown. His constitution, all biographers agree, was delicate, and he had a sensitivity to any stimulant which sometimes—but not always—caused him to become excitable to the point of madness. It has been conjectured that after such a well-attended final lecture in Richmond, he celebrated overly much and the alcohol-induced mania led to exposure, madness, and death.

Others believe that, having left Richmond alone with a considerable sum of money from his last public appearance, a sum which disappeared some time before he was found in Baltimore, he'd been accosted by thieves who got him drunk, then took everything he had and left him penniless and incoherent.

In 1852, some three years after Poe's death in Baltimore, Maria Clemm, Poe's beloved "Aunt Muddy," lamented to a friend that all her financial worries would be over if she could only find the means to make her way to Louisiana. To the best of anyone's knowledge, Poe had never been to that state, nor had the family ever known anyone there.

afterword

From the time I began to develop my taste in reading, I recall Edgar Poe.

The Poe of those deliciously overwritten and horrific stories that I would read again and yet again for the shivers they gave me. Poe, the poet of marvelous cadences and strange juxtaposition of metaphors, of images. And as my youthful obsession with his works grew, of Poe—the man of a short and tragic life marked so depressingly by the loss of one beautiful woman after another.

In my research for this novel, I discovered a different Poe. A Poe who loved to entertain children. A Poe of well-tuned wit and marvelous, often self-deprecating, humor. A Poe of intermittent madness and black despair, who managed to create a huge volume of work in spite of this and give a wealth of literature to a new country.

Poe only used the name "Allan" once in his life, yet his foster father's name remains forever attached to his. And for all his beliefs that his foster son would never amount to anything, it is the only reason we recall John Allan today.

Poe would have found this irony hilarious.

In my search for Poe the man, the hero of this book, I am thankful (again!) to Poe expert Mark Paul Stehlik for letting me borrow from his extensive Poe collection as well as for suggesting the balloon trip. Of all the books I read in researching this novel, I would recommend *Poe—The Man,* a two-volume collection by Francis Winwar for its look at his day-to-day life, and *Plumes in the Dust* by John Evangelist Walsh for its intriguing premise that Poe was not the celibate, eternally platonic lover that earlier scholars had believed him to be.